Brilliance

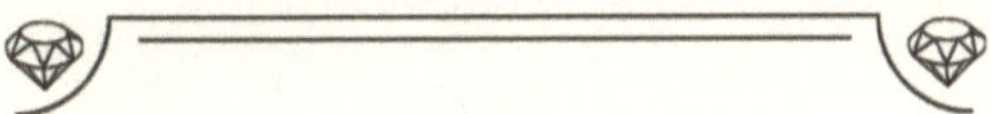

Diamonds of the First Water

SYDNEY JANE BAILY

cat whisker press

Boston

This book is a work of fiction. Names, characters, places, and incidents either are products of the author's imagination or are used fictitiously. Any resemblance to actual events or locales or persons, living or dead, is entirely coincidental.

Copyright © 2023 Sydney Jane Baily

All rights reserved under International and Pan-American Copyright Conventions.

No part of this book may be reproduced or transmitted in any form or by any means, electronic or mechanical, including photocopying, recording, or by any information storage and retrieval system without written permission from the publisher, except for the inclusion of brief quotations in a review or article.

Second Paperback Edition, 2025
ISBN 978-1-957421-65-0

Published by Cat Whisker Press

Cover: Dar Albert, Wicked Smart Designs
Book Design: Cat Whisker Studio
Editor: Chris Hall

DIAMONDS OF THE FIRST WATER

OTHER WORKS

The RAKES ON THE RUN Series
Last Dance in London
Pursued in Paris
Banished to Brighton
Gretna Green by Sunset
The Lady Who Stole Christmas

The RARE CONFECTIONERY Series
The Duchess of Chocolate
The Toffee Heiress
My Lady Marzipan
The Gingerbread Lady

The DEFIANT HEARTS Series
An Improper Situation
An Irresistible Temptation
An Inescapable Attraction
An Inconceivable Deception
An Intriguing Proposition
An Impassioned Redemption

The BEASTLY LORDS Series
Lord Despair
Lord Anguish
Lord Vile
Lord Darkness
Lord Misery
Lord Wrath
Lord Corsair
Eleanor

PRESENTING LADY GUS

THE BLACK KNIGHT'S REWARD
with Marliss Melton

DEDICATION

To Debra Arnold Codd

As I finish this final book that I'll write while in my travel trailer, I recall you were the last one to see us off on our adventure. Your special, thoughtful friendship has always touched my heart and made me grateful.

Thank you!

ACKNOWLEDGMENTS

I wish to express my gratitude to my editor on the Diamonds of the First Water series, Chris Hall. Her comments, suggestions, and corrections made each and every book better.

And another massive dose of appreciation to my sister, Toni Young, for reading through the messy first drafts. By poking holes in my stories and pointing out consistency errors, she was immensely helpful.

I couldn't have written these books half as well without their assistance.

INTRODUCTION TO
DIAMONDS OF THE FIRST WATER

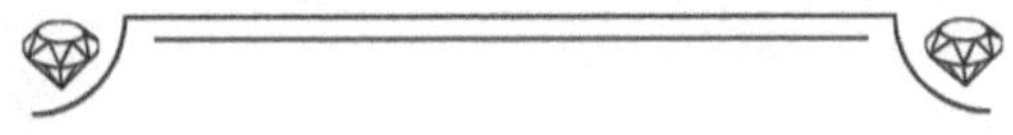

Once upon a time, an Irish family by the name of O'Diamáin emigrated to England from the north of Ireland, from County Doire to be specific. You may know the area as Derry or even Londonderry if you are thinking of it after King James I granted the city a royal charter.

Felim O'Diamáin, who was the youngest son, sailed across the Irish Sea to make his fortune, bringing his pretty wife and two young children with him. As the story goes, they stopped over on the Isle of Man for a perfectly peaceful night before landing at Ravenglass the next day and traipsing through the Lake District.

Another version swears they took the shorter but far more dangerous route north, across the sea to Portpatrick, finding themselves in the southernmost part of Scotland. From there, if they indeed came that way, they headed east toward Gretna Green. Not for any quick anvil marriage, mind you, but to traverse the border to England.

No one knows for sure the veracity of either tale, nor particularly cares. Once they arrived in England, Felim did very well for himself, as did his descendants.

At some point during the twelve-year reign of George I, another O'Diamáin by the name of Liam was made an earl for his devoted service to the Crown. During those years in the early eighteenth century, King George also created a few dukes, at least one marquess, some barons, a single viscount, and other earls. But we're not interested in any of them, although some may have helped to quell the riots that ensued when Hanoverian George outmaneuvered any pesky residual Stuarts hoping to claim the English throne.

Nevertheless, our interest lies with Liam. With his new earldom came much wealth and land, specifically in Derbyshire. And naturally, a title. However, George I, being of Germanic descent, didn't find the Celtic name of O'Diamáin tripped easily off his tongue. Neither did he master Gaelic or Manx, for that matter. In any case, with a little persuasion and an extra thousand acres, Liam became William, the Earl Diamond, as his male descendants have been known ever since.

Over the years, the earls have enlarged the original house to be an impressive manor, always named Oak Grove Hall, which is the translation of their long-ago home of County *Doire*.

Generations later, while inheriting the earldom and all its assets, Geoffrey, Lord Diamond and his beloved wife, Caroline, have wealth of a different nature as well—five healthy children: Clarity, Purity, Adam, Radiance, and Brilliance. They are known as the Diamonds of the First Water, at least by their parents.

This is Brilliance's story . . .

CHAPTER ONE

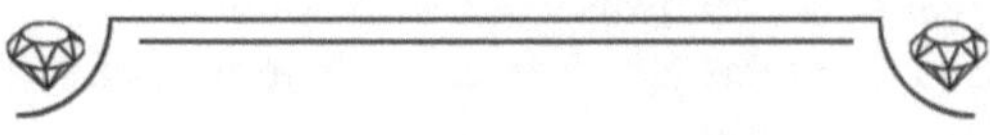

Brilliance knew she was going somewhere she ought not go. And it wouldn't be the first time she had simply followed an inclination without giving it much thought. However, the compelling music of a piano being beautifully played drew her from her intended destination.

After arriving at Lady Twitchard's country house party a mere two hours earlier, Brilliance had taken tea in her assigned room, rested as one did after travel, then washed off the dust off the journey before changing for dinner into a lightweight, pink, silk gown with white flowers around the neckline and the hem. Belinda, her personal maid, had expertly combed and styled her dark hair, sweeping it into coils on either side of her head while leaving down and loose as many curls as a single lady dare get away with.

Having yet to see her best friend, Martine, also a guest for the week, Brilliance was hurrying toward the noisy drawing room, its double doors standing open and welcoming. However, her footsteps slowed at the closed conservatory door, and she found it impossible to continue along the passageway.

Pushing open the door in so deliberate and quiet a manner as to have her bursting with the effort to rein in her curiosity, she discovered a man seated at a highly polished grand piano with his back to her.

Brilliance wasn't so silly as to believe in love at first sight. After all, she had seen plenty of handsome men at numerous assemblies, and she hadn't loved a single one of them. However, she well knew her parents' own romantic story. Lord Geoffrey Diamond and Lady Caroline Chimes hadn't instantly fallen head over heels in love. Rather, Brilliance's father had nearly knocked her mother on her bottom. Falling rear end over heels was another matter entirely in the arena of love. Regardless, they'd felt an immediate attraction upon that initial meeting.

Thus, an unexpectedly strong attraction at first sight was something Brilliance understood and believed in . . . yet she'd never thought it could be fashioned by music. In this case, whatever the gentleman was playing, something she'd never heard before, was drawing her forward. Moreover, she could not take her eyes off the pianist.

There might not be anything spectacular about him. At least, not that she could see. He had light brown hair that came over the collar of his worsted wool, charcoal-gray evening coat. His broad shoulders sat atop a long torso that indicated he was tall.

He seemed to be staring straight ahead out the conservatory window to the twilight gardens beyond, looking neither at his hands nor at any sheet music while he played.

Both his bearing and the beauty of the music quelled her normal exuberance. Brilliance walked softly and stayed silent, even keeping her lips tightly closed, rather than rushing forward and exclaiming how the music touched her deeply. Moreover, she fisted her hands against the front of her bodice to stop herself from clapping.

Eschewing the plush chairs lined up along one wall, she remained standing, inching a little closer, then closer, without realizing it until she was directly behind him.

After another few moments, the stranger froze, his hands resting lightly upon the keys.

Despite her cream-colored, kid-skin slippers making no sound on the woolen rug, which covered all but the outer two feet of the polished wooden floor, he seemed to know he was no longer alone.

Stiffly, he turned and fixed her with a sage-eyed stare through metal-rimmed spectacles that caught the lamplight. His visage was comely, indeed, but with a most severe expression for someone producing such lovely sounds.

Quite certain she had been quiet, nonetheless, Brilliance circled around to stand at his side.

"I am terribly sorry to have stopped your playing, sir. It was truly delightful." If he promised to continue, she would take a seat. Before she could encourage him to do so, he spoke.

"Was not the door shut?"

Brilliance nodded. "It was. But I could still hear you."

"If you could hear the music from the other side of the door, then why did you feel it necessary to enter?"

Brilliance considered it a very good question, one deserving an answer. But it also struck her funny, as many things did. Her sisters and brother thought her a little flighty or giddy, but their opinion didn't change the fact that people were often amusing.

She shrugged and gave in to the urge to laugh.

Unexpectedly, this made him rise to his feet. She'd been correct in imagining him to be tall.

"Are you laughing at me?" He looked down his nose to where she came only to his necktie. In size, she was between her sisters, Clarity and Purity, who were diminutive, and Radiance, who was a wee bit taller.

"No, sir. Not at all." Brilliance hoped he would introduce himself, despite the inappropriateness of their being alone. The late-July house party had only recently begun. Guests were still arriving, and as yet, they'd had no gathering, neither formal nor informal, during which introductions could be made.

"I assure you I laugh only because I am happy. We are at the start of a week full of merriment. And in answer to your question, I can only think that I came in rather than remaining in the hallway because I was curious. I wanted to *see* the source of the music. Wouldn't anyone?"

"No," he shot back. "Music is for your ears. What is there to see?"

Another good question. She nearly told him what she saw was a handsome, albeit inexplicably irritated man.

"I think when listening to music," Brilliance explained, "looking upon the musician is particularly satisfying. It enhances the deep emotion imparted by the notes."

"Balderdash," he muttered. "I assume you are a guest of my cousin."

"If your cousin is Lady Twitchard, then I am."

"I believe the others are gathering in the drawing room despite possibly hearing my playing as they passed by. So, no, miss. *Anyone* would not simply barge in through a closed door."

Brilliance sighed. *What a crabbed, humdrum fellow!* "You are exceedingly pleasant to look at, sir. It's a shame your nature doesn't match your appearance."

His expression came over as shocked, but he said nothing in return.

She took a step back. "I suppose you play only for yourself. A miserly musician who could delight others but prefers to hoard his talent."

Still, nothing but an arrogantly raised eyebrow on his part.

Should she have such talent, Brilliance vowed she would share it. She was not skilled musically at all, despite her parents offering her lessons. Purity was the only one of her sisters whom one might declare musically gifted and had managed to convince their parents to set aside an ancient square fortepiano that her mother had inherited. A spanking new piano arrived one day for all the sisters to practice upon.

Yet precisely as her mother, Clarity, and Ray had done before her, Brilliance took lessons for two years and had given up.

Nevertheless, she appreciated a good musician, or in this case, a superb one.

"I shall leave you to your solitude, sir, for the price of a question. How did you know I was here?"

She waited. He stared. She waited longer. *Was he going to be so rude as not to answer?*

Finally, she shrugged and walked toward the door, which she'd left ajar. After all, an earl's daughter had to protect her reputation.

Yet before she slipped out, he spoke.

"I vow I could feel your impertinent gaze and smell your perfume—like summer roses—wafting toward me."

"Did it?" Brilliance sniffed. "Sadly, I have been wearing it for a year, and thus cannot really smell the lovely fragrance anymore. Perhaps I should take a break from it."

She expected no response, but surprisingly, the gentleman said, "The scent suits you."

Brilliance nodded, happy that he'd changed from surly to friendly.

But then he ruined it by adding, "A showy flower with a heady fragrance, without subtlety or nuance. One might say overpowering."

Her mouth had dropped open, and she snapped it closed. She wished she hadn't told him he was handsome. Obviously, he considered himself such a rum duke he thought he could be insufferably rude.

"You forgot to mention the thorns, sir."

For some reason, this made him smile. Not broadly. Merely a small wry one.

Without another word, she departed.

VINCENT WAITED UNTIL THE door closed before he resumed his seat on the piano stool. His cousin, Alethia, who was closer to the age of his parents than to him, had confessed to a shortage of single men at her house party. Some blasted damber had bowed out at the last minute, and since he was close at hand, living for the summer in his Joyden's Wood estate, she had begged him to round out her dining table and keep her numbers even.

When he was fresh out of Trinity College, his cousin's husband, Colonel Twitchard, had gifted Vincent an introduction to his acquaintance, the Hungarian pianist, Franz Liszt. Heading at once to Weimar, Vincent had been accepted as a student of the famed composer. For his cousin and her husband's kindness, he would always be in their debt. Being a guest at their party full of simpering females and randy bucks had seemed a small price.

Yet he hadn't expected to be trading barbs with one of Alethia's other guests within a half hour of his arrival.

Where had he left off? Pushing his spectacles farther up his nose, he considered the piece he'd been playing from memory, seeing the notes in his head right up until the instant he had smelled the lady's sumptuous floral scent.

Nuisance female! He had another half hour, at least, before all his cousin's guests arrived and gathered in the drawing room. Placing his hands upon the keys, he recalled the irritating young lady said she found him handsome. Moreover, she had stated it aloud, as if they were known to one another. *How extraordinary!*

Maybe she was a bit of a climber or a would-be mushroom. She was certainly pretty enough to catch his attention. In any case, he had plenty of time to speak with her later, yet precious few minutes to replay a piece he wasn't entirely confident he had perfected. Written years earlier, even then, he had doubted its worthiness of being set to paper. Thus, it remained only in his thoughts.

The thing about playing without the notes in front of him was that even a memory as superb as his own could play tricks once in a while. He had liked the sonata better a month earlier, and now, he wasn't as taken with this section.

Was that how he'd originally composed it?

Not for the first time, he considered overcoming his reluctance and writing down the sonata. Perhaps he finally would when he reached his country estate a mere two miles away. He had another week to think about it.

For even if overnight, he decided he wished to transcribe every note in his head, he could do nothing about it. Alethia would tan his hide if he left, even for half a day. Once committed to a house party, one was truly committed—or be labeled an arse as the missing male guest would be. Why, the man would probably never receive another social invitation. And when it was a case of family acting as the hosts, the consequences for neglecting social obligations in favor of personal desires would be even worse.

CHAPTER TWO

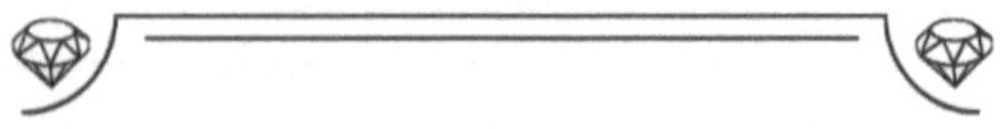

Brilliance waited in the drawing room for the pianist to enter. While chatting excitedly with Martine, who had already pointed out another guest her friend fancied with curly blond hair and very straight teeth, Brilliance couldn't help keeping an eye on the door.

Eventually, minutes after everyone else had already come in and been introduced, the pianist strode through the open doorway. She could see he wasn't shy, not a wall-prop by any means. Thus, he had stayed away simply because it had suited him. It was as plain as the patrician nose on his face.

After letting his glance flick around the room, landing momentarily upon Brilliance, he greeted their hostess, his cousin if he'd spoken true. Then he stood stony-faced while she made his introduction.

"Since my cousin was detained from joining us earlier," Lady Twitchard said, covering for his standoffishness with a vague turn of phrase, "allow me to introduce you all to Lord Hewitt."

He gave a bow as if that was the end of it.

Brilliance hardly thought that fair to the rest of them.

"How will he learn our names," Brilliance asked, "if you don't bring him around and introduce your cousin to each of us individually?"

A murmur from the guests—the female ones, at any rate—indicated she may have said something the others were thinking. Why no one else had said so, however, for the life of her, Brilliance couldn't imagine. It was always better to speak one's mind.

In any case, Lady Twitchard appeared to agree.

"Well considered, Lady Brilliance. And you are quite correct. We shall put off dinner *another* fifteen minutes while I make sure my cousin learns each and every one of your names."

Lord Hewitt, as Brilliance now knew him, pierced her with a look that might have flattened a less formidable soul. It bothered her not one whit. In fact, she thought him amusing, like a tiger in a top hat. He'd hoped to set his own rules and flaunt society's customs, but instead, he would be made to go through the somewhat nerve-racking ceremony of being introduced to unknown people with whom one would spend the next seven days.

What's more, they were expected to recall each other's names immediately. She was already confusing Lady Georgiana with Miss Newton and Mr. Denham with Lord Patterson. They were a higgledy-piggledy purée in her head. *Who was who?*

She returned his glare with an affable smile. He would surely enjoy the party more if he learned his fellow guests' names or suffered through the attempt as she was doing.

While Lady Twitchard made the rounds once again with her cousin by her side, the rest of the guests chatted and drank sloe-gin punch. Brilliance and Martine resumed their discussion, thinking it remarkable that they didn't know another soul there, although they had, at least, seen some of them at London assemblies. Soon, Lady Twitchard and Lord Hewitt approached.

"Lady Martine, may I present Lord Hewitt?" their hostess said. "Her father, Lord Flowers, is a coffee importer."

The pianist took hold of Brilliance's friend's hand, then released it with a toneless, "Enchanted."

When it was her turn, Brilliance was about to admit to Lady Twitchard that she'd already encountered Lord Hewitt, but he beat her to the revelation.

"I have met this one already," he told his cousin.

This one? Brilliance had disturbed his serenity, apparently. Something she was good at doing. She felt Martine stir beside her.

"How so?" Lady Twitchard asked.

"*She* barged in while I was practicing."

Brilliance studied her hostess's visage. Instead of shock or annoyance, she saw only amusement.

"How clever of you to initiate contact with my prickly cousin!" Lady Twitchard told her.

"Clever?" he scoffed.

"I was drawn to his playing," Brilliance confessed. "Although we didn't get so far as to exchange names, as that seemed improper whilst alone."

"Quite correct. Lady Brilliance, may I present Lord Vincent Hewitt?"

"Indeed, you may." She held her hand out to him, not certain he would take it. After the briefest of pauses, he did, gently grasping hold and bowing over it in a polite fashion before dropping it like a hot coal.

"An unusual name," he remarked.

"Oh, no, my lord. I think Vincent is a fine name. Or did you mean Hewitt?"

She vowed she detected a hint of a smile playing about his lips. Lady Twitchard laughed outright, as did Martine.

"Lady Brilliance is the youngest daughter of the Earl Diamond," their hostess continued. "And it seems magnificently fortuitous that I have seated you together for dinner."

Lord Hewitt raised an eyebrow and something devilish appeared in his—*Brilliance leaned closer to get a better view behind his spectacles*—his gray-green eyes. Even if he wanted to protest, and Brilliance hoped he didn't wish to, he could not since Lady Twitchard took hold of his arm once again.

"My cousin will return to escort you to the dining room in a few minutes. I have a less prickly gentleman for you tonight, Lady Martine," she added.

"Prickly," Lord Hewitt protested. "How am I prickly?"

Lady Twitchard rolled her eyes. "Come along. We must continue with the introductions."

Brilliance watched them depart, excitement tingling through her at being Lord Hewitt's dining partner for the next few hours. She hadn't expected such good fortune, but he had already turned out to be the most entertaining gentleman at the house party.

"An early conquest," Martine said.

"Nonsense," Brilliance shot back, but she liked the idea.

In less time than it took her to empty her glass of punch, Brilliance's arm was taken—rather stiffly—by Lord Hewitt. Lord Twitchard, who styled himself always as "the Colonel" ever since becoming Colonel of the 1st Regiment of Life Guards at least two decades earlier, had shown up in the drawing room just in time to escort one of the female guests to the dining room. Naturally, a male guest, whose name Brilliance had forgotten, made ready to escort Lady Twitchard. Brilliance and Lord Hewitt took their place behind them near the front of the line, perhaps due to him being the hostess's cousin.

Moreover, when they reached their seats, their place cards were fairly close to the head of the table, too. It was all most exciting. As the fifth child of five, Brilliance was never usually at the head of anything. At least, she hadn't been until the others had, one-by-one, married and moved out.

Once seated, having removed her gloves and placed her napkin over them on her lap, she settled in for the fun of dining with a group of strangers. Single strangers, except for their hosts. The company was to her liking, and she was assured of lively conversation and a delicious repast.

She said as much to her dining partner when he was equally settled in his chair, with his gloves stripped off and his spectacles slipped into his pocket.

"I hope you are correct, Lady Brilliance. Although from first glance and after enduring introductions, this may be a gathering of ninny-pates and dullards, present company excepted."

She laughed. "I appreciate the exception and would extend it to my good friend, Lady Martine. Besides us, however, if your hasty initial impression is correct, then thankfully, we have one another with whom to converse. So far, although you are a little rude, I do not find you to be in the least dull."

He blinked his sage-colored eyes before saying, "Thank you."

The Colonel lifted his glass of claret and gave the briefest of disinterested toasts to everyone's health. This was followed by Lady Twitchard offering a more effusive welcoming speech, laying out all the amusements they would have over the course of the week.

Through both toasts, Brilliance couldn't help watching Lord Hewitt's hands. His fingers were ever restless, tapping the table linen with one set of five, pattering the wine glass stem with the other.

She imagined his brain was equally active. She wished her own was similarly—at least on a single purpose. Rather, she knew herself to be somewhat scattered. Books, except for the most enjoyable ones, were often left unfinished. Needlepoint sat in a basket at home incomplete after years, and Brilliance couldn't conceive of the discipline necessary to compose an entire piece of music. She could barely write a journal entry without losing interest.

Maybe she should ask him if he had any tips on becoming more focused. She waited a minute as he was conversing with his cousin. As soon as there was a lull, she addressed him.

"Lord Hewitt. A word if you will be so kind."

VINCENT TURNED TO HIS pretty, brown-haired dining companion on his right.

"Yes, my lady."

"How do you keep your mind upon one thing so long as to produce, for instance, what you were playing today?"

"A sonata."

"Sonata. What a lovely word," Lady Brilliance exclaimed before repeating it. "*Sonata.*"

As her mouth formed the syllables, his gaze was captivated by her pink lips. It took him a moment to reply.

"It's Italian," he said, finding himself wishing to chat with her despite how she'd interrupted him earlier in the conservatory. Moreover, he ought to be annoyed that she'd made him bow over the five other ladies' hands as well as hers, then meet the other five gentlemen making up their party.

Taken around the room like a show pony!

Of course, he knew it was his duty as a fellow guest, but he could have learned their names as was necessary.

"What does it mean?" Lady Brilliance inquired.

"Mean?" he asked, taking in the rich cobalt shine in her eyes.

"In English, my lord. Sonata—something about the sunshine, perhaps, the way some music makes you think of a sunny day in June."

Was she teasing him? Her innocent expression indicated she was not.

"The word refers to something that is sounded rather than sung, which is a *cantata.*"

"Cantata," she said, then smiled. "Another lovely word. It makes me think of someone running quickly across a field. Maybe I should take up Italian. I have only ever tried to speak French."

Then she laughed, although he could not imagine why.

"That's funny, is it not, my lord? For obviously, I am speaking English and not French. In fact, I found French to be extremely difficult. All those tedious verb conjugations and every word having different endings. It made my brain hurt. Is Italian much the same?"

He nodded. She was a bizarre creature indeed. She didn't seem to be a chuckle-headed cake exactly, yet nor would he say she was particularly quick-witted. Perhaps somewhere in the middle, a bit of a jingle-brains.

"I believe all the so-called romance languages are similarly arranged," he explained.

"Romance languages," she echoed. "I wonder how English is described by other people. It seems a very romantic language, too, wouldn't you say? We have fine words for love and tenderness and being sweet on one another." She sipped her wine and beamed happily.

Amazingly, Vincent could tell she was not acting coy nor flirting by bringing up those words. She was genuinely trying to make sense of the world. *How refreshing!*

"That's not the type of romance intended," he explained. "The term means languages based upon those in the Roman world, those derived from Latin. I believe you'll find our own is considered a Germanic language."

She frowned. "That cannot be correct."

To his discomfort, she turned to the gentleman on her left. "Did you know that English is considered to be Germanic?" Not waiting for an answer, she turned again to Vincent. "Are you sure? Why isn't it called an *Englic* language, and is German under the same umbrella?"

She shrugged as if it were entirely beyond her.

"I am no linguist," he said. He couldn't fathom how they had strayed so far from discussing the sonata. *What had she asked him?*

Then he recalled her question.

"In truth, my lady, I can only tell you that I have no problem maintaining a singular focus on music. Quite the contrary. I find it difficult to tear my thoughts from it."

"You are talented, and thus, you can keep your mind upon it." She cocked her head. "Or is it because you keep your mind on music that you are so talented? Or did I just say the same thing twice?"

"No, I don't believe you did," he said politely.

"In any case, I have not yet found anything that holds my attention long enough to be good at, nor been good at anything long enough to hold my attention."

His head was beginning to pound like the notes at the low end of his beloved piano. And they weren't even at the fish course.

"I have never heard of you as a professional musician," she said abruptly. "But you wrote the piece yourself, didn't you?"

"Yes," he agreed, feeling the old, familiar annoyance wash over him. He hated the path of their conversation, knowing where it would lead.

"Your music should fill concert halls, my lord."

It already does, he nearly snapped. But that would rip open an old wound and lead to much explanation.

"I have other interests and duties making claims upon my time. I am in Parliament."

"Pish," she said.

"Pardon me?" Vincent asked.

The lady gestured with the hand that held her fork. "Anyone can be a statesman, but not just anyone can write music."

"Compose," he corrected her, watching flecks of gravy fly off the end of the silver tines onto his cousin's snowy white table linen.

"Yes, compose," she agreed, *"and* play piano so flawlessly."

"Be that as it may," he began, but she was turning away to her right again.

Vincent heard her ask, "Wouldn't you like to hear some beautiful music, a sonata, played for you after dinner?"

"No," Vincent said a little too loudly, for the entire table fell silent. He glanced at his cousin. "My apologies," he said, addressing her querying expression. He didn't say anything else because there was nothing more to say.

Lady Brilliance turned back to him as the chatter resumed.

"Is something wrong?"

"You cannot offer my composition to others like offering up a plate of roast beef."

He ought to have realized this would tickle her which, by her winsome smile, it did. Vincent had to speak more plainly.

"The sonata you heard belongs to me, and only I may decide who hears my music and when."

She nodded. "I understand."

"Do you?" he blurted.

"Indeed. If your sonata had been published and played publicly, like Mr. Ambrose Castern's music"—he stiffened at the mention of his most bitter enemy, but she didn't notice—"then it becomes the property of the world, and one may hear it whenever someone with enough talent can play it. In such a case, music more resembles a painting in a gallery. The artist can no longer control who sees his canvas."

Vincent realized he'd drained his wine glass and tapped it to indicate his desire for more, which thankfully came quickly at the hands of the nearest footman.

"Oh, I should like more, too," Lady Brilliance said enthusiastically. She seemed that type of person—all in for a penny as much for a pound.

With that settled, Vincent decided to get his dinner partner off the topic of music altogether.

Although he was only at Bexley Hall as a favor, and while he was certain he would never see any of these people again apart from his own cousin, he would make an attempt not to be an utter arse. He must show an interest in his dining partner.

"Naturally, I have heard of Lord and Lady Diamond, but I was unaware of you." Belatedly realizing that smacked of discourtesy, he added, "That is to say, I know nothing about you or whether you have sisters and brothers."

Moreover, Vincent couldn't deny—despite his first impression of Lady Brilliance as a nuisance, albeit a pretty one—he found her company tolerable.

"I have three older sisters and one older brother. And you, my lord?"

"An older sister and a younger brother."

"I am relieved for you," she said.

An odd statement, to be sure, until she added, "I find my family to be the source of my greatest happiness."

That surprised him, given his own less-than-joyful relations. While he was close with his mother and on good terms with his stepfather, his sister had left for Belgium upon marrying five years earlier and had never returned. His younger brother enjoyed Cambridge so much, he was residing there despite no longer being a student.

"I may as well tell you that my name is the worst of the lot," Lady Brilliance remarked into his silence.

He wasn't sure how to reply. "It is, as I said before, an unusual one."

"I don't mind that. What is most vexing is how rarely it is used. If one is going to be given a name by one's loving parents, for goodness' sake, use it. My sisters are lucky. The eldest, Clarity, could be called Clare, yet no one ever does. Still, it would be a real name. And my other sister, Radiance, is often called Ray which, to me, denotes sunshine, a perfectly acceptable name. My other sister, Purity, is always called precisely that, and she wouldn't have it any other way. No one would call her Pure, as that's just a word, not a name. And then there's Adam, who is naturally called Adam."

She sipped her wine and looked around as if the conversation was over. Vincent almost didn't prod her to continue, but he found himself wanting to know the answer.

"May I ask, what does your family call you?"

She turned back to him and sighed. "Bri. It is dreadful. Not a name, not a word, merely a sound."

He nodded, then recalled something. "There is that soft French cheese, Brie de Meaux, made just east of Paris."

She frowned. *Had he insulted her?* Where before, even earlier that evening, he hadn't cared one way or the other, he now had no desire to be insolent, especially not over her name. After all, it was hardly her choice.

"I admit that I don't know anything about this cheese," she said, "nor am I sure that sharing a name with the product of a cow really makes it any better. Have you tasted it? Is it good?"

"It's delicious," he told her. He'd eaten it in France and when visiting his sister in Belgium. "It is not like cheddar, much softer and creamier, sometimes even sweet. You can get it in London, I assure you. I don't think the English knew much about it or cared until the famed banquet during the Congress of Vienna."

Her expression indicated she had no idea of what he spoke.

"Go on," she said.

"Lord Talleyrand was an excellent diplomat. While everyone was divvying up nations, he thought to calm the temperaments with a cheese contest. Each country at the bargaining table was invited to contribute their native cheese to the banquet. Naturally, Lord Castlereagh chose Stilton to represent the British. And who doesn't love it with a hunk of fresh bread and some watercress?"

"No one, I would warrant," Lady Brilliance said.

"However, it was the Brie that was unanimously declared 'Le Roi des Fromages'."

"The king of . . .?" she queried.

"Cheeses," he supplied the translation.

"Truly? Or are you teasing me?"

He couldn't help smiling. "God's honest truth, my lady. Brie is the king of cheeses, declared so by all the statesmen of Europe and the United Kingdom. Or, in your case, the Queen."

She shook her head. "Still, would I rather be called a word like *pure* or *ray* or named for cheese?"

"Then I shall address you only by the full title of Lady Brilliance."

She nodded. "You are not insufferable as I believed upon our initial conversation."

Vincent startled. Everyone thought such things about others, but one rarely heard oneself spoken of in such a manner.

"I hope I am *not* insufferable," he said.

She smiled again, a dazzling effect, causing her deep blue eyes to sparkle in the dining room's candlelight.

"Will you take part in the evening's entertainment?"

She had switched topics so quickly that he almost missed it.

"No, decidedly not."

"I can hardly credit our hostess has something better forthcoming than your piano playing."

He doubted there was, but still, he wasn't going to be paraded out like a monkey on a leash playing cymbals. He did not perform on demand. He did not perform at all!

"Regardless, I am *not* part of the evening's entertainment."

"Another evening, perhaps?" she asked. "It would be selfish of you not to share your talent."

He gaped. "You cannot tell someone they are selfish for not playing the piano."

Lady Brilliance shrugged her slender shoulders, bare due to the fashionable neckline of her dress. *How the devil did those little lace and satin sleeves stay up on her arms?* Vincent wondered.

"Why would you deprive people of hearing your talent?" she persisted, and he was irritated to find them back on the topic of music. "Many, if not most, would love to be able to play with such skill. You can, therefore you should."

She blinked at him, waiting for him to agree, he assumed.

"*Should* I? You speak as though I were blessed with piano playing like a gift that I opened for Christmas. Since I have it, I ought to share it. I spent years learning and practicing."

"Precisely. And for what purpose if not to perform for others?"

Vincent was squeezing his wine glass stem so hard, he feared he would shatter it.

"Perhaps for myself," he ground out and then turned away. He did not have to explain himself to this chit named for cheese.

Striking up a conversation with Alethia, he could practically feel Lady Brilliance staring at his right ear. He ignored her. And that's what he would do for the rest of the evening if at all possible.

CHAPTER THREE

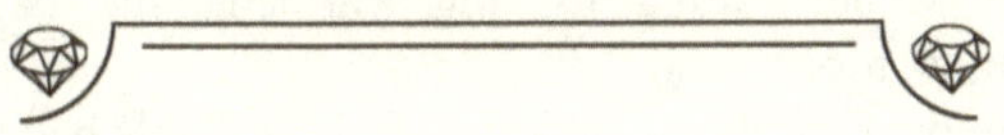

The poor man! Brilliance had heard of actors afflicted with stage fright, a term she'd learned when attending a play at Covent Garden only to be disappointed by the absence of one of the primary cast members. Her mother had waved down the play's manager, a harried individual in a worn top hat, who bowed low when realizing he was speaking with a countess.

"Stage fright," he had told them succinctly. It had derailed the performance.

Brilliance's mother had sent the actor some fruit the following day by way of a cheering gift.

Brilliance could not imagine any other reason why Lord Hewitt wouldn't wish to share his music with the rest of them. It would explain his annoyance with her earlier when she had interrupted his solitary playing.

For he could not be in any doubt as to his superiority of talent over everyone else in attendance. The possibility that there were two gifted pianists at the same house party was improbable, if not utterly unlikely. Moreover, she was equally certain that many of the ladies present and undoubtedly some of the gentlemen would give a drawing room performance before the party's end. Some would play the piano, others the violin or flute. Some would sing, and a few would give a dramatic recitation. It was expected when gathered in the country.

And Brilliance had been to her fair share of gatherings where talent was decidedly lacking but made up for by a performer's enthusiasm. Nobody minded a flat note or two if the singer's heart was full, nor a stuttered piano performance if the player continued with jovial determination.

Why, she had once seen a young lady be sick upon her slippers while waiting to sing, yet sing she had, and beautifully, too.

Moreover, while the basket of fruit probably had little to do with the Covent Garden actor's recovery, he had, in fact, made it onto the stage the following night to high acclaim. Thus, Brilliance intended to assist Lord Hewitt in any way she could.

That night, since the guests had arrived only hours earlier, some from afar, they had little demanded of them beyond attending the dinner and relaxing in the drawing room. A very light and early supper would be served at eleven. And then, of course, they could retire to their beds.

In the drawing room, cards were provided without much interest, along with a chess board, and plenty of creamy syllabub, despite it falling out of favor lately, as well as coffee, tea, biscuits and cake, which did garner some enthusiasm. Most talked in small groups, getting to know each other. For those literary-minded, there was the library, but no one seemed inclined to reach for a book that night.

And of course, Brilliance knew there was a conservatory, but she imagined it was already occupied by Lord Hewitt, probably with the door barricaded. She, for one, had no intention of bothering him again, not until the following day at the earliest.

Although after a moment's thought, she asked the footman at hand what type of fruit Lady Twitchard had. Thrilled to learn of fresh oranges, she requested one and placed it outside the conservatory door with a simple note.

"For Lord Hewitt." She could, in fact, hear him playing the same tune as earlier.

Not willing to sit on one of the drawing room settees after the coach ride and the lengthy dinner, Brilliance instead opted for a stroll of the upstairs gallery.

Gladly, she accepted the company of Martine and another two ladies, new to her but amiable so far. They were all four of a similar age and had seen one another at events during the Season, but never before until that evening had they been formally introduced.

They strolled the long hallway created when the enfilade, or long series of rooms stretching from one side of the house to the other, had been closed up. It made for an excellent place to display paintings.

"Any prospects?" the blonde Miss Newton asked a little forwardly.

Brilliance instantly loved that about her since she had wondered the same thing. However, before she could jump into the conversation and say how intriguing she found Lord Hewitt, Martine squeezed her hand and spoke first.

"I think it's early for that," she said.

Her tone reminded Brilliance of her sister Purity, but she appreciated the cautionary reminder to hold her tongue, for she was often apt to speak without thinking. If the others knew she was at all interested in Lord Hewitt, they would watch her every move. The most innocent of gestures might be misconstrued.

The other young lady, a pale brunette, Lady Georgiana had a somewhat wolfish grin in the flickering lamplight of the landing. And she seemed ready to discuss the male guests.

"I think Lady Twitchard did a grand job with the invitations. I see more than one man with a fine face and figure. Not to mention the latecomer, Lord Hewitt. I thought him to be well worth waiting for."

"Really?" Brilliance asked, knowing it was ridiculous to let even the thinnest thread of jealousy weave its way into her heart, having known the man only a few hours.

Nevertheless, perhaps because she'd been alone with him or perhaps because they had dined beside one another, she felt a tad proprietary. Moreover, she was curious as to how strong a match the other ladies were willing to make.

"If any gentleman over the course of the next week indicates a desire to form an attachment, will your parents allow you to make your own choice and encourage his courtship?"

"My parents trust Lady Twitchard," Lady Georgiana said. "Elsewise I wouldn't be here. Any guest of hers, and a cousin no less who is also a viscount, shall be considered a good catch. Don't you all agree?"

"I do," said Miss Newton. "And Lord Hewitt is handsome, to be sure, but I thought Lord Patterson to exhibit the very pinnacle of manly beauty as well as having a perfectly gentle way of speaking."

Since this *pinnacle* was the same blond-haired gentleman who had also caught Martine's hazel eyes, it occurred to Brilliance how a small country party of eligible single people could quickly devolve into competition and bruised hearts.

"One must guard oneself against forming an attachment too swiftly," Martine said, "and doing so upon first impressions is the least reliable."

Brilliance looked at her friend's slight frown and knew she was hoping to save Lord Patterson for herself. Perhaps she could help with some advice straight from Purity's lips.

"Surely the gentlemen themselves will disclose in some subtle manner with whom they are forming an affinity, thereby saving an eager female from making an egregiously embarrassing misstep. One would hate to appear overly interested in the wrong direction."

The others considered such embarrassment and nodded. And then they turned their attention to the impressive art collection on the walls of Lady Twitchard's long gallery. They strolled in silence for a few minutes.

"It's a little *spooky*," Miss Newton remarked, indicating the wall lamps that illuminated only circles of floral-patterned paper and parts of dark oil paintings.

That was only the second time Brilliance had heard the word, with both occurrences being that year. It was a perfect term for what it denoted, and she hoped to find an occasion to use it herself.

"The gallery warrants a daytime visit," came a male voice she recognized at once. A little shiver of excitement raced through her as Lord Hewitt appeared from the gloom at the other end.

"I thought you were in the conservatory," she said, watching the lamplight flicker on the glass of his spectacles.

All eyes turned to her at such a disclosure of awareness as to a certain guest's whereabouts. *Too late for discretion*, she mused, unbothered.

"I was," he agreed. "Oddly, when I came out, I tripped over an orange."

The other ladies laughed, but Brilliance peered up at him.

"Did you eat it?" For she wasn't sure how the fruit might help, but eating it was undoubtedly an integral part of the stage-fright cure.

"I have it in my pocket for later," he assured her.

"Very good," she said, waiting expectantly for him to declare his reason for being there.

He turned to Miss Newton. "While it is difficult to see the detail in this light, if you return tomorrow, you will view some Flemish paintings with amazing artistry, mainly in the fabric and lace," Lord Hewitt promised. "And fruit," he added, sending Brilliance a quick glance. "As well as the lifelike feathers on hens and partridges. I promise there is nothing in the least frightening."

"We can only hope there's time," Lady Georgiana said. "Tomorrow's schedule is spanking full, leaving little time for dillydallying between sunrise and sunset."

"I am sure my cousin will allow all you ladies time for a little dillydallying," he said. "If you will excuse me, I will let you continue your promenade."

Just like that, he disappeared through a doorway with the knowledge of someone who had been in the country manor previously and knew his way around.

They all remained silent for a moment, gazing after him. Miss Newton spoke first. "I believe he paid me especially kind attention. Having heard my remark about the atmosphere of this gallery, he went out of his way to reassure me."

Brilliance didn't think that to be the case at all, but she wasn't going to argue. In fact, Lady Georgiana put up a little opposition of her own.

"He was equally attentive to my words about the schedule."

Martine made a *tut-tutting* sound. "His lordship was being polite to everyone in similar measure. I don't think he gave anyone any reason to feel particularly favored. Are we going to continue walking or return downstairs?"

"I think we should return to the drawing room," said Lady Georgiana. "If the other gentlemen are gathered there, then the remaining ladies are enjoying a lopsided quantity of attention."

"Indeed," agreed Miss Newton. Without another word, they hurried back the way they had come.

"I would just as soon go back, too, if you don't mind," Martine said.

"Not at all. I'll join you. Let me fetch my wrap, and I'll meet you there. I know it's July, but my shoulders are cold."

"How we suffer for fashion," Martine quipped and disappeared in the same direction as the other two.

Brilliance looked along the hall. There was quite a bit more to the gallery, but it was even darker. She certainly didn't fancy going ahead alone, nor did she wish to retrace her steps since the ladies' chambers were at the back of the house in a wing mirroring the gentlemen's. In her experience in this type of country manor, she needed to bisect the grand house.

Thus, without much forethought, she put her fingers on the handle to the closest door, the one through which Lord Hewitt had disappeared, and opened it.

VINCENT WAS PEELING THE orange while he walked, dropping the peel into his pocket. His cousin had obviously recalled his love of the juicy sweet fruit. Thoughtfully, Alethia hadn't disturbed him while he was playing. The house party wasn't going to be such a terrible inconvenience after all.

Coming upon the bevy of beauties lurking in the dimly lit corridor had startled him. He'd expected all the guests to be in the drawing room. In any case, he knew better than to remain in their midst. Before he realized it, one of them would start having designs on him. Thus, he'd made his escape quickly, although he hoped he had not been rude.

The passageway, used mostly by servants, led directly back to the gentleman's quarters, the shortest route, in fact.

Alternately cramming a slice of orange into his mouth and whistling a tune between bites, Vincent reached the end of the long corridor and stepped out into the spacious, carpeted hallway. The only other person in sight was a footman making sure the lamps were lit. A few more yards, and he was at his own door.

Inside his room, he shrugged out of his jacket and flopped onto the bed. The option to skip the supper was tempting. He might fall asleep before eleven. After all, he was fairly sure there would be other vacant seats that first night, the only one in which guests were given leeway to forgo an otherwise obligatory gathering.

Thus, he had just stretched out on the bed when there was a light tap at his door. If Vincent was lucky, the footman might be offering gentlemen a glass of brandy in their rooms.

"Enter," he called out.

Lady Brilliance walked in, took a look at where she was, and stopped in her tracks.

CHAPTER FOUR

"What the devil?" Vincent exclaimed before he could stop himself. "You cannot be in here." His feet hit the floor, and he was standing, arms crossed, in front of her in seconds.

The lady looked him up and down. "No, I suppose not. I saw you enter as I came out of the long passage. So convenient to traverse the house thusly, don't you think?" She looked down at the area rug underfoot, glanced at every piece of furniture in his room, even the bed, and then finally set her gaze upon him again.

"Why are you here?" he demanded.

"You are in a state of undress," she pointed out.

For the briefest moment of terror, he thought maybe he'd taken off his trousers before reclining. Luckily, however, he'd only divested himself of his coat and necktie.

"I am, indeed, because this is *my* bedchamber."

"The corresponding corner room in the other wing," she said, her gaze fixing on his bare collarbone, "on the ladies' side, is a sitting room."

"Yet this isn't!" he practically shouted. *Why wasn't she fleeing in shame and embarrassment?* "Not only shouldn't you be in my chamber, you shouldn't even be in this hall. What happens if you step outside my door and are seen?"

Lady Brilliance shrugged. "I know it would look bad, wouldn't it? But I would simply explain—"

"That you followed me into my room! How would that help?"

"*Hm.* I see what you mean. Perhaps you should peek out first and make sure no other gentlemen are lingering, and if the way is clear, I shall slip out."

"Very well." Vincent scooted past her, not bothering with his coat after all. The primary concern was getting her out of there.

He cracked the door only the width of his left eye. To his immense consternation, another two fellows were walking along. One was speaking, then the other broke out in laughter.

Vincent shut the door and turned, only to find Lady Brilliance so close her nose pressed against his chest. Unthinkingly, he reached out and grabbed her shoulders. If she was trying to throw herself at him, he would keep her at bay.

Yet she blinked up at him, her intense deep-blue eyes absolutely guileless.

"I was trying to see past you. But your shoulders are so wide, you blocked out everything."

His gaze fixed on her ridiculously rosy lips, even as his grip on her upper arms relaxed. He ought to release her instantly. Instead, almost of their own accord, his thumbs caressed her warm, bare skin below her silly half sleeves, which he could push down with a puff of breath. Goosebumps rose under his fingers.

"You're cold," he said, wondering at the husky tone of his voice. He cleared his throat.

"No," she replied, her gaze not wavering from his. "I mean, I was previously a little chilled, which is why I am here. I am looking for my wrap. Not in *your* room obviously. I was going to my own. I confess I took the same path as you, and then, as I stepped into the hallway, I saw this door swing shut."

"I see." He was still stroking her skin. And while he knew he should unhand her, the moment was so surreal and unexpected that Vincent held on. "There are two other guests in the hallway."

"Then I suppose I must stay a little longer," she said.

Vincent marveled at the appearance of her tongue, darting across her lower lip. A fascinating little movement that indicated she was not quite at ease.

It was his fault. He was behaving badly. Finally, he dropped his hands from her, despite the impulse to draw her closer and kiss her.

He attributed his errant inclination to being alone with one of the prettiest females he'd ever seen. One without an ounce of self-preservation, it seemed.

She didn't step back, even with nothing keeping her close.

"Do you know something, Lord Handsome . . . I mean, Lord Hewitt?" Her cheeks pinkened at the adorable slip of the tongue. "I thought you might be about to kiss me."

His own cheeks were undoubtedly taking on a ruddy hue as she read his thoughts. She wasn't quite so adorable, gazing up at him, her teeth once more tugging on her own lower lip. More like a hunter, with him the unsuspecting prey.

"Let me look again." Vincent turned away from her and peered out the door once more. The corridor was thankfully empty. "We are in luck," he said before feeling her bare, ungloved hand on his arm, searing him through his shirt sleeve.

"Are we? Let me see?"

He barely had the chance to move sideways when she pushed around him and looked out. Her back was practically pressed to his front, and her fragrant hair was under his nose. He sniffed in the heady aroma of roses and something else. Carnations perhaps?

Lady Brilliance giggled. "Are you smelling my hair?" She turned in the space between them, her breasts brushing his arm, and his restraint snapped. With his hands resting on either side of her head, he leaned in, making the door click closed once again.

With her back flat against the door, she looked up. "Why, you *are* going to kiss me! How exciting!" Then she shut her eyes and waited.

Although the moment struck him as funny, it didn't diminish his desire one whit. While trying to remain somewhat of a gentleman and not touch her body with any part of his, Vincent claimed her mouth. His lips slanted across hers, and he felt her gasp in a quick, hot breath.

In the next moment, her arms worked between them until she was doing what he would not allow himself—she was tracing her fingers up his chest until they finally rested at the back of his neck.

"*Mmm,*" she hummed, and the sound stroked the length of him.

The kiss, itself, was slow, but the surge of longing raced through his body like a spark of fire.

Sweet Bedlam! She was lucky he truly was a gentleman in manner and not in name only. If not, he would have her on her back upon his bed in seconds, with her décolletage drawn down to expose her breasts and her satin skirts tossed up half a minute after.

Still, he didn't raise his mouth from hers. Not yet. Not before he allowed them another few moments of bliss while he traced his tongue across her lips. She parted them.

He had to accept the invitation. *It would be rude not to!*

Sliding his tongue along hers, soon he was gently sucking it. Finally, he felt her hands pressing gently against his shoulders. She had come to her senses. She ought to slap him at the very least, denounce him to his own cousin as a rogue at the worst—and get him sent home on the first night.

Suddenly, he hoped she didn't.

Looking down at her, half expecting to see ire and outrage, instead, he saw a tentative smile.

"You tasted of sweet orange. You ate my gift."

"*Your* gift?" he echoed. "I thought it from Lady Twitchard."

She shrugged. "That was a perfectly splendid kiss. Shall we do it again?"

Now that some modicum of sanity had returned while they conversed, Vincent was determined to get her on her way to safety.

"No."

"What?" she exclaimed. "Not ever? Wasn't it done well? I thought so. Didn't you like it? Was my breath not fresh? I vow I chewed on the sprig of mint after the last meat course."

Realizing he was gaping, he finally let himself touch her, only to put his finger under her chin and tap her mouth closed.

"Silence! You must get out of my room, or you'll be sent back to London in disgrace. Do you want that?"

"No," she said, sounding reasonable. "Then we could never kiss again. I shall go." Turning, she nearly yanked open the door until he stopped her.

"Wait!" Determining the hallway was empty, he said, "You ought to run until you are on the other side of the main stairs, then there will be little risk of someone assuming you were in this wing."

"Very well."

He started to crack the door wider when she said, "My very first *paramour*! Isn't it exciting?"

With that, leaving him shocked once more, she hurried out.

Vincent didn't wait to see her progress, as his open door would ruin everything should it be noticed. Instead, he closed it firmly and faced his empty room.

What the hell just happened?

BRILLIANCE FOUGHT TO KEEP from skipping. Yet taking Lord Hewitt's advice, she walked as hastily as possible, without losing a slipper, all the way to the ladies' wing. Then she could catch her breath and reflect on what had occurred.

Her first real kiss. *And what a kiss!* While trapped in the hollow between his arms, scenting his cologne, a peppery fragrance of juniper, vetiver, and . . . manliness, she had closed her eyes—the better to feel every whisper-soft sensation, as well as the harder ones, too, such as the back of her head on the door and the persistent ache that blossomed low in her belly.

She had wanted to curl her hips against his. Moreover, she had yearned to feel his fingers touch her skin. *Anywhere!* Instead, the gentleman had kept his hands frustratingly off her.

That had been her only complaint on an otherwise magnificent kiss. His lips were obviously meant for hers. Why, their mouths fit like two pieces of a puzzle with nothing left over.

Surely that could mean only one thing—they were destined for one another. All traces of tiredness from the long day vanished. Brilliance could hardly wait for supper when she would see him again.

CHAPTER FIVE

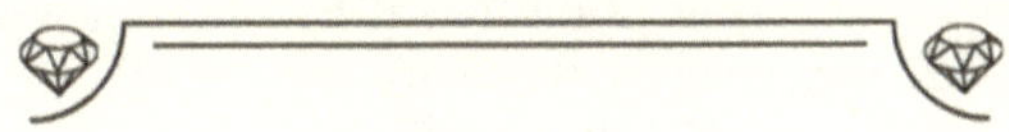

Seeing sunshine upon opening her eyes the following morning, Brilliance let the memories rush in. She was *not* at her home on Piccadilly in London. She was in Bexley and about to have her first full day at Lady Twitchard's country manor. And she had already been kissed.

What more excitement might possibly be on the horizon?

As that question buzzed in her busy brain, she was up and, with the assistance of her maid, Belinda, dressed in a lovely morning frock. Within a quarter of an hour, she headed downstairs.

Some guests would be strolling the property or taking tea in the gardens, but Brilliance had always been fond of stoking her inner hearth with a cup of chocolate and, at the very least, a coddled egg or two before starting her day.

The previous night's supper had been held in the same pink salon in which they'd been told to take their breakfast. It was a nice change from one long table in the dining room. Four tables were set up around a white marble font. Instead of water, it contained a lovely display of living plants.

"Good morning," Brilliance said to one and all. However, a brief inspection of the room's occupants indicated neither Lord Hewitt nor Martine was there. In fact, only two gentlemen were as yet eating.

That was a bit of a letdown, as Lord Hewitt had not put in an appearance at the previous night's light supper of soup and bread, either. Brilliance had tried not to let her disappointment ruin the fun of being up late at a party without a chaperone or her parents or siblings. She had enjoyed the soup while being showered by Martine's questions.

"Where on earth did you disappear to?" her friend had asked.

"Lost," had been Brilliance's truthful answer, but Martine had given her the horse-eye.

"A rather long time to go from the gallery to your room," her friend had declared. "I made it back downstairs and chatted with the others and still you didn't reappear."

Brilliance had simply shrugged until her friend had given up, deciding there was nothing to know.

Now, as the two gentlemen rose to their feet, Brilliance hesitated in order to determine the protocol. *Should she take a seat or go to the sideboard and help herself?*

"The footman just went off to get more toast," said the blond Lord Patterson. "But there is no standing on ceremony. Allow me," he added.

Picking up a clean plate from the sideboard, he lifted the silver lid off the first chafing dish.

"Coddled eggs or scrambled?"

"The first, please." Brilliance went to join him.

"Bacon or sausage?" he asked upon lifting the second lid.

"Why not both?" she asked. "Otherwise, I might not make it until dinner."

"We don't want you passing away from hunger," he said, matching her teasing tone before placing two rashers of bacon and two sausages on her plate.

"There are sweet onion tarts, too, and creamy potatoes," he added as they strolled along the sideboard.

"Perhaps if I have room," she said, taking a seat beside the one he had vacated. "Thank you."

She helped herself from the chocolate pot, proclaiming it, "Superb."

"Everything is of the finest quality," agreed Lord Fincham, whose name she remembered because his face reminded her of a bird.

"Especially the guests," said Lord Patterson, nodding at her. "I am happy to be among so many nice people."

Brilliance approved of his friendly disposition. She hoped he would return her best friend's interest. If possible, she would help matters along.

"I am glad to have your company, my lord, as my lovely and very sweet friend Lady Martine must still be abed. Were you introduced to her?"

"Indeed, I was. The lady with the mole on her neck," he said.

"The same," Brilliance agreed. "I think it is a pretty birthmark."

"I suppose it can be considered such, by some."

Brilliance wasn't sure he sounded all that approving.

"Your clear complexion is deemed far more desirable," the gentleman added.

Oh, dear. She had no interest in the golden-curled lord. She must take his attention off herself.

"What is the first item on our day's schedule? Lord Fincham, do you recall? Silly me, I forgot to look."

"For the gentlemen, nothing more taxing than strolling down to the stream, although undoubtedly carriages will be offered, too," Lord Fincham responded. "We are fishing."

"And the ladies?" she asked.

"I believe you ladies will have the opportunity to paint," said Lord Patterson. "For my part, I would be happy to watch *you* paint for hours."

Noooo! "That sounds dreadfully dull for you," Brilliance said.

Luckily, Martine entered. Again, both gentlemen rose. However, with the footman having returned, Lord Patterson didn't need to play the server this time.

Regardless, Brilliance had hoped he would wait upon her friend as he had done for her. He did not.

"I didn't realize how late the time was," Martine remarked, taking a seat. "I vow I sleep more deeply and longer in the country than I ever do in Town."

"It's not all that late," Brilliance said. "I think the majority of people are still abed."

"That's a relief." Martine took a sip of chocolate. "My, that's delicious. And restorative. In any case, I thought it was later because Lord Hewitt is already practicing in the conservatory."

Brilliance sat up straighter. The man was dedicated, indeed, if he would play before breakfast.

"Lord Patterson tells me we are painting this morning."

Martine nodded, then turned to him.

"Do you paint, my lord?"

He laughed unnecessarily. "No, what a notion!" His tone was derisive, as if he had never noticed that most of the famous painters in the world were male.

"The gentlemen are invited to fish," Lord Fincham repeated.

Brilliance thought him superior in disposition and wished Martine would switch her interest to the birdlike man.

"My eldest sister and my brother adore fishing," Brilliance told him. She wondered if Lord Hewitt would fish and whether female guests could eschew the finer arts, of which she had no skill, in favor of the rod and line, of which she also had no skill. At least, with the latter, her lack of prowess was less noticeable.

As more guests arrived, they chatted about the week's upcoming events, including the final evening's ball. After Lord Fincham left, Brilliance decided to do Martine a favor by leaving her alone with Lord Patterson for a few minutes as no one else had come to their table.

Unfortunately, as she rose, his lordship quickly stood, too.

"I hope you will excuse me." She ought to have come up with a reason beforehand. Yet Martine was looking at her with gratitude and understanding.

Rather than retaking his seat, however, Lord Patterson looked as though he was going to escort Brilliance from the room. She would have to be forceful.

"I hope you will keep my very good friend, Lady Martine, company. And I shall see you both outside in a little while."

His lordship appeared disappointed, but he regained his chair. That settled, Brilliance considered taking a plate of food to Lord Hewitt until she decided she was being presumptuous. Still, a bowl of cherries, already pitted by the scullery maid, could hardly be unwelcome.

With the offering in hand, she returned to the conservatory door.

Sure enough, Brilliance could hear him. Surprisingly, this time, she knew the music he was playing. Not his own, but the work of Mr. Ambrose Castern, of whom everyone was familiar. For a while, this particular piece was played not only at his concerts but at those of other pianists. People clapped when they heard the opening notes, knowing what was to come.

With less hesitancy than the day before, she opened the door.

Lord Hewitt's back and his same upright posture greeted her. And after a few moments, the same cessation of playing. However, this time, when he turned, he didn't look nearly as irritated, although perhaps the tiniest bit hesitant.

For her part, she didn't feel the least unnerved by the fact that when last she'd seen him, they'd had been pressing their mouths against one another's.

"I brought you some cherries. Without stones," she added.

He rewarded her with a small smile that tickled her down to toes.

"What a lovely smile you have, my lord."

It grew broader. "Thank you. It's very kind of you to say. But why did you bring me cherries?"

"Because I didn't see any other fruit," she confessed, hoping he wasn't embarrassed. "My mother once sent a large basket of fruit to an actor. It seemed to help him tremendously."

His brow furrowed. Yet in the next instant, he took the bowl from her.

"Again, I thank you."

Brilliance was thrilled he was willing to try to cure his stage fright. "Is it your habit to skip breakfast?"

If it was, then should they marry, she would have to keep herself company by reading the morning paper while drinking her chocolate.

"Not at all," he said, "I simply lost track of time. I didn't intend to play this morning, but somehow, here I am. Have I missed it altogether?"

"I am sure your cousin won't starve you." Brilliance went to the large windows where she could see guests gathering on the lawn. "But I believe it is nearly time for the first entertainment. Do you intend to fish?"

"Do you?" he asked.

She spun around with interest. "If you are inviting me, then I will. I am not as good as my eldest sister and my brother, but perhaps not as terrible as my other two sisters."

"I haven't fished since I was a boy." He looked pleased at the prospect while popping berries into his mouth.

"I am sure you shall easily recall how to do it. You have a magnificent memory, after all," Brilliance told him. "I am most impressed by how well you were playing Mr. Castern's piece when I entered."

To her amazement, Lord Hewitt's expression darkened. Any hint of happiness disappeared, and he slammed the porcelain fruit bowl onto the piano.

With disbelief, she watched a few of the juicy red cherries "escape" as she fancied their quick movement. For it appeared as if they'd hopped over the rim of the shallow bowl before rolling across the smooth surface of the piano and falling to the rug below.

"It isn't *his* music," Lord Hewitt hissed.

Was he teasing her? "I beg to differ, my lord. I have heard it many times, and that was the very same. I am certain you can compose something as good if you put your mind to it."

She decided to pick up the cherries. Lady Twitchard would not be pleased to find stains on her carpet should someone stand on them. Nearly as bad as spilling a glass of burgundy wine on a cream-colored table linen. Brilliance had done that, too.

Crouching low to retrieve the wayward fruit, she almost missed his next words.

"Leave me in peace."

"It won't do to let these remain on the rug," she began before realizing what he had said. Having quickly picked up the errant berries, she rose.

"I beg your pardon?" Brilliance asked, dropping them back into the bowl.

"I asked you to leave." His tone was sharp. "I have music to practice."

"What about fishing, or even a mouthful of breakfast?"

"Out," he said, rudely lowering himself onto the stool and giving her his shoulder.

Cherries certainly affected him differently than an orange, which had put him in a good mood. She did not like the foul one that had come over him.

He was apparently jealous of Mr. Castern.

It seemed petty and beneath a man of honor, especially one with such talent. About to tell him that very thing, Brilliance restrained herself, albeit with difficulty. Instead, she left without another word, taking the bowl of cherries with her.

What's more, she would try her hand at painting. *Again!* There was no point in dragging her skirts to the possibly muddy stream if Lord Hewitt was going to remain in the conservatory.

FISHING! WHAT A POINTLESS waste of time unless one intended to catch something substantial for one's dinner. However, Vincent knew what was in the nearby waters that flowed through Alethia's estate toward the River Cray—nothing but small dab. Maybe some trout if one was lucky.

Besides, he didn't want to stand there tossing in a line and hook when he could be practicing.

For what? came the unkind voice in his head. *Or for whom?*

Regardless, he ran through the sonata again. *His* sonata. One of his favorites, originally named for a young lady as beautiful and treacherous as King Arthur's Guinevere. *Lydia.* Naturally, the scoundrel, Ambrose Castern, had changed the title.

Unexpectedly, Vincent made a mistake halfway through. Beginning again, he found himself looking down at the keys. That didn't help. He made another mistake, hesitated, and then ground to a halt.

Lady Brilliance!

His normally sharp concentration was shattered. And it was the lady's fault. What with her damned cherries! She obviously had sawdust between her ears.

Luckily, when he stormed into the pink salon, no one else was there. He poured himself a cup of lukewarm coffee, which put him in an even worse mood. Then he had some hard toast, a piece of cold gristly bacon, and a rubbery sausage before giving up.

He ought to be a dutiful guest and join the fishing party. Instead, he wandered into the back garden, finding it blooming with ladies and their easels.

"Why are you looking like a thunder cloud?" his cousin asked him. From her vantage point on the terrace, Alethia was overseeing the others in lieu of painting. Vincent knew her to be quite skilled and not one to risk bruising her guests' tender psyches.

"Because I am trapped at your party," he shot back.

Alethia didn't look the least upset, nor even insulted.

"Mr. Warbly, please go help the lady by the delphiniums," she said to the painting master she'd hired. "Her painting looks more like a giraffe than a flower, don't you think?"

Then his cousin turned her attention to him.

"Who spat in your tea this morning?" Alethia asked.

"What a disgusting thing to say." Vincent spied Lady Brilliance by the rose arbor. "Are there no gentlemen here?"

"Apparently not," she said pointedly.

He blinked at her. She raised an eyebrow. Finally, he relaxed.

"I apologize for being out of sorts. It must have been the lumpy mattress."

"I own no lumpy mattresses," she protested.

He wasn't going to mention a pretty lady who set his teeth on edge.

"Is the Colonel at the stream, too?" Vincent liked his cousin-in-law. Colonel Twitchard was a no-nonsense man of action whose only weakness was his wife. And while the man didn't understand the finer points of composing music—*"how can you string all those notes together in any order that sounds pleasing?"*—he was still a good one with whom to hash out anything troubling.

Yet the one thing Vincent had never spoken to Twitchard about was what troubled him most. The Colonel would never have allowed his music to be stolen!

"Yes, my husband is fishing. Why aren't you?"

Vincent shrugged. He was behaving badly, but he couldn't enjoy himself until he'd apologized to Lady Brilliance.

"I may head down to the stream in a few minutes," he said. With no further explanation, he stepped off the terrace and ambled toward Lady Brilliance by a circuitous route around his cousin's whimsical topiaries and past the other painters as if he had no particular destination.

He thought some of the paintings were quite good. One of the ladies from the gallery, Lady Georgiana if his memory served him, and it usually did, looked up at him as he passed.

"Take a look at my attempt, Lord Hewitt. But be kind."

Since she was inviting him to look, he knew it would be good. Yet she continued in her false self-deprecation.

"We cannot all be as talented as Mr. Turner."

Her painting was certainly not similar to Turner's, which were all light, shadow, and impressions of objects. But it was skillful nonetheless in a more pedantic and realistic way.

"That is the very likeness of those flowers, my lady. Precisely done." He couldn't be more enthusiastic, since her painting had no personality, merely a representation of the flowers in front of her. It would have been better as a sketch, in fact.

Lady Georgiana seemed pleased with his words, offering him a coy tilt of her head as she said, "Why, thank you, my lord. I never expected such praise."

Nodding, Vincent continued on, hoping not to make eye contact or be brought into any more conversations with these females. Finally, he came upon Lady Brilliance. Approaching from behind her, he was able to spy her canvas while she was as yet unaware.

It was beyond anything he'd ever seen in its absolute atrocity. If he could not see the roses in front of her, he would have no idea what her subject was. Shaking his head, he recalled he had little experience in the world of art. *Who was he to judge?*

Unfortunately, that thought did not help. Even if he had never seen a painting before, he would know in his bones how terrible this one was. The stems growing directly up from the ground were too short and thick, while the roses looked like salmon-colored, misshapen mushrooms. And unless he was sadly mistaken, she had put one of those pieces of fruit she was always giving him—a large, dimple-skinned orange—in the distance.

Coming closer, he circled around until he was in her field of vision. "Good day, Lady Brilliance."

Looking up at him, she shaded her eyes with her hand despite wearing a bonnet. He noticed she had paint on her cheek and her ungloved hand and now on the brim of her bonnet.

"Good day, Lord Hewitt. I should be angry at you and shun you with silence, but what is the point in that?"

He'd never met such an affable female. She entirely lacked the veneer of game-playing that covered even the nicest ladies upon occasion.

"No more point to it than fishing in a rain barrel, in my humble opinion," Vincent said before clearing his throat. "I came to apologize for my earlier outburst. I am sorry for spilling the cherries and for chasing you away."

Her smile was breathtaking.

"Perhaps your mood was brought on by a bout of peckishness," she said. "That's why I always go straight to the breakfast table when I awaken. A cup of chocolate and something nourishing staves off any bad moods or headaches."

Although he knew his lack of food had little to do with his earlier anger, he nodded.

"I went to the salon and had some toast and coffee. And you are correct, I am much improved."

"And yet, here you are amongst the ladies instead of with the gentlemen. Are you going to claim an easel, too?"

"No, I shall not. I haven't the patience, nor the skill for it." He wished he hadn't mentioned skill. For she glanced at her painting and then back at him, her expression clearly questioning.

Vincent hated to lie to her, so he said nothing. He merely rocked on his heels, put his hands into his coat pockets, and squinted into the distance as if something had caught his attention.

"You haven't yet remarked upon my painting," she said. "Where are your eye-glasses?"

Perhaps they would help, but he feared his spectacles would only bring her disaster-in-oil into clearer focus. Withdrawing them from his pocket, he donned them and looked at her work of art once again, trying not to flinch.

"An *interesting* composition," he said. "I particularly like the orange. You've captured the fruit's roundness and color."

Her eyes widened, and she studied her own painting in silence for a long moment. Stepping back, he did the same from his vantage over the back of her bonnet. When her shoulders began to shake, Vincent feared the worst.

Lady Brilliance was devastated, sobbing and distraught. *It was all his fault!*

CHAPTER SIX

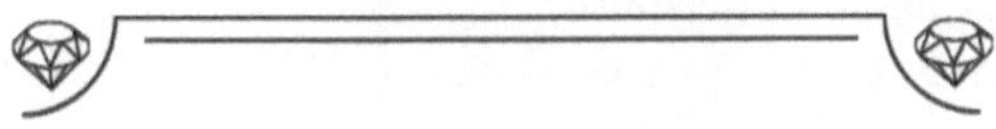

"**L**ady Brilliance," Vincent began, wishing he'd eaten his own shoe rather than insult her.

Suddenly, her laughter burst forth, bringing him instant relief. In fact, she laughed so hard she dropped her paintbrush onto the grass and covered her face. He feared she would convulse with the heartiness of her humor.

Finally, she lifted her head and gave herself a little shake.

"That, my lord, is the sun," she managed to say. "Truly, I thought it the best part of my dreadful creation. Make no mistake, I am fully aware that I have less-than-no talent for oils. Or watercolors, for that matter. I would have been insulted had you tried to flatter me and make a silk purse from my sow's ear of a painting."

"If you tell everyone it is an orange, then it shall be a triumph," he suggested.

Should he tell her that she now had even more paint upon her face? It didn't diminish her beauty at all, but females were fussy about such things.

"But what of these terrible roses?" She retrieved her brush and used it to point at one of the ugly blooms.

"Sadly, there is nothing you can say about those that will make them appear any better."

The painting master chose that moment to come over.

"I hear merriment from this quarter, usually the happy sounds of tri—"

He broke off when he got a good look at Lady Brilliance's painting. "Triumph," he finished flatly, glancing at Vincent who shrugged.

"It is magnificent," the master added. "Like a primitive cry of rosy passion."

Lady Brilliance was chuckling again, and Vincent couldn't contain a snicker. It earned him a warning glance from the painting master.

"Any attempt must be encouraged," he said. "Besides, the orange is well done. The large citrus looks positively juicy."

The laughter that burst out of them both seemed to offend the instructor, for he immediately strode away to another guest.

"I think I would like to try my hand at fishing," Lady Brilliance said. "If it's not too late."

With that, she dipped her brush into the black daub of paint on her palette and in a shaky hand scrawled the word "Brilliance." It took up the entire lower right corner and even curled up the side.

He would have sworn a child had painted it. *How delightful!*

Sighing mightily, she rose to her feet, set her palette on the stool behind her, and wiped her hands on a dry rag that did little to clean them. To his amazement, she turned her back and drew on a pair of lightweight summer gloves, directly over the paint stains.

"I can hardly do any worse at the stream," she said.

BRILLIANCE WAS THRILLED THAT Lord Hewitt had sought her out. They were back upon a solidly friendly footing, and she was hopeful by the end of the day, they might share another passionate kiss.

Perhaps in the throes of a *primitive passion*, as the painting master had said.

"Do you need to change?" he asked, offering her his arm.

She hadn't considered doing so. Purity would, of course, admonish her for not putting on a less diaphanous gown for going to the stream's edge.

"I am not bothered," Brilliance told him. "Unless I offend you for not doing so."

"Not at all," he assured her. "I simply recall that ladies like to put on a new gown for every occasion."

"We often do, don't we?" Flirting outrageously, she leaned on his arm, knowing her breasts were squashed against him. "I shall tell you a secret. Changing our dress is primarily a way to show off our wardrobe to the other ladies. I don't think the men even notice whether we are in blue or pink or cream, silk or satin or cotton."

He nodded, his gray-green gaze dipping to her neckline briefly before locking on her own eyes once more. Brilliance found herself fishing for a compliment more eagerly than she intended to fish in Lady Twitchard's stream.

"For instance, have you noticed what I am wearing today versus yesterday?"

He coughed and again his glance flickered over her. "Yesterday evening, when we first met," Lord Hewitt said, "you were wearing a pale pink gown. Today, you look lovely in that shade of sunshine."

"Shade of sunshine?" she repeated. "You *are* a poet, my lord. This pastel yellow makes me happy."

"What about last evening's rosy pink?" he asked.

"That color makes me happy, too."

"I ought to tell you, then," Lord Hewitt began, sounding a little hesitant, "since my hints about changing your gown did not work, you have paint here"—he touched her cheek, making her flinch—"and here"—he touched her nose, which made her smile—"and even above your eyebrows. Also, if you examine your hands."

Brilliance sighed. "What about my bonnet?"

"A little," he said. "Barely any."

"Drat! And I tried to be so careful, too. By chance, would you have a spare handkerchief you might not mind sacrificing?"

"Indeed, yes," he said, bringing one out of his coat pocket as quick as a whip. It had an elegant blue *H* embroidered on one corner.

"I shall spit on it, but then you must do the wiping, my lord."

This was not the impression Brilliance had wished to make, needing to be cleaned up like a toddler. Nevertheless, she spat twice onto the cloth and handed it back to him. A little gingerly, he wiped her cheek and then, with more effort, scrubbed at it. In this same way, they cleaned the rest of her face.

"My bonnet will have to wait," she said, handing him the soiled handkerchief, which he stared at a moment before shoving back into his pocket.

Finally, they were on the path to the stream, just the two of them, and knowing how clever he was and how she had ruined her painting and managed to get covered in paint, she desperately wanted to say something interesting.

"My father is in Parliament, too. Is yours?"

"He was, and infamously so. Twenty years ago, he had a torrid affair with the wife of the then Prime Minister. It became public. They fought a duel, but luckily no one was injured. Except for my father's political career. It was dead."

"Your mother must have been very cross."

"She was, but my father passed away seven years ago, and she has happily remarried."

Brilliance considered that. "Your career as a member of Parliament shall seem quite stellar in comparison."

"That is a good way to look at it," he agreed. "I can hardly do worse, and anything I do that is better than trying to shoot the Prime Minister will put me in good standing amongst my peers."

"Tory or Whig?" she asked.

"I say," he declared. "That seems rather personal."

"Not for two people who have kissed. Surely." Her words made him look around them in case there were any eavesdroppers. Finding none, he simply nodded.

Brilliance smiled to herself. Men were strange when it came to politics and finances. Moreover, she didn't particularly understand the difference in the political parties nor care which way he leaned. Thus, she changed the subject.

"I very much like roasted chicken," she confessed. "I adore peas and potatoes but am not fond of mushrooms."

During the silence that followed, she hoped he would reciprocate with likes and dislikes of his own so they could better get to know one another.

When he didn't offer up anything, she asked, "What about you, my lord?"

"What *about* me?" he asked.

"How are we to grow more used to each other and progress to an agreeable understanding if we don't learn more about one another?"

He faltered in his step, and she had to relinquish her hold on his arm when he stopped walking altogether.

"Progress to an agreeable understanding?" he said doubtfully.

Brilliance had an inkling she might be rushing ahead of the gentleman. *But the kiss!* While she could already imagine loving him and setting up a home together, even bearing his children, she realized he might still be considering a long courtship.

Regardless, at that instant, they were alone betwixt the manor and the stream. Thus, in a copse of birch, with the only sound being the guests up ahead, sounding jovial in their fishing endeavors, she faced him.

Her mother would be appalled that her youngest daughter was flagrantly flaunting the proper behavior of a single female at a house party. And normally, with Lord

Patterson or *any* of the other male guests, she would never dream of walking alone. But this was their hostess's cousin, so he already had a measure of endorsement.

What's more, Lord Hewitt played hauntingly perfect music, which spoke of a deep and spiritual nature as well as a fine mind. Besides, he had pushed her out of his room to safety when he could as easily have compromised her beyond any redemption.

They were all good reasons as to why she looked up at him and said, "Kiss me."

Behind his spectacles, his eyes widened. "My lady." He looked around them as if fearing witnesses.

Gracious! He was unexpectedly shocked. She hoped he didn't think her loose.

"I assure you, my lord, I have never asked the same of any man."

"You asked me similarly last night."

"Yes," she agreed. "I find you intriguing, fascinating, and attractive beyond measure. I confess when you are near, I feel as though I would like to kiss you more than anything."

His eyes grew rounder.

"Young ladies of your class do not speak in such a manner," he said.

Brilliance couldn't help the long sigh. "I believe you are correct. I am unusual, to be sure. But for the life of me, I cannot seem to retrain my nature to be . . . false."

"False?"

"Isn't it false to pretend disinterest? What about if I paid equal attention to the other male guests, hoping to make you jealous? I know I wouldn't like it one jot if I saw you paying special attention to the other female guests."

"I see what you mean by false, yet some would say you might want to be a little more reserved, to exhibit a measure of restraint."

"Some have definitely said that," Brilliance conceded. "Mostly my family. But why?"

"Because you are as likely to get hurt as not. What if I were a cad, a rogue hoping to take advantage of you?"

"Are you?" She knew the answer.

"No. But what if I simply have no interest in you while you have laid your heart bare?"

"Do you?"

"Do I what?" he asked.

"Do you have no interest?"

After a brief hesitation, he said, "No."

"*Oh.*" Brilliance felt a wave of disappointment, then thought perhaps she was misunderstanding him. "No, as in you do *not* have 'no interest' in me, or no, you have no interest in me?"

He stared at her, frowning. "Even if I have an interest in you, I am precluded by decency and good manners from telling you on the second day of our knowing one another. It is simply prudent to hold oneself and one's feelings private."

"Prudent?" she echoed. "I detest prudence. It is like stuffing a lacy handkerchief in one's mouth."

Lord Hewitt rolled his eyes and shook his head.

"You are a singular female to be sure."

Then he wrapped his fingers around each of her shoulders, held her firmly in place so she couldn't step closer, and lowered his mouth to hers.

"*Mm,*" she sighed, feeling like a cat in the sunshine. She'd been wondering if the kiss was exactly as she'd recalled— delightful and exciting. *It was!* Lord Hewitt smelled manly, although Brilliance wasn't certain what the fragrance was. And his lips were perfectly firm against her own, making her feel . . . desirous of something more.

Squirming under his restraint, she wanted to press her body against his, but he was stopping her every attempt. Nevertheless, she would enjoy herself. Parting her lips, she relaxed and tilted her head as he had done in his bedroom.

As she'd hoped, he slanted his head in the other direction, and their kiss deepened.

In the next instant, his hands moved from her shoulders to her back. Lord Hewitt drew her close and pressed her curves to his hard planes. In a twinkling, she had her fingers entwined in his hair at the back of his neck.

When his tongue touched hers, she could not hold back the moan of pleasure. Apparently, the sound brought his attention back to where they were. Releasing her swiftly, he stepped back, although she would have liked to explore the scintillating sensations a while longer.

When she opened her eyes, not realizing she'd closed them, Brilliance saw his glasses were crooked and his hair mussed. *Had she done that?* What's more, he now had a little paint over his right eyebrow where her bonnet had rubbed.

"Never mind," Brilliance said, reaching up to smooth his hair for him. And then she spat on the thumb of her glove and used it to scrub at his forehead.

Through it all, he remained motionless, although his gray-green eyes tracked her every move.

Satisfied there was no trace, she asked, "Do *you* like roasted chicken?"

For an instant, he continued to stare at her as if he thought her a mad woman. Then he straightened his glasses and offered her his arm once more.

"I do," he said as they began to walk the path again. "And peas and potatoes."

A warmth spread through her. How perfectly they were matched until he added, "But I also enjoy mushrooms sauteed in butter with salt and pepper over a piece of toast. A most satisfying meal."

She shuddered. "I can overlook that."

"I am not certain I understand—"

The trees parted, and there was the fishing group.

"Look, there is Colonel Twitchard and the others." At once, it was obvious she was the only female who had ventured to the stream.

The male guests fluttered around her eagerly, especially Lord Patterson, who drew her away from Lord Hewitt to help her prepare her rod.

"The fish are biting," he said with enthusiasm.

She went with him to the stream's edge, glancing back to see Lord Hewitt already in conversation with their host, Colonel Twitchard.

"I am delighted you joined us. I am sure you will have great luck at this," Lord Patterson said, oozing flummery. "Why, the fish will be fighting one another to bite your hook."

Brilliance frowned. "I think you are speaking nonsense. Surely the fish cannot see who is holding the rod. And why would they be any happier to die at my hands than at yours?"

He fell silent, looking like a disciplined dog, and guilt pinched her. Yet she couldn't abide too much of the fawning flattery that men thought women wished to hear. Refusing to apologize for her reasonable question, she let it hang in the air between them and lowered her baited hook into the stream.

Brilliance hoped he would leave her in peace to contemplate the ideal morning she'd already had—or at least, the ideal encounter in the trees. It had turned around all the unpleasantness of the conservatory and the dismal failure of her painting, although she had never much cared about her inability as an artist.

In fact, she had plenty of other inabilities, and she had no doubt that many would be on display before the week was out.

CHAPTER SEVEN

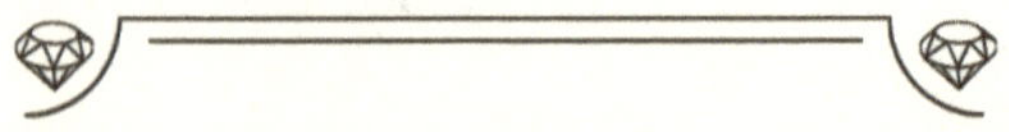

That evening was the first entertainment in the conservatory. Brilliance had presented Lord Hewitt with an apple and another orange during the day after returning from the stream. He had pocketed both with a bemused expression.

"I shall have to determine what to give you in return, my lady," he said.

"I need nothing," she assured him. "Why would I?"

Brilliance hoped her mother's remedy was easing his stage fright, but there was no way to be certain. All she could do was push Lord Hewitt a little each time the opportunity presented itself. To that end, she penciled in his name on the performance sheet that had been resting upon the table in the drawing room all afternoon.

Between dinner and supper, when they were all gathered in the music room, after an uncomfortably ear-splitting operatic performance by Lady Georgiana, who had the lungs necessary but no ability to control her notes, Lady Twitchard glanced at the roster.

Brilliance noticed her expression of surprise. Then their hostess looked over at her cousin. Still, she hesitated.

At last, she said, "Lord Hewitt, do you intend to play for us?"

Brilliance, along with everyone else, turned in his direction to where he was seated between two female guests. His cheeks blazed a ruddy color.

"I do not," he said emphatically.

"Oh, do play us a tune," the lady to his left said. It was Miss Newton, and Brilliance hoped he would be courteous and do as she asked.

He crossed his arms and ignored her.

"It is only that your name appears next on the list," Lady Twitchard said.

"How can that be?" he demanded, unfolding his arms. "That's impossible!"

Brilliance knew she ought to say something. She had embarrassed him *and* their hostess. But she couldn't quite get herself to confess in front of everyone. Regardless, by the way Lord Hewitt's sidelong glance pierced her where she sat, he had ascertained it was her doing.

"Moving along," Lady Twitchard said, "Lady Martine will play the piano."

Brilliance had heard her friend play before and settled in for a pleasant performance. After another lady sang quietly but on key and one of the gentlemen gave a dramatic reading from a translation of Homer's *Iliad*, the evening's performances were at an end.

"What of Lady Brilliance?" came Lord Hewitt's deep voice, cutting through the rustling sounds as people rose to their feet.

"Her name is not on the list," Lady Twitchard said. "No guest may summon another to perform."

"Is that so?" Lord Hewitt said.

Brilliance understood the meaning of his message. And then she had an idea.

"I *will* play something," she offered. Perhaps she could show him how little there was to fear, and also how grand was his skill compared to hers. Rising to her feet, she stared straight back at Lord Hewitt. He merely shrugged.

"To put it mildly," she said as she approached the piano, "I am not very good, but neither was Lady Georgiana, so I suppose it is acceptable to inflict myself upon you. We are all amateurs and among friends, are we not?"

Everyone resumed their seats except for Lady Georgiana, who walked out with her head high. *Oh dear!* Brilliance hoped she hadn't offended her. She had assumed the lady knew how dreadful she was and opted to perform, anyway.

From Lady Twitchard's stack of music, she picked out something that didn't appear too difficult. Settling herself on the stool, Brilliance spread the sheets out and began.

Luckily, she remembered how to read the notes, at least some of them, but she was painstakingly slow to work out each one and its corresponding key. She ignored the black ones entirely. Not at all sure the tune was recognizable, even to herself, she soldiered on with long hesitations between notes, keeping her left pointer finger on the music so she wouldn't lose her place while letting her right hand do all the work.

After a few minutes, which probably was only three but felt like thirty, Brilliance stopped. She might have still been in the middle of the last page, but she could not continue punishing the other guests. She had done her best, but it was painfully obvious she was no better at playing the piano than she was at painting or at fishing. She hadn't caught a single thing in the two hours she'd stood by the stream. And now, she'd butchered a popular piece of music beyond recognition.

Still, everyone clapped as they had for each of the other guests while hastening to their feet and hurrying from the room.

Brilliance stayed back. She would have to apologize to Lady Georgiana when next she saw her, hoping the lady had gone ahead to the drawing room where they would play cards.

When the conservatory emptied, Lord Hewitt was still there.

"I cleared the room quickly, didn't I?" Brilliance remarked. "The others feared another clownish nick-ninny was going to try to perform after me."

He eyed her speculatively. "That was brave of you."

"Not particularly," Brilliance disagreed, wanting to play down the courage it took in case he didn't have it himself. "I imagine, however, it would have been far easier for me and much more enjoyable for the listeners had I *your* talent."

"Indubitably," he agreed. "You are probably the worst piano player I have ever had the misfortune to hear."

"And you are among the best," she said. He showed no emotion. "You *seem* like a reasonable man," she added.

"I am."

"But you're not," she pointed out. "You have this immense talent and refuse to share it."

"You ought to put it out of your head." He crossed his arms. "I choose with whom I shall share my music."

"A music miser!" she declared.

Instead of annoying him, he grinned. Then he laughed before retorting, "I suppose that can be etched upon my headstone."

She pursed her lips. "I am sure in the end you would like something more complimentary, such as 'A gifted composer.'"

He sighed. "You are like a dog with a bone. Besides *in the end,* as you say, I won't give a fig about what is written."

"Do you enjoy charades or pantomimes?" she asked.

"Of course. I am not a savage."

That surprised her. After all, those party games were as like a performance as not, and often with much more sport being made of the performer.

"Indeed, I am quite good at them," Lord Hewitt continued. "Shall we be partners tonight?"

The man was a conundrum. Feeling a little miffed that she had embarrassed herself for nothing, Brilliance shrugged and strolled past him.

"Cards, tonight, my lord," she reminded him. "Charades are tomorrow evening."

CARD GAMES WERE GREAT fun. Brilliance adored playing them. By midnight, when they were all bidding each other good night and leaving the drawing room by ones and twos, her only regret was that Lady Georgiana was still standoffish. Although the young lady said a polite "good evening" to Martine who stood nearby, her gaze passed over Brilliance as if she were invisible.

When she tried to apologize, Lady Georgiana snubbed her and walked out of the room. In the morning, Brilliance would try to make amends.

"A good first day," Martine remarked as they climbed the stairs.

"It was, wasn't it?" Brilliance agreed. "And so many activities to come." They made their way to their wing, with half a dozen guest rooms for the single ladies.

"You seem taken with Lord Hewitt," Martine remarked since they were alone.

"He is a dash-fire gentleman, don't you think?"

Martine shrugged delicately and said, "I prefer the fair looks of Lord Patterson, but I think he has eyes for you."

Brilliance sighed. "I am not the least interested in him. I am sorry if he sees some unintended encouragement on my part."

"Men need little actual encouragement in my opinion. They want what they want, or whom they want." She sighed. "But tread carefully with Lord Hewitt. He has deep, still waters if you ask me."

With those words, her friend kissed her cheek and entered her room.

Puzzled by Martine's remarks about Lord Hewitt's water, Brilliance heard a door click closed as she passed. When she reached her own room, she undressed by herself, having dismissed Belinda for the evening after her maid helped her change for supper. Exhaustion quickly took her to the Land of Nod.

When Brilliance awakened, finding Belinda already opening her window curtains, she recalled what they would be doing as a group after breakfast. *Riding.* While she admired horses, as for being atop one, she hadn't much practice. When younger, she'd been timid about the distance from the saddle to the ground, and while eventually overcoming her aversion, Brilliance hadn't pressed herself to become a skilled horsewoman.

Regardless, there was one thing about riding she could look forward to—her new tawny-colored riding outfit, with its sable-brown piping. Belinda was laying it out across the bed for after breakfast. If Brilliance had to ride horseback in order to wear it, then that was the price she would willingly pay.

Hopefully, Lord Hewitt would find her fetching.

Breakfast was a hurried affair that morning, as most were eager to get underway. And their hostess had instructed her staff to put out a meager fare compared to the previous morning's generous offering.

Eating toast and jam with Martine, Brilliance kept her gaze trained upon the door but saw neither hide nor hair of Lord Hewitt. However, while discussing the meaning of deep waters with her friend, she noticed Lady Georgiana enter. Still trying to make amends, Brilliance waved her over.

"Good morning," Brilliance addressed her. "The chocolate is delicious this morning, won't you have some?" And she made to pour the lady a cup from the pot on their table.

Lady Georgiana sniffed. "I prefer tea," and she kept on walking, taking a seat at a neighboring table with Miss Newton.

Brilliance sighed. "I only wanted to offer her my sincere apology."

"Let her eat her breakfast in peace," Martine advised. "There will be plenty of time today to say you are sorry. It was dreadfully rude of you, by the way."

Brilliance felt tears prick her eyes. "I must learn to think before I speak," she agreed. "But I will make it up to her." After another slice of buttered toast and a dish of strawberries with cream, they rose to leave, with Brilliance giving one more look toward Lady Georgiana.

"Leave her for now, Bri," Martine advised. And they went upstairs to change before meeting the other guests in the stable yard.

Finally, Lady Twitchard disclosed their destination to be Roman ruins. "Let us hope none of us lose our way, for I think you will all find them interesting."

"Like a treasure hunt," Brilliance said to Martine, "but without any treasure."

"Without any treasure," her friend repeated, "but the treasure is the main part of the hunt." Her tone was light and teasing. Martine was clever in a way Brilliance knew she herself was not, but her friend seemed never to mind her lapses in intellect.

However, Lady Georgiana, in a navy-blue riding habit that set off her blonde curls to perfection, overheard. "And thus *not* like a treasure hunt at all," she said, shaking her head as if Brilliance were the stupidest creature alive.

Lord Hewitt, who had just arrived at the stable, took Brilliance's thoughts away from the mean-spirited lady. He looked fine indeed in his riding clothes. Before she could greet him, the Colonel gave a loud whistle to secure the guests' attention.

"Everyone, find a partner, male or female," he said. "Let us ride before the sun gets too high in the sky."

Bold as brass, Lady Georgiana strolled toward Lord Hewitt. "I love riding," she declared. "Will you partner with me, my lord?"

"I shall, my lady," he responded.

Drat! Brilliance had let two opportunities escape her, both to apologize to Lady Georgiana and to partner with Lord Hewitt.

"You are stuck with me," Martine said, following Brilliance's gaze toward the couple who preceded them to the mounting block. One by one, they were given a suitable horse, deemed so by the head groom after he asked each guest a few questions as to his or her ability.

"I certainly insulted the wrong person," Brilliance said after she and Martine were assisted in mounting their horses—gentle mares, for Martine wasn't much of an eager rider either.

"I know you didn't mean to be hoggish," her friend said, "but unquestionably, you put her back up."

"And yet I cannot believe she didn't know how terrible she was," Brilliance said, trying not to fall off the horse nor choke the poor animal by drawing back on the reins. "Lady Georgiana has heard someone singing well before, hasn't she? I knew what an awful pianist I was."

"Not everyone is as self-aware as you are," Martine said.

"I suppose you're right. Look, there is your Lord Patterson." The blond gentleman was riding beside Miss Newton.

"Not *mine*, by any means," Martine said. "I have gone right off him. He has nothing to recommend him but his looks."

"He sits a fine horse," Brilliance remarked, and her friend began to chuckle.

"Sweet Bri, you mean he has a fine seat."

Brilliance was shocked. "Do you mean Lord Patterson's posterior? How can you tell from this angle?"

"No, I mean—" Martine didn't finish. "Never mind. I hate to say it, but in my conversations with him thus far, I thought him self-absorbed and shallow."

Brilliance agreed but wouldn't have said anything in case her friend had been enamored.

Martine shrugged. "Lord Hewitt has a fine seat, too."

Brilliance startled. He was up ahead in the main group while she and Martine had been among the last to mount up. His back was arrow-straight, and his riding coat of dark gray fit him perfectly.

Although she was always grateful for Martine's loyal friendship, Brilliance couldn't deny a part of her wished she was riding beside Lord Hewitt. He seemed to be speaking animatedly about something to Lady Georgiana, who was hanging upon his every word, and she longed to know what he was so enthusiastic about. It wouldn't surprise her if the lady—and all the other female guests—were growing a *tendre* for the pianist.

That would be awkward indeed, for Brilliance could well imagine warning them away from the gentleman who was swiftly and thoroughly capturing her attention in a way no man had ever done before.

The instant attraction in the conservatory combined with their kisses were assuredly a sign of destiny.

Suddenly, Lord Hewitt turned as if feeling her gaze. He tipped his hat in her direction before facing forward again, and a pleasant warmth spread through her. It quickly died when Lady Georgiana turned as well, smirking smugly as if she knew of Brilliance's interest.

"If I can see that you are aware of Lord Hewitt's good qualities," Martine said, "then others can, too. Including Lord Hewitt, himself. That would give him too much power over you, I fear. Proceed with caution, Bri. I urge you most adamantly."

Brilliance nodded. She would not deny the truth, at least to herself, yet she knew it most improper to mention the kisses even to her good friend. Martine would disapprove of her distinct lack of caution, and Brilliance would hate to lose her friend's respect no matter how full her heart already was with . . . something special for him.

"Let us speak of anything besides men," she suggested to Martine.

They brought up the rear, trotting, cantering, galloping, and walking. By the time they reached the ruins, forty minutes later, Brilliance was ready to dismount and wouldn't care if she ever rode again.

"Was it your first time riding?" Lady Georgiana asked loudly, her tone dripping with antagonism. "You looked positively petrified. So stiff and awkward. We feared you might topple off at any moment." Then she allowed Lord Hewitt to assist her in dismounting, giving no doubt as to whom she meant by "we."

Brilliance stopped herself from sticking her tongue out by clenching her jaw. After all, it was her own fault. She had made an enemy, one who would bring up her every flaw— and Brilliance knew she had many. Suddenly, the week stretched out before her as one long opportunity to be derided and mocked.

Moreover, she didn't like the way Lady Georgiana had launched herself off the side of the horse, so Lord Hewitt had no choice but to catch her, nor the way she seemed to slide down his body.

Waiting atop her mare, hoping he would also help her to dismount, instead Lord Patterson arrived first.

"May I offer you assistance?" he asked.

She glanced to where Lord Hewitt was taking Lady Georgiana's arm, turning toward the ruins.

"Yes, thank you, my lord." Unfortunately, as she unhooked her leg from the upper pommel, her treasured new skirt caught, making her tumble awkwardly onto him.

Lord Patterson yelped, trying to keep them both from toppling over, and succeeded in drawing every eye their way. With most of her riding habit still above her head, Brilliance could feel the cool air on her legs and let out a matching yelp of surprise.

Even Lord Hewitt and Lady Georgiana turned back toward the ruckus. The lady burst out laughing, and Brilliance was further from wanting to give her an apology than ever.

With a vicious tug, she managed to free her skirts from the saddle. Ignoring any continued snickering, not daring to look in Lord Hewitt's direction, Brilliance smoothed the front of her habit, no longer wondering if he found her fetching. She only hoped the horse had hidden her nether regions from any of the guests on the other side of it.

"Are you steady now?" Lord Patterson asked, his own cheeks having ruddied somewhat at her clumsy display.

"Yes, thank you. I appreciate how you kept me from ending up prostrate at your feet. Shall we go see the ruins?"

As a group, Lady Twitchard's party guests swarmed what once was a Roman farmhouse as well as a nearby personal family temple. Lord Hewitt had disappeared ahead, still being monopolized by Lady Georgiana. Martine was speaking with their hostess probably about the ruins, as her friend had an interest in history.

For the better part of ten minutes, Brilliance climbed over low walls and tried to imagine what would have happened in each area of the farmhouse. Lord Patterson remained doggedly nearby, jabbering in her ear about his own estate in Norfolk, until a female guest dropped her fan beside him. It was an obvious ploy, indicating the lady's interest, and for which Brilliance was exceedingly grateful.

While he retrieved the fan, she excused herself and escaped at a quick pace toward some wild shrubs. When Brilliance rounded a clump of golden dock growing up in the middle of a stone wall, she entered what was left of the pagan temple, which would have belonged to the farmer and his family.

Lord Hewitt stood in the center with his back to her. *Alone.*

Brilliance sighed. It seemed they were destined for one another after all. She picked her way across the rutted ground, about to say his name, when Lady Georgiana poked her head through an archway closer to him. At once, her gaze fell upon Brilliance, and she smirked.

"There you are, my lord," the lady called to him. "I thought I had lost you. I am ready to move on. It has grown too crowded here."

As Lord Hewitt turned, he caught sight of Brilliance. But Lady Georgiana had already reached his side.

Stopping in her tracks, Brilliance wished there was something she could pretend to be admiring or looking at, any reason at all for her having been behind the gentleman other than quietly studying him.

Fixing her gaze on the smallest of crumbling alcoves as if she was looking at the famed Roman Colosseum her brother had once visited, she tried to appear casual.

Then she heard him address her. "Lady Brilliance, Lady Georgiana and I were about to stroll to the top of the hill and see the view," he said. "Would you care to join us?"

Us? Brilliance would rather gnaw her own arm off than tag along.

"Thank you, no."

By then, other guests had made their way into the temple. Bringing up the rear was Colonel and Lady Twitchard.

"Good day, everyone," she said. "I hope you have already worked up an appetite. Please come this way."

She and her husband stepped through a stone archway and disappeared around the half wall. As other guests trailed behind, they exclaimed in delight at something just out of sight.

Brilliance watched Lord Hewitt and Lady Georgiana follow. At least now they couldn't go on their private stroll. When Brilliance went through the arch, however, and passed the half wall, she found a rustic picnic area had been set up by Lady Twitchard's capable staff.

"It *was* a treasure hunt of sorts," Brilliance said when she joined Martine, happy that soon she would enjoy a glass of lemonade. Even happier that Lady Georgiana's intent to be alone with Lord Hewitt had been thwarted.

In no time, the guests were seated on two large woolen blankets, the ladies all tucking their skirts around their legs and the gentlemen trying to sit in a manly fashion.

Brilliance loved a country outing and a meal outside, but the juxtaposition of indoor elegance with raw nature struck her as funny.

Her ladyship's elegant tableware had been laid out, and platters of all manner of food, including sliced meats and salads and vegetable dishes were offered where simple sandwiches would have sufficed. The only thing their hostess hadn't tried to offer were hot dishes.

Napkins were provided and polished silverware, the latter making Brilliance begin to chuckle.

"What is amusing?" Lady Georgiana asked from across the blanket where she sat a wee bit too close to Lord Hewitt. "What can possibly *not* be to your liking?"

Oh dear! Brilliance looked at Lady Twitchard, who had paused in taking a bread roll to learn the answer.

"*Everything* is to my liking, which is why I laughed with joy," Brilliance answered, earning a smile from their hostess. "Who can be cross and serious at a picnic?" she returned pointedly, hoping Lady Georgiana would stop being such an arse.

Her hope was futile when next the young lady addressed her again.

"I heard that your piano playing was egregious beyond all belief and that I was fortunate to have missed it."

There was a small, collective gasp as gazes swiveled between the two females, eyeing one another across the spread of food. Brilliance supposed it was what she deserved, but it occurred to her that Lady Georgiana's words were reflecting badly upon their speaker. If the young lady wasn't careful, she would lose all the sympathy gained by Brilliance's own careless remark.

Hardly knowing how to respond, or whether she should say anything, Brilliance couldn't stop her eyes from seeking out Lord Hewitt's.

Had he been talking about her while riding with Lady Georgiana?

In the end, Brilliance decided to handle it the way she had hoped Lady Georgiana would have handled an errant remark.

"Why, yes," Brilliance said, "I believe you were fortunate indeed."

Lady Georgiana nodded and helped herself to a minced lamb tart. Everyone seemed to be waiting for the next salvo.

"Since you did me a favor by driving me from the conservatory during your awful performance, I forgive your rudeness," Lady Georgiana continued.

Brilliance had wanted to offer an apology first, yet having been already publicly forgiven, it now seemed pointless.

"Thank you," she said, not feeling the least grateful since Lady Georgiana hadn't behaved with an ounce of graciousness. Without stopping to consider, Brilliance added, "If only you had done me a similar favor."

By the look on Lord Hewitt's face, a mixture of surprise and then obvious mirth, Brilliance knew she had been impudent again. This time, purposefully, too, unable to help herself. She was feeling as green-eyed as Othello where he was concerned.

By Lady Georgiana's frown, she was still working out the latest insult.

Brilliance was beginning to wish fortified wine had been served instead of lemonade. Even if it hadn't soothed Lady Georgiana, it might have made it easier to stomach her.

When they had all eaten their fill, Lady Twitchard let her husband draw her to her feet. As everyone rose, Brilliance dreaded an announcement that they were to immediately remount their horses.

"The weather is proving amenable," their hostess said. "Please take your time wandering around the area. Not a furlong away are more modern ruins of a twelfth-century abbey."

She pointed in a westerly direction.

"And to the south, if you climb the hill, there's a lovely view of the valley beyond."

Brilliance was readjusting her bonnet since the ribbon had come loose under her chin when Lord Hewitt appeared beside her.

"Will you take a stroll with me, my lady?"

CHAPTER EIGHT

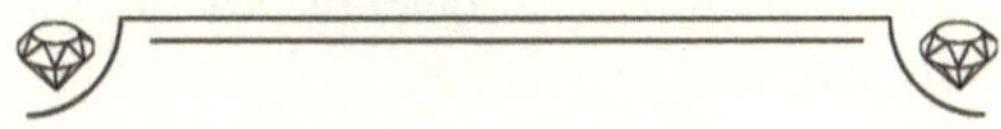

Looking up into his gray-green eyes, her entire being flooded with happiness.

"Gladly," Brilliance said. But she couldn't help peering past him to make sure their walk would not be a threesome. Fortunately, Lady Georgiana was engrossed in a conversation with Lord Fincham. Thus, she followed Lord Hewitt away from the picnic.

They didn't touch. He didn't take her arm, yet they walked companionably close, seeming to mutually decide to go to the abbey ruins.

There was much more remaining of the medieval structure than the Roman ones. Brilliance walked along a decrepit nave, ignoring the field mouse that scuttled ahead of her. There was still a section of the altar. And on her left, the wall and roof were partially intact, containing some of the clerestory window framing, although there was no glass left.

"It's lovely," she proclaimed.

He smiled. "Lovely in an accidental way, I suppose. Not lovely like a female dressed for a ball."

"Yes, that's precisely what I meant." She thought it a romantic place and tried to imagine the abbey when it was whole, perhaps with light streaming in through stained glass, replete with devoted nuns and clerics. Maybe they held weddings there and baptized children.

"You look far away in your thoughts," he said.

She shrugged. "It is easier to picture what happened in the abbey than in a Roman farmer's temple."

"I agree, although—" he broke off as others came in behind them. "Shall we move along?" he asked.

Nodding, they left through one of the large gaps in the wall.

"Would you like to see the southern view that my cousin mentioned?" he asked.

"I would." They began to walk up the gentle incline behind the abbey. Brilliance considered her handsome guide. "I just realized you must have seen all this before. The ruins and the view. Your home is not too far away, is it?"

"My estate is about half an hour by fast horse, and I have visited my cousin's manor house all my life, so yes, I've seen the view from the knoll." Then he added, "But not with you."

That made her smile. Lord Hewitt was being kind and friendly. She hoped it lasted. She would try not to do anything that annoyed him. As long as they didn't stumble across a piano, that shouldn't be too difficult.

As if reading her thoughts, he asked, "Did you write my name on the list of performers yesterday?"

That might engender his ire, but she had to be honest. "I did."

"Why?" His voice remained even. "What did you hope to accomplish?"

"I knew you would hear others who weren't as talented, and thus, by the time your name was called, I hoped you would have gained the confidence needed to play for us."

She held her breath. Instead of looking irate, however, he started to laugh. Finally, he took her arm and tucked it under his. The warmth and strength of him took her breath away.

"Is that why you humiliated yourself with your piano performance? In order to bolster me?"

"Why, yes." And then she shook her head. "I knew it was bad, but was it truly dreadful?"

"Beyond dreadful. It was painful to listen while you picked out the notes. You nearly succeeded in your goal, by the way."

"Did I?" she asked, relishing his body alongside her own as they continued to climb toward the plateau.

"If you had gone on much longer, I might have had to push you aside and at least play three notes in a row without pausing."

"Your intrusion would have been welcome, I assure you. I couldn't have continued if I had looked behind me to see the faces of my captive audience." She ought to be mortified at how poor her musical abilities were given her companion's great talent, but his lack of arrogance left her unbothered. "The two times I have seen you playing, you were doing so from memory. Can you read music?"

"I can," Lord Hewitt said. Then he raised an eyebrow at her. "And a lot better than you, by the way."

She laughed, taking no offense as, clearly, he meant none. "Have you written out your own music so others can play it, too?"

The man beside her stiffened, changing from relaxed to tense in the space of a heartbeat.

"That's the last thing I want to do." His tone was terse.

Lord Hewitt was a mystery, and the only way to understand a mystery was to ask questions. "Why?"

"That is not your concern," he snapped. Then he shook his head, apparently releasing whatever tension had got hold of him. "I apologize for sounding harsh. Yet while I am mentally capable of keeping my music in my head, I shall continue to do so."

Curious and more curious, she thought.

"Careful," he said, drawing her past a small gully and around some chickweed bushes interspersed with purple marsh orchids. "We're almost there."

"I would just as soon our destination were far away and that we had hours before I had to get back in the saddle. The best horse is harnessed to a swift carriage."

"You don't like to ride?" he asked.

Brilliance realized it was a mark against her and perhaps even a deterrent to securing Lord Hewitt's fond admiration. Gentlemen, especially noblemen, appreciated women who could ride with them in Hyde Park. *What could she say?*

"I don't mind it," she hedged, determined not to lie to him, "and it's possible I shall grow more comfortable with practice. Today's ride was a little long, and in truth, I found it rattling. Nerve-racking, if you will. Probably the way you feel about performing in public."

He didn't say anything to that, but after a thoughtful moment, he patted her arm.

"If we can ride out again this week, you may, as you said, feel increasingly at ease as you gain experience."

What a generous offer! She hoped it was because he wanted to be with her, not because he wanted to spend more time riding horses.

"I would like that," she said. "To be honest, I would like any time we spend together, be it on horseback, walking in the tall grass as we are now, or otherwise."

VINCENT HALTED AT THE top of the rise, looked up at the blue sky with its few puffy white clouds, and smiled to himself. Lady Brilliance was unlike any female he'd ever met. He had spent the entire morning in the presence of Lady Georgiana, and the difference between the two ladies was stark.

While Lady Georgiana was pretty with a practiced skill for conversing upon many topics, she was also coy and flirtatious. And where Lady Brilliance was concerned, the former was downright vindictive. Lady Brilliance, on the other hand, was forthright and honest in a direct, effortless way that most people, in his experience, simply were not. It left one far too vulnerable, but she seemed unaware of that. Or brave enough not to care.

Moreover, her emotions, sometimes even her thoughts, were plainly apparent. *How did she go through life being so transparent?*

"There you go again," he said finally, looking into her indigo eyes.

"Where am I going?" she asked.

"Without an ounce of guile, speaking about us spending time in each other's company with an utter lack of self-preservation."

"I don't understand," she said. "Why would I wish to be deceitful with you, and from what would I need to preserve myself?"

That struck him funny. When he laughed, she did, too.

"You have a pretty laugh," he told her, "and you laugh often, which is nice."

She shielded her eyes from the sun and continued to look up at him.

"Not too much, I hope, like a braying donkey."

With Lady Brilliance being so earnest and affable, he wanted to take her in his arms despite it being broad daylight outdoors. He also had to swallow some ridiculous words, which ought not to be spoken lightly or too soon.

Such as how attracted he was to her and how much he enjoyed her company, both amusing and refreshingly off-kilter.

Clearing his throat, he said, "That thought never crossed my mind. You are not at all like a donkey." Vincent drew her in front of him. When she looked as though she were about to melt against him for another kiss, he turned her around so her back was to him.

"Now look out there," Vincent ordered, letting his hands rest lightly upon her shoulders. "Do you see the next valley where the stream appears as a ribbon of shimmering gold?"

"That's entirely accurate and so cleverly described," she said. "Yes, I see it."

"My home is next to those woodlands."

"Is it?" she asked before trying to turn in his arms.

The minx! But he held her firmly in place since other guests were approaching. He could hear them chattering as they came around the gully behind them. All he had to do was move so he wasn't touching her.

"Perhaps you can see some of my home's chimneys," he said and took a step backward. "It's possible." *If one were a bird in the sky.*

Lady Brilliance raised her hand to the rim of her bonnet once again, staring into the distance. But then she laughed, spun around, and barreled toward him.

Vincent had to grab hold of her upper arms before she knocked him over.

"You're teasing!" she exclaimed. "Kiss m—"

Lady Brilliance interrupted herself, undoubtedly catching sight of other guests. He turned and groaned. Sure enough, four others had stopped to stare at them, including the sharp-eyed Lady Georgiana, Lord Patterson, Miss Newton, and Lady Martine.

While Lady Brilliance put space between herself and him, she seemed unaffected by being caught standing close.

"Come see," she called out, her voice perfectly natural, holding her hand out to Lady Martine. "You can *almost* see Lord Hewitt's home from here."

Easing the awkwardness, the lady came forward and took her friend's arm. Together, they looked out across the shallow valley, soon joined by the other guests, although Lady Georgiana had given him a withering glance as she'd drawn near.

"His home is past the gold ribbon," Lady Brilliance announced. "Can you see any chimneys?"

"No," Lady Martine said and turned back to look at Vincent with a raised eyebrow.

He coughed. The lady thought he had lured her friend up there on false pretenses. It was clear as day.

"How disappointing," Lady Brilliance said. "Shall we have an outing to your home one afternoon, Lord Hewitt?" she asked without turning.

He startled at her boldly inviting herself and others. Hopefully, Alethia had every day booked with activities from morning till night. In truth, Vincent had no wish for a passel of strangers to descend upon his estate. Luckily, his cousin and the Colonel had just crested the hill.

Having received no response from him, Lady Brilliance wasn't shy about asking Lady Twitchard the same.

"Will there be an opportunity to visit Lord Hewitt's country home?"

Vincent knew he must be wild-eyed as he caught his cousin's questioning gaze. She recognized his reluctance to play the host and deflected the eager young lady.

"Since my cousin is here," Alethia said carefully, "and came directly from London, his home is still closed up, probably with little in the way of food or niceties."

Lady Brilliance looked at him for confirmation.

"Sadly, it is true," he said. And it was. After the party, he would be going to Joyden's Wood directly. By then, his minimal country staff ought to have everything open, aired, dusted, polished, and stocked. He would be blissfully free from Parliamentary duties as well as from prying females who barged in when he was losing himself in his music. Or rather, when he was finding himself. For while playing the piano, with the notes in his head sounding clear, resonant, round, and rich through the instrument, only then was his mind at peace.

The rest of the time, he could hear any music he merely thought about. With his perfect pitch, the notes played inside his head as precisely as if he were at the piano. That almost never ceased, although sometimes he wished it would.

Vincent glanced at the most disturbing, intrusive woman he had ever met. Lady Brilliance was staring directly back at him. He felt her clear, penetrating gaze like a punch to the gut.

What the devil? She was so plainly wishing they were still alone that he feared the others would see it on her lovely face, too.

He clapped his gloved hands to distract and call attention to himself. Unfortunately, he hadn't planned anything to say. Thus, after an awkward pause, he asked, "Are we finished here?"

His cousin shook her head. "Are you eager to get back on your horse? I know you've seen all this before, and no one will mind if you wish to leave. But some of my guests are only now making it this far." She looked at the others gathering on the top of the hill.

"Was the view worth the climb?" asked Lord Fincham, cresting the plateau.

"Indeed, it was," said Lady Georgiana, but she was staring at Vincent, not out over the valley.

"Tell us what we're seeing," demanded Lord Patterson. The Colonel began to point out landmarks as far as the eye could see.

Suddenly, Lady Brilliance was at his elbow. "I am ready to return and would be pleased to ride back with you."

He sighed. She was not a strumpet, but no one would be faulted for thinking her one. *Had she no sense of decorum?* But her blue eyes in the mid-day sunshine bewitched him, and her hopeful smile was impossible to destroy with harsh words.

"If your friend accompanies us, then I shall happily be your guide."

A shadow crossed her face. He'd thwarted her attempt to be unaccompanied. Oddly, he didn't put her in the same class of female as Lady Georgiana, or the many others who tried to manipulate or coerce a man. Lady Brilliance genuinely seemed to like him and merely wished to spend time together.

As did he.

However, he would be a blackguard to kiss her again or even be alone with her. In a few days, she would be returning to London, and he didn't want her to leave with false expectations or, worse, a broken heart.

Far worse than that would be if they let desire take them too far, and she went home ruined. Vincent wasn't prepared for the Earl Diamond showing up on his doorstep demanding he marry this peculiar young lady.

"I will go, too," Lady Martine said.

"So shall I," Lord Patterson declared.

Thus, the four of them strolled back to their waiting horses. Easily, they paired up with the ladies riding ahead and the gentlemen behind.

Vincent thought he had satisfactorily deferred any and all issues until Lady Brilliance turned in her sidesaddle to address him. "Do you really think your home is in such a state of disrepair that we cannot visit?"

He cursed the range of movement that riding aside gave a female, as she could as easily turn her torso and speak with him as she could look forward.

Lady Martine coughed loudly.

"Are you well?" Lady Brilliance asked.

"Yes," she said, "merely some dust in my throat. What is on Lady Twitchard's schedule for this evening?"

Bless her heart, Vincent thought, *for distracting her persistent friend.*

"Charades," responded Lady Brilliance. "I do so love them, although I often am stumped by the riddles."

"Then we must be partners," Lady Martine said, "and help one another."

"I had hoped to partner with you," Lord Patterson said.

Vincent eyed him. *What was the man about?* One didn't show favoritism when two ladies were present.

"To which of us do you speak?" Lady Brilliance asked, now looking back at him.

"Why, to you," Lord Patterson said.

Vincent felt a niggling prickle of propriety, which he hastily dismissed. Rather than her paying him undue attention, she ought to partner with the other man. Otherwise, tongues would start to wag.

"I am afraid that is impossible," Lady Brilliance said, "for yesterday, Lord Hewitt asked to be my partner."

Vincent nearly groaned. She made it sound so premeditated, as if he had purposefully claimed her for himself ahead of time. In fact, Lord Patterson gave him a sidelong look that had lost its friendly demeanor.

Nevertheless, Vincent didn't gainsay her. He was, in fact, pleased with the arrangement. And luckily, Lord Patterson showed he wasn't an utter looby by extending his offer to Lady Martine, thereby averting an awkward moment. While the lady accepted, to Vincent's eyes, she didn't seem too keen upon the idea, either.

Lady Brilliance appeared not to notice. "Aren't we a merry foursome? If only there was a way to know the riddles in advance. Why, we would be the champions of the charades."

Was she openly declaring she would cheat? Vincent shook his head. He was a little on edge not knowing what she might say next. When she looked back at him once again, he cringed in anticipation.

"I, for one, would not mind seeing your home even if your furniture is sheeted and your pantry bare."

To this bold statement, all eyes turned to him, and Vincent would gladly wring the lady's slender neck.

CHAPTER NINE

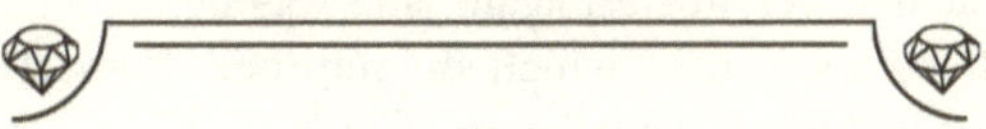

Brilliance hoped Lord Hewitt would make her happiness complete. She would hate to return to London at the week's end without having seen his home, seeing how it was so near.

His reluctance was obviously due to some worry over the estate's inferiority. *The tortured man!* The hesitancy was probably stemming from the same place as his reticence over playing the piano before an audience. His lordship lacked self-confidence and self-worth, two matters from which she had never suffered despite being considered something of a shallow-pate, even a little light between the ears.

Once, as a child, she'd been called a "pig-widgeon" by a playmate. Upon asking her mother what that meant, Lady Diamond said, "It means that little girl resents your sweet nature and has no kindness in her heart. As long as you have both, then you shall always be admired."

"I believe we should adhere to our hostess's itinerary," came Lord Hewitt's measured answer.

She sighed. Perhaps she would take it up with Lady Twitchard. Mayhap there was a way to put the pianist's home on the schedule.

The four of them rode in companionable silence, broken only when Lord Patterson spoke, mostly about himself, occasionally asking a question which only led back to another of his own stories. He was the opposite of Lord Hewitt in every regard. And unfortunately, more often than not, when Lord Patterson did wait for an answer, Brilliance realized he was speaking to her.

It was a good thing Martine had already stated her disinclination for the man. Not everyone could find an immediate meeting of the minds and emotions as she had found with Lord Hewitt.

Glancing back at him again, she was heartened by him giving her a warm nod, which she returned. Even that brief exchange had her heart pumping faster. Perhaps they would elope to Gretna Green as her parents had done. *How romantic!*

At the Twitchards' manor, they found the staff ready to cater to their every need despite the rest of the guests and their host and hostess as yet being away. After Brilliance and Martine changed from their dusty riding clothes, Brilliance headed directly to the conservatory.

It was empty. She would love to have heard Lord Hewitt play again. It occurred to her that her hostess might have sheet music for the famed Castern piece, "The Hummingbird," which Lord Hewitt had been playing the day before—the one he had denied was Mr. Castern's.

Disappointingly, she didn't find it in the stack of music. In less than five minutes, however, she had located the butler.

"Mr. Ramsey, how close is the nearest town?"

"There is the village of Bexleyheath, only ten minutes away by horse."

Brilliance considered a moment, recalling it was on their schedule for a visit the following day. "Is it tiny?"

The butler nodded. "Yes, my lady. Only a single main street, although its shops are of the best quality and stocked regularly."

"Is there a music store?"

"Are you in need of an instrument?" he asked.

"Printed music," she explained.

He shook his head. "You won't find any in Bexleyheath, my lady."

Brilliance wasn't ready to give up. "Is there a larger town not too far away?"

"Indeed, my lady. Dartford would have what you seek."

"Could I give a footman coin enough to purchase sheet music?"

"That is unnecessary, my lady. Lady Twitchard has instructed that all her guests' needs be taken care of. If you write down what you seek, I will handle it directly. By tomorrow at the latest."

"This is the most accommodating house party I have ever attended," Brilliance told him, earning a satisfied nod from the head of the household staff before she left him.

CHARADES WERE AS DIFFICULT as ever she found them. *How was anyone supposed to make sense of the riddles?* Brilliance made suggestions to her handsome partner, but invariably Lord Hewitt gave his own answers for their team. And he was usually correct!

Embarrassingly, she'd even forgotten the answer to the riddle Ms. Austen had made famous by putting in her acclaimed novel *Emma*. Their hostess read it aloud.

"My *first* doth affliction denotes, which my *second* is destin'd to feel. And my *whole* is the best antidote for that affliction to soften and heal."

"Isn't it something about sponge cake?" Brilliance asked, which engendered hearty laughter, not only from Lord Hewitt but from all those within hearing. Lady Georgiana was loudest of all.

Brilliance's cheeks heated, but upon learning the answer was *woman*, she laughed, too.

"*Wo*e plus *man*," Lord Hewitt explained.

Brilliance shrugged. *A woman was nothing like a sponge cake except for being soft in places.* Ms. Austen hadn't given the answer either. Maybe she hadn't known. In any case, the rest of the riddles might as well have been in French, the way all the complicated rhyming confounded her.

Expectedly, she did no better with the second riddle that was purportedly easy for its plain language:

"My *first* is an animal most useful have you vermin, my *second* is an article of speech as common as the first letter, my *third* should be used every day lest you give an appearance of dishevelment, and my whole is a place for the dead."

"Something about mice and a hairbrush," she guessed.

"Very close," Lord Hewitt said encouragingly. He even winked at her, which she appreciated.

"Cat-a-comb," Martine called out a second later.

Brilliance leaned close to Lord Hewitt, breathing in his clean smell. "I am sorry you have such a wretched partner." Fortunately, he didn't seem the least bothered by her incompetency.

Brilliance supposed she should forgo charades in the future along with painting and fishing.

She sighed, wanting to contribute to the evening's entertainment. Before the next charade was offered, she told the gathering, "I know a funny jest. What smells the most in a chemist's shop?"

"The nose," Lady Georgiana responded, sounding utterly bored. A few people chuckled, nonetheless.

"Why, yes," Brilliance said, "but you were supposed to let *me* give the answer." *Had Lady Georgiana spoiled her joke on purpose?*

On the other hand, when it was time for a pantomime charade, Brilliance successfully made Lord Hewitt guess both an umbrella and a walking stick. Acting was always easier than solving riddles.

Feeling redeemed, she didn't mind when their partnership came in fourth place for points earned. And the evening concluded even more delightfully with cucumber salad and stewed duck for supper, one of her favorites.

The following day, after a mid-morning game of croquet, which was so close to pall-mall Brilliance didn't know why anyone bothered changing the name, she followed the other guests to the shaded back terrace for lemonade. Lord Hewitt had been behind her team, of course with Lady Georgiana stuck to him like pitch, and finished their round later. Thus, Brilliance had procured an extra glass and was keeping an eye out for him when Lady Twitchard's butler approached her.

"I have secured the musical score you requested, my lady."

"Have you? How wonderful."

"It is in your room," Mr. Ramsey added.

"Thank you!" Thrusting her half-empty glass into his hands as well as the one for Lord Hewitt, she rushed to the main staircase.

As good as his word, "The Hummingbird" sheet music lay upon her bureau. It looked very complicated. However, having heard it played often, Brilliance could hum parts of it and might be able to pick out the tune.

Surely, Lord Hewitt would admire her determination while also being inspired by seeing the music in print. If she could play a little of Mr. Castern's wonderful composition, then she hoped Lord Hewitt would write down one of his own for her to learn to play.

VINCENT COULD NOT BELIEVE his ears. *His* sonata was coming from the conservatory's open door. *Plonk, plonk, plonk.* A second later, he shook his head. No, it wasn't his music. Simply something that sounded a little like his melody. Then again, yes, it was his! *Wasn't it?*

Drawn toward the room, he knew whom he would see at the piano by the long pauses between the notes that made her torturous to listen to. Sure enough, Lady Brilliance was on the stool.

Plonk, plonk, plonk.

The dark-haired young lady was hunched over the keys, her left elbow upon the piano case, while she studied the page before her and picked out the notes with her right hand.

The page!

Striding forward, Vincent couldn't believe his eyes. *"The Hummingbird" by Ambrose Castern.* He felt ill just looking at it.

Her head swiveled to look up at him an instant before he snatched the printed sheets from the piano's music rack.

"Lord Hewitt, please put those back."

He couldn't take his eyes off the staves filled with the notes he'd composed years earlier. And then red fury clouded his vision.

"Please, my lord. I wish to practice this lovely piece that you were playing recently."

He stacked the pages together and tore them in half.

"No!" she shrieked, rising to her feet. "That was meanly done of you."

He looked down at her. "Where did you get this? I am certain my cousin did not have it."

"From a shop." Then she stamped her foot, distracting him. "Why did you tear them up? You had no right!"

"I had every right," he ground out, but then he stopped. *Did he want to confide in this particular female?*

"You are jealous of Mr. Castern?" she asked.

"No!" he shouted nearly as loudly as she had.

"I am glad to hear it, for you shouldn't be." She laid a hand upon his arm. "Why don't you write your own on similar sheets with all those helpful lines—"

"Staves," he said curtly.

"I had no idea there was a name for them. Let me see." She reached out her hand.

Unthinkingly, he returned the pages to her. Quick as lightning, she ran around the other side of the piano.

"Thank you. I shall use some glue or whatever our hostess keeps on hand to repair these. Elsewise, I will never be able to practice."

"Return them at once," he ordered, going around the piano and holding out his hand.

The minx darted out of reach. Vincent tried again, but she kept eluding him. Like children, they were running around his cousin's piano. Finally, he ground to a halt.

"Give those sheets back to me."

"No, they are mine," she said, lifting her chin to infuriate him further.

He gave chase again. "I do not wish to hear you play that music."

"How rude! If I practice, I will get better."

He lunged toward her, but she scurried away once more.

"Practice something else!" he said, gritting his teeth against the urge to scream.

"This is the very reason you should write down your music, in order that anyone can play it whenever they desire."

He nearly growled. That was another reason he did not want to write it down. Then anyone could play it, control it . . . steal it!

With that thought, he dove low and scrambled under the piano table, making Lady Brilliance shriek again. He had his hand on the toe of her kidskin slipper, but she managed to tug it out of his grasp and scamper away. Instead of remaining near the piano where he could reach her, she went toward the window.

"Ha!" he exclaimed, knowing she was trapped.

"Stop this," she insisted, running into the curtains.

"Give me that music," he ordered again as he rose to his feet and began stalking her.

"No!" She had her back to the window. Her cheeks were pink, and her eyes looked a little wild, stirring something in his blood.

"You cannot escape," he told her, "and I will take back those pages."

Instead of being reasonable and handing them over, Lady Brilliance quickly rolled the half sheets and stuck the cane-shaped tube of paper down her décolletage between her ample breasts. Only the top of the pages was still visible.

Well! The encounter was becoming less irksome and more entertaining.

"Let me pass," she ordered, but he would vow she was enjoying herself by her satisfied smirk.

"Or what?" he asked, crossing his arms.

"I don't know," she said. "I suppose we have achieved a checkmate, which I have never done when playing chess."

"You haven't done it today, either." He took a step closer with his palm out. "Give me that music."

Raising her hand to ward him off, Lady Brilliance implored, "Lord Hewitt, be reasonable."

He longed to toss the torn pages into the nearest hearth. Since it wasn't lit, however, he would take them to the large oven in Alethia's kitchen.

"I am past being reasonable." Taking another step, he was slipper-to-boot with her, able to see the instant when her pupils dilated.

His gaze fell to her sweet, kissable lips.

Twice wasn't enough, he realized. But first, the music. Reaching forward, his fingers hovered over the valley between her lovely breasts.

"What is going on here?" came his cousin's voice.

CHAPTER TEN

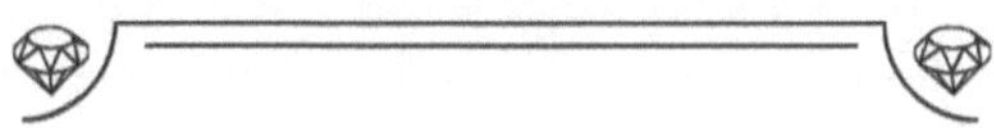

Brilliance couldn't move, trapped between Lord Hewitt and the curtained window panes. But he stepped backward, swift as a hare. At the untimely interruption, disappointment trickled over her like cold rain. Almost certainly, he had been about to kiss her again, and she had been more than ready.

She waited, wondering in what way he would answer their hostess, while keeping her own mouth closed. After all, Brilliance didn't owe anyone an explanation as Lord Hewitt was the one behaving oddly.

"The lady had something in her eye," he said finally.

"Did she?" Lady Twitchard asked before fixing her glance on Brilliance. "Why don't you come with me? If it's an eyelash, I'll use the end of my handkerchief to remove it."

"Sometimes blowing hard works, too," Brilliance said. "But my eye is fine." She didn't want to lie to their hostess and felt ashamed of Lord Hewitt for lying to his cousin.

"If you'll excuse me, I am going to my room," she said to Lord Hewitt, tapping her chest. He glared at her, but Lady Twitchard could not see his face.

Brilliance edged around him, nodded to their hostess, and hurried from the conservatory.

A mere three feet from the room, however, she turned back, recalling her need for something to repair the torn pages. Standing in the doorway, unnoticed yet not at all hidden, she was privy to her hostess's first words.

"What was that all about?" her ladyship demanded of Lord Hewitt, her back to the door. "I've never had to worry about you trying to compromise any of my guests before."

"I was not," he declared, then noticed Brilliance had returned. He gestured with his head until Lady Twitchard turned.

"I am sorry to bother you, my lady, but would you have any glue?"

Her ladyship frowned, while Lord Hewitt's eyes narrowed.

"No glue for her," he said.

Lady Twitchard gawked at him. "You have lost all sense of civility. You will frighten the young lady."

"Oh, no," Brilliance defended him. "Even when he was chasing me around the piano, I wasn't truly scared of him."

"Chasing you around the—" Lady Twitchard broke off with a shake of her head. "Come along, Lady Brilliance. I will find you some glue. If not, perhaps sealing wax would work for your project."

She took a few steps toward Brilliance before rounding upon her cousin.

"And you! Stay away from this sweet earl's daughter, or you shall answer to me!"

BRILLIANCE MANAGED TO STICK the pages back together, fairly confident they were in the right order after matching up the torn edges. But there was nothing she could do with them except put them in her traveling trunk. If she returned to the conservatory, Lord Hewitt would, as likely as not, waylay her again.

It had occurred to Brilliance to ask Lady Twitchard whether she knew some reason for her cousin's strange behavior, particularly regarding this popular musical piece. Yet that seemed rather sneaky. She would far prefer Lord Hewitt explained his actions to her directly, but that meant they needed to be alone once more, which was not the easiest to accomplish.

Putting the entire matter aside, she vowed to enjoy the party for the days that were left and be entirely agreeable to the nobleman in question. She even requested an entire bowl's worth of assorted fruit, whatever was ripe, pleased to receive sliced melon, raspberries, and a couple of small peaches.

Self-consciously, she knocked upon his door and left the offering, knowing she couldn't actually go in. The first time had been an honest mistake. Brilliance wouldn't be able to claim that a second time. She would be truly a wanton woman.

However, she could—and would!—spy on him from the neighboring linen cupboard. After a few long moments, Lord Hewitt opened his door and nearly stood in the bowl. Then he looked up and down the hallway, making her gasp when his spectacled gaze seemed to land on her hiding place.

But all he did was shake his head, retrieve the fruit, and go back into his room.

The following day was a sporting day with bow-and-arrow competitions—another thing at which she wasn't spectacular, although she managed to actually hit the straw target once in twelve tries. Afterward, all the guests played croquet again, seeing how there was a cooling breeze. After a light meal, many were going riding since the countryside was so lovely.

By then, Brilliance and Martine had decided a lengthy promenade would be fine as five pence. Having left the veranda, they were alone in the extensive terraced gardens.

"You like Lord Hewitt," her friend said, not making it a question.

"I do," Brilliance declared, seeing no reason to pretend otherwise in Martine's confidence. "Isn't he magnificent?"

"I do not know about *magnificent*," Martine said. "After all, I don't know much about him at all. Do you?"

"Only that I fancy him above all others."

Martine appeared shocked. "Does he feel the same?"

"I don't know," Brilliance confessed.

Martine sighed. "You haven't told him, have you?"

Brilliance thought back to what she had said. "Not really."

"But you wear your heart upon your sleeve more than anyone I know," her friend chided. "He probably knows. Therefore, you mustn't let him be alone with you or allow him to make any advances."

Brilliance swallowed the words, *Too late for both*. Instead, she asked, "Why?"

"Country parties are far more relaxed than anything we do in London, don't you agree?"

"I do." They had far more freedom, not to mention opportunities for improper mischief, should both parties be agreeable. Unfortunately, Lord Hewitt had retreated since the last incident in the conservatory. Pleasant enough, yet he was managing to keep her at a distance.

Martine was still warning her. "Thus, he might take advantage of you in any number of places."

Brilliance sighed, thinking of a few where she would be happy to oblige.

"He might ruin you," Martine declared, halting Brilliance's happy wool-gathering, "and then where would you be?"

"Perhaps his wife," Brilliance said.

Martine stopped in her tracks. "We have but little time left. Even if we had another week, I would say that isn't nearly enough time to get to know one another properly for considering a lifetime together. And if he is the type to get you alone and steal your virtue, then he is *not* the type who would offer his hand. I fear you would be at Fiddlestick's end."

"Do you really think so?" Brilliance hadn't considered that possibility, not after he'd sent her from his room that first night. "He seems all square, as they say, although I am not sure why *square* means *upright*. Nonetheless, a true gentleman." She paused, thinking of his captivating eyes and his devilish smile before adding, "A dash-fire, rum duke, to be sure, but also a gentleman."

"Don't you think that is what he wishes you to believe?"

This made Brilliance laugh. "No, I don't think he cares what I believe. I think he simply wants to be left alone in the conservatory to play music."

"Maybe he remains in there brooding, as a trap to lure you in." Even Martine cracked a smile after uttering such a nonsensical statement.

And then, as if conjured by their words, Lord Hewitt came walking toward them.

"Well met," Brilliance spoke first as soon as he was within a civilized distance.

"Good day, ladies," he greeted them both. "You didn't fancy riding, I take it."

"No, my lord. Nor you, it seems?"

"I rode," he replied, "but only as far as the village upon a brief errand, and now I intend to—"

Brilliance didn't get to hear his lordship's intent for Colonel Twitchard appeared from behind a tree as if he'd been waiting there all along.

"Just the man I wanted to see," he said. "Good day, ladies. Come along, Hewitt. This way."

Lord Hewitt appeared surprised by the encounter and by being summoned. However, he gave a shallow bow to Brilliance and Martine before heading off with their host.

Nearly that same scenario played out more than once over the next few days, when either Lady Twitchard or her husband would arrive a moment after Brilliance and Lord

Hewitt entered into close proximity. Obviously, his cousin and her husband were attempting to keep them at a distance.

And it was beginning to annoy Brilliance. After all, their time under the same roof was limited and diminishing with each passing day. Taking matters into her own hands, she decided to come upon him when their hosts least expected it.

Thus, after supper, when they had all bid one another good night, she kept a watchful eye on Lord Hewitt. Wherever he went, she had decided to follow, even into his bedchamber.

Naturally, Martine was by her side as they headed toward the stairs with the other ladies in front and behind them. With relief, she saw Lord Hewitt slip into the conservatory instead of going up to bed. She could do nothing in that instant except appear to go to her room.

"Good night," she said to Martine and wandered along the hallway toward her own bedroom door. Waiting until it seemed all the other female guests had retired, a mere two minutes, she turned back to the staircase, deciding to risk the terrible things her friend had warned her of—ruination and all that.

No one was on the stairs, thankfully, and Brilliance went directly to the conservatory, quietly pushing the door open. She stifled a gasp at seeing Lady Georgiana and Lord Hewitt standing so close they must be breathing the same breath.

Lady Georgiana was going up on tiptoe, and Brilliance stepped back, for she couldn't bear seeing the frothy blonde's mouth on her pianist!

She closed the door, and it made a loud *snick* that had her scrambling for a place to hide in case the conservatory's occupants ventured out to see who might have been spying on their private moment.

Brilliance was shaking as she dashed across the hall to the open drawing room. Luckily, it was empty. Peering through the door's hinge, she watched the conservatory door open quickly. Lord Hewitt appeared first, looking hither and yon, up the staircase and down the passageway toward the back of the manor.

He frowned. Then he reached behind him and yanked Lady Georgiana out into the open. She looked flushed and flustered, and Brilliance's stomach sank. She knew that look, having worn it herself each time she'd been kissed by Lord Hewitt.

Her pianist!

"Go now," he ordered, "before someone sees you."

Lady Georgiana didn't move. Instead, she lingered, which was a dangerous risk, then reached out her ungloved hand to stroke his cheek. Brilliance's heart ached, realizing how completely she had assumed he was hers and that she was the only female who had caught his interest.

Lord Hewitt reared back out of reach. "Stop it. If someone comes now, we shall both miss the ball, and you'll be sent back to London in disgrace."

Brilliance shook her head. Those were the words he had used when telling her to leave his bedroom. Clamping her hand over her own mouth, she waited.

Lady Georgiana seemed to think that threat enough to finally get moving toward the stairs. She glanced around her once more before speaking. "I would not miss the ball and the opportunity to be in your arms for all the tea in China. Good night, my lord."

With those words, she went unhurriedly up the stairs with her full skirts swaying suggestively. And Lord Hewitt watched Lady Georgiana all the way until Brilliance could no longer see her progress. Finally, he went into the conservatory and closed the door.

A part of her still wanted to follow him into that room. It would be a pathetic act, if she did, with Lady Georgiana's perfume undoubtedly still hanging in the air and her spittle on his mouth. That thought soured Brilliance's stomach.

It was not her place nor her right to offer a jealous tirade. Worse would be if he tried to calm her with seduction.

Regrettably, she could well imagine yielding to his charms and letting him kiss her again.

Straightening, she considered what she was doing, hiding behind a door, spying through a crack. She was Brilliance Diamond, who never behaved in a sneaky fashion. *What had come over her?*

Yanking open the door, not caring how much noise she made, Brilliance stomped up the stairs and along the women's wing to her room, slamming the door closed behind her.

CHAPTER ELEVEN

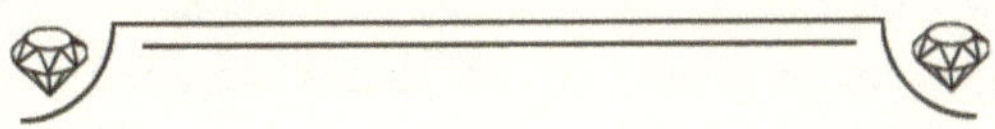

The next day was their last full day. In the evening, they would enjoy a grand ball. Brilliance ought to be melancholy over the former and happy at the latter. Instead, she was simply vexed and puzzled.

Martine noticed it over breakfast. "You have barely spoken two words."

Brilliance sipped her chocolate. "I am sorry for being such poor company."

Lord Hewitt entered at that moment, followed an instant later by Lady Georgiana, as if they had walked down the stairs together. It was quite possible they had arranged to meet that morning.

Brilliance hunched over her plate of coddled eggs and bacon, as yet untouched.

"Is *he* the reason?" Martine asked. "Or is it *her*?"

Brilliance would not say that it was both of them together that was the problem, so she said nothing. To her amazement, Lady Georgiana came over and drew out a chair beside Brilliance as if they were the best of friends.

"Can you believe we are nearly at an end to this delightful party?" she asked. "I vow the week has flown by." She poured herself a cupful from the porcelain teapot. "I don't know about you, but I shall certainly miss the other guests."

Brilliance realized that Lady Georgiana was staring across the room to where Lord Hewitt was filling his plate. Her stomach twinged as it had the night before. As if he sensed being watched, he turned, scanned the room, and nodded in their direction. And then he began to walk over, holding his laden plate steadily in one hand.

"Good morning, my lord," Lady Georgiana was the first to greet him.

"Indeed it is, my lady. We have a practically empty schedule today."

Lady Georgiana laughed as if that was the funniest thing she had ever heard. Brilliance felt Martine's leg press against hers, obviously wondering what was unfolding before her eyes.

"Surely the opportunity for last discussions with those whom we have become *close*," Lady Georgiana said, batting her lashes at the gentleman, "also makes the day a promising one. Not to mention the ball tonight."

Lord Hewitt nodded, pouring his coffee and stirring in some crystallized sugar. "And good morning to you, ladies," he said, taking in both Martine and Brilliance, who had yet to speak.

"Good day," Martine returned, now tapping her knee against Brilliance's.

She supposed she must make an effort. "Good morning, my lord. You seem to have a greater appetite for breakfast than usual."

He glanced at his plate before sending her a handsome grin, which made her curl her toes within her shoes. "I confess I hadn't realized anyone noticed whether I broke my fast with eggs or with nothing at all. But you are correct, this morning I am famished."

"What might have brought on this hearty appetite?" Lady Georgiana asked, in a too-familiar, teasing tone.

Brilliance rose to her feet before she knew what she was doing.

"Excuse me," she said to Martine. "I shall see you . . . later." Without awaiting an answer, or even remembering to wish the others a good day, she strode from the room.

In truth, the day had much to offer despite Lady Twitchard and her staff being entirely consumed with preparing for the evening's ball. The printed schedule to which they had all been slaves the entire week was woefully thin. Regardless, there would still be croquet, and even *jeu de Paume* if guests wished to don a thick leather glove and hit a ball back and forth. They could fish, too, or use the bows. And, as always, there was riding.

None of it interested her. Brilliance knew she was sulking. Most of the other guests would enjoy the outdoor activities and then, if they'd exerted themselves, take baths to ensure they were refreshed and sweet smelling for the last festive dinner and dancing.

Any staff not needed in the kitchen or for the final decorations in the ballroom would be kept busy lugging hot water and portable copper tubs to each room in turn. While there were a few dedicated rooms for bathing, those would be reserved for the Colonel, Lady Twitchard, and perhaps Lord Hewitt since he was family.

For the first time, Brilliance felt homesick, thinking of the splendid cast iron tub at her home on Piccadilly. She wandered outside, through the gardens, and down toward the river. Tomorrow, by nightfall, she would be back with her parents, but she would be changed.

Surely in her two decades, she had never experienced such a range of emotions, and in such a short time, too. Choosing a pebble, she threw it as far as she could to watch the rippling on the surface of the gentle stream. It was satisfying, so she did it again with a larger rock.

"You will scare the fish," came Lord Hewitt's voice.

Brilliance gasped and whirled to face him, heart immediately pounding.

"My apologies," he said. "I did not mean to frighten you."

"I was wool-gathering, a nasty habit."

"And throwing stones," he pointed out. "Is that also a habit?"

She didn't answer. In her mind, she was imagining him kissing Lady Georgiana. "Why are you here? *Without* a fishing pole?"

"*You* don't have a pole," he pointed out.

"I didn't come to fish." She looked around. "I didn't even mean to walk this far."

"I didn't come to fish, either," he said. "I was looking for you."

Brilliance almost gasped a second time. She wasn't normally a dramatic person, but his gaze was unwaveringly direct. And they were alone.

Just as he had been with Lady Georgiana.

"I am surprised your lady-friend isn't with you."

"My lady-friend?" he asked quizzically. Then he barked out a laugh. "Do you mean Lady Georgiana?"

Brilliance was mortified. She had sounded irrationally, humiliatingly jealous. Dignity was not always necessary, nor even pride. But being pitiful was beyond the pale. Turning away, knowing she could not speak civilly to him when he was so casual with his kisses, she began to walk back the way she had come.

"Here now, where are you going?" Lord Hewitt fell into step beside her. "Are you angry with me? You didn't seem so at supper last night, but at breakfast, you had lost every ounce of friendliness."

"I am not to be trifled with," she said through gritted teeth, increasing her pace so she would pass quickly through the copse of trees.

"I am no trifler," he said, but she kept walking.

"Lady Cheese," he called after her, his tone teasing, but that only made her angrier. "Giver of fruit and fabulous kisses," he added.

She halted. *Damn the man!* When she looked back at him, his gray-green eyes were welcoming and happy behind his spectacles, and his mouth—*so perfect*—was in a half smile. She took a step toward him.

"You say you are not a trifler, but you were hidden away in the conservatory kissing Lady Georgiana last night, and now you have the gall to joke about kissing me! I shall report your behavior to your cousin."

Brilliance turned away, but suddenly he had closed the distance and grabbed her arm.

"Release me," she demanded, giving a little tug to free herself.

"I have not kissed Lady Georgiana," he stated. All traces of humor had vanished. "You have no reason to believe me, except I shall be insulted if you don't. What's more, I have *never* kissed two women at the same party. That would make me a trifler, indeed!"

Brilliance considered his words. "Oh," she said finally, believing him both because she wanted to and because he was too affronted to be lying. At least, she hoped so.

"You may release me now," she said.

His eyes narrowed. "Will you run away like a frightened rabbit?"

"No."

He let go of her.

"Do you deny she came to the conservatory after everyone had gone upstairs to bed?" Brilliance asked, needing to know the entire truth.

"I don't deny it, but she came uninvited. And I sent her back upstairs as soon as I sussed out her game."

"I see."

He took hold of both her hands. "I believe you *did* see. I heard a noise. Was that you?"

"Perhaps," she said, letting him draw her toward him.

"And what were *you* doing creeping downstairs?" he asked. "Were you meeting a lover?"

Her cheeks heated. He had caught her. Lord Hewitt knew she had intended to do exactly what Lady Georgiana had done.

"If you had slipped into the conservatory, I promise you, I would not have thrown you out as I did her."

"Why?" she asked, looking up at him. She wanted him to compliment her, and it must have shown.

"Well, that is a first," Lord Hewitt said. "Lady Brilliance is flirting with me. Shamelessly, too. I would have kept you locked in the music room with me until all hours. And if you do not know why, then I will show you."

Without warning, he kissed her. Without a thought, she snaked her hands up to rest behind his neck while his hands spanned her waist.

Brilliance had learned a few things that week, such as how to tilt her head and make her mouth fit against his perfectly without their noses bumping. She'd learned it made the kiss better to part her lips. But when his tongue began its quest, she slid hers into his mouth, surprising him.

It was a delicate dance, and while they performed it, her heart was pounding so hard that the noise filled her ears like a drumbeat. Why it should be pleasurable to crush her breasts against him, she could not explain, but it was. In fact, she could not get close enough.

How long they kissed, she couldn't say. Leisurely, he raised his head and she sighed. Then, seeing how her bonnet brim was half over her left eye, she started to straighten it.

"I nearly forgot!" he exclaimed. "I bought you a gift."

"Whatever for?"

"For all you have given me, all the fruit and the friendship. And simply because I wished to." He reached inside his coat. "There was not much selection in the village, and now we've crushed the silly thing."

Lord Hewitt handed her a decidedly flat but lumpy parcel of creased tissue-paper.

Not the least hesitant, she tore it off in two seconds. "A bonnet," she said softly, staring at the folded hat in the lightest cotton. "And the prettiest shade of blue."

"To match your eyes," he said.

"Thank you. I adore it." She undid the bow under her chin and wrenched off the cream and pink bonnet she was presently wearing, tucking it under her arm. Giving the new one a shake that didn't succeed in removing its many wrinkles, she set it atop her head.

"How does it look?" she asked.

"Beautiful, albeit crumpled. I am sure your maid will tend to it." He took hold of the blue ribbons dangling down. "Meanwhile, allow me to tie these for you, my lady."

Brilliance felt his fingers under her chin as he made a lopsided, clumsy bow. As soon as he had finished, she went up on tiptoe and kissed him again.

Instantly, heat curled through her body, increasing when he pressed one of his thighs between hers. Lost in the ardor of their embrace, she was hampered only by the cotton of her day dress from feeling his firm leg against her most intimate part.

Voices had them springing apart, with Brilliance sucking in a shocked breath while Lord Hewitt tugged at his coat sleeves.

"Walk toward them," he ordered, "and I will go back to the stream. I shall come find you, and we'll go riding."

She did as he suggested without hesitating, only wishing large animals weren't going to play a part in the rest of her day.

She hurried forward, meeting Colonel Twitchard and a cluster of the male guests carrying poles.

"Well met," said the Colonel. "Would you care to join us?"

"No, thank you," Brilliance said. "I walked this far, and that was far enough." After all, she had already made her catch for the day.

WHEN VINCENT CAUGHT UP to Lady Brilliance twenty minutes later, having skirted the fishing enthusiasts entirely, he found her already wearing her riding habit. Unfortunately, she was surrounded by other guests who all intended one last ride before they dispersed by late morning the following day. Most of them were going back to London. If they liked riding, then this was a far better place than Hyde Park or St. James's, although with less chance of being seen by the right people.

His cousin was among those standing in the stable yard.

"There you are," Alethia said. "Go change, and we'll wait unless you have other plans."

Lady Brilliance's gaze was upon him, almost rueful, but there was nothing for it except to join the group.

"I am surprised you are riding," he said to his cousin. "After all, you are putting on a ball tonight."

"I am thoroughly organized, and my staff even more so. We shall be ready. A ride will clear my head."

Vincent hurried inside to change. He hadn't brought his valet, but he was well able to look after himself, and took no longer than five minutes. Upon his return, however, his cousin had coupled the riders, including Lady Brilliance, who was to ride beside Lord Fincham. He dreaded to discover his partner was Lady Georgiana, much relieved to see it was, in fact, Lady Martine.

"You are more at ease in the saddle than your friend," he remarked when they had set off across the fields.

"I suppose I am." After hardly any hesitation, she asked, "Speaking of my friend, what are your intentions, my lord?"

He was shocked. Lady Brilliance's forthright manner was apparently contagious. Or perhaps that was why she and Lady Martine were friends, birds of a feather and all that.

"The answer should come easily," she added. "It is not a riddle."

"I was only wondering whether Lady Brilliance asked you to ask me, or if playing the part of a parent was your own idea?"

"Hardly a parent," she said. "Simply a concerned friend. Lady Brilliance is one of the sweetest, candid, most genuine people I have ever had the fortune to meet. I cherish her, as she deserves."

As she deserves. Vincent considered that. "Don't you, and all of us for that matter, deserve to be cherished?"

Lady Martine smiled. "I suppose you are correct, my lord."

At that moment, Lady Georgiana who was riding ahead turned and gave him a hungry stare. The woman was not subtle. What a shame he had no interest in a quick flyer against some convenient wall, for he had a notion she would be willing—albeit with some serious strings attached, such as the leg-shackling chains of marriage.

In any case, the lady caused no rise in him. If Lady Brilliance had given him such a look, he would have felt it searing him down to the soles of his riding boots.

Lady Martine cleared her throat, reclaiming his attention. "I caution you against trifling with Lady Brilliance in the short time you have left. Even if I am powerless, you may recall who her father is."

There was that word again, *trifling*. It put Vincent's back up. While he had engaged in some passionate kisses with the lady, he had not forced her! Nor would he ever lose control and compromise her virtue.

"In that particular regard, I am in no fear of the earl, and you need not be concerned for your friend. I believe she and I are like-minded."

To his surprise, Lady Martine shook her head. "Oh, my lord. That is highly doubtful. No one has a mind like Lady Brilliance. Have you noticed how she has a tendency to say what she is thinking? Her heart is similarly open. Too easily won over, I believe. At least, once she has let it become inclined in one direction over another. She is wonderfully frank, but also trusting and in some regards, naïve. She lacks . . . defenses."

He appreciated Lady Martine's warning, her worry for her friend, and her discreet language.

More than that, Vincent found himself pleased, exceedingly so, at the prospect of Lady Brilliance opening her heart to him. It had been a mere sennight, but the devil take him if he wasn't absolutely captivated by her.

"I shall remember what you have said, my lady. And I thank you for it."

While he enjoyed Lady Martine's thoughtful company, he was glad when they reached the first rest area, where the stream fed into the River Cray. While the horses drank, they were able to switch partners.

As Lady Georgiana made a move toward him, straight and swift as a blackbird, he ducked and wove his way through the riders, avoiding her, until he arrived at Lady Brilliance's side. She was laughing over something her companion, Lord Fincham had said.

The lucky chap! Vincent wanted to knock him flat.

Her eyes widened when she saw him. "How was your ride, my lord?" she asked. "I admit that I am becoming more at ease with each long journey."

"That was hardly long," Lord Fincham said. "In fact, with you as my partner, it seemed monstrously brief."

Bleh! Vincent hoped Lady Brilliance didn't appreciate such drivel.

"Then the next part of your ride will return to the normal scheme of time," he told the man. "Because Lady Twitchard has announced we are all to switch partners. And Lady Brilliance is now mine."

"*Egads!*" Lord Fincham said, looking around. "Then I must make haste and find my new one before all the pretty ladies are taken."

Vincent and Brilliance watched him go, heading straight to Lady Georgiana, who was staring back at them with a glowering expression.

"That wasn't nice of him," Lady Brilliance said. "At least he ought not to have stated it aloud. Any of the ladies can be good company regardless of their looks. And in truth, I don't think there is an unattractive one here."

Privately, he thought there was an assortment of horse-faced, big-eared, snaggle-toothed, scraggly-haired ladies along with the few pretty ones, such as Lady Martine and Lady Georgiana. However, Lady Brilliance was the only breathtaking beauty at the party.

Aloud, Vincent said, "He is an insolent blackguard who should have kept his miserably mean thoughts to himself."

"Oh my," she said. And then her laughter bubbled up again.

He was glad he had been the one to inspire it. What's more, it was infectious, and he laughed with her. A life with her by his side would be one of happiness, he was certain.

"Shall we ride?" he asked, as others were starting to gain their saddles.

"If we must," she replied. Then she leaned closer until he could catch her intoxicating floral scent. "I wasn't lying about enjoying riding a little more each time, but I am happier to be *your* partner than Lord Fincham's. Or anyone else's here, for that matter."

He beamed down at her, feeling honored. And when he assisted her into the saddle, he felt something else. Touching her, lifting her, sliding her foot into the special leather slipper stirrup—all these incidental encounters left him hard as a piano leg.

In turn, this made climbing into his own saddle a tad painful. But she was worth it!

CHAPTER TWELVE

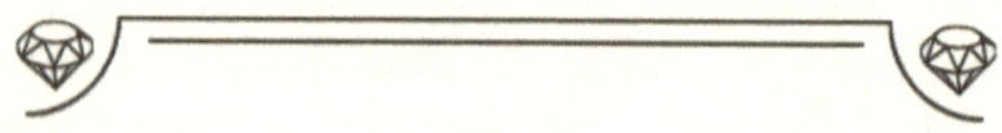

Brilliance was bursting with excitement at the notion of being in Lord Hewitt's arms once again. Dressing for the ball, she vowed she was trembling all over, awaiting their first dance. Riding side by side earlier in the day had been delightful, too, as they talked about anything and everything. However, at the point where they turned and headed back to Lady Twitchard's estate, their hostess made them switch partners again.

Brilliance had a notion it was only because she was riding with Lord Hewitt. Worse, she had been paired with Mr. Denham, whom she had not spoken with since the first evening's introduction assembly. He made up for lost time by proving himself a tedious chaff-cutter, rattling on enough to jaw her dead.

By the time she was back in her room, luxuriating in a lukewarm bath before the six o'clock dinner, Brilliance had forgiven Lady Twitchard. She was merely protecting her female guests as a good hostess should. Surely at the ball, though, even Lady Twitchard must concede there was no harm in dancing.

Brilliance descended the main staircase as slowly and gracefully as she'd been trained and walked through the east wing toward the ballroom. All the while, she wished she could run. Dressed in the gown she'd saved for the occasion, gold silk slid softly over her skin, neckline to hem, with a fitted bodice and little cap sleeves. The entire effect was softened by an overlay of paler gold lace tatting. Feeling splendid in the London modiste's creation, she couldn't keep the smile from her face as she followed a trail of well-dressed men and women through the open double doors.

Dozens of candles in wall sconces set before mirrored disks and hundreds of candles in chandeliers suspended high overhead, dripping with crystals, lit the room like bright sunlight. Brilliance had seen the maids early that morning cleaning each and every crystal teardrop with vinegar.

The floor, previously covered with thick carpets, had been exposed and polished with beeswax. It shone, too, to the point one could gaze down and see one's reflection. Everything was sparkling and glittering, like being inside a jewelry case.

Colonel and Lady Twitchard were just inside the doorway, greeting their guests.

"Everything is spectacular," Brilliance told them. "I am grateful to be here."

"We are grateful for your presence," her hostess returned, although the Colonel was busy with his snuff box rather than noticing his guests.

Nodding, Brilliance moved on, hoping to find Martine who had already left her room when Brilliance went to look in on her. Before she saw her friend, however, she spied Lord Hewitt.

If she'd been alone, Brilliance would have gasped at the way the sight of him in his black tails affected her. Her heart squeezed, and her stomach twinged. This had to be how her parents felt upon first seeing one another . . . or at least, when her father had helped her mother to remain standing after knocking into her.

Her feet took her involuntarily toward him. When he turned and noticed her, his eyebrows rose above his spectacles, and then he smiled.

Oh, that smile!

And then Lady Twitchard stood between them. Her hostess must have raced from her post greeting guests in order to block Brilliance. But the woman, no matter how well-intentioned, was *not* her mother. Brilliance would not allow herself to be deprived of the delights that could only be had in Lord Hewitt's arms.

Thus, with barely a moment's hesitation, she said, "Good evening, again, my lady. Did I mention how wonderful your ballroom looks?" And she skirted her hostess as if edging around a prickly raspberry bush, finally reaching Lord Hewitt.

Immediately, he grasped her gloved hand and bowed over it.

"You are exquisite, my lady. Dare I say radiant?"

She shrugged. "That is more aptly said of my dear sister, Ray, but I appreciate your kind words."

He frowned and removed his glasses, slipping them into a pocket. "Let me try again. The *brilliance* of your beauty outshines every other female here."

"Oh, I like that very much," she said. "Thank you. And you look very fine, my lord. So handsome, I could swoon— if I were the swooning type."

His cheeks flushed an impressive shade of rose. "Thank you." His gray-green eyes gleamed in the candlelight.

"Hewitt," said Colonel Twitchard, sidling up from nowhere. "Would you care to—?"

"I will do whatever you wish," Lord Hewitt said, "*after* I have danced with this lovely lady. You cannot expect me to leave her standing here." Then he gestured to her. "Just look at her, Colonel."

"Yes, I see," their host said. When the Colonel actually took in Brilliance's appearance, head-to-slipper, his eyes widened.

She smiled at his admiring expression—it was sweetly unexpected. Then the cornet player, seated on an oval platform in the room's center, gave the signal for the start of the first dance—a few short blasts. The sound reverberated along her spine, and Lord Hewitt took her arm and led her to where the other dancers were lining up.

The rest of the musicians, a pianist, a violinist, and a cellist, began to play. Brilliance finally had her heart's desire, dancing with Lord Hewitt. After a few turns around the room, she told him, "Although I believe you are a superior musician to the pianist, tonight, I am glad you are not playing on the dais."

"Why, thank you, my lady."

"Can you believe we have known one another only a week? I vow it feels longer. Tomorrow, I shall be sad to say goodbye to you."

He startled. "Perhaps we will meet again in London."

Brilliance had hoped for something more reassuring. While she knew she shouldn't ask him outright, still she could determine his future whereabouts.

"When are you returning to London?"

"In the autumn," he said, keeping his gaze steadily upon her.

She thought of all the events she might attend in the next two months.

"I may be betrothed by then," she said sadly. How terrible she would feel if Lord Hewitt were to come back into her life after she had grown a *tendre* for another man. But then, if she had given her heart to someone else, she wouldn't feel quite so terrible, after all. Yet Lord Hewitt might be devastated.

"I only tell you that because I have a full social schedule planned. I would hate for you to decide I am the woman you most admire in all the world only to leave it until it is too late."

He looked as if he were choking, but a moment later, he recovered and merely shook his head.

"You are as outrageous as ever."

"Am I?" Brilliance was puzzled. "I am simply trying to save you from heartache."

"In that case, I am most grateful." His hand holding hers squeezed a little harder while the other pressed firmly against her lower back.

Was he telling her something? She sighed.

"I hope we may have another dance before the ball is over," Brilliance said. "Moreover, unless we put our heads together, I doubt we shall find the opportunity for another kiss."

Lord Hewitt faltered abruptly, and Brilliance nearly crashed into him before he resumed the flow of the dance.

Then she couldn't help repeating, "Put our heads together! That is funny." She chuckled. "For it is precisely what I would like us to do, but your cousin and the Colonel have been successfully playing chaperone for the better part of two days, have they not?"

He nodded, saying nothing.

"We could try tonight," she volunteered as the music ended.

Lord Hewitt escorted her from the floor in thoughtful silence, and pain stabbed at her heart. He wasn't going to give her any encouragement, it seemed. *How odd!* She'd been sure, at the beginning of the week, that they were destined for a mutual understanding and a lifetime of love.

Just before he turned away to find his next partner, he caught her gaze. "Will you do me the honor of a second dance later?"

Speechless, Brilliance nodded. Hope flooded her. Lord Hewitt did care for her.

He did!

NOT FOR THE FIRST time, Vincent found himself thinking what an uncommon woman Brilliance Diamond was. It was practically a miracle that she had grown up in the bosom of the highest echelon of Britain's social strata without absorbing its oft-times cunning ways and while not taking on its lowlier nature of prevarication or subterfuge.

Moreover, despite an intriguing quality of innocence about her, she seemed to have emerged into the full-flowering of female maturity without being battered and injured. It was almost as if no one would think to take advantage of such an open and willing soul. More likely, she had been incredibly fortunate.

The exact opposite to his own scarred psyche. He hadn't tried to throw himself off a bridge as composer and pianist Robert Schuman had done, plunging into the Rhine during a fit of melancholy. But the betrayal three years earlier had scarred him greatly enough that Vincent didn't know what he could offer a sweet lady who was telling him openly she would like to keep company.

That evening, the angelic essence of Brilliance was accentuated and amplified by her glittering golden gown. Upon first seeing her walking toward him, stunned by her appearance, Vincent had thought her the embodiment of all that a man could want in a woman—her spirited beauty and a sense of genuine sincerity, along with her blue-eyed gaze shining with eagerness.

But her question had caught him off guard. A part of him wanted to promise her he would seek her out in London. And he knew he would be disappointed to learn of her betrothal. Yet she could hardly expect him to declare an inappropriately premature intent out of fear that she would be snapped up by someone else.

Could she?

On the other hand, he could not imagine a more suitable female. She lacked a few of the artistic graces one often found in an educated female of the upper class. Brilliance couldn't sketch, paint, play music, sing, shoot, use a bow, or do needlepoint. She was better in a carriage than on a horse but, self-admittedly, not a good driver.

Regardless of her shortcomings, she seemed as capable of being an excellent wife as any woman he had ever met. More so!

When the ball was half over, Vincent claimed her for their second dance. Her smile as he'd approached caused him a pang of . . . regret, perhaps? That he didn't have a similarly trusting nature. That he couldn't sweep her into his arms and tell her how she interested him to the point of having spent the entirety of the ball watching her. While he was partnering other ladies and she danced with the other gentlemen, she still claimed all his attention.

When they began a slow waltz, for which he was exceedingly grateful, a question tumbled from his lips. "Have you ever had your heart broken?"

Without hesitation, she said, "No, my lord. I have never had my affections engaged to such an extent that it could be broken." She gave a small shrug, barely discernible while they were dancing. And then she stared into his eyes. "But I am not, at this moment, ignorant of how that might feel."

Before he could think about why he had asked her such a personal question, she sent it winging back at him, "Have you?"

Brilliance was so painfully honest, how could he not honor her similarly? Moreover, he had been the one to bring up the delicate subject.

"Yes," he confessed.

Her gorgeous jewel-tone eyes widened, and he could practically see her curiosity flickering in their depths along with her sympathy. And to her credit, that was what she first professed.

"I am sorry to hear that. I heard something of your pain in your playing."

He hated to think his past still managed to leak out of him, as if he were a badly patched wine barrel.

They twirled around one end of the room, moving as if they were one entity.

"If only we could be as the animal kingdom," she added.

He smiled despite himself. "Your meaning?"

"Oh, my lord, it is well known that many birds, and I am sure other creatures as well, simply decide to become mates and then are perfectly satisfied staying that way for the rest of their days."

He nodded.

"Not love at first sight, I warrant, but something deeper," she continued. "They agree to build a nest and watch over their eggs, and to do that over and over for the rest of their lives. Very mature, if you ask me, doing their bird duty."

"Bird duty," he repeated, biting back a laugh. She was speaking matter-of-factly, but he could sense there was a profound truth buried therein.

"Yes," she said emphatically. "Even though it seems impossible that they fell in love upon first deciding to be partners, reasonably thinking, they must love deeply during the course of their lives while caring for one another and for their babies. Don't you think?"

"We are still talking about birds, aren't we?"

"Indeed," she said.

Vincent considered. "It makes sense that they are not indifferent to one another."

"Indifference," she scoffed. "That's a tepid notion. But we have strayed from the point," she said.

He had never carried on such a conversation while dancing. What's more, he had forgotten the point.

"Which is?" he asked.

"Swans don't worry over hair color or the daintiness of the lady's feet. They don't waste time leaving calling cards and paying fifteen-minute visits so they can discuss the weather. They don't spend months dancing around the subject before forming an attachment. Nor do they then, with a cruel and fickle nature, decide upon another."

Vincent considered. "Surely that is because they have shorter lifespans and because . . . well, they are birds!"

She heaved a large sigh, which was a beautiful sight in her dress. "I suppose. Did you love her quite ardently?"

He startled. Brilliance had changed the subject, or rather brought it back to heartbreak so swiftly she left him dazed. She had finally given in to her curiosity, and he had to admire the duration of her restraint in questioning him.

Luckily, the dance ended before he could form an answer. Nevertheless, while they walked, she looked up at him expectantly. In fact, Brilliance nearly collided with another guest, but Vincent tugged her aside in time.

"No answer," she mused.

"The discussion during dancing ends with the dance," he said, hoping that sounded like a societal truism.

Her pretty mouth formed a small *O*.

"Is that a rule? I had no idea." Then she smiled. "Maybe we should have a third dance at the evening's end."

He couldn't help grinning at her words. She wished to glean the details from him and wasn't trying to hide it. Yet since he felt relaxed and happy with her, he would prefer to focus on the present than get mired in the past. For him, it held something more insidious than a single fickle female, worse even than simple treachery, although Lydia had been treacherous enough.

"Would you like to take a stroll in the garden?" he offered. "Perhaps another look at my cousin's topiaries?"

He shouldn't have asked her. Given their brief intense history, he knew what would happen, as did she. If Lady Brilliance agreed, she would expect a kiss, and Vincent would gladly grant it. He was, in fact, nearly desperate to embrace her again. His cousin had been very effective in keeping them apart except for earlier by the stream. And when not her, then the Colonel.

Suddenly, they had almost run out of time, and he wasn't ready to see the back of her as she climbed into a carriage and rode away.

"Despite the freedom I have enjoyed all week," Brilliance said, "because I am at a ball, my instincts have me looking around for my mother or one of my married sisters."

"House parties are an anomaly unto themselves, are they not?" he said. "Yet at this one, because my cousin is an upstanding woman who takes her duties as hostess very seriously, there have been few hijinks."

"Hijinks?" she repeated, allowing him to lead her toward the terrace. "Do you mean of a lascivious nature?"

He said the most carelessly frank things to Brilliance Diamond upon topics he wouldn't dream of bringing up with other ladies, such as heartbreak or the loose behavior of the average house guest. Vincent had caught Lord Fincham in a steamy embrace with Miss Newton, and Lord Patterson *in flagrante delicto* with a chambermaid.

Neither shocked him particularly, except he recalled thinking how glad he hadn't discovered Brilliance in any such vulgar position—unless it was with him. Even then, he couldn't imagine her going along with something like Patterson's ill-advised and hackneyed tumble on the floor of one of the bathing rooms.

Thus, he had to question his intentions by taking her out into the darkness. *Not lascivious!* He felt something more honorable than that. At least, he liked to think so. All of Lady Martine's warnings returned, like a swarm of wasps.

Changing his mind at the door, Vincent halted with his hand on the small of her back. "Perhaps it is too chilly after all."

"Nonsense," Lady Brilliance said, thrusting open the door and stepping outside. "The air is warm tonight. Besides, look, the lamps indicate our hosts' intent for their guests to enjoy the outdoors, don't you think?"

Vincent looked around.

"It's not as though we are alone out here," Brilliance continued.

She was right. He had been rather rakishly wanting to get her outside where they could have some privacy, not taking his gaze from her gold-clad, fairylike form long enough to see that others were enjoying syllabub and sherry out of doors.

He relaxed, glad she wouldn't suddenly realize he had maneuvered her into an unsavory situation like a predator.

"There you are!" Alethia said as if he had done that very thing and completed the dastardly deed behind a hedgerow.

"Come now, Cousin. We are simply enjoying this splendid July night. You cannot fault us for joining our fellow guests out of doors."

Alethia frowned and then understanding dawned. "No, of course not! I only meant I was glad to find you. I've had news from London that affects all of us."

CHAPTER THIRTEEN

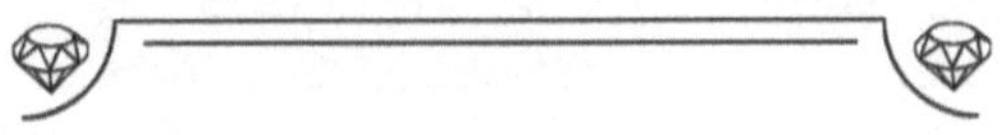

"What has happened?" Brilliance asked.

Lady Twitchard held up her hand, showing more than one unsealed message. "Another cholera outbreak."

Brilliance gasped, her thoughts turning to her loved ones.

"Do not worry. Although it is a terrible thing regardless of whom it affects, this outbreak is on the east side of the city. I have already heard from your family, along with messages from nearly every female guest's parent or guardian. While each of your situations is different, Lord and Lady Diamond have asked that you remain with me while they pack up their home and assist your siblings as they pack theirs. Everyone who is able to do so is fleeing London for their country homes, and as soon as your parents are established at Oak Hall—"

"That's Oak Grove Hall, my lady," Brilliance corrected her. "In Derby."

"Yes, exactly. When they are in residence at your family's country estate, then they will send for you." Addressing her cousin, Lady Twitchard added, "Your mother and stepfather are also well."

Brilliance glanced at Lord Hewitt, who was silently watching. "Then this isn't my final night, after all," she said.

His visage in the light of the outside lamps gave nothing away. While she was not at all pleased that cholera was ravaging the city, she hoped Lord Hewitt was not unhappy to learn he hadn't yet seen the last of her.

"Indeed not," Lady Twitchard said. "You may stay as long as you need. I must go speak with the rest of my guests. Two other young ladies will also be staying, and the rest are going directly to their family's manorial estates."

"And what of the gentlemen?" Brilliance asked, keeping her gaze on Lord Hewitt.

Her ladyship was already walking away from them, but she halted. "No male guests are staying on after tomorrow. They have no need. All of them can go to their country estates without waiting for family or chaperones."

Then Lady Twitchard moved on to the next group.

"A strange coincidence," Brilliance said. "Don't you think?"

"How so?" Lord Hewitt asked, snagging them each a glass of syllabub from a passing footman.

Brilliance felt a pang of guilt at the thought of enjoying something as frivolous as the frothy, old-fashioned drink when people were suffering. But it was not the first outbreak in her lifetime, and it most certainly would not be the last. Londoners, indeed all her fellow countrymen, were made of strong stuff. Whatever happened in the next few weeks, it would not break their spirit. Of that she was certain.

Finally, she took a long draught and then answered him.

"Given what we were discussing earlier while dancing. Do you recall, about returning to London and how I hoped to see you there?"

He nodded. "You have cream on your upper lip."

"Do I?" She licked across it in a quick sweep despite knowing good manners dictated she find her handkerchief and wipe it away properly.

"It looks delicious," he added, his voice dropping lower.

She smiled and sighed. "It is. Try yours."

"I meant your upper lip," he said.

Her breath caught, and they enjoyed a long look, which she doubted she would ever forget. And still, she would love to invite him to try it, to lick it from her lip if at all possible.

Thus, she took another sip and watched him drink his.

"Now neither of us will be in London," she mused.

"Yet nor will we be here together," he pointed out. "I am one of those pesky male guests who shall be tossed out tomorrow."

Drat! "Surely your own cousin wouldn't mind if you stayed on."

"I wouldn't dream of doing such a thing," he said. "That would be an imposition. The party will have concluded, and I shall be ready to go home."

He didn't sound in the least bit bothered at leaving her behind.

"And besides those relations Lady Twitchard mentioned, have you anyone else to worry over in Town?" she asked. For her part, she would feel a little anxious until she knew her parents, sisters, and brother, along with their spouses and children had all vacated Mayfair.

"Neither of my siblings live in London. My mother and stepfather will undoubtedly go to their favorite spot, a small manor due east of here, in Kent. Although my mother adores the seaside, so perhaps they will go all the way to the coast."

"I love watching the ocean," Brilliance told him, but she was distracted by the inevitable occurrence of being in the Twitchards' massive manor without the possibility of running into Lord Hewitt around every corner or in the dining room, drawing room, or one of the smaller salons. It would be empty, indeed.

"By the way, seeing as you will remain in Bexley a while longer," he interrupted her thoughts, "I would be most honored to have you come visit my home."

Had she heard him correctly?

"That would make me exceedingly happy," she told him. "When shall I come?"

He chuckled. "Let us first finish my cousin's ball without wishing the night away."

Suddenly, the future seemed brighter again, and the pallor of parting and of the frightening sickness somewhat dissipated.

"You are correct, of course."

Grabbing for his empty glass, Brilliance set it along with her own on the stone wall beside them. And then, she took hold of his hand.

"Come along, my lord. I am ready to dance."

WHILE SAD TO SAY goodbye to Martine who had been summoned to her family's estate in Surrey, Brilliance was equally excited at the prospect of going to Lord Hewitt's country home. And knowing she would do so softened the pang she felt at seeing him depart the following day.

One by one, her fellow guests left until it was only Brilliance, Miss Newton, and—unfortunately—Lady Georgiana. She wished they had never had a cross word. On the other hand, she hadn't been "treated" to another session of the girl's singing, so perhaps falling out with her had been worth it.

Now that Lord Hewitt had left, Brilliance found herself haunting the conservatory. She even brought out the repaired sheet music and spent a frustrating few hours picking out the tune. While doing her best, the piece still scarcely sounded like Mr. Castern's famed work.

Lady Twitchard entered upon hearing her playing.

"How are you coping, Lady Brilliance?"

"Coping, my lady?" She rose from the stool.

"Stuck here without any planned activities. My husband and I lead a rather dull existence when we are in the country. But compared to our hectic schedule in London, being quiet here is the desired goal. Perhaps not for a young lady though."

"I do not mind. You have an extensive library, and there are the other two ladies, although we do not share a close friendship. I believe they went riding and didn't ask me to join."

"You were improving your musical talent, and good for you." Lady Twitchard eyed the torn and glued pages. "What is that piece you were playing?"

Brilliance couldn't help laughing. "I suppose my musical talent, as you say, has not improved at all, elsewise you wouldn't need to ask. It was Mr. Castern's 'The Hummingbird.'"

"Oh dear," her ladyship said. "Is that what had my cousin all up in arms earlier in the week? Did he tear those?"

"Yes, my lady. I don't understand why, do you? I heard him playing the music, so I thought he liked it, but he denied the tune he played was 'The Hummingbird,' despite it being unmistakable."

"Lord Hewitt is a remarkable composer," Lady Twitchard said. "And years ago, he wrote a piece that sounded much like 'The Hummingbird.' Or my cousin claims *exactly* like it."

Brilliance frowned. "He wishes he had published his version first, I imagine."

Lady Twitchard shrugged. "Something like that. You will have to ask *him* the particulars for I do not gossip. Would you care to take tea with me?"

"I would. Thank you."

Brilliance hoped Lord Hewitt soon sent word inviting her to visit his estate. She would find it difficult to wait, knowing he was nearby. If given no choice, she was willing to break the etiquette that guided so much of her life, but she would much prefer that he be the one to communicate first.

Luckily, she didn't have to set pen to paper and do anything that would make her sister Purity have a fit. The next day, two letters arrived addressed to Brilliance. One from her dear mother assuring her everyone was well while stressing the need for her to stay put.

And the second—she tore it open to read Lord Hewitt's brief but welcome words:

Lady Brilliance,
I have sent word to my cousin that I am serving tea and a light luncheon at noon tomorrow with the expectation of your company along with that of the other stranded guests. I hope you will attend.
Hewitt

Her emotions wavered between excitement and chagrin. Going with Lady Georgiana was not in the least desirable. Brilliance had spent hours playing cards with her and with Miss Newton the previous evening until she thought they would wear off all the marks, and still Lady Georgiana held a grudge.

Regardless, Lord Hewitt had singled her out with a private note, and thus Brilliance could ignore the other girl's discontent.

When the time came the following day, she was ready with her gloves and new bonnet on, waiting in the front hall before the others appeared.

"Oh!" Lady Georgiana exclaimed. "Are *you* going, too?"

As if she didn't know! They had discussed it over dinner the night before. And Lady Georgiana had gone so far as to speculate why Lord Hewitt was eager to see them all again so soon.

"Perhaps he has fallen in love with one of us," Miss Newton had said, sticking her fork into a roasted potato with some vehemence.

Lady Georgiana had looked thoughtful and pleased at the prospect. Perhaps that was why the two of them had overdressed for a midday meal, but Brilliance was too polite to mention it.

Lady Twitchard appeared, and they set off on their excursion in their host's closed traveling coach. Despite the sunny skies, it was prudent not to rely on them staying that way. Plus, they would arrive in a far less dusty state.

Discussion among the four females turned to fashion fairly quickly. They had all seen the magazines from Paris, and how the skirts were predicted to grow fuller, even more bell-shaped with layer upon layer of fringes by the following spring. And wide horizontal stripes on rows of ruffles would be seen on the streets of London.

"I sometimes wish we could go back to the simpler gowns of our grandmothers, with the high waist and a single petticoat," Miss Newton said. "I have four on today, and my gown is still wilting."

Lady Twitchard, who was at least fifteen years older than any of them, laughed. "As one ages, the many layers, not to mention the shape of our current fashion, serve to hide multiple flaws, including too many helpings of syllabub and sponge cake with cream."

"While I have no trouble keeping my slender figure," Lady Georgiana remarked, "I agree it would be easier to enjoy a warm summer day such as today with a loosely flowing gossamer gown and a roomier bodice." She slid her hands over her layered, blue cotton bodice.

Brilliance did, in fact, admire the high waistline and loose drape of the dresses from the beginning of the century. But she thought the current style was preferable. "At least we don't have to wear the farthingale and hip pads from our great-grandmother's time. And their tall wigs seemed most uncomfortable and liable to make one's head hot."

The others nodded in agreement.

"Given our current form-fitting fashion," Miss Newton said, "perhaps we shall be fortunate if Lord Hewitt has a terrible cook."

Lady Twitchard chuckled. "I cannot attest to my cousin's staff, but I believe he hired a new female cook last year. Tight waistline or not, let us hope she knows her way around the kitchen."

"She probably does," Brilliance said, "or she would hardly be considered a cook."

When Lady Georgiana and Miss Newton started to laugh, Brilliance merely shrugged. *What had got into them?*

"It is simply a figure of speech," Lady Twitchard said. "I am certain Lord Hewitt's cook is a real cook."

Brilliance felt her cheeks warm. *Were the others laughing at her?*

She was well aware that occasionally she got the wrong end of the walking stick, but there was no excuse for the other ladies' rudeness. Fortunately, the trip was short, as Lord Hewitt had promised, and Lady Twitchard soon announced they were nearly there.

Brilliance started looking out the window, ignoring the chatter, especially when they went through an adorable village and then turned off the passable road onto a tended gravel drive.

"With this special treat," Lady Georgiana said, "I am almost grateful for the cholera."

Brilliance exchanged a shocked look with Lady Twitchard while Miss Newton giggled but declared, "That's wicked!"

And then they rocked to a halt before a manorial residence of Georgian brick under a tiled roof, with two stories of windows seeming to wink in the midday sun.

"It's lovely," Lady Georgiana said. "Any woman would be proud to be its mistress."

"I cannot wait to see the grounds," Miss Newton added. "I do so enjoy a fine rose garden. Not that there could be any finer than yours, my lady." She sent a glance to their hostess.

And then a footman opened the door. Lady Twitchard descended first, followed by the other two.

When Brilliance came blinking out of the carriage into the sunlight, she paused. She didn't much care about the fineness of Lord Hewitt's house or his gardens. But she couldn't wait to see the man again.

Thus, when his front door opened and he came out, she felt a strange lightening of spirit. Even in this new place, seeing him gave her a feeling of peacefulness and familiarity.

"Greetings, ladies, welcome to Joyden's Wood and to my home, Mirabel Manor." His gray-green eyes took them all in.

Brilliance hoped his gaze would linger a little longer upon her person, but she was unsure whether it did.

"Mirabel," repeated Lady Georgiana softly. "Why, that's the prettiest name I ever heard for a house, and it suits your home perfectly."

Brilliance would agree if she could take her gaze from Lord Hewitt.

He greeted each of them in turn, almost as if they were strangers. Lord Hewitt bowed, they curtsied.

Brilliance's pleasure would be very great indeed, if only Lady Georgiana hadn't somehow been the one in front, taking the arm he offered as he led the way into his home.

CHAPTER FOURTEEN

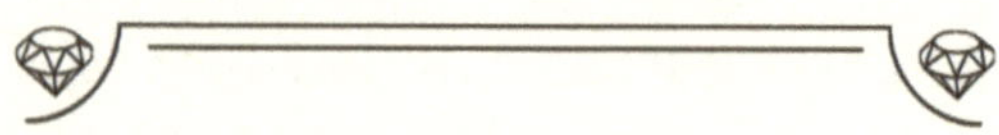

They did not dally in his entrance hall, nor go directly into a drawing room. Rather, they traversed his home front to back, finally stopping before paned doors leading to an elegant brick-and-stone terrace.

With honesty she hoped did not offend, Brilliance told the back of Lord Hewitt's handsome head, "I can see why you were ready to leave Lady Twitchard's home, as elegant and comfortable as it is, in order to return here."

Then she glanced at Lady Twitchard, "Meaning no disrespect, my lady."

Lady Twitchard merely nodded. "I have always thought Joyden's Wood to be a lovely spot. You have maintained the house well, Cousin."

"Thank you," Lord Hewitt said. "I hope you ladies are famished, as my cook has everything prepared. However, if you prefer to take a tour first, then she can, with some persuasion, hold the meal."

Brilliance did not mind whatever they did. She was still waiting for that moment when he gazed directly into her eyes. Perhaps then, her appetite would come roaring back.

For the moment, she would rather be alone with him more than anything else—certainly preferable to trailing along while Lady Georgiana monopolized all his attention, or worse, watched while her fellow females pretended they had the tiniest birdlike appetites when she knew they could eat as much as any man.

Lady Twitchard made the decision for them. "I am ready for a cup of tea and a smattering of both savory and sweet."

"Grand," he said. "I thought, given the weather, that we would eat outside."

Miss Newton clapped her hands. "How clever of you, my lord. I love eating outside. Why, if I had my choice, I would take every meal out of doors if it meant having a view of *your* estate, my lord."

Brilliance could not help rolling her eyes. "Even if it were thick with frost?" she wondered aloud.

Miss Newton sent a sour look her way.

"You have not yet seen the view from my back terrace," Lord Hewitt pointed out.

"Undoubtedly, it is lovely," Lady Georgiana professed, "with a name like Mirabel."

"What if it were the ugliest parcel of land in all England?" Brilliance couldn't help asking. "Would you still want to sit outside? What if you were looking at five-foot weeds covered in bugs? Or a rubbish pile of old bones?"

Paling, Miss Newton made a face, and Lady Georgiana appeared downright annoyed.

"Why would you mention vulgarities when we are about to dine?" she asked. "And why would you insinuate, even in jest, that his lordship would have any such thing in his garden?"

Had she insulted him? Brilliance was ready to apologize, but his expression was amused, not angry.

"I tell you what, Lady Brilliance," Lord Hewitt said, finally addressing her directly and stepping closer so the others could not see his face, "I think we should go right outside and see if the view suits you."

And then, to her delight, he winked before placing her arm on his. She sighed. It was so very nice to be touching him again and to be touched by him.

"How wise of you," she said, "although I confess that I don't give a fig about seeing the sights from your terrace. It is the company that brought me here today."

He put his free hand over his heart. "How kind of you to say."

That earned her a dagger-sharp look from Lady Georgiana.

But Miss Newton managed to get in front of Lord Hewitt. "Naturally, it is your company that brought me here, too, my lord."

"So not merely my terraced lawn and pretty gardens?"

Miss Newton laughed as if he'd said the funniest thing. Brilliance thought both girls were addlepated. They hadn't behaved nearly so strangely when there were more gentlemen around. It would seem the scarcity was bringing out their competitive nature.

What a pity for them that she had already kissed him!

A naughty thought, but true nonetheless. Brilliance didn't worry for an instant that they could usurp her in his affections. After all, he had already told her she was the loveliest woman at the country party, and they were no prettier than they had been all week. Besides, not that she thought Lord Hewitt cared, but she had heard men greatly appreciated the sizable dowry of an earl's daughter.

Sometimes, it was simply good to be Brilliance Diamond.

And then they stepped out the rear of his house, and she exclaimed at its beauty.

"Why, how clever of you to have both cultivated and natural gardens," she said.

"It makes it interesting, to be sure," he said. "Which do you prefer?"

Brilliance looked at the various elements, the tidy rose garden, the soaring arbors, the wildflowers in clumped displays interspersed with fountains and birdbaths. And topiaries grander even than Lady Twitchard's.

"The harmony makes it difficult to choose," she said, "but the wildflowers certainly hold their own. I suppose they speak to my own nature, the part that exasperates those who wish I would behave predictably."

Silence met her words until Lady Georgiana made a sound of exasperation and spoke up.

"I don't mind saying I prefer the fragrant roses. They are the perfect floral embodiment of England, after all."

Miss Newton agreed, "Besides, I cannot tell the difference between a wildflower and a weed, but I always know a rose."

Brilliance rolled her eyes. *Drivel! Could they not for one moment say something original or have a unique thought?*

Lady Twitchard spoke up. "I, also, think it brave to blend the two. Some will say it is an unforgivable juxtaposition. For my preference, I wouldn't have the courage to let my gardens be natural, not even in the smallest part."

Brilliance laughed. "That's peculiar, isn't it? Worrying over whether nature is too natural."

Lady Twitchard laughed, too, and they dropped the subject.

Lord Hewitt drew out a chair for his cousin while a footman seated the rest of them at a round, white rattan table. They had cold chicken and ham sandwiches followed by freshly baked lemon cookies.

"Your cook knows her way around the kitchen," Brilliance said, trying out the term.

"Thank you," Lord Hewitt said. "I will pass on your praises to her."

"On the house tour," she continued, "we shall see if your housekeeper knows her way around the bedroom."

Lady Twitchard gave a small gasp while Miss Newton and Lady Georgiana burst out in inexplicable laughter. Lord Hewitt merely coughed into his napkin.

"What did I say?" Brilliance asked.

"Never mind," Lady Twitchard said. "Another cup of tea?"

VINCENT HAD SURPRISED HIMSELF by inviting the small group of females so soon after leaving Alethia's. And if he were honest with himself, had he been able to invite only Lady Brilliance, he would have.

That in itself bore examination. He had grown used to the lady's company over the course of the sennight. His first day and night in his own home had felt a little lonely. That might be attributed merely to having been surrounded for a week by other people, but it was Brilliance's presence, speaking with her, hearing her laughter, looking at her animated face—all those things he had greatly missed.

Now, seeing her in his home, he thought she belonged at Mirabel just as well as the roses in his garden, the whimsical mat of dark green ivy he allowed to climb up the eastern side of his home, and the wildflowers she'd admired.

Trying not to let emotions run away with him, still, he was determined to have a few minutes alone with her. He would have to enlist Alethia's assistance, not to mention her permission.

Thus, when they were in the middle of the tour of his house, on the second floor where a back bedroom gave a panorama of his gardens and the fields beyond, he managed to hold his cousin back.

Lowering his voice, he asked her, "Would you be amenable to allowing me five minutes to speak privately with Lady Brilliance?"

She gave him a long look, her eyebrows raised.

"Give me credit, Cousin," Vincent said. "I would hardly ask you to give me leave had I poor intentions."

"What *are* your intentions?"

He wished he knew. "I would simply like a moment of her time. I want to express my admiration for her and see if she might like to come visit me again." He paused. "*Without* the other ladies."

"I see."

"If I try to pay a visit to her at Bexley Hall . . ." He trailed off.

"The other ladies would learn too much," his cousin surmised, "and begin to wonder if anything had occurred over the past week."

"Precisely," he said. Vincent kept his gaze on the three females peering out the window. He'd told them they might be able to see the same ruins where they'd enjoyed their picnic. "Your tone is not entirely approving."

Alethia sighed. "I wish you were speaking with her mother rather than with me."

"It is not as if I am asking for her hand," he said. Although he now believed they might continue along a path with an engagement as the natural progression. And then, of course, marriage.

Lady Hewitt. That sounded beyond satisfactory.

"I think she may be the one," he heard himself saying aloud.

His cousin looked over at her three charges. "I think she's a rare find. Just make sure you don't ask her, *not* without her parents' permission."

"Of course not."

"Then I shall help you in any way I can." Alethia left his side to go over to the three young ladies.

He couldn't hear what she said, but Lady Georgiana and Miss Newton answered exuberantly in the affirmative and then departed the room with Alethia. Lady Brilliance was left standing by herself.

She looked at him. "Did *you* make that happen?"

She was astute and unafraid. He admired her more and more, but he was curious.

"What did my cousin say to them?"

"Lady Twitchard asked if they wished to see your bedchamber."

The deuce! "She did not! Did she?"

"She did." Lady Brilliance was smiling broadly.

He thought of those ladies gawking at his private space, examining his pillow to see if there was an indent from his head, perhaps even finding a stray stocking or cravat.

"But that's my personal space. She cannot—" Vincent stopped and took a breath. "Why didn't you go with them?"

"Because I would far prefer spending my time with you."

Putting his head back, he laughed from deep in his belly. She was a gem, indeed.

Brilliance spread her hands. "After all, if things turn out well between us, then I'll be seeing your bedroom for myself when it is only the two of us."

He sobered quickly. They were thinking along the same lines, but it still was alarming to be in the company of an absolutely plain-spoken female.

"I take it you can imagine it being *our* bedroom," he said.

"I don't see why not," she said. "Although it would be nice to have a chamber of my own, to get away from you."

"Get away?" He felt almost affronted. "Why would you want to do that?"

It was her turn to laugh. "When we have an argument, for instance, and you are too pigheaded to see that you're wrong."

"I'm not sure I care for the term *pigheaded*. Maybe I wouldn't be wrong."

"See," she said, "that sounds pigheaded to me. Of course you would be wrong. Why else would I need to get away from you? My mother oft needs a break from my father."

She nodded sagely. "Or I might simply need a place to collect my thoughts, perhaps to quietly read a book or take a nap. This room, for instance, seems ideal."

Lady Brilliance glanced around, and they both ended up looking at the bed.

Vincent's imagination had them naked and entangled on the counterpane in under two seconds.

"Would I be allowed to come find you in here?" he asked. "Perhaps to apologize for my pigheadedness?"

Together, they still looked at the bed. He had never noticed how comfortable it appeared, nor how inviting.

"I think that would be acceptable," she said, her tone a little husky.

He wondered if her thoughts matched his, with him rising over her, his knee nudging her legs apart before his body settled between her thighs. He longed to see her smooth stomach bowed with anticipation and her breasts arching ripely for him to worship.

"Then that would be a good compromise," he agreed, not having expected to be discussing living arrangements. But that, he realized, was quintessential Brilliance, taking him on a path along which he knew not whether it would end.

"Where would you go?" she asked.

Vincent frowned. "Where would I go when?" he retorted.

"There might be some situations in which I might make you want to tear your hair from your head."

"How clever of you to deduce that you might not always be right," he said.

She shrugged. "You might simply not see the rightness at first. In any case, if we were sharing a bedroom, then where would you go?"

"There are plenty of other rooms, including my study. Would you like to see it?"

"We ought to catch up with the others," she said. "We have been alone long enough to shred my reputation should anyone spend a moment thinking about how we vanished from the group. Time enough that we might have reclined upon that bed and been very improper."

Now he wished he hadn't wasted the time jabbering when they could have been behaving improperly. But he had promised his cousin something. He couldn't recall, except he wouldn't blurt out a marriage proposal.

"Will you come visit again?" he asked as they stepped into the hallway. "Without the others, I mean?"

Her smile was glorious. "I have no notion how that will be possible without the cooperation of Lady Twitchard, but I am amenable to doing so should the circumstance arise."

Vincent would ensure that it did.

CHAPTER FIFTEEN

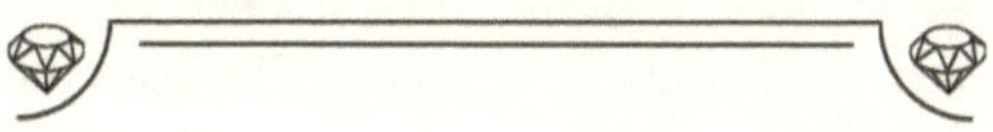

Brilliance wrote to her father and mother as soon as she returned to Lady Twitchard's. Ever dutiful and honest, she knew her parents should be apprised of a gentleman's interest in her, especially seeing how they had discussed married life.

As to finding a way to see him again alone, that was beyond her ability.

And then everything worked out even better than she could have hoped. When she went down to breakfast two mornings later, there were trunks in the hall.

"Has someone arrived?" Brilliance asked the housemaid.

"No, my lady. Two guests are leaving." And she hurried away in the fashion of busy maids who always seemed to have somewhere else they needed to be.

Brilliance went with equal speed into the breakfast salon. Sure enough, both Lady Georgiana and Miss Newton were dressed for travel.

"Why are you leaving?" she asked, taking a seat and nodding to the footman to pour her a cup of chocolate.

"We have been invited to another house party," Lady Georgiana said, her smug expression leaving no doubt as to her mood. "Didn't *you* get an invitation?"

"No." Brilliance found it impossible to sound the tiniest bit sad. Inside, she was simmering with excitement.

"Are you terribly mortified at being left behind?" Miss Newton asked, spearing a morsel of sausage on her plate.

Instead of answering such a disingenuous question, Brilliance asked, "Where are you going?"

"To Richmond, to the home of Lord and Lady Boyer."

"I've never heard of them," she said. *Why were the girls so excited?* It wasn't as though they were going to Syon or Devonshire House.

"Nor had I," Miss Newton said, "but somehow, they have heard of us. Party orphans due to the cholera."

Brilliance bit her lip. *What rubbish!* She wasn't going to try to dissuade them from going, though. Far from it! "How kind of them to take you in."

"Not just take us in. They are hosting us properly with a ball. And they have two single sons," Lady Georgiana added.

Miss Newton nodded. "We are to stay in a home with two single gentlemen!"

"How fortunate for you." Brilliance truly hoped this was some fortuitous event that led them to both finding matches. *Wouldn't that be magical?* In any case, they clearly preferred to have two men residing under the same roof over sharing a single viscount who lived a half hour carriage ride away.

"I hope you won't be bored here without us," Miss Newton said.

"Oh no," Brilliance replied. "I doubt your departure will make much difference to me."

By the thunderous expression on their faces, she'd been a trifle too honest. But all she could do was wish them well and hope that Lord Hewitt soon invited her over again.

"WE ARE TO DINE WITH my cousin this evening," Lady Twitchard said the following morning. "That is, if you are amenable."

"I am. Very much so. I hold Lord Hewitt in the highest esteem."

"Then I shall send word back."

"I look forward to it." Brilliance wondered how she would pass the hours before they set off in the Twitchards' carriage.

"Perhaps you would like to take the response back to him yourself, go early, and spend the day in my cousin's company."

Brilliance wondered if she could have heard her correctly for it was a most unusual thing to suggest.

"My lady, that would be my most fervent wish, but I can hardly believe you find it acceptable for me to do so. Not that many days ago, it seemed that you and Colonel Twitchard were colluding to keep your cousin and me firmly apart."

Lady Twitchard looked uncomfortable. "I got a little above myself, as they say. I thought my cousin might be playing you falsely. But I don't think that any longer. Rather, I know he has genuine admiration for you. And vice versa, if I understand your sentiments correctly."

Brilliance nodded. "Lord Hewitt and I do share a strong mutual admiration."

"Then let me not to the marriage of true minds admit impediments."

"How well put," Brilliance said. "So poetic."

"Shakespeare," Lady Twitchard said. "From one of my favorite sonnets."

Brilliance felt a little embarrassed. "I am sorry to say I have never memorized any of his works."

"That is neither here nor there. You have other grand qualities." They stared at one another for a moment.

Brilliance was glad Lady Twitchard didn't try to come up with any of those qualities because she knew her list of accomplishments was short, and her attributes were restricted to a pleasant personality and above-average good looks. Regardless, she tried to always be a good daughter, a true friend, and a congenial guest. One day soon, she hoped to be a loyal fiancée and then a loving wife.

"In any case," her hostess continued, "Lord Hewitt sent a letter that was extremely polite yet also compelling, resulting in the somewhat unconventional day that lies ahead. My cousin is persuasive when he wants something."

Lady Twitchard left it hanging in the air that what he wanted was . . . Brilliance.

Thus she found herself packed off with her maid to spend the day at Mirabel Manor, with the understanding that Colonel and Lady Twitchard would arrive within a few hours.

"Should I take a change of dress?" Brilliance thought how her mother might disapprove of her sitting down to dine in the same gown she'd traveled in and worn for hours.

"Do you see?" Lady Twitchard remarked. "You have a very sound head upon your shoulders. I think, under the circumstances, you will be forgiven for not changing. However, I see nothing wrong in taking another gown since you'll have your maid with you."

By mid-morning, she was bundled into a small conveyance with her maid and a change of clothes and driving to Lord Hewitt's home.

It was most unusual, as Lady Twitchard had said. Many times, Brilliance wondered if her parents would approve, in particular, her father.

Regardless, a short while later, she was met at Lord Hewitt's front drive, not by a footman but by the viscount himself, helping her down from the carriage.

"You came," he said, sounding excited and charming her down to the toes of her favorite, soft blue shoes.

As if there had been any doubt that she would!

"I thank you for the invitation. Your cousin and the Colonel will be along in a few hours."

"Isn't that wonderful?" he said, not taking his gaze off her.

"I have brought my maid," she added, in case he thought her entirely without morals.

"Isn't that wonderful, too?" he repeated. "I am sure she will enjoy spending the day with my staff. Come along, let us introduce her to my housekeeper, and then we'll figure out what we want to do first."

"After the carriage ride, I would like to take a stroll and exercise my legs."

"May I join you?" he asked.

Brilliance burst out laughing. When she could speak easily again, she said, "The first time I saw you in Lady Twitchard's conservatory, I would never have thought you to have a jolly sense of humor."

"I am serious when playing, it's true."

"Oh yes, you were fierce, and you chased me off. Twice."

They entered his front hall, and she gave her lightweight short mantle to his butler.

"I may always be that way when concentrating on music. In fact, I can almost guarantee I will be," Lord Hewitt said. "I work best when I forget myself, almost as though my physical body were unimportant except for my fingers. They are merely the conduit which sends the music from my brain out into the world."

"I will try to remember not to disturb you when your brain is sending music," she promised.

After Belinda was dispatched to the servants' quarters, they started their exploration of his estate. In companionable silence, they traversed the gardens to a clipped lawn and, eventually, to the same waterway that wended its way through the Twitchards' property farther north.

He had a gentlemanly hold of her arm, and she felt perfectly safe.

"Now that we are friends," she asked, "will you play for me?"

He hesitated, which made her a little sad. *Didn't he trust her not to judge him?* And even if she were the harshest possible critic, the arbiter of all that was good in the realm of music, still he must know she would not find any fault with his playing. *Had his stage fright not improved even a little?*

"Have you been eating plenty of fruit?" she asked.

"Lady Brilliance, I hope this doesn't sound pudding-headed, but why were you making gifts of oranges, cherries, and such?"

"Isn't fruit a well-known treatment for stage fright?"

"If it is," he said, "I have never heard of it."

She sighed "Perhaps you needed to *know* about the treatment in order for it to work. I am dreadfully sorry."

He shook his head. "Do not be sorry. I do not now, nor have I ever suffered from stage fright."

Astonished, she stopped in her tracks. "Don't you?"

"No. I promise you."

"Not even a little bit?" she asked.

"No," he repeated before tucking a strand of her hair behind her ear, making her shiver.

"Well, then I am absolutely flummoxed. Why won't you play?"

With his sage-colored eyes gazing into hers, he vowed, "I will play for *you*."

"A piece of music I have never heard before," she pressed as they began walking again. "For it must be something *you* have written."

"You are a demanding minx. And the answer is yes. Come, let me show you a particularly lovely spot."

As if England itself were conspiring to make everything perfect, the weather was warm, the sky cloudless, and an abundance of birds were swooping to catch insects. They paused at a bend in the stream.

"Can you truly see the Roman ruins from that back bedroom?"

"No, but from the attic you can make out the nearby trees, I imagine."

"Then you lied." Brilliance hoped he didn't make a habit of bending the truth to get his way.

"I did. I wanted to ask Alethia if she would allow me to have a few minutes alone with you, and I needed her to help me make it happen."

"It worked. Lady Georgiana and Miss Newton could talk of nothing but *your* bedroom on the ride home. In fact, they lorded it over me."

"How are they faring?" he asked.

"You needn't sound so innocent. I have no doubt you arranged for them to be whisked away to someone else's home."

His handsome face broke out into a grin. "I did. Are you angry?"

"You know I am not, or you wouldn't be smiling like a fiend."

He looked as though he were trying to regain a measure of concern. "I hope you won't be lonely while staying at my cousin's."

His arms unexpectedly slipped around her, and she leaned against him.

"I don't mind my own company. And I assume you will come visit me at Bexley Hall or invite me here again."

Before he could say anything more, she had to ask Lord Hewitt the question she had wondered about ever since Lady Twitchard told her she was to spend the day with him.

"Are you courting me?"

Brilliance felt him tense.

CHAPTER SIXTEEN

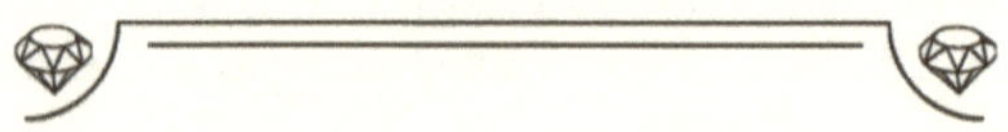

As usual, Lady Brilliance didn't mince words. Out of habit, Vincent's first thought was that he didn't want to mislead her. Yet, for the first time in a long time, her words were precisely in line with his wishes. He did, in fact, intend to court her. He did not have to dredge up those tired and trite words about enjoying the lady's company while hoping she didn't expect more from him.

Today, he could acknowledge that *he* was the one who wanted more.

"Yes, my lady, I would like to court you."

"That's good," she said. "Then you may keep your arms around me, and you may kiss me."

He needed no further invitation. However, when he leaned down, she asked, "You want children, do you not?"

He froze. That was a little further into the future than he had been pondering. There was the engagement, probably three months, then the wedding, followed by the honeymoon period as they settled in and got to know one another. And maybe after a year of being careful in the marriage bed, then they could allow nature to take its course.

"I ask because I have enjoyed being one of five. I like a large family."

Then she curled her fingers into the hair behind his head and drew him down a little closer.

His eyes crossed while trying to look at her face a mere two inches from his own.

"Yes, a few children will be most welcome," he said. And finally, he claimed her mouth.

She tasted like mint, which must be due to her tooth powders because he couldn't imagine she'd chewed on mint with breakfast. But he forgot that as he molded her curves to his body and thought it astonishing how perfectly they fit. He couldn't get her close enough and imagined a day when they would be bare skin against bare skin. If he had to marry her to accomplish that, so be it!

Happiness blossomed inside him at the idea of marrying her. The search he hadn't even been aware of was over. And it had happened so easily. What's more, he knew full well she would never betray him—Brilliance was frank and forthright. And he was a lucky man to have won her affections.

"Do you think we could lie down here on the grassy bank?" she asked. "I confess my knees are trembling and ready to collapse."

"Yes," he said. "No! We mustn't. That would break the trust placed in us by my cousin. But you are so delectable." He squeezed her waist. "Blast it!"

She giggled as he warred with his conscience. "Hold my hand, Lord Hewitt, and we shall stroll back and keep the trust placed in us, for which I am very grateful. If we were in London, it would be impossible for us to even promenade alone."

Vincent was equally grateful. "I have a surprise," he blurted when they were nearly back at his home. "I hope you're ready for a small nuncheon."

"I am indeed."

He drew out her chair at the same wicker table, glad his cousin and the other two females, who had looked at him as though he was a juicy piece of beef, weren't there.

Opening his back door, he called out to whoever was within listening range, "We're ready for the cheese and bread. And we'll have wine. Wait." He looked back at Brilliance. "Tea or wine, my lady?"

The sun was on her bonnet, the very same one he'd given her. Her blue eyes gazed at him, and he vowed he felt pure adulation for this woman on his terrace.

"Tea, please. Unless . . . no, I think wine if it's red. Thank you."

"Claret," he yelled out, then realized his housekeeper was standing close. "Thank you, Mrs. Mullens."

When the trays came out laden with rolls and butter, cheese and sliced apples, and a carafe of wine, Brilliance clapped.

"A wonderful surprise. I thought we wouldn't be eating until Colonel and Lady Twitchard arrived."

Feeling giddy with happiness, he said, "The food isn't the surprise. Or rather, it is, but not all of it. Here, look at this." He lifted the domed lid of the cloche. "For you, my lady. Brie!"

"Yes?"

"No, not Lady Bri. Brie," he said, but she frowned. "This cheese. It is Brie." He pointed at the creamy slices on the plate. "From France."

"Oh, Brie!" And she laughed her delightful laugh again.

Vincent adored making her happy. He enjoyed watching her taste the nutty, smooth cheese for the first time, and he wanted to kiss the bread crumbs from her lips.

"It is like nothing I have ever tasted. I am the luckiest Diamond after all to be named for such deliciousness. I vow I could eat this every day for the rest of my life."

"I vow I could eat *you* every day for the rest of mine."

She dissolved into a fit of giggles, and he was grateful she didn't understand the salacious thoughts inflaming his passions.

"I think wine was the correct choice," she said. "Warm, milky tea would not have been nearly so good as this claret."

"Agreed. But then, have we disagreed about anything?"

A shadow crossed her face, and he knew it was about his music, but he wasn't ready to discuss "Sonata in A," which he'd once foolishly called "Lydia" and that idiot had named "The Hummingbird." It would only put a blight on this otherwise perfect day.

On the other hand, he was ready to grant her request.

"Will you do me the honor of listening to some of my music?"

She pushed her chair back and was on her feet before he could even stand. "The honor is all mine, my lord."

"Vincent," he said.

She tilted her head and considered. "How funny. I recall now when your cousin introduced you, I was thinking of a hundred other things, of how handsome your face is and how attractive your velvet gray eyes are. I have thought of you as Hewitt until this moment. However, Vincent suits you nicely."

There were so many compliments in her words, he felt his cheeks warm. But all he said was, "Thank you."

He took her into the room he never took anyone, not for many years, not since Lydia and Ambrose obliterated his trust. Strangely, he felt a little shy.

"I noticed when I was here last," she said, "you did not invite us to see this room. Thus, I am doubly honored."

Somehow, she understood! He relaxed and looked around his conservatory with her. It held little except his piano and a bench, which he preferred to a stool, and a divan. When the music overwhelmed his brain, he often reclined upon it with closed eyes. Sometimes, the notes would sort themselves out more easily than if he remained doggedly at the piano keys.

"I thought it would be strange having someone else in here, but I feel perfectly comfortable with you."

Instead of seating herself on the sofa, she went to his piano and leaned against it with her elbows propping her up, facing where he would sit.

"Now I feel a little *less* comfortable," he quipped.

She smiled. "I thought you didn't suffer from stage fright."

"I don't. But above anyone else, I want you to like my music."

Brilliance rolled her eyes but had a satisfied look on her face. "Go on," she said, encouraging him with a gesture of her hand. "Please. Play as though I am not even here."

But that was nigh to impossible. Quite without an ounce of self-consciousness, she was leaning over, giving him a thoroughly distracting view of the upper curves of her beautiful breasts. For a few moments, his mind emptied of music, and all he could think of was burying his face between their bounty.

"Vincent," she prompted into the silence.

"Very well," he said. "But I also feel like the rudest looby for taking a seat while you stand."

"Stop procrastinating," she ordered.

Vincent thought playing might be different, but it wasn't—as his fingers depressed the keys, the world around him shrank and dwindled until there was only the music. It had been that way since he was very young.

His parents had possessed an ancient pianoforte with the old style of black keys and white sharps. It was more for decoration than for playing, as neither his mother nor father were musically inclined.

Vividly, he still recalled the first time he'd knelt on the stool, which had nearly toppled over. Steadying himself, hours had passed while he explored each note. Something inside him already knew how to put them together.

Within a year, his parents had bought him his first modern piano from Broadwood & Sons with gleaming white keys and shiny black ebony sharps. He had watched with fascination as the tuner opened the case and made sure each key was true to tone. And then Vincent had spent every waking hour at the magical instrument. His mother's calls to the dining table or even to bed had fallen on deaf ears.

With lessons while he attended Harrow, where he first met Ambrose Castern, he had begun to compose long pieces. Later at Trinity College before going to study with Liszt, he had relied on music to carry him through all his other studies, which he often found pointless and boring.

And then he had fallen in love.

He stopped playing suddenly, feeling breathless, recalling the desperation of his music being taken from him. That pain trumped the heartache over losing Lydia. When his gaze fell upon Brilliance once again, he drew in a long breath, and smelled her tantalizing fragrance.

"Is something wrong?" she asked.

"No." Vincent made sure he was sitting up straight, and he played another piece, one he hadn't thought about for years.

To his delight, after a few stanzas, Brilliance sat on the edge of the bench beside him. When it was over, she clapped. He hadn't heard anyone clap for his playing in a long time.

"It was beautiful," she said. "Was that something new?"

"No. I have not composed much lately. It was an older piece, over a decade."

She appeared shocked. "You wrote that music when you were a youth?"

"Sixteen," he said. "Not so young."

"Young for such depth of emotion."

He shrugged. "When I was at Harrow, I wrote a *barcarolle* for orchestra. That was much more difficult. How did that go?" His fingers remembered more than he did and soon, the lively piece was coming back to him.

When he reached the end of the piano solo, he stopped.

This time, she didn't clap. Instead after a long moment of silence, she said, "That was magical. How can you make a piano seem like a wistful lover? It was romantic and expressive. Actually, I don't have the words to describe your music." She touched her hand to his shoulder. "Why don't you compose any longer?"

Vincent rose to his feet as if he was sitting on hot coals. "It's not important. For the past few years, I thought I had said everything I needed to say through music."

Standing, she eyed him carefully. "Then you have many more works to share?"

"I do. For years, the music flowed out of me like . . ."

"Like a river?" she asked, moving closer.

"It was never that easy, but it was steady. Perhaps a constant trickle, more than a deluge. Themes, feelings, tempo, as soon as I had completed one piece, I was already composing the next."

Unthinkingly, he reached out and let his hands span her waist before pulling her against him.

"It has been too long since I kissed you."

He felt her laughter ripple through her body. They both knew it had only been a few hours. But as long as she was willing . . .

His mouth claimed hers. Within seconds, their passion heated to boiling. With the tip of his tongue requesting and being granted entrance, he slid it between her lips, his heart beating hard in his chest. When her tongue tentatively stroked his, he groaned before sucking it gently.

This was definitely not what his cousin would approve of, but Alethia had to have expected it, nonetheless.

When they broke apart, breathing hard, she stared, wide-eyed. Then she put a hand to his cheek. "I believe you have much more music flowing in you."

Vincent wanted to kiss her again, *not* talk. He wanted to sink his fingers into her hair while he lowered his mouth to hers. But if he didn't start talking, then they would soon be in a compromising situation that would remove any choices for both of them.

Leading her to the divan, he tugged her hand until she sat beside him. "You're correct. I do still have many melodies inside me." Suddenly feeling exposed, even vulnerable, he added, "Very recently, I have begun to compose again."

She smiled. "I am very glad."

"I might as well," he added. "The music plays regardless."

Brilliance cocked her head in question.

Could he explain his busy mind? He could try. "Sometimes, I desperately need a little peace and quiet," Vincent said. "Whether I am composing or not, there is constantly music playing."

Brilliance looked around the otherwise silent room of his conservatory.

"It seems very peaceful," she said, reaching out a delicate bare hand and laying it atop his where it rested on his knee. He felt her touch like a flame burning through him.

Yes, he had fallen hard for this woman. And he wanted her to understand him, as much as he wanted to learn every nuance of her nature.

With his free hand, he tapped the side of his skull. "I constantly hear music in here."

Her curious expression was adorable. She leaned closer. "That makes me want to put my ear to yours."

Her ear? "What do you mean?"

"So I can hear it, too," Brilliance said without irony.

Vincent refused to laugh at her. She was so purely earnest and sweet. "I am explaining it poorly. The curse of having perfect pitch—"

"I confess I don't know what that is."

"Meaning, I inherently know how each note sounds. I can tune an instrument quite easily by matching the string to the sound I hear inside my head. Although I use a tuning fork to verify."

She nodded. "The smallest fork at the place setting. Alas, I use it only for prawns and occasionally cockles."

He stared, his mouth slightly open, until Brilliance grinned at him. "I know what a tuning fork is, my lord. Go on."

Relief flooded him, and he felt ashamed. Would it really have mattered if she didn't know what one was?

"Anyway, the fork has nothing to do with—" he began again.

"One could call it a *pitchfork!*" she said and laughed heartily at her own joke. "Perfect pitch, tuning fork. Do you see?"

"Yes." He had heard the play on words before but never from the lips of such a delightful lady. Vincent knew he had a foolish expression on his face. *How could he live without this ray of pure sunshine in his life?* "You are clever."

She beamed at the compliment. "Please continue telling me about music. I won't interrupt again."

"I like it when you interrupt. Besides, all I am trying to explain is that I hear either my own music or great works I've studied playing in my head, even when I don't want them to, even if I would rather be quiet. Upon going to sleep, for instance."

"A nuisance, I imagine," she agreed.

"In truth, the curse of perfect pitch is a gift," he confessed, "and I would not trade it. I believe it explains how Beethoven could compose even after he went deaf. I merely would like to turn it off at my bidding."

"*Hm*," she murmured, cocking her head. "Are you hearing music now?"

Vincent had a stunning realization. "No, actually, I am not!"

CHAPTER SEVENTEEN

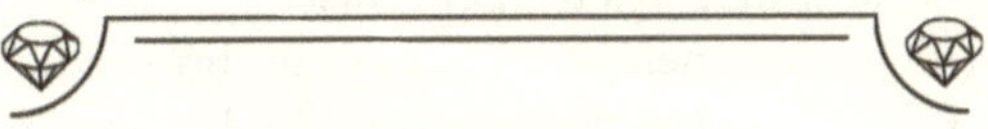

Whenever he talked with Brilliance, nothing interrupted his focus upon her, and his senses were engaged, not divided. Extricating his hand from under hers, he captured her face between both of his palms. When her bonnet impeded his movements, he unfastened the bow at her chin and lifted it from her glorious dark hair, setting the hat on the table in front of them.

"You, my lady, have become the music in my head when you speak, your voice like lilting notes, offering respite from the symphonies always pounding in my brain."

"Truly?" she asked. "*Lilting* notes. Are you offering me flummery, my lord?"

He shook his head. "I am not. I swear it."

Vincent traced her mouth with the pad of his thumb while still cradling her head. It was a small journey from touching her lips to leaning down and kissing them. And he made that journey swiftly.

"*Mmm*," she moaned softly under him.

The sound was intoxicating, making him feel reckless as he gave in to the strong desire coursing through his veins.

Pressing her back, they were now nearly horizontal on his divan, where he often stretched out either trying to recall a measure or for a refreshing nap. It had never occurred to him that he would one day have an exquisitely soft and shapely female under him upon the red velvet cushion.

He never broke the kiss, but instead, slanted his head and nibbled on her plump lower lip.

She slid her hands to his shoulders, and he settled in as best he could with her taut skirts being the only impediment. In truth, they were formidable. He could not feel the heat of her core, nor learn if she were on fire with passion for him. Regardless, he had no doubt she could feel the length of his arousal resting against her inner thigh.

Behaving extremely badly, Vincent brushed the hair from her forehead and then lifted his body enough to slide his hand between them and cup her breast. Just as his thumb had caressed her mouth, now it played across her nipple through the thin summer fabric of her gown and petticoat.

"*Oh!*" she exclaimed. "I like that."

Her nipple pearled satisfyingly under his touch, while he nibbled a path along her chin and down her arching neck. Vincent wanted to suck her stiffened rosebud between his lips—and his better self warred with his baser one as to how much he could get away.

Before he could give in and draw her peaked nipple into his mouth or explore more of her luscious physique, he heard carriage wheels on his drive. His frustration soared.

With haste, not lingering in case his capable butler entered the room to announce his visitors, Vincent rolled off Brilliance. Not catching himself in time, he ended up flat on his back on the Persian carpet, staring at his conservatory ceiling.

Brilliance's warm laughter rained down on him, and he joined in. The tension of pent-up desire dissipated a little, enough for him to rise somewhat inelegantly. Then reaching out his hand, he drew her to her feet before surveying her quickly, head to toe.

She looked, frankly, a little frowsy. Her lips were extra red, and her curls were no longer smooth but frizzy. Then there was the matter of her neckline.

"Your gown is a little . . . uh"—he gestured with his pointer finger—"askew."

"Is it?" She sounded dreamily distracted.

"And your bonnet is missing," he added.

He heard Mr. Jordan's polished shoes, accompanied by others, on the tile floor beyond the closed door. *Why hadn't they left the door open?* That was an egregious error!

"Quickly now." He snatched the silly telltale bonnet off the low table and captured her hand. Together, they ran to the other end of the room.

Opening the door built into the wall and covered with the same red and gold-flecked wallpaper as the rest of the room, he shoved her through into the narrow servants' passage.

He heard his butler's light tap.

"That door to the right," Vincent told Brilliance. "Go through and into the small salon across the hall. There's a standing mirror. Return by the main hallway."

He hesitated until she went in the right direction, although moving too slowly for her own good. Then he closed the door.

The tapping repeated.

He ran to his piano and sat once more upon the bench.

"Come," he called. Hearing people enter his conservatory behind him, Vincent ran a hand through his hair, while hoping nothing about him was in great disarray. He dare not look down.

Instead, he turned to face his cousin and the Colonel.

BRILLIANCE FELT AS THOUGH she were floating on clouds while examining herself in the looking glass. How fortunate Vincent kept one in the violet-and-cream chamber with a lamp and two wingback chairs in plum-colored velvet.

There were bric-a-brac on shelves, some books stacked on the floor, and a generous-sized wooden lap desk with pages on it, but she determinedly didn't allow herself to become distracted. After all, she'd recalled hearing a carriage, and undoubtedly, her hosts had arrived.

While Lady Twitchard must have anticipated a kiss or two would occur, she couldn't have predicted what had happened in the conservatory.

"Look at yourself," she said and tugged up the neckline of her gown until it lay evenly across her chest. Her body was still sizzling and humming—not to mention throbbing, too, in places.

And she couldn't wipe the smile from her face.

It must look as though she'd allowed no liberties to be taken, nothing greater than a kiss, anyway.

First, she took the pins out of her hair and considered the wreck of her ringlets, skillfully crafted by Belinda.

Belinda! It had been hours since she'd thought of her maid. Seeking her out to repair the damage would be impossible as she might run into Lady Twitchard, or even any of Vincent's staff—people who might one day be her own servants. She didn't want to give them a questionable early impression. Brilliance would have to come up with her own solution.

Her curls were decidedly wispy and frayed, and many had straightened. Having no comb, nor any other accoutrements, there was little she could do but scrape her messy locks back with her fingers and wind them around into a bun. It took her three tries for any semblance of order, and then she rammed in the pins. Her hair wasn't truly styled, nor was it even particularly kempt, but it would have to do.

Resetting her bonnet, she tied it in place, hiding as much as she could under the fashionably small cotton and lace creation.

What an eventful afternoon it had been, she mused. Truly enlightening in many regards, both musically and otherwise. Mostly the *otherwise* part interested her, as she'd learned more about the man who had captured her heart. He was so talented and knowledgeable—in kissing and such.

Finding herself beneath the hard, strong body of Vincent Hewitt, Brilliance had momentarily lost herself and forgotten her surroundings. She could gladly have stayed there for hours, feeling his heat sink through her gown, relishing the weight of him pressing her into the divan, enjoying both his mouth upon hers and his skillful touch on her breast. *Her breast!*

She widened her eyes at her own reflection. Why, she'd been reduced to a quivering heap of sensation.

"Delightful!" she exclaimed, smoothing her gown with her hands one last time before crossing the room to the door. The swish of her gown moved the air and in turn swept the pages from the lap desk.

Halting, she bent down to retrieve them and realized what she held.

With only the tiniest of hesitancies, Brilliance folded the sheets before sliding them under her gown and into the pocket hanging beneath. Satisfied, she left the little salon and made her way along the passage toward the foyer so she could enter the conservatory from the main hallway.

"Here she is," Lord Hewitt remarked at her entrance. Colonel and Lady Twitchard were seated on the very same sofa on which—

Her gaze darted to him. With her mouth suddenly dry, she cleared her throat.

"I apologize for taking so long. I hope I didn't keep anyone waiting."

Despite having been underneath him, Brilliance didn't feel a modicum of awkwardness when she looked into his eyes. She adored him and hoped they would have the opportunity to repeat the experience in the very near future.

"I thought you brought another gown to wear for dinner," Lady Twitchard said.

Only then did Brilliance recall it, still folded in a case, somewhere in the house with Belinda. If she had feared for her wits before, she could expect to lose them entirely when mesmerized by Vincent Hewitt.

She shrugged.

"I think she looks perfect just as she is," her brand new suitor said.

Brilliance knew she was the luckiest woman in the world.

"Be that as it may," Lady Twitchard continued, "you cannot wear your sunbonnet to the dinner table. You must remove it."

Vincent's expression appeared stricken. She probably wore a similar look.

"Must I?" Brilliance asked. *Why hadn't she thought of that?*

Lady Twitchard laughed as if Brilliance were speaking in jest.

"Shall I go find my maid and change after all?" she offered.

"No, no," said the Colonel. "We don't stand on ceremony. I don't see what the fuss is about over wearing a blue bonnet, but I am hungry. I know what happens when you ladies go off to change, and I won't allow it."

With such a decree, Brilliance could do little but untie the ribbons under her chin and remove it. Lady Twitchard didn't gasp, but her gaze sharpened. *She knew!*

Brilliance resisted putting her hand up to her severe bun, knowing her hostess had recalled the pretty curls that had cascaded around it earlier. Sighing, she couldn't meet Vincent's eyes in case her cheeks turned scarlet. Instead, she walked stiffly with the others into the dining room.

Dinner was exceptional, and Lady Twitchard had to compliment her cousin on his *superior* cook. All in all, when Brilliance and her hosts made their way home, she had to consider it one of the best days of her life, the bonnet incident notwithstanding.

And in the morning, she wrapped up Vincent's handwritten music she'd *borrowed* and sent it to the village for the afternoon post to London.

Although she knew he didn't like to write out his music, seeing that he had done exactly that had sparked an idea. If Vincent had any doubt of his superb talent, it would dissipate once he could see his own music professionally printed, just like Mr. Castern's.

Brilliance was convinced he would be gratified.

CHAPTER EIGHTEEN

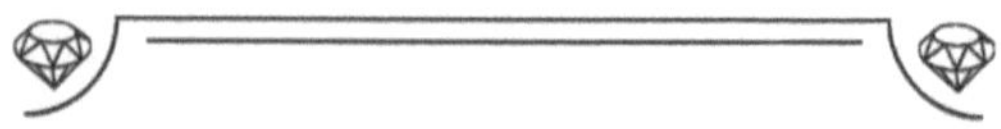

Brilliance spent the next day wool-gathering at Bexley Hall. She even wrote to Martine in Surrey, telling her little of the personal details while conveying her great affection for Vincent. The following day, he came to his cousin's home for dinner, and they were allowed time alone in the conservatory.

Again, he played a private concert for her, and she considered him the most gifted pianist who had ever lived. And obviously, he must also be the best kisser, for she could not imagine better.

The day after, she received a letter from her mother, saying they'd heard only good things about Lord Hewitt's reputation as a Parliamentarian. Naturally, they said nothing about his musical abilities since they could have no idea about that aspect of his life. *How could they when he hid it?* More than anything, she wanted the world to know of his immense talent.

Lord and Lady Diamond expressed their relief at leaving the city in two days. Since Brilliance could not travel all the way to Derby by herself, her mother had accepted Colonel and Lady Twitchard's gracious offer to bring her, partly in their coach and partly by train.

Brilliance set down the thick sheet of stationery covered in her mother's exuberant handwriting onto the sofa beside her. Her emotions were mixed. She loved her family's country estate and always welcomed the chance to stay there. Moreover, she looked forward to seeing her parents. But she would be sad at the conclusion of this exciting interlude.

On the other hand, while this time had been idyllic for her, she knew it had been prompted by misery at home, and she fervently hoped the cholera would disappear as quickly as it had arrived.

When she left Bexley, she would have to wait until she and Vincent were both in the city again to see him, unless he made the trek north to Derby. Brilliance swallowed her sadness, reminding herself she was a grown woman. She had waited a lifetime to find him, and she could easily wait another month or two before they could resume their courtship.

If only the sheet music would return from London in time for her to give it to him, she would be content to leave. When a package arrived the following day from Boosey & Co. on Old Bond Street, she asked Lady Twitchard's permission to make one last visit to see Vincent.

Hurrying Belinda into the carriage, she descended before anyone could even open the door to Mirabel Manor. As Mr. Jordan opened the grand front door, Vincent came out of the conservatory, still tugging on his coat.

"I have been composing!" he announced.

"Aren't you always composing?" she asked when he took her arm and led her back into the room, closing the door behind them.

So improper, but she was now too familiar with his staff to bother about first or fourth impressions. She hadn't even had to tell Belinda to go to the kitchen. Her maid had disappeared down the passageway as soon as they'd entered the house.

"I am *not* always composing. I am always playing and going over my old music. But when I awoke at two o'clock this morning, I heard the notes of a new piece. Clear as a flawlessly cast bell."

Brilliance winced. "And now I have interrupted you! I ought to have sent word of my intent, and you could have told me to stay away."

"I would never have said that." Vincent still had hold of her arm, and he brought her to the infamous divan, which she could hardly look at without blushing—despite how well they had behaved since then.

"After all," he added as she seated herself and he relinquished his hold, "I'm only writing music again because of you."

"Because of *me?*" Brilliance looked up at him. "Am I your muse?"

"Indeed, you are," he replied as if it were the most natural thing in the world. "The sonata I'm writing was inspired entirely by you. I am trying to capture your essence in music."

Her essence? A little shiver ran up and down her spine. "May I hear it?"

Vincent looked as if he were fit to burst. He was even hopping excitedly from one foot to the other. "It is not finished, you understand, barely even started, but I was hoping you would ask." His face was alight with eagerness.

Brilliance thought him greatly changed in a fortnight. "You appear so very different from when first I laid eyes upon you."

"Do I? How so?" He sat upon the piano bench.

"Younger maybe?" she said. "No, that's not it, or at least, not only that. You look at ease. And, dare I say, happy?"

"I am happy. You make me so."

"I am glad. Play for me."

And she sat silently, having to remind herself to breathe, while he played. A few times he paused, once to say something incomprehensible to her about the first movement not yet having a conclusion, and again, he halted to scold himself over a mistake she could not detect before he stopped and lifted his fingers from the keys.

"That is all I have so far."

"Clapping seems inadequate," she said. "I cannot believe this didn't exist until . . . until this morning. It sounds perfect and complete."

"It is hardly that!" But he was beaming. "Did I capture a little of Brilliance Diamond?"

"That is not for me to say. It sounded joyful and light."

"That *is* you! The woman I have come to . . . to admire beyond all others. Then I will title it 'Essence of Brilliance.'"

She found it nearly unbelievable—that they two should suit one another so perfectly—and wished they had more time before they separated.

"I received a letter from my mother yesterday. Your cousin and the Colonel are taking me up to Oak Grove Hall in two days."

His expression sobered. "Derby is one hundred and fifty miles away. I consulted a surveyor's map."

Her heart sputtered. "That was quite premeditated of you. Are you planning to visit me?"

"I was thinking about doing precisely that." Vincent left the piano and drew her to standing. "After all, I should . . . that is, I *want* to speak to your father."

He sounded as if he dreaded the prospect despite saying he wanted to.

"Lord Diamond is not the least bit frightening. And when I tell him of your magnificent gift—composing music that represents *my* essence—he will be most impressed." *How fortunate that today she had a present for Vincent in return.*

When he wrapped her in his arms, she wished that day could end with a proposal. Truthfully, she thought it a little old-fashioned to insist upon speaking to her father before he asked her properly to marry him. Regardless, she was more interested in hearing his declaration of love because she desperately wanted to say it back to him.

The gift she was about to present would probably make clear how dearly she loved him and how he already held her heart.

"You look thoughtful," he said. "And beautiful."

"Thank you," she replied. "As usual, you are very handsome. Since you have put your arms around me, will you draw me closer, please, and kiss me? After that, I have a present for you."

"More oranges or cherries?" he teased. Then he patted her backside. "Are you hiding fruit in your skirts?"

She laughed. "I am not. Kiss me first, and then I'll show you what I have brought."

He leaned down and did as she asked, taking his time to kiss her slowly and thoroughly until her heart was beating so loudly she could hear it, certain that he could, too. His skillful hands palmed her rear end through her layers of shift, petticoat, and summer gown, tilting her against him.

She would swear her body was pulsing everywhere!

When he drew back, he said, "You don't need to ask me to kiss you. It isn't a chore, but a privilege. One I am happy to have the honor to do. One I can imagine doing every day."

Was he going to propose right then?

She waited, but he did no such thing, and so she broke free. On the other end of the divan, under her reticule was a large envelope. Picking it up, she clasped it to her chest for a moment, beyond excited, and then handed it to him.

"What's this?" he asked, already reaching in and sliding out the contents.

"Your music!" she exclaimed. "Printed at a London music publisher."

Vincent stared at the top page of printed sheet music. His eyes grew wider, and then his cheeks took on a ruddy hue. He drew spectacles from his pocket and put them on slowly with one hand.

"My music," he repeated at last, his voice a harsh whisper, sending a trickle of alarm through her. "How?" he demanded. "Did you steal it from me?"

"Steal it?" Brilliance was puzzled. "Well, I guess I did, but not to keep. The original music is safely in the envelope." Since he was frozen, staring at the printed page, she gingerly took the envelope from him, reached in, and withdrew the pages.

"I am sorry. They are creased, as I folded them."

"To sneak them out of my house."

"Yes," she agreed. It sounded nefarious when he put it like that. "I wanted you to see your work in print. Now anyone can buy it and play it."

He closed his eyes for a long moment. When he opened them he asked, "The title? Where did it come from?" His tone was unwaveringly flat, while his finger ran over the words "The Starling."

"I . . . I made it up because yours had no title. But I have no idea what this sounds like, so I don't know if it is more of a falcon or a sparrow."

"I see. And yet you didn't put my name on it. Why did you have it published anonymously?"

"I wasn't entirely sure you would approve of your identity being known as the piece's composer. Perhaps you think a minister of Parliament should not also dabble in musical composition."

"Dabble?" he repeated. "You would steal my music and have it printed for the world to see, but you have integrity when it comes to protecting my identity. How curious."

Brilliance was beginning to realize that he wasn't at all pleased by her gift from Boosey & Co.

"Are you angry? They are a reputable music publisher, I assure you. Should I have instructed them to put your name on the music?"

"You shouldn't have taken it and had it published at all. Angry doesn't begin to cover how I'm feeling." He tossed the pages onto the divan beside them before striding to the piano, keeping his back to her. "What if the piece was unfinished? What if I hated it and had no intention of ever letting anyone hear it?"

"Do you hate the piece?" she asked.

"That isn't the point. It was not yours to send to London. And now that you have published it anonymously, what if someone else claims to be the composer?"

"Why would someone do that?" she asked, going closer and putting her hand on his arm. Vincent flinched.

"You are like a child!" After uttering those hurtful words, he stormed from one side of the room to the other, pacing. "A willful, careless child! Except far worse because you can do the damage of an adult. An immature, foolhardy, reckless adult," he fumed. "I cannot even call you spiteful because you would have had to think this through with malevolent intent, and I know you to be too much of a dunderhead for such calculated malice!"

Brilliance's eyes pricked with tears. When a single one escaped and rolled down her cheek, she dashed it away with the back of her hand.

"Oh no you don't!" he said. "That's an old trick. You can appear as pathetic as you like, but I shall not take any notice. I clearly told you my performing was against the pluck and that I had an abhorrence to transcribing my music, let alone having it printed. Didn't you believe me? Or did you rush ahead with utter disregard for my wishes?"

Brilliance had no defense. There was nothing she could say to bring back the friendly, loving Vincent of moments earlier. Thus, she stayed silent, unable to think of any excuse for her actions, which had seemed so appropriate until he'd pointed out that they were not.

Still, she ought to offer an apology, even though she didn't understand why he was so upset.

"I am sorry to have—"

"I suggest you return to my cousin's home without delay." He went to the window. When he turned, she could hardly see his face for the summer sun at his back. But she knew his expression was twisted with anger. "And I must request that you do not return. If you come knocking at my door, I promise you shall not be admitted."

Snatching up the printed pages, he strode from the room without a backward glance.

"I love you," she whispered over the sound of his footsteps as he crossed the front hall. She could still smell his cologne, rich and peppery, the one that always made her tingle.

Looking around, she had nothing to retrieve except her reticule, which she slid over her wrist. Then she inspected her hat, making sure it was still on and relatively straight. Even though he was being beastly, she could see now that she deserved it. She had overstepped. *Again!* And this time, unlike when she'd put his name on the list of the evening's entertainers, it seemed there were no more chances, no further forgiveness.

If she'd been a different sort of female, she would sink to the carpet in a puddle of hysterical waterworks. In truth, she felt like sobbing, but she would wait until she was back in her room at Lady Twitchard's.

Although she might allow herself a little cry in the carriage on the short ride back. Sure enough, as soon as she and Belinda were in her host's borrowed conveyance, Brilliance turned her face to the window and let her tears spill over and course unchecked down her cheeks.

Two days later, without any further communication between them, she departed Bexley for Oak Grove Hall in Derby.

CHAPTER NINETEEN

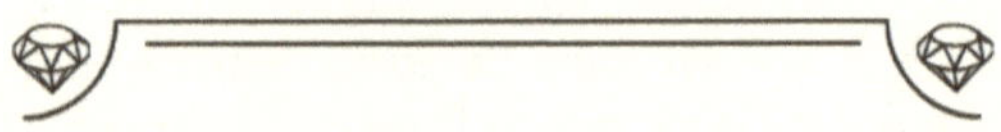

Vincent ignored the missives from his cousin. He expected a heartfelt request for forgiveness from Brilliance, but one never came. Not that it would have made any difference. She did not understand how egregious her betrayal. Moreover, she apparently thought a barely uttered apology—while he was too blisteringly furious to listen—had been enough.

She was wrong. He had trusted her! A mistake he would not make again.

"Fool me twice," he muttered, as he wrote to London in an attempt to get his music recalled. Hopefully, the only copy was the one sent to Brilliance. After all, there couldn't be much call for an anonymous sonata with an asinine title.

As Vincent discovered, Brilliance had given the publisher his real name and his address. Any questions or royalties were to be directed to him. However, she had not told anyone at Boosey & Co that he was the composer. Still, under Vincent's authority, the publisher agreed to stop printing more copies, but there was nothing he could do about those already distributed or sold.

Within a week, he tried to put the entire incident behind him . . . except now Brilliance was gone. Not only from the southeast of England but from his life. And with each day that passed, he missed her more and began to regret his outburst and the boiling fury that had caused him to say some inexcusable things to her.

In truth, he had been angry at her as much for the betrayals of the past as for what she had inadvertently done. And in his heart, he knew it was he who owed her an apology.

Should he go to Lord and Lady Diamond's country house in Derby? He had no idea whether Brilliance would wish to see him again after the cruel dressing down he'd given.

Vincent supposed the more important question was whether he could forgive her duplicity enough to take up where they left off. He had been prepared to propose marriage.

Now he wasn't sure she was any different from Ambrose or worse, Lydia. Or worse again, Ambrose. He could never decide which betrayal cut deeper—that of his ladylove or his best friend—although ultimately, he knew he loved his music more than he had ever cared for Lydia.

And what about Brilliance? He simply never imagined, with her openness and frank speech, she could deceive him as she'd done. It had shaken him to his core.

His heart hardened, and he made his decision. Better to have found out her true nature before he went hat-in-hand to speak with her father.

And better still that he should remain alone rather than tie himself to someone he could not trust, no matter how much he missed and yearned for her.

"She stole my music and sent it to London. I do not know how you can defend her," he said over dinner with Alethia and the Colonel one evening. Unfortunately, every time he went to their home, he was reminded of Brilliance around every corner.

His cousin had just opined how she thought Lady Brilliance's intentions were good. At Vincent's words of reprimand, Alethia sighed and looked to her husband for his opinion. The Colonel tugged his earlobe absently before picking up his knife and fork, saying nothing.

"The lady was bewildered but apologetic when the Colonel and I took her to her parents. It was a long, awkward journey," Alethia added.

Vincent would probably have forgiven her if he had been in the carriage, and thus, he was glad he hadn't been. *How many times could he be taken for a fool?*

"In any case, I do not know how you can still be thinking of her as if it happened yesterday," his cousin said. "Lady Brilliance seems to still consume your every waking thought. Therefore, either you passionately hate her, or you are madly in love. Which is it?"

Vincent opened his mouth, then shut it. Then he shook his head and rolled his eyes at his cousin's ridiculous statement.

"Neither," he groused before taking a large sip of wine. "I am allowed to be outraged, am I not?"

"It has been weeks," the Colonel reminded him. "Speaking of which, when are we all going back to London? I fancy a little excitement after so much quiet."

Vincent stopped listening as husband and wife discussed the autumn parties, the year-end festivities, and whether they would stay in the city right through the Christmastide or come back to the country.

He would be in London at week's end for a parliamentary session and his mother's birthday. His stepfather always had a large gathering for his beloved Lady Winthrop, and Vincent broke his own staunch rule once a year to perform publicly for her and her guests.

Beyond that, he rarely attended balls or parties unless a good friend was throwing the affair and had promised a bevy of beauties. Also, his friends made sure that two people were never in attendance, Lydia and Ambrose Castern.

Now he would have to avoid Brilliance Diamond, too. Not because of a similar loathing that he felt for the other two, but due to the uncomfortable sensation that he hadn't behaved well where she was concerned. He had been downright vicious, and the man who had spewed venom at her in his conservatory was not the person he thought he was. It certainly wasn't the person he intended ever to be again.

Despite still thinking she was absolutely in the wrong for taking his music, he recognized that she had intended no harm. As far as he could tell, not much harm had been done, either.

Except for their tattered friendship.

BRILLIANCE HADN'T EXPECTED THE swift and terrible end to her romance with Lord Hewitt. *Heartbreak was monstrously awful!* It was made infinitely worse because *she* had caused the rift. If only she could have left well enough alone. She'd been wrong about his stage fright, wrong about him being happy to see his own music in print, and wrong about him loving her so entirely that he couldn't live without her.

She had even been wrong about fruit!

And she was having to accept the fact that she could and would live without the man she loved.

After all, even if he forgave her, she now knew he thought her to be a sapskull, a dunderhead, basically too stupid for him.

But the publisher had assured her, given how she'd provided Vincent's name at the outset, no one else could take credit. Vincent had made it seem as though she had given his composition away to the world, as if another musician could claim ownership.

How had her best attempt failed, sending her to Weeping Cross? She still wasn't certain.

In any case, if Vincent's heart was broken, if he missed her, then he could have written to her. Instead, weeks had passed, and people were starting to return to London. While the latest outbreak had been in the poorer area of Soho, directly east of Mayfair proper, it was close enough that those living in the wealthier neighborhoods were still nervous. Her parents were considering their return in another fortnight after daily scrutiny of the newspapers.

"A water supply at the crossroads of Broad Street and Cambridge Street has been determined as the source of the cholera," her father read over breakfast. "Consequently, the pump handle has been ordered removed by the eminent physician John Snow."

"That capable nurse, Miss Nightingale, is treating many patients at Middlesex Hospital," her mother added.

A miracle, Brilliance thought, that someone had isolated and identified the problem in a city the size of London. Her only hesitation over returning to their Piccadilly home was that Vincent wouldn't know where she was. *What if he came to Oak Grove Hall looking for her?*

"Stop moping," her mother said for the umpteenth time.

"I am not moping," Brilliance protested. "I am sulking."

"Then stop sulking. You had a summer romance. You are not the first, nor the last girl to place her hopes in a man who turned out not to appreciate her."

Brilliance had not told her parents all the details, only that she had inadvertently disappointed and angered Lord Hewitt. Thus, he would not be paying a visit anytime soon. At least when they reached London, she would be nearer to him by many miles and have all her old distractions. The Crystal Palace had reopened, and there were new plays and concerts for the upcoming winter.

And, of course, there were balls. More opportunities to wear her gold ballgown. As so few people had seen it at Lady Twitchard's home, it was practically new.

After nearly eight weeks in Derby, they moved home, and Brilliance engaged herself in all the activities of the final three months of the year. There was no shortage of entertaining diversions, and she tried her best not only to enjoy her friends but also the gentlemen who paid her attention.

"I am so glad everything is back to normal," Martine said as they stood together at Lord St. Claire's ball, having admired each other's gowns. Nearby, their mothers were busy catching up on their personal news.

Her friend had arrived in London a day after Brilliance. Seeing Martine for the first time since Bexley Hall caused many memories to come flooding back, both pleasant and not. It must have been the same for Martine, who remarked, "Neither of us found a match in the country. Lord Patterson was a scoundrel!"

"How do you mean?" Brilliance asked.

"Because he did not favor me over the other ladies."

They laughed. That hardly made him a scoundrel, merely a man of dubious taste in women. For Martine was superior to anyone as far as Brilliance was concerned.

"Then you were fortunate," she said, "because the more we came to know him, the more insufferable he became."

"How true," Martine agreed. "I thought, however, given your happy letter to me, that you had made a conquest," she added, tapping her toe as the musicians warmed up before the first dance.

"A conquest?" Brilliance repeated, her throat suddenly dry. She didn't wish to discuss Vincent. That had been more of a stunning defeat than anything.

"Yes, with our hostess's cousin. While I thought Lord Hewitt a bit intense, even severe, he brightened around you. But then your sweet nature makes everything better."

Brilliance couldn't help hugging Martine, even as tears welled in her eyes.

"That is very kind of you. I am grateful to have you as my dear friend."

"Why the emotion?" Martine asked, looking surprised. "You must know what a delight you are and how much you are admired."

Brilliance could only shake her head, her throat clogged with sentiment. Briefly, she had let Vincent's harsh words dim her own confidence, but she had quickly rallied. For she was a Diamond and had been comfortable in her own skin, assured of her worth, all her life.

Thus, when the ballroom manager, hired by Lord and Lady St. Claire to handle the occasion, brought two handsome gentlemen over for introductions, Brilliance lifted her chin and prepared to dance. The ball had begun in earnest.

MANY HOURS LATER, BRILLIANCE fell into bed, happily humming the final tune in her head. While she had never stopped thinking of Vincent, she had, at least, smiled, which she hadn't done in ages. She had also danced for the first time since the Bexley ball—her last dance being with *him*—and yet, she had managed to feel a measure of contentment with some of her partners.

Not one had provided the immediate attraction she'd experienced upon first seeing Vincent in Lady Twitchard's conservatory. Yet she had to accept she might never experience such a swift and definite yearning again.

And she would accept it, for Brilliance still intended to become a wife, and the sooner she stopped mooning over the man she had lost, the better.

Besides, she desired someone who saw her the way Martine did, with admiration and genuine affection. Brilliance snuggled in her bed, deciding she would settle for nothing less—certainly not someone who considered her a dunderhead.

And that made it easier the following day to look through the calling cards and allow a gentleman whom she'd danced with the honor of visiting her.

Lord Redley was the son of a friend of her parents. She had met him once before in the spring. And after they had danced at the St. Claires' ball, she realized he was a good man. It didn't hurt that he was handsome in a classic way, with trimmed brown hair and a strong jaw. His brown eyes were not distorted nor obscured behind spectacles.

How she missed those steely spectacles and the mesmerizing gray-green eyes that looked through them!

Seated beside her mother with her suitor opposite, Brilliance said yes to nearly everything Lord Redley asked. Thus, by the time he left precisely fifteen minutes later, she had agreed to a concert at Canterbury Hall two nights later. Just across the Thames in Lambeth, the massive venue seated seven hundred people with multiple musical offerings over the course of an evening.

How coincidental—and even a little uncomfortable when she recalled Vincent's obvious envy—that one of the performers turned out to be Mr. Ambrose Castern. The pianist was charming. He stood on the edge of the stage and chatted with the audience before playing. He gestured to the box at the upper right of the stage and thanked his devoted wife for always being there. And then he played, captivating every person to the point of absolute silence, where even breathing seemed too loud.

When he began "The Hummingbird," his best-known work, Brilliance could feel the swell of joy roll across the audience.

For the first time ever, it made her sad. Vincent had played it just as well, and his cousin had said he'd written something like it. Watching the mesmerizing man on the stage, making so many listeners happy, she couldn't help but think how it could as easily be Lord Vincent Hewitt, using the gift with which he had been born.

Mr. Castern ended his concert with a new work. While clearly in his same style, leaving her in no doubt it was his composition, it had a delightfully romantic tone.

She sighed. Romance made her think of Vincent. As she walked to the carriage between her mother and Lord Redley, Brilliance knew she would have to tame her wayward desires. She was determined to do so, resolute in her intent to get over her summer romance and move on with her life.

Which was all very well and fine until an invitation arrived from a most unexpected hostess.

CHAPTER TWENTY

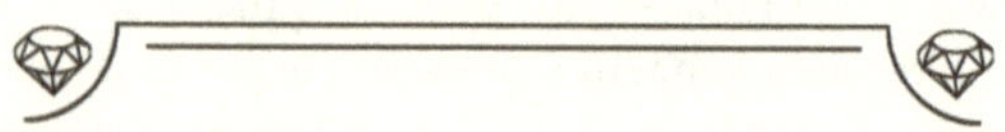

"Are you certain you want to go to Lord and Lady Winthrop's home?" Carolyn Diamond asked her daughter.

"Mother, we have been over this. I was invited, and it would be rude to turn down an invitation when I have no excuse."

"How about not having your heart wounded by seeing their son again?"

Brilliance couldn't wait to see Vincent at his parents' home. It was the only reason she wished to attend the birthday party on Davies Street, a stone's throw from her eldest sister, Clarity's home, and a slightly longer throw from Purity's.

So what if it hurt as long as she laid eyes on him once more.

Brilliance wore pink satin trimmed with pale-gray buttons and piping and pale-gray gloves.

"I wonder if he asked his mother to invite you," Lady Diamond said. "That would bespeak of his continued interest."

Privately, Brilliance thought it highly doubtful, given the last time she saw him.

"Good evening, my lord," she greeted Lord Winthrop, Vincent's stepfather at the entrance to the drawing room.

"Many happy returns of the day," Brilliance added when meeting Lady Winthrop. She had the same sage-colored eyes as her son. Instantly, Brilliance's heart tightened painfully in her chest. Maybe her mother had been right.

"How good of you to come," Lady Winthrop said.

"I was honored to be invited but puzzled." Brilliance decided she might as well determine why she was there. "I don't believe we have ever met, nor are you known to my parents."

"Oh no, I think not," Lady Winthrop said, while her husband was already greeting the older man behind Brilliance in the receiving line. "My late husband's niece, Lady Twitchard, said you got along well with my son at her July country party. I hope you don't mind, but since Vincent is attending, I thought it a nice surprise for him to have one of his own acquaintances amongst all of us older folk. And from how Alethia described you, you do not disappoint."

Brilliance felt her cheeks grow warm. Now she was certain that Vincent was unaware of her attendance. Most certainly, he would not think it a "nice surprise" and would have told his mother she was not welcome.

Nevertheless, she was there. And he was . . . right beside her!

"Mother, I am sorry I'm late." Vincent leaned in and kissed his mother's cheek before taking his place beside her. Only then did he turn toward Brilliance.

If she hadn't been so anxious, she might have laughed at his utterly stunned expression.

"What good timing," Lady Winthrop said. "I have only just met Lady Brilliance, a friend of yours, I take it."

Feeling the line of guests pressing at her side, Brilliance ignored how he remained speechless. Nodding to him, she murmured, "Good evening, Lord Hewitt," before moving along.

If he didn't ask a footman to show her out, then there would be time later to speak. Or maybe they would ignore one another all evening.

However, she didn't have long to wait. As they gathered in the Winthrops' drawing room, with sparkling wine being handed out to toast their hostess's health, Vincent approached.

"Good evening, Lady Brilliance. You look well."

"I wasn't sure you would speak to me," she said.

"Yet you came anyway," he pointed out.

"I hoped to see you regardless of whether we conversed."

"Why?"

She sighed. "I am not a wilting violet, afraid to face someone who might not be thrilled with me. But we were . . . friends. And ever since that moment when we were no longer . . . friendly, I have missed you."

He apparently approved of her honesty for he offered a tentative nod. After a brief hesitation, he said, "Then I am glad you came, if only to overcome the last impression I gave you. I was not myself."

Inside, Brilliance could have wept with the relief that washed through her. Even if they could no longer enjoy the same level of closeness as they once had, she felt better knowing Vincent did not hate her. She wanted to apologize again but was reluctant to bring up the incident and ruin the truce. Thus, instead, she pretended as if they were simply acquaintances on a good footing.

And due to Lady Twitchard, they were dining partners, as well.

"Thank goodness my cousin didn't mention certain other guests to my mother, such as Lady Georgiana," Vincent said.

"I am certain you would have behaved as politely as you are with me," Brilliance said. For he was treating her with extreme politeness, nothing beyond, no references to anything intimate having ever occurred between them.

As the courses rolled on, however, she started to feel melancholy. Maybe it was worse being near him after all, when she had thought it would make her happy. The loss of their friendship was now starkly evident.

"You have gone quiet," he said after a few minutes of her silence.

Brilliance nearly blurted out Lord Redley's courtship but stopped herself. Vincent might think she was trying to make him jealous, which she would be. *And what could be worse than him not showing an ounce of jealousy?*

She also bit back her words praising the concert she'd attended. If it had been any other musician, Vincent might have been interested. But she would seem to be taunting him if she mentioned Ambrose Castern, although she didn't know the reason.

With her tongue tied, Brilliance maintained her silence except when Vincent asked her a question. And he was as likely not to as to do so, spending half his time speaking with the female on his other side, as a good guest should.

On her left was an older gentleman who was hard of hearing. After a few attempts at conversation, she simply smiled at him. Thus, despite being next to the man she loved at his parents' dining room table, Brilliance was starting to wish she had not come.

That all changed when his stepfather commanded the table's attention by raising his glass and tapping its stem with a spoon.

"I thank you all for coming to celebrate my wife's birthday. Welcome to all our old friends," he nodded to many, including the somewhat deaf guest beside Brilliance, "and to a few new ones."

To Brilliance's amazement, Lord Winthrop nodded at *her.* Then he toasted to Lady Winthrop's health, and they all drank. After which, she spoke.

"Thank you, my love, and I, too, wish to thank you all for coming. Tonight, we have our yearly special treat. My son, Lord Hewitt, will give a short concert following the meal."

Brilliance stifled a gasp, turning to stare at him. He glanced down at her and shrugged.

"I can hardly say no to my mother, can I?"

"Honestly," she said, "I thought you could say no to anyone."

He smiled wryly. After the pudding course, they all went into a large salon upstairs. The piano situated sideways was more modest than Lady Twitchard's or Vincent's own, but he sat upon the stool, looking quite at home.

Brilliance realized he had probably been playing on this piano his entire life. As she took a seat, she could easily imagine the young child climbing onto the stool and picking out notes for the first time. And then he began, and all her thoughts fell away.

"'Essence of Brilliance,'" she murmured, recalling how he'd hoped he had captured something of her nature.

"What did you say?" asked the gentleman beside her. He had remained by her side on the short walk from the dining room to the salon and taken the next seat.

"*Shh,*" she said, feeling rude, but she didn't want to miss a note. Vincent had said it was unfinished two months earlier, but she recognized the first part. It seemed he had continued to work on the piece. It had three movements, starting deliberate and unhurried with the section she remembered, then speeding up in the middle, before finishing slowly.

He had altered it, making it less light-hearted, more somber. She wished she understood how, but the notes in the middle section left her unsettled and a little sad, while the end was wistful.

Everyone rose to their feet when the final notes died away, and the applause was loud. Vincent's mother darted forward as he stood and bowed. She grabbed his hands and kissed his cheek.

Brilliance wished she could do the same, although she would aim for his mouth. Regardless, he did glance her way. When their gazes met, she was infused with hope. He looked as he had in the past, relaxed and smiling, and as if he played a private concert every night, instead of once a year.

When he raised an eyebrow over his spectacles, she tried to decipher the message he was sending but couldn't. His mother thanked him and asked him to continue.

"I shall if you release my hands," Vincent said.

Everyone laughed, and Lady Winthrop resumed her chair in the front row beside her husband. It might have been the flickering gas lamp, but Brilliance thought Vincent winked at her before he sat once more on the stool.

"Another recent composition," he said, and then he began to play.

At first, Brilliance simply enjoyed the music, but soon, she knew she'd heard it before. And with awful realization, she knew when, where, and by whom.

Ambrose Castern had ended his concert with this music, his new work.

Brilliance began to feel ill. Maybe it was the large helping of the rich cabinet pudding with raisins and cherries buried under thick creamy custard which she had scoffed during the dessert course. In any case, she wanted to cover her ears.

At its conclusion, the applause was even louder. And then little by little, people rose to their feet and filed through the doorway, invited by Lord and Lady Winthrop to the drawing room for brandy or sherry.

When the room emptied, Vincent was still standing by the piano.

"What did you think?" he asked.

Brilliance took a breath. She was in his parents' home. She must conduct herself like a polite guest, even as she wanted to rail at him for stealing the piece and going to the trouble to memorize it.

Was "Essence of Brilliance" *even truly written by him?*

"The music you played for me in your home—"

"The one you inspired," he interrupted.

"Yes, am I wrong in thinking you have changed it?"

"I told you at the time it wasn't finished," he reminded her. "And after what transpired, I realized it was a tad frothy."

"I see." He no longer considered her simply a joyful, light-hearted person.

"I hope you don't mind," he said.

"Not at all. It is *your* music, isn't it?"

He smiled slightly. "I actually wrote it for you."

She bit her lip. *Should she remain silent?*

"What are you thinking? Some unflattering thoughts, I warrant, by your expression. Am I to understand you did not like it?"

"I enjoyed it," she said. "And since *you* wrote it, as you say, you may change it as you wish."

Vincent frowned at her words. "I suppose I may. What did you think of the second piece?"

Brilliance was wringing her hands, not something she usually did. Dropping them to her sides, she said, "I enjoyed it very much." *Sweet Mary!* She couldn't leave a lie between them. "I liked it the *first* time I heard it, too."

"The first time?" His frown deepened. "You couldn't possibly have heard this before."

"Yet I have. I heard it at its public debut by its composer."

He cocked his head with obvious confusion.

"Ambrose Castern," she added. "He concluded his concert at Canterbury Hall with this piece. He called it 'An Enchanting Dream.'"

REALIZING HOW THAT WAS possible—because of *her*—a sense of despair rushed through him. He had spent the last few hours during dinner talking himself into believing he could still have a friendship with Brilliance Diamond. *More* than friendship, if he was honest with himself. What she had done hadn't been so egregious after all, he'd decided.

Now, however, he knew the ramifications of her publishing his music. And the worst possible outcome had happened. *Ambrose!* Moreover, no one would ever believe it was not the work of the popular composer and pianist.

"'An Enchanting Dream,'" he spat out. "A ridiculous name thought up by a ridiculous man."

"Why?" she asked. "Why are you playing *his* music?"

"It is mine!"

"That makes entirely no sense."

He wondered why she seemed truly angry. *She* wasn't the one who had been stolen from.

"You write beautiful, intricate music. So why would you . . ." She trailed off, unable to say the words.

"You had best leave. You are calling me a thief! That's rich, coming from you. And under the roof where I was raised, too."

Without another word, Brilliance turned and left. Vincent assumed she would first take her leave of his parents because she was a properly raised lady of the *ton*. By the time he had collected himself and swallowed the worst of his anger, she had departed the residence.

At one time, he had thought she was the one person who would believe in him.

He wouldn't make that mistake again.

CHAPTER TWENTY-ONE

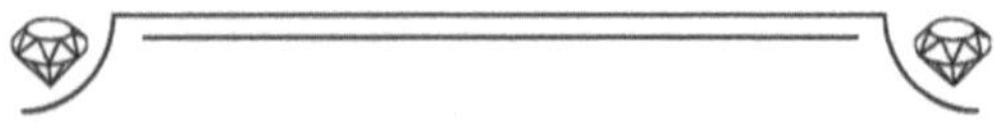

Vincent knocked on Ambrose's door early the next day. Too early for polite visiting hours but also too early for the blackguard to be out and about. If he had to drag him out of bed himself, he would.

A housekeeper answered.

"Tell Castern that Lord Hewitt is here to speak with him."

He heard the gasp through the open doorway and strode past the housekeeper.

Lydia was standing in her drawing room, looking as lovely as ever. And she was wearing only a jade-green silken housedress, belted at her slender waist with her golden braid over her shoulder.

"Mrs. Castern," Vincent greeted her pale face. "Where is your husband?"

"You cannot simply burst in here," she began. "It goes against all civility, and at this early hour. Why, it's not yet ten."

"Civility be damned. Neither you nor that plagiarist you married know anything about the word. Call for Ambrose, or I'll go upstairs and wake him myself."

She pursed her lips. Pretty pink lips that he had spent half a year kissing. Half a year trusting the lies that came from them.

"My husband had a concert last night, a very successful one. The Queen herself called for encores."

"And I just bet he gave her one."

"I did, indeed," came a familiar voice.

Slowly, Vincent turned. There was no way he would ever see Ambrose Castern without first seeing his old and dear friend for the briefest of instants.

They'd met at Harrow and also attended Trinity College together. Their paths were similar since they were both pianists. Yet Ambrose had never been much of a composer. He ought to have had a successful career in an orchestra playing other people's work. Instead, the scroof had decided to have a successful and lucrative career as a soloist playing Vincent's work.

There were times when it still seemed like a bad dream. If only he would awaken to find his compositions still strewn about his conservatory and salon at Mirabel where Lydia had stolen them during her single visit. If only he had published them sooner under his own name, rather than continuing to polish them to perfection.

"Your encore was mine," Vincent pointed out.

Ambrose's eyebrows rose. "Now you are making a jest, and a poor one at that. Just because you believe some of my pieces have a passing resemblance to some of yours, you cannot go claiming every work as your own. I haven't been near your home for years."

"You didn't need to." Vincent would not go over the old accusations that had led nowhere. Ambrose had always refused to speak the truth even when the two of them were alone. Instead, he focused on the current egregious theft.

"You simply found my latest piece, mistakenly published, and are now passing it off as your own. I suppose you have spies out to all the music publishers and shops awaiting something anonymous you can sink your claws into."

Ambrose laughed, and Lydia joined in. It was infuriating. The only saving grace was that she hadn't ended up as

Vincent's wife. Whether she actually fell in love with Ambrose in the brief time the three of them were together at Mirabel or whether she saw in the ambitious pianist something she didn't see in Vincent, he would never know. All he knew was that she left for London along with anything he had ever foolishly transcribed onto paper.

A month later, Ambrose had his London debut, playing to great acclaim. "A masterful composer and superb pianist!" screamed the headlines in capital print. Of course, Lydia was always there, basking in the adoration of her husband and of the audience to whom he never failed in introducing her. She loved the limelight as much as, if not more than, her husband.

"A friend of mine published one of my sonatas recently, and apparently, *you* are now playing it in concert and passing it off as your own."

"Preposterous," Ambrose said. "I wrote every note." But Lydia didn't look so convincing in the way her eyes widened.

"You had a piece published anonymously?" she asked. Then she shook her head, rolling her eyes as if it served him right to have it plagiarized.

Vincent liked to think she had some morals, somewhere deep down, a little shame for what she'd done, unlike his former friend, who would never admit to anything.

"If that is why you came, merely to hurl more wild accusations like you did three years ago, then you wasted a trip." Ambrose relaxed onto the sofa, showing his lack of manners by sitting when his wife still stood.

"I let the other infractions go," Vincent started.

"There were no other infractions," Ambrose declared, "and there was nothing you could do if there had been."

"Vincent," Lydia said softly, snagging his attention. "Music was meant to be played and heard."

Vincent laughed, not hiding the bitterness in his tone. "Is that how you live with yourself?"

Shaking his head, he crossed the room to the door. "Stop playing it, Ambrose. You have blundered this time. I can prove the piece is mine. I won't even make you publicly renounce your authorship. Just stop playing it."

Ambrose rolled his eyes and looked away. Vincent looked at Lydia. *What could she do?* He stormed out, hoping Ambrose took him seriously. If not, he was prepared to fight.

BRILLIANCE WAS SHOCKED WHEN Belinda tapped on her door and told her who was downstairs in the drawing room.

"How do I look?" she asked her maid. "Never mind. That is of no matter." She paused. "But how do I look? I wish I'd worn a brighter color today."

"Peach suits you, my lady. You look beautiful."

"Thank you. But I shouldn't have asked. It's not like you would ever say I looked dreadful. Would you?"

And then she dashed from the room, trying to slow her steps so she didn't appear to be hurrying to see Vincent. But her heartbeat was not cooperating, beating more quickly the closer she came.

"Good day, Lord Hewitt. To what do I owe this unplanned visit?"

"Good day, Lady Brilliance. I am here to ask a favor."

A favor! He had some nerve. She would give him that. He had all but thrown her out of his mother's birthday party. Regardless, she wouldn't stoop to uncivil behavior.

"I am happy to speak with you. Would you care to take tea with me?"

"No, thank you."

She took her favorite seat at one end of the blue sofa. "Won't you sit, please?"

He did, taking the wing chair opposite.

"I am surprised you are here." Brilliance squirmed slightly, wishing they had tea service after all, so she had something to do with her hands apart from wringing them on her lap.

"Frankly, I am surprised to be here, but I think you are the only one who can help me. I know I have behaved badly toward you—"

She raised her eyebrows at the understatement.

He looked grim. "I apologize and take full responsibility for not being in better control of my temper."

"Before you say any more, my lord, while we are both calm and have our wits about us, I must apologize once again for taking your music from your lap desk in the salon. I folded it and tucked it into a pocket tied to my petticoat. I must have known I was doing something naughty and unwise, or I would have asked you if I could send it to London."

While she wished he had handled it differently, and not been so quick to become livid, Brilliance had thought a great deal about how she would feel if someone took something of hers. Even for a good purpose.

"Will you forgive me truly and put it behind us?" she asked, trying to still her hands in the fabric of her skirts.

After a brief pause, he said, "If you will accept my apology, then yes, my lady, I will. Besides, you could not have possibly understood how I felt because I never told you about what happened in the past."

"I have time now," she offered.

He nodded and tugged at his necktie. "Will you believe me, that is the question?"

"Why wouldn't I?" Then Brilliance recalled with reddening cheeks how he had already made some statements about his music that she had refused to believe.

He must have recalled those instances because he shrugged. "Because it sounds fantastical, even to my ears. How could I expect you to accept what I tell you on faith?"

Brilliance made a decision. "Because we are friends, I shall accept what you tell me."

Vincent stared at her unwaveringly through his spectacles while a small muscle jumped on either side of his closed jaw. Then he nodded.

"I have been lied to by someone who professed to be my friend before. My closest friend, in fact, turned out to be my worst enemy."

"Ambrose Castern?" she asked.

"How did you know?"

"When his name has come up, each time you've grown exceedingly cross."

He nodded. "The short of it is that we've known each other for years. He had access to my home. And at the first opportunity, he arranged to steal every scrap of music that I'd committed to paper."

Brilliance couldn't help the gasp that escaped her. "How awful."

"Since I had never played any of it publicly, he could claim it as his own."

"Even 'The Hummingbird'?"

"Yes," he croaked and then cleared his throat. "That piece, *my* 'Sonata in A' made his reputation as a brilliant composer."

"And it is yours," she said softly.

"It is."

"Yet you cannot prove any of the works he plays are yours."

To her amazement, Vincent gave a half smile. "Because of you, I believe I can."

"Me?" Brilliance managed finally to release her fingers and still her hands.

"The piece I played at my mother's birthday, the same that you heard Castern play in concert—that's the one you took from my salon and published."

She gasped again. "Oh no!" Then she closed her eyes. "I feel sick to have betrayed you."

He rose to his feet and came over to sit beside her on the sofa. In a quick movement, he stripped off his gloves and took one of her hands between his.

"We have moved beyond that, haven't we?" he asked.

She nodded, trying to quell her tears of guilt.

"As it turns out, it is only because you saw the handwritten sheets in my home and then sent them to London that I can prove prior ownership. It would be better if you had declared me the composer when you gave it to Boosey & Co., but at least you gave him my name and address as the owner."

"And I can vouch that I took the music from you. I didn't even know what it sounded like."

"Which brings me to this." Vincent released her hand, which was a shame because she was enjoying his touch very much. He withdrew folded pages from his pocket. "I brought the music, which I call 'Il Rinnovo' and you called 'The Starling.'"

"And which Mr. Castern called 'An Enchanting Dream.'"

Ignoring that, he asked, "Do you have a piano?"

"Why, yes." Jumping up, Brilliance said, "Follow me." And as she took him through the house, she realized she ought to have had a chaperone instead of speaking alone with him, but it was too late for that. If one of her parents were home, it would be a different matter.

"In here, Lord Hewitt. It's not really a conservatory, but my mother occasionally still tries her hand at the piano, so she keeps it. My sister, Purity, is quite good and used to play it often before she married and moved out."

Looking at the instrument now, always dusted and polished by their household staff, Brilliance hoped he didn't find it too inferior.

"It is unlikely to be in tune," she added.

"That is no matter. You will recognize the piece, I think."

He spread the first two pages out on the piano's music cradle and without hesitation began to play.

She remained silent through the piece, realizing he hadn't turned the pages, but finished the movement from memory as he had at his parents' home.

"Yes, that is what Mr. Castern played," she said, feeling morose at having had a part in the nefarious pianist getting his hands on Vincent's work.

"I know. I went to his concert last night after I had already been to see him. I told him in no uncertain terms that he must stop playing this piece. It is too late for the rest of my work but—"

"Why do you say that? I think you should use this latest act of plagiarism to force him to admit to the rest of it."

He shrugged. "I think people will always believe my work is his because they have heard him play it on the stage. That goes a long way to validating his ownership. It made you think so."

Guilt pinched her again. "Then you must play it, too," she declared.

He started to shake his head. Losing her temper, she stomped her foot. "I won't let him get away with this. I shall demand he confess."

To her surprise, Vincent smiled. "I only want him to cease playing this latest piece. 'Il Rinnovo' is important to me. That is why I came today. Although I demanded he remove it from his repertoire, he played it anyway. I am hopeful you will accompany me to consult with a solicitor. I believe you can swear to a statement about what you know, and then we'll present it to Castern. If he knows what's good for him, he will listen and do as I have asked before I take him to court."

"It is infuriating," Brilliance said. "But *your* music, 'Il Rinnovo' and 'The Hummingbird,'—"

"It is *not* 'The Hummingbird,'" he protested.

"Very well, your 'Sonata in the Hay.'"

"Sonata in A," he corrected. "That means I wrote it in the key of A."

She blinked and smiled sheepishly. "I thought it was a romantic piece about two lovers in the hay. I could tell you a story about my eldest sister—" Brilliance broke off, clamping her teeth on whatever she was saying, knowing her cheeks were turning bright red.

"What were we talking about?" She frowned. "Oh, yes. You cannot let him keep the rest. All the music Mr. Castern plays, all of it has a certain similar quality."

"Because it all came from my brain," he reminded her. "Similarly, you can tell a piece by Beethoven or Mozart or Haydn just as easily."

Brilliance bit her lip, then released it with a squeaky sound. "You perhaps can tell them apart, and many other learned people, too, I am sure. But I cannot." She wished it wasn't another failing to add to her list, right after fishing. "And do you have more music?"

"Nothing transcribed. I am ashamed to say I destroyed the few pieces that I found still in my home. Burned them in the hearth."

She shook her head at the horror.

"I know it sounds drastic," he explained. "But I was crushed to learn all my compositions had walked out the door. At the time, it seemed the only way to protect those that remained. After all, the music is still in here." He tapped his head.

She sighed. "Better it was out here," she reminded him. "The point of music is not to drive you insane playing over and over inside your head. It is to delight the listener, whether moving us to smiles or to tears."

"Mrs. Castern said something similar. To excuse her husband's plagiarism and betrayal."

Brilliance wanted to confront the woman on Vincent's behalf. "That is no excuse for stealing." She recalled the concert. "Mr. Castern paid tribute to her as he has done at each of his concert's I have seen, which numbers three in the past two years. He always looks up at her in the box and mentions her name and claps along with the audience."

"I guess he loves her very much," Vincent said, rising to his feet. "I will make an appointment with a solicitor if you agree to come."

"Tell me when and where, and I will meet you."

"With a—"

"With a chaperone," she promised. "I will behave properly."

Being an earl's daughter wouldn't hurt either, Brilliance mused. And best of all, it seemed she had her friend again.

She only wished, when he had taken his leave, he'd given her some small indication that the events of the past hour would put them back upon the path they had been on before. One in which they gave each other their hearts and decided to live a life together.

CHAPTER TWENTY-TWO

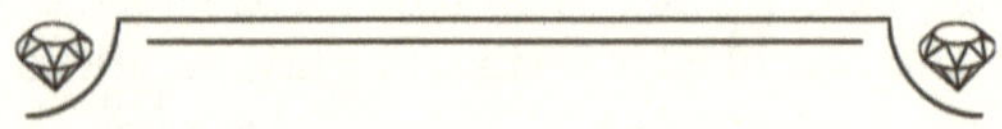

Brilliance wore a dress of solemn charcoal gray and brought Lord Diamond along to meet with Vincent's solicitor at Lincoln's Inn. It was an odd way for her father to meet the man she loved.

"My lord!" Vincent said upon realizing it was the earl who accompanied her. He even bowed.

Brilliance smiled at his discomfiture. She had seen the same reaction all her life when people met Lord Diamond. He was an earl with a formidable presence, tall and quick-witted, while retaining a thick head of dark hair, streaked with a little gray.

Vincent inclined his head, but her father stuck out his hand for a proper handshake.

"I understand you have been robbed."

"Indeed, I have," Vincent said. "Although intellectual property is trickier than going to the constable and explaining how my horse was stolen."

"Was your horse stolen, too?" Brilliance asked. *Poor Vincent, he was the unluckiest man.*

"No, Lady Brilliance, I was just making a point that the intangible is not usually the purview of the police."

"Isn't it?" Brilliance was glad her father had come for she feared she was already starting to lose the thread of Vincent's explanation.

"Lord Hewitt is correct, but a solicitor should be able to put the fear of God and of lengthy litigation into the perpetrator."

Walking in front of the two gentlemen, Brilliance let a clerk lead them to the lawyer's office. In a very few minutes, she was explaining the part she played in allowing Vincent's music to fall into the hands of Mr. Ambrose Castern.

"I used to admire him greatly. After all, what a pleasant name. Ambrose, I mean. It makes me think of strawberry jelly in a ring mold with chunks of real fruit. I'm sure you know the type," she said to the solicitor, an older man who was watching her with dark eyes and a slightly open mouth.

"Jelly?" he asked. He looked to Lord Diamond and to Lord Hewitt and back again. "What is the meaning of this?"

Brilliance turned to the earl. "Father, you know what I mean, don't you? That dessert which Cook makes in June? Although I suppose it could be another type of jelly, such as lemon." She paused and thought of the name *Ambrose*. "No, definitely strawberry jelly, which is very nice with fresh cream on top and a sliver of sponge cake underneath."

"My daughter is correct. That is one of my favorite desserts, too."

Brilliance nodded, glad for her father's assistance. "And Mr. Castern has an equally nice face to go along with his name," she continued. "Who would ever imagine he could be as bold as Lord Mayor Brass, stepping onto a stage and playing someone else's music? I can't imagine doing such a thing, can you?" she asked the solicitor.

When he didn't answer, she added, "And yet that is precisely what he did. I was at the concert with Lord Redley as my escort." She glanced at Lord Hewitt, who might have been under the impression she had gone to the concert with her parents.

Did he mind? Did he care?

"Lord Redley is the eldest son of the Earl, Lord Pettigrain," she explained to the solicitor.

"A good man," Lord Diamond said. "I am speaking of the father, mind you, but it goes for the son as well. Pettigrain has doubled his family fortune since claiming the title. And his son, if rumors are true, will double it again."

"I wouldn't know about that, Father." Then Brilliance again addressed the solicitor. "Lord Redley and I have been keeping company for weeks."

"I fail to see the relevance," he said.

Brilliance considered and then nodded. "I suppose there is none at all, except I would not have been at the concert if not for him."

Then she managed to close her mouth and stop talking until the lawyer asked her another question. But she couldn't help sneaking a glance at Vincent, who looked somber. He sat up a little straighter when he noticed her looking his way.

However, when the meeting was over, he merely thanked her and her father for coming and climbed into his carriage.

"I HAVE BEEN DEPOSED," she told her sister Radiance. "It was exciting to have the solicitor listening to me carefully and taking down my true and lawful statement. Only think how my own words may help Lord Hewitt regain his music."

They were walking along the path beside the three dinosaur islands at the new location of the Crystal Palace, which had recently reopened with an Egyptian exhibit. Both sisters preferred the original structure at Hyde Park to the enlarged one on Penge Peak next to Sydenham Hill.

Regardless, it was a good outing nonetheless with the innovative glass and steel building being the perfect place to promenade on a rainy afternoon.

"I hope Lord Hewitt was dutifully appreciative," her redheaded sister said. They had taken advantage of a break in the rain showers to tour the massive exterior exhibit featuring extinct animals, designed and sculpted by Benjamin Waterhouse Hawkins. Ray was intimately familiar with it as the scientist directing Mr. Hawkins was Sir Richard Owen, a dear friend of her husband.

Edward Lockwood, who suited Ray perfectly in Brilliance's estimation, had invited her to join them weeks earlier to see the Crystal Palace being rebuilt and to watch the dinosaurs being painted in place.

"Can you believe these beasts once roamed all over?" Brilliance asked, changing the subject.

Vincent *had* been grateful, but it wasn't as though he had been overly effusive about it. After all, she'd caused the mess in the first place. And even if he had wanted to take her aside and declare his undying gratitude, he couldn't. Her father had kept a watchful eye on the two of them.

Besides, there had been that embarrassing moment when she had explained to all three men how she'd folded up the pages and lifted her skirts to deposit them in her pocket. She didn't want her father thinking too much about his youngest daughter's actions.

"I cannot imagine how these animals were raised. How could there be a stable big enough to hold them?"

Radiance halted and turned to her. "Bri, dear, there weren't any people at the time of the dinosaurs. They never lived on earth at the same time as us, so we never had to put them in a pen or a stable."

Brilliance looked past her sister at the large creatures. "I am sure you are correct, because you are smart and know so much, but if no one has ever seen them, then how do we know what they looked like?"

Ray tucked Brilliance's arm under hers. "I shall tell you about fossils if you tell me how you ended up alone in a room in Lord Hewitt's country manor."

Brilliance stumbled. She didn't want to discuss that. Her sister was far too clever. "Do you know there is a cheese named *Brie*?"

"I do," Ray said. "So, am I correct in thinking you fancy Lord Hewitt?"

Brilliance had not succeeded in distracting her even for a second.

"Brie is soft and creamy and divinely delicious."

Ray laughed. "Is that how you tell your sister to mind her own business?"

Brilliance sighed. "I admire Lord Hewitt greatly. Quite naturally, we had a falling out when I took his music and had it printed."

"Naturally," her sister agreed. "But that one incident, especially since you meant no harm, could not possibly stop true love. At least, it should not, in my opinion."

"True love?" Brilliance mused. "Honestly, Ray, my heart had firmly decided upon Vincent Hewitt. And I thought he felt the same. However, he set me aside rather easily and so swiftly my head was spinning. I didn't have time to convince him I didn't intend any harm. Moreover, he has not given me any indication since meeting again in London that he wishes to take up where we left off."

She looked at the dinosaur statues. "I suppose he puts me in the same category as his best friend who stole his music and has built a career of fame and fortune on Lord Hewitt's work."

"But it's *not* the same at all. You didn't try to benefit from his music. You were only trying to help him." Ray sighed. "What does Father think?"

"He seemed impressed by him. He invited Lord Hewitt to dinner, not in person, but in writing after we discussed it privately on the way home."

"Did he?" Ray nodded. "Why, that is a good sign."

"He thought Mother might like to meet him. But he also said he wants Lord Hewitt to sing for his supper. And to tell you the truth, I don't believe Lord Hewitt can sing at all."

"It's a saying, Bri. You remember, from 'Little Tommy Tucker'? Did Father mention Mother's piano?"

"Yes."

"There, you see? Father probably wants to hear Lord Hewitt play something to make certain for himself that he is truly a composer and not a charlatan."

"A charlatan! As if I would take up with such a person." Then she shook her head. "I am greatly relieved about the singing, but I am not at all sure Lord Hewitt will play for his supper, either."

VINCENT HADN'T FELT NERVOUS going to a dinner party since . . . Come to think of it, he couldn't remember ever being nervous. After all, why would someone in his position of life have a reason to feel anxious, even at the prospect of dining with an earl? It wouldn't be his first, nor his last. He had even dined with a duke.

And in the House of Lords, he rubbed shoulders with all his peers.

And yet, this was different.

The Earl Diamond was legendary as was his family, his father and his father before him, and so on. They were always on the right side of history, in favor with the royal family, and generally looked at as altruistic, shining examples of *noblesse oblige.*

His own family seemed almost shabby in comparison.

"Ridiculous!" he muttered to himself as he dressed.

This dinner was no different from any other meal he'd had in someone's home. Except, of course, as far as he knew, he was the only guest and would be dining with the parents of the lady who had enthralled him for months. He had been ready to ask for her hand before the debacle.

And now?

She was helping him sort out the disaster she had created. But still, he appreciated it. And more than that, he still found her to be the most intriguing of females. No one since Lydia had made him want to spend huge amounts of time in her company, merely talking, listening, and learning about her.

No one else made him feel quite so hot and protective at the same time, either. Brilliance was like a piece of intricate music he wanted to play over and over, sussing out all her nuances.

And so, despite worrying that her parents might have the wrong idea—for he was no longer ready to jump into marriage or even an engagement with such an impulsive creature as Brilliance Diamond—he couldn't deny he was still firmly intrigued by her.

Wearing a black suit of worsted wool, he arrived at the Diamond home on Piccadilly and lifted his hand to the brass knocker. The door opened before he could take hold of it.

"Good evening, Lord Hewitt. Please come this way."

He followed the butler into a drawing room that reminded him of his parents' own elegant yet comfortable parlor.

Lord Diamond rose to his feet, as did Lady Diamond and her daughter a moment later.

"Good evening, my lord," Brilliance said, stepping forward so eagerly, Vincent thought she was going to hug him. Instead, she held out her hand, which he took, bowed over, and released, feeling her give his own a little squeeze before she let her arm drop. *Encouragement, perhaps.*

She looked lovely as usual in the palest lavender, wearing a velvet gown since the evenings had turned chilly. It set off her thick dark hair, which he longed to see completely loose.

"You have met my father," she said.

He bowed to Lord Diamond.

"Allow me to introduce you to Lady Diamond," she continued. "Mother, may I present Lord Hewitt?"

Her mother had similar facial features, but the resemblance stopped there. Her vivid red hair was swept up and decorated with a strand of pearls and emeralds that matched her rich green eyes.

"My husband and I are so pleased you accepted our invitation, my lord." Her hand went out to him, which he hastened to take. "I hear you are as talented as you are good looking."

"Mother," Brilliance retorted.

In her gown of royal purple, the countess was like a showy *pizzicato* piece, whereas her youngest daughter . . . Vincent thought Brilliance's manner and words were more like a smooth *arpeggio*.

The ladies took their seats once again, and he was offered one next to Brilliance.

"I hope you don't take offense, my lord, but my parents would very much enjoy hearing you play the piano tonight, either before or after we eat. Would you be so kind? You will be relieved to know you do not have to sing."

"Sing?" he repeated, still considering her request that he perform, waiting and wondering why the usual irritation didn't materialize.

Brilliance nodded to Lord and Lady Diamond. "Like Tommy Tucker."

He couldn't help his smile. "I see. You mean for my supper."

"Why, yes," she stared at him with that look that made him feel invincible. "How clever of you, my lord."

A sweet nature, he thought. Like *dolce* music.

The butler returned with a tray of glasses and a full wine carafe.

"Shall we toast to our guest's health?" Lord Diamond asked. "And most particularly to the successful resolution of his legal case."

"The solicitor seemed confident of victory," Vincent said. "Thanks to Lady Brilliance's testimony."

She shrugged delicately, looking pleased with herself.

"It is my understanding," said her mother, "that you burned some of your written music."

Hearing it out loud was mortifying. "I did. I admit that I wasn't in my right mind at the time."

"In your left mind, perhaps," Brilliance quipped, but by her placid expression, he couldn't tell if she was making a joke, so he didn't smile.

"Truly, I wasn't thinking straight."

"Crooked thinking," she murmured and sipped her wine.

"Ah . . . indeed. I should have let my anger pass." Many times, he wished he had. He addressed Lady Diamond. "But as I told your daughter, I have it all still in my memory."

"Isn't that amazing?" Brilliance asked. "Why, I can hardly recall what I read in the morning's paper, and Lord Hewitt remembers entire sonatas."

"Lately, I have considered transcribing all my lost music again," he said.

Brilliance tried to clap, but her wine glass prevented her. "That is very good news."

"The sooner you publish it under your own name, the sooner it is protected under international copyright," Lord Diamond said. "Are you going to try to regain the authorship of your other pieces, too?"

"I don't see how I can do that," Vincent said. "I believe that horse has left the barn."

"Now what are we talking about?" Brilliance asked.

But her mother ignored her. "I don't think you should give up. It was wrong of Mr. Castern when he stole your work, and it is just as wrong today."

"I will think about how I might be able to do that," Vincent said, hoping they were not going to discuss his messy personal issue any longer.

Luckily, Brilliance was also ready to move on with the evening.

"I don't believe you answered my request," she said, "regarding playing the piano tonight." And her admiring gaze made him feel as if everything might turn out for the best after all.

What's more, a new sensation of wanting to play for the sheer enjoyment he might bring to this family resounded through him.

"If I am not delaying our dinner, then I would be honored to play for you now," he said. Surprisingly, he meant it.

Dolce, indeed.

CHAPTER TWENTY-THREE

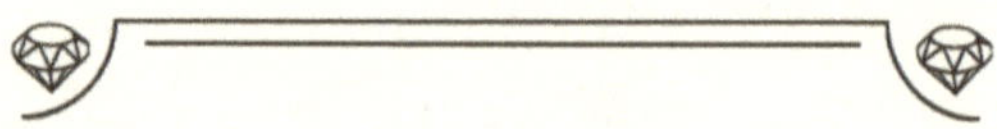

"You cannot be serious!" Ambrose Castern declared as soon as he was shown into Vincent's study. "You are sending lawyers after me? What next? Scotland Yard?"

"You cannot barge into my house," Vincent said. "Not like in the old days. Although knowing you have been served by my solicitor and are a mere octave away from justice finally coming down upon your miserable, conniving head, that alone gained you entrance when otherwise my butler would have closed the door in your sorry face."

Ambrose threw himself into the only empty chair. "Everything looks exactly the same." His friend used to be a steady fixture in Vincent's house, the first year after he purchased it, before . . . everything.

"Why wouldn't it?" Vincent asked, not wanting to have a civil, social discussion with the person who had betrayed him.

"I guess you had no reason to alter it. My wife had my entire house repainted and refurnished directly after we married. Cost me a bloody fortune!"

The wretch could only have brought up Lydia to be irksome, to wound Vincent as best he could. Strangely, even though the thought of her used to cause a pinch of pain, at that moment, he no longer gave a fig.

Seeing her again as Ambrose's wife had taken the shine off her nob, as it were. She was better in his memories than in the real-life person.

It was a relief to feel that way. On the other hand, Ambrose was also better in the past. In person, his old friend was now nothing more than a whining, light-fingered diddler. And a weasel to boot.

"Since you paid to redecorate your house using money you made from my music, you must excuse me if I don't give a damn. And I am certain you didn't come to discuss my home's furnishings."

Ambrose stopped the pretense of being friendly. His sly face sobered.

"I came because I received a threatening letter from your solicitor. It is absurd."

"What is? How once again you stole my music? Or the part about how I want you to confess publicly?"

"Both. All of it. Even if I had purchased an anonymous piece of music, and I am in no way saying I did, I had no idea it was yours. That was purely bad luck."

"It honestly doesn't matter, does it?" Vincent asked, trying not to lose his tenuous hold on serenity and on his temper. "The point is you knew it was not yours."

"It sounded like mine," Ambrose grumbled. "I could tell that it would when I first read the sheets."

"You mean it sounded like *mine*!" Vincent reminded him. "Because it is. Luckily, I am in a position this time to prove that I wrote it. But if the music hadn't been mine, you would be getting away with stealing from some other sad bleater."

He knew the black ache in the soul when forced to listen to someone passing off one's work as his own. He wouldn't wish that on anyone else. Looking at Ambrose now, with his boyish face and quick, darting eyes, a shiver of pure disgust danced up Vincent's spine.

What a slithering snake! It was galling to have been fooled for years by this man who had pretended, convincingly, to be a loyal friend.

Leaning back, Vincent put his booted feet upon his own desk, feeling for the first time since Ambrose had stolen his music that he had the absolute upper hand.

"I don't know why you do it, either. Pure laziness, I suspect, because I recall you had some spark of ability. Small talent, perhaps, but not completely negligible. Why don't you simply compose your own music?"

Ambrose's face twisted. "That's easy for you to say."

"Easy? Easy!" Vincent exclaimed, realizing he was fisting his hands, belying his relaxed position. So much for serenity. "There is nothing easy about composing. And it was made far more difficult after you, my so-called friend, took all my work. It deflates one's powers to produce and create. Something you wouldn't understand since you are always taking, not making."

Ambrose didn't even have the decency to appear the least chagrined. "The music was just sitting there anyway, being wasted."

Vincent caught his breath. It was the closest Ambrose had come to confessing. Unfortunately, it was so dismissive of any responsibility, his words had Vincent seeing a red haze.

"If I play my music only for myself or even my blasted horse or if I choose never to play it at all, that is *my* choice. My pieces weren't like spare dinner plates, which you needed at a party."

Ambrose shrugged, looking sullen. "I have already played that new composition in concert, and very well, too. The audience loved it, and they loved my rendition. What can I say now that won't break their hearts and make them hate me?"

Vincent couldn't maintain his *sangfroid* another moment. His composure snapped as he swore a blue oath. Uncrossing his ankles, he lowered his legs slowly to the floor and rose from his desk.

"You may not understand why, and God help you for your lack of understanding, but I don't care about any of that. They *should* hate you. I hate you!" He halted. "No, I don't really. I despise you, and now that you must admit to the world what a fraud you are, I pity you. Almost."

Ambrose stood quickly. "Save your pity. You'll need it for your little Diamond lady when I'm finished with her."

Vincent's feet carried him around the desk and ran him directly into Ambrose before he could even think what he was doing. Sweeping the worm backward until he heard Ambrose's head connect with the study wall, Vincent pressed his forearm across the stunned man's throat.

"Hewitt," Ambrose croaked, scrabbling at Vincent's arm, but he kept applying pressure until his adversary's eyes bulged.

"You will do nothing to her," Vincent ground out, seething with fury. "You won't try to contact her, you won't speak to her, you won't so much as look at her. If you do, I'll break every bone in your hands."

Ambrose paled—either from the threat or from lack of air. Either way, Vincent was finished with him and stepped back so he could breathe.

Grabbing at his own throat, Ambrose rubbed the skin above his necktie as if to soothe it.

"That was rash of you. I could charge you with assault."

"You could," Vincent said. "Why don't you go ahead and try? In the meantime, get out of my house. And I shall look for that public confession in *The Times*. Otherwise, to the Court of Chancery we will go."

Opening his study door, he stood back so Ambrose could leave.

He brushed by without another word.

AFTER THE SUCCESSFUL DINNER with her parents, Brilliance had expected Vincent to send his card requesting to see her or perhaps send an invitation to a social event.

For a few days, nothing happened, which was a disappointment. She went to a ball with Lord Redley and didn't bother looking for Vincent, since she hadn't seen him at any of the Season's festivities, neither in the spring nor since returning to London.

But the following morning, their butler brought her a calling card on his silver salver.

Jumping to her feet, Brilliance read it swiftly and asked, "Is Lord Hewitt waiting?"

"No, my lady. His footman bought the card with a request to see you later today if you are free. At two o'clock. Would you like me to give the man a reply?"

"Thank you, Mr. Dunley. Please tell the footman to tell Lord Hewitt that I will be here at two o'clock and shall expect him."

"Very good."

Thus, she had to wait on pins and needles for the correct hour, knowing Vincent to be a punctual sort of person. The clock had not yet struck the hour when she heard Mr. Dunley admitting Vincent to her home.

Appearing in the doorway, Brilliance waved at him.

"Do come in. Please bring the tea service," she asked the butler who was collecting Vincent's coat and hat.

And then, after greeting, at last, they were seated in the drawing room. *Alone.*

He pushed his spectacles up his nose. "Should you request a maid or your mother?"

"I don't see any need. I vow I have snuck a peek at each of my sisters as they entertained a suitor without a chaperone. And Mr. Dunley will be in momentarily with the refreshments. It is not as though he will find us in an embrace."

She smoothed her skirts, then looked up at him. "Will he?" *Oh, dear.* She definitely had the tone of longing and hope in her voice.

"No," he said quickly.

Drat! It occurred to her, despite the happy butterflies in her belly, that Vincent hadn't come on a social call as she had hoped. But she'd been wrong before.

"Did you come today in order to begin courting me once more?" She might as well ask.

"No," he said again, looking uncomfortable. "I came because I was paid a visit yesterday by Ambrose Castern."

Now she understood. He was there to tell her the results of the solicitor's letter.

"Did you and he work things out satisfactorily?"

Mr. Dunley came in promptly with the tea service since they'd been preparing for the exact moment of Vincent's arrival. The tea was perfectly steeped and ready to pour, the milk was in the cups, and there was a plate of delectables.

Vincent said nothing while she poured for them both and offered him the plate with biscuits and small custard tarts.

He took the tea but waved away the plate. "Thank you, but no."

"The tarts are very good, my lord. I would warrant they are as fine as the baked goods your cook made for us at your Joyden's Wood estate."

They stared at one another, both recollecting being at his country home. She would love to recapture the sentiment of the best day of their short friendship.

He cleared his throat. "I have no doubt."

"Well, you must doubt, my lord, until you taste. How could you not? Anyway, our cook will be insulted."

"Very well." Vincent leaned forward, snatched a tart from the plate, and took a large bite. As he chewed and swallowed, his face changed, becoming less tense. With him looking more relaxed and friendly, Brilliance could just observe him silently.

She, too, ate a tart. Strangely, she was content simply looking at him without the need to make the usual polite prattle in order to keep the quiet moments at bay.

"This is nice," she said before taking a sip of tea. "Perfect. Sometimes, there is nothing better than a cup of tea. Please drink yours before it grows cold. And then tell me about Mr. Castern's visit."

Vincent sipped the tea, and then, oddly, he began to smile. "How do you make me happy by doing nothing but being yourself?"

She shrugged, although basking in his compliment. "It's *not* me. It's the tea and tarts. Who wouldn't be happy with these? I don't think I have ever cried while eating a custard tart."

He set his cup down. "I assure you, it *is* you. Lady Brilliance, I know we have had a rocky start, but I want you to know that I hold you in the highest esteem."

She felt her cheeks warm. "And I, you, my lord." The day was looking up. "Are you courting me after all?"

His long hesitation gave her the answer, and she wished she hadn't asked again. Moreover, despite what she had only just said, Brilliance could easily imagine crying while eating a tart and letting warm salty tears fall into her tea. She wanted not to be in love with the man seated opposite, but it was so very difficult to rein in her feelings when he was being pleasant.

When he was saying kind things about her.

When he was looking so dash-fire handsome he made her toes curl!

"What about Lord Redley?" he asked, answering her question with one of his own. "And his wonderful father with their ever-growing income? Gold sovereigns blossoming like weeds in a field," he finished by mumbling under his breath.

The notion of money growing in a field struck her funny. Her amusement grew when she considered that Vincent could have said any type of flower. *Weeds! Was he jealous?* He seemed to want an answer.

Brilliance liked Lord Redley. She didn't love him. She might come to love him, and in any case, she had no intention of living as though she had no prospects left. She had prospects a-plenty.

"I have been keeping company with Lord Redley. We were out last night in fact." *What more could she say?* "He is a good dancer."

"A good skill to have," Vincent said tightly, then sipped his tea, appearing out of sorts again.

"I suppose if one is at a ball, yes, it is," she agreed. "But it is a common skill, unlike yours and Mr. Castern's."

Vincent blinked and set his empty cup on the table. "I am a fool. I had nearly become distracted from why I wished to speak with you. When Ambrose Castern came to my home, he didn't seem ashamed and apologetic as one would hope. In fact, he was threatening."

Brilliance felt blood rush into her head.

"He threatened you? After stealing your work? How dare he!"

That would not stand, as long as she was Vincent's friend. She was an earl's daughter. While she didn't put on airs, and wasn't really sure what that meant anyway, she knew her father was powerful. And by some reason of association, she had a little power, too.

"How can I help?"

Vincent shook his head. "You misunderstand. He did not threaten me," he said. "He threatened you."

CHAPTER TWENTY-FOUR

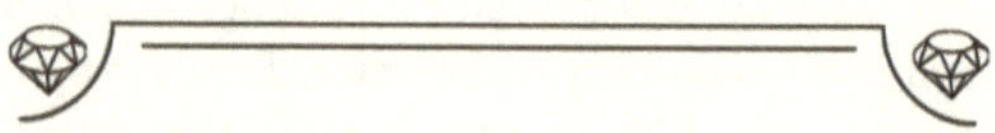

Brilliance wished they had spent more time talking about the high esteem in which Vincent held her. Instead, as soon as he'd explained how Mr. Castern had made vague threats, Vincent said he had come because he felt it was his duty to warn her.

"Your duty," she echoed softly, thinking that didn't sound very romantic.

"If he tries to pay you a visit, deny him. Or if you do somehow find yourself in his company, make sure your father is with you. Will you promise me?"

"I promise." She went over it in her mind. No visiting with Ambrose Castern except with her father present.

And then Vincent had left without inviting her to a play or a concert or even dinner at his parents' home. Disappointed, she ate another custard tart after he left, which cheered her a little.

At the week's end, she was dressed and ready for a night out with Lord Redley. They were going to his widowed aunt's home for dinner and dancing, and thus, she wouldn't need a chaperone except for the carriage ride. Her parents allowed her to take Belinda for the short journey.

Reminding herself that she had prospects, and a good-looking one at that, Brilliance dressed in sapphire-blue velvet and put a smile on her face.

"I have a surprise for you, my lady," Lord Redley said when they reached his aunt's mansion on London's outskirts.

Brilliance perked up. "Do you?"

As soon as they went through Lady Danson's receiving line and entered the drawing room, she clapped her gloved hands.

"How wonderful of you, my lord."

"What have I done?" he asked, taking two glasses of claret off a tray and handing her one.

"The surprise," she said. "Unexpectedly seeing my good friend Lady Martine in your aunt's home is quite a treat. I hope we are seated close at dinner."

Upon seeing her, Martine hurried forward, and soon, they were discussing winter festivities.

"My parents are having a Christmas ball, but you must know that," Brilliance said. "I think invitations have gone out."

"Indeed they have, and I have received mine already and replied," Martine said. "We must get together and discuss the latest cold-weather fashions soon. I shall need a new gown for the occasion."

Brilliance spent more time speaking with her friend than her suitor, until Lord Redley said, "Your surprise is here."

"I thought Lady Martine was my surprise."

"In truth, I didn't know anything about her, but my aunt seems to know everyone this Season. She is a patron of the pianist we saw in concert. I know how much you enjoyed his music, so I asked her to invite him tonight."

As Brilliance realized whom he meant, a chill passed over her. Turning, she saw their hostess beside Ambrose Castern, who was accompanied by his wife, the lovely blonde woman from the theater box.

The other guests in the drawing room broke out in spontaneous applause when Lady Danson introduced him. Shocked by his sudden appearance, Brilliance refrained from clapping. Her first thought was that she ought to leave.

She had promised Vincent she wouldn't be in Mr. Castern's company without her father. On the other hand, she was surrounded by other people and escorted by Lord Redley. She didn't feel in the least threatened.

What she felt was angry. More so when Lady Danson invited them all to toast Mr. Castern's latest successful run of concerts and his new composition, "An Enchanting Dream."

After the cheers died down, Brilliance heard herself ask, "Have you spoken to the newspapers yet, Mr. Castern?"

His light-brown eyes flickered over her as did his wife's cool blue ones.

"About what, dear lady? I don't believe we have been introduced."

"Oh, pardon my rudeness," said Lord Redley's aunt. "Before any more conversation about Mr. Castern's fame in the papers or in person, let me bring our honored guest around the room to meet each of you personally."

Brilliance could hardly wait, tapping her toe as the pianist and his wife went from person to person with Lady Danson making the presentation. Although a flurry of nerves was starting to make her stomach churn at the upcoming confrontation, while standing between Martine and Lord Redley, she felt perfectly safe.

And then he was before her, Vincent's former friend and current nemesis.

Lord Redley's aunt said, "This is Lady Martine. Her father is Lord Flowers. And this is Lady Brilliance, the youngest daughter of the Earl Diamond. And this is Lord Redley. He is my nephew."

Brilliance saw the instant Mr. Castern realized who she was. His smile froze upon his face, giving him an oddly Jack-o'-lantern appearance. His wife also stared, mouth slightly open before she snapped it closed and looked to her husband for his next reaction.

"How good to meet you all. Your aunt has been very kind," he said addressing Lord Redley.

"Lady Brilliance and I saw you recently in concert. Will you be playing for us after dinner?"

"He will, indeed," Lady Danson said. "Anyone who hasn't had the good fortune to make it to one of his concerts will be treated to his latest composition."

"How thrilling," Martine said.

"Then you haven't spoken to *The Times* or the *Morning Herald* yet?" Brilliance asked again.

"In fact, I have," Mr. Castern said, nodding to those around him. "I was interviewed by *The Times* recently."

"I read that," Lord Redley said. "That's how I knew you were acquainted with my aunt."

"Yes, he mentioned my patronage," Lady Danson gushed.

Even though Mr. Castern was trying to make eye contact only with Lord Redley, Brilliance made him look at her with her next words. "It doesn't sound as though you confessed yet to plagiarizing Lord Hewitt's music as you were supposed to."

As if all the guests were listening to the small group rather than merely the few people around Brilliance, the entire room fell silent.

"I beg your pardon," said Lord Redley's aunt.

"Bri, what are you saying?" asked Martine, touching her arm. "Everyone knows Mr. Castern is a brilliant composer. No one else knows Lord Hewitt plays the piano."

"I know," said Ambrose Castern. "He is an old friend from school. A gifted pianist, but a little jealous of my success."

Brilliance gave an unladylike snort. "He is not in the least jealous of you. Even if he were, that doesn't change the fact that you stole his music."

She heard the gasps but didn't let it stop her. "You received a letter from his solicitor, and to prevent legal action, you were supposed to confess to *The Times*."

She turned to Lord Redley who looked a strange shade of puce, perfectly matched by his aunt's aghast expression.

"I know for a fact he was supposed to publicly confess," Brilliance added.

To her astonishment, Mr. Castern laughed. "I must say, considering I came to give a free performance, I find this particular guest to be a puzzling inclusion to our evening."

"Puzzling and insulting," said Mrs. Castern. "I think we should leave."

"No, please don't," said Lord Redley's aunt before looking pointedly at Brilliance.

In the silence that ensued, Brilliance realized the import of her hostess's stare.

"Are you wanting *me* to leave?" She was half mortified, but also strangely fascinated. "I have never left any party at its start. I am not sure my parents will approve of my returning home so soon."

Lady Danson appeared to waver. "I cannot offend Lord and Lady Diamond," she moaned. "I shall be shunned."

"Oh, no," Brilliance said. "They would never shun you. They will, of course, wonder at your choice of a guest of honor, seeing how he is a man without any. And they will be utterly perplexed as to how I could be thrown out of your home before I even got to taste the quality of your pottage."

When Lord Redley's aunt groaned with dismay, he became her champion, turning on Brilliance.

"I must insist you apologize to Mr. Castern for disparaging him and to my aunt for frightening her with . . . with becoming a social pariah due to your impressive lineage. That is not at all fair."

His aunt moaned again at the notion.

"I intended to frighten no one," Brilliance protested. "Nevertheless, I am telling the truth. I have even been deposed on the matter." She finished with a nod to those who were watching.

Martine squeezed her arm. "I know you thought Lord Hewitt to be most admirable this past summer, but he has filled your head with fabrications."

Brilliance wished she had spoken to Martine about all that had transpired recently, but she hadn't had the chance.

"He hasn't, I assure you. You are my good friend. You ought to believe me over this charlatan." She looked at Mr. Castern again. "It's a very fine-sounding word, *charlatan*, but doesn't mean anything near as regal as it sounds."

"I know what it means," Mr. Castern said, his eyes flickering from her to those around them.

"I do not mean to be harsh with my language," Brilliance continued, "but you are a thief, after all. 'An Enchanting Evening' was composed by Lord Hewitt."

"That's nonsense," said Lord Redley, speaking more harshly to her than he ever had. "You and I went to Cambridge Hall and watched him perform it."

"We watched and listened, certainly, but what does that signify?" Brilliance asked. "We didn't see him write it. Did we?"

Appearing exasperated, Lord Redley reminded her, "You loved every minute of the concert. That's why I thought you would enjoy this evening. Instead, you are behaving like someone who ought to be locked up in Bedlam."

Brilliance couldn't help laughing at his dramatic delivery. But Martine didn't join in, and quite obviously, she didn't approve.

"I will leave with you," she offered, holding Brilliance's arm more firmly.

"Then I shall be two females short at my table," Lady Danson complained.

"That is true," Brilliance said, feeling a little sorry for their hostess. Her own mother would not appreciate an uneven number of guests, either. The seating would be a nightmare. "It would be easier if Mr. and Mrs. Castern left."

"This is outrageous!" said Mr. Castern.

"Outrageous," repeated Mrs. Castern, taking a hostile step forward. "Do you realize my husband has played for the Queen and her Prince Consort?"

"Sadly, your husband was playing Lord Hewitt's music," Brilliance shot back. Pulling her arm free from Martine's grasp, she, too, took a step closer.

"What's more, my sister solved a jewelry forgery for Queen Victoria and Prince Albert two years ago, and her husband was granted a barony because of it." Then she looked at Lady Danson. "So you see, my family and the royal family are as close as this." Brilliance clasped her hands together, holding them up like a cudgel.

Their hostess took a step back. Brilliance was exaggerating slightly, but she was rather fed up with having to defend herself.

"If you wish to hear the music from Mr. Castern's concert, then you should send word to Lord Vincent Hewitt on King Street. While he is hesitant to perform in public, I assure you, he does not have stage fright."

Then she crossed her arms and awaited the fall out of her lengthy diatribe.

Lady Danson remained speechless, Lord Redley shook his head, and Martine muttered, "Bri, we should go." The rest of the guests around them started to discuss the issue, taking sides over who should remain.

Finally, when the awkwardness was at a boiling point, Mr. Castern spoke.

"I believe we shall take our leave, Lady Danson. I could not possibly play tonight, anyway. Perhaps another time."

Lady Danson nodded. "I will be in touch. And I do so apologize for what has happened here tonight."

In the end, the couple left swiftly without saying goodbye to anyone else. And then, as soon as the drawing-room door closed behind them, every eye turned toward Brilliance. Some faces were curious, others hostile.

She considered her older siblings, each of whom would have handled the situation differently. Clarity would have been loath to make anyone unhappy and thus probably have said nothing at all. Purity might have spoken out, but she would have left directly after having made the hostess uncomfortable. Adam would have invited Mr. Castern outside to speak privately upon the matter and maybe come to fisticuffs. And Ray . . . she would have already been to the man's house and somehow made him confess before he could come ruin the party.

Brilliance sighed. "I, too, am leaving."

Lady Danson pursed her lips and lifted her chin. She was more than a little angry, and Brilliance felt sorry. After all, it wasn't Lord Redley's aunt's fault that she'd been duped the way all of London had.

Leaning close, she whispered to Lady Danson, "Please do not worry. You shall find there are no recriminations from the Diamond family where you are concerned. I simply don't want to be the recipient of quite so much resentment all evening. I imagine that is bad for one's digestion."

When Martine made to go with her, Brilliance stopped her friend. "Stay so our hostess doesn't have such a hole at her table."

After a brief hesitation, Martine nodded.

Addressing Lord Redley, Brilliance knew their brief association was at an end. Still, she hoped he would do the gentlemanly thing. "Will you loan me your carriage so my maid and I can go home? I shall send it back directly."

"Of course. But . . . you don't really have to leave, do you?"

That surprised her. "How sweet of you, but I think it's for the best." Once more to her hostess, she added, "You really ought to contact Lord Hewitt to learn the truth."

Then, head high, satisfied she had done her best on Vincent's behalf, Brilliance left the party, offering the silent guests a little wave from the doorway and a smile. After all, she was a Diamond.

Reading *The Times* the following day and the one after that, Brilliance realized Mr. Castern had dug his heels in like a stubborn donkey.

"Father, I believe I will be going to court."

"You don't have to," the earl said, "if you think you might be uncomfortable. However, I believe it is the right thing to do."

"Especially if you intend to marry the man," added her mother.

Brilliance raised an eyebrow. "Do you think Lord Hewitt wishes to marry me, after I've caused him so much consternation?"

"Unquestionably!" Lady Diamond said, stirring her chocolate. "At least he has come out from the shadows. His talent was being wasted, and now, because of you, he has no choice but to claim his music." Her mother sipped and then added, "He owes you a debt of gratitude for ensuring that greatness is his only option."

Brilliance laughed. "I do not think Vincent . . . I mean, Lord Hewitt sees it like that. He was content to be only a statesman and to allow his music to remain in his head."

"Except for what was already stolen," her father said. "Imagine how that must have eaten at Hewitt every day, knowing some rascal was earning money at his expense. I would have had to call him out."

Brilliance hoped Vincent would come to appreciate having the whole thing brought into the public eye. If he did, then there might be a chance for them to have a relationship again.

Even more of a chance since her other prospect had let her disappear into the night without even offering to escort her home.

CHAPTER TWENTY-FIVE

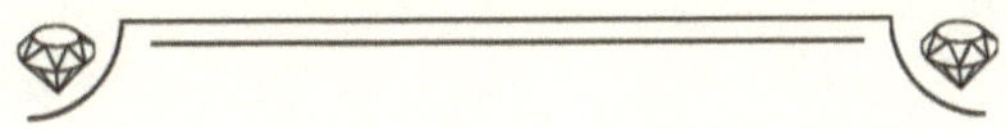

Vincent read the morning edition of *The Times* each day before going to Parliament, and every evening as well. Nothing from Ambrose. He had allowed him to get away with plagiarism for so long, the rascal was not taking him seriously.

After five days, he wrote to his solicitor and told him to move forward by filing with the Court of Chancery. That meant Brilliance would have to be summoned. It shouldn't worry him, except it did. She was so damnably unpredictable.

It was hard to trust her to maintain the correct amount of gravitas, all the while worrying she wouldn't talk about trying to cure stage fright with fruit or go on about pitchforks. Shaking his head, Vincent finished the letter, signed and sealed it, and rang for his butler.

He ought to send a missive to Brilliance as well, letting her know he was proceeding with the lawsuit and, thus, a trial. On the other hand, it would be better to contact her after he received a court date and time, which could be weeks, if not months into the future.

Honest with himself, he couldn't wait that long to see her again. Recalling Lord Redley, however, Vincent didn't want to poach on another man's land. He frowned. That wasn't sound thinking. Brilliance was an unattached, self-governing female. Until Lord Redley proposed, then Vincent could pursue her.

Was that what he wanted to do? *Damn right, he did!*

Thus, he drew out a fresh piece of stationery.

Dear Lady Brilliance,

Will you come to a play with me this Friday evening? I will see what is being offered at Theatre Royal. Haymarket, of course, not Drury Lane.

Yours,

Hewitt

He looked it over and smiled. The tepid, terse, almost disinterested missive hardly captured the emotions swirling inside him. Regardless, he sent it off to her. In person, he could impart how warm his feelings for her still were.

To his relief, she accepted. With excited anticipation, as if he were escorting her for the first time, he directed his carriage to the Diamond residence. Under her parents' gaze, he escorted her to his carriage, along with her ever-present maid.

"I never told you what we were going to see," Vincent said as soon as they were underway to the theater. "What if it is a play you have already attended?" He was suddenly thinking of her heading out for an evening with Redley. Perhaps at its conclusion, they kissed. She was an eager kisser, as he'd experienced.

"I have not been to many plays," Brilliance said. "The only one I have seen lately, a few weeks ago, was *Guy Mannering.* Is that what we're seeing tonight?"

He sighed with relief. "No."

"That's good," she agreed. "Although seeing it again with you would be different. In any case, as long as we are not seeing a tragedy by Mr. Shakespeare, I am sure I will enjoy it."

The devil take him! His relief drained from him, but all wasn't lost. "How about a comedy by Shakespeare?"

"Did he write any comedies?" Brilliance asked. "It seems everything of his I have seen had many bodies piling up on the stage by its end."

"Did you see *Hamlet*?" he asked.

She nodded. "I confess I had no idea what was happening during most of it. Regardless, the scene with the witches was very well played. I have also seen *King Lear*. I could not keep the characters straight in my mind, but they all seemed most treacherous."

"This play has no murders in it," he promised her. "It is called *Twelfth Night*."

"Like the Twelfthtide? I shall try to make sense of it then, but I'm afraid the tricky Elizabethan language often confuses me. If you don't mind my asking occasionally what is going on, then I will enjoy it immensely. And I love the intermission." She gave a small chuckle. "I could say the opening of the curtain and the intermission are my favorite two parts of a play."

Vincent wouldn't have interrupted her for a block of gold, waiting for whatever she would say next.

"The curtain, due to that moment of anticipation when something magical is about to happen," she explained. "And the second because everyone is always in such a good mood."

He could not deny she spoke the truth. "Perhaps that is because the audience members are stretching their legs after a long start to the play and also because they are finally allowed to enjoy a glass of wine."

Brilliance's laugh was contagious, and Vincent joined in. Even her maid smiled from the corner of the carriage.

Vincent felt like the luckiest man alive, escorting Lady Brilliance. As soon as she gave her black wool cloak to the coatroom manager, revealing a gown of silver satin beneath, every male eye turned to admire her figure.

His mouth going dry, Vincent swallowed with difficulty. As her gown glittered in the lamplight, she sparkled like a diamond, but he would bite his tongue off before saying anything so trite. Yet he could tell her the truth.

"I have never seen a lovelier lady in my life."

Instantly, her cheeks turned rosy, and a smile bowed her lips. With her blue eyes sparkling up at him, she said, "Thank you. I am better than a wedge of cheese, I guess."

"Indeed, my lady, you are. Tastier, too."

His words caused her blush to deepen, although Vincent knew she could not imagine how far beyond the taste of her lips his thoughts were leading him.

They went into the auditorium rather than lingering in the lobby. While he wanted to show her off, she wanted to get to their seats and read the playbill.

"Then I have a chance of understanding what I am about to see."

"I don't think you will have any difficulty," he said, taking her arm and leading her into box seats. Her maid took one of the two spare seats behind them. Once Brilliance was settled and perusing the program, he tapped it to get her attention.

"The play goes along like this: Viola, although disguised as a man, is in love with Orsino, who is in love with Olivia. But she is in love with Cesario, who is really Viola's male disguise."

Brilliance shook her head. "I shall be utterly lost about five minutes after the curtain rises," she said and closed the playbill. "I ought to have studied more when my mother sent me to school. Or at least tried to listen to my tutor instead of wool-gathering."

"What were you thinking about when you weren't being an attentive student?" he asked.

She grinned. "You will think me odd, perhaps. I was making up stories about people living up there." She pointed up.

"On the roof?" he asked.

That seemed to tickle her greatly for she began to chuckle. "No, not upon the roof of the Theatre Royal." She kept laughing. He adored her joyful nature. "My tutor had told me about the solar system. Don't look so surprised, my lord. I know a little—sometimes very little—about many things. Mostly trivial things. And so, when I was supposed to be listening but found myself bored, I would imagine people on the other planets, riding fish instead of horses or flying like birds rather than walking. Indeed, I thought up entire new civilizations."

"That sounds as important as anything your tutor was teaching, even Shakespeare."

She shrugged delicately. "When I grew tired of colonizing planets, then I imagined people living deep underground and how they might spend their days without sunlight."

Vincent was fascinated. "How did they?"

"How did they what?"

"Spend their days without sunlight?"

"Are you really interested?" she asked. When he nodded, she said, "I have never told anyone about my silly musings. I gave the underground dwellers strong lamps made out of worm oil, like sperm whale oil, but they were squeezing fat worms instead. Then I decided that, having never seen the sun, they wouldn't need lamps after all. They just existed in the darkness but with all their other senses working perfectly."

"Maybe they wouldn't even have eyes," he said, warming to the topic of creating new worlds.

Brilliance scrunched up her face. "That's distressing to think of, my lord." She glanced around, and he saw when something caught her eye. In fact, she gasped softly.

"They are here," she said. "Mr. and Mrs. Castern."

Vincent's good feelings evaporated, and he followed where she gazed. Sure enough, Ambrose and Lydia were in a box on the other side, obviously being hosted by a nobleman. He realized it was the Duke of Monmouth.

Vincent couldn't blame the old duke. After all, everyone celebrated Ambrose and had done so since he'd first burst onto the concert stage three years earlier. *Who didn't enjoy fine music and thereby want to fete the person who played it?*

"The sooner we go to court, Chancery not Buckingham Palace," Brilliance said, "the better. The last time I went to dinner, I was disbelieved while trying to explain that Mr. Castern was a plagiarist."

The hair stood up on the back of Vincent's neck. "Excuse me, my lady. What are you saying? Moreover, why am I only just hearing about this disturbing event?"

She shrugged. "Lord Redley escorted me to his aunt's home. She is Lady Danson, who, as it turns out, is a patron of Mr. Castern. I assume that means she gives him money, and he pretends to like her more than he likes other people."

"Just so," Vincent muttered. "Have I ever told you how clear-thinking you are?"

"No," she said. "Only that I am an immature adult and a dunderhead." Her words hung in the air between them, like cannon balls—heavy and dangerous.

"Before we say anything else, I want you to know I was out of my head. Hurt by what I thought was your betrayal, I was not thinking rationally." Vincent took her hand. "I know you to have an original mind, one which I admire and hold in the highest esteem. Your thoughts are precious and perfect. Will you forgive me? More than that, can you try to forget my vicious tirade?"

He thought she would take a minute to consider his apology. She didn't. Instead, she nodded instantly. "I will try to forget what you said. Even if I cannot, I won't keep a grudge, although I did for a while. And I forgive you because I have come to understand how I overstepped, albeit unintentionally."

"Thank you." He desperately wanted to kiss her. Perhaps she could raise her fan and he could duck behind it, but as he looked around, he saw her maid's brown eyes trained upon her mistress. *Perhaps not.*

"Regarding the dinner party, I am sorry you had to experience such unpleasantness. I know what it is like not to be believed."

Brilliance rested her gloved hand on his leg in sympathy, and he suddenly couldn't breathe, with sizzling heat radiating from where she touched him and beyond.

"It wasn't too bad," she assured him. "In the end, Mr. Castern and his wife left first, but seeing how people were not pleased at how I had called him a thief, I departed, too. I don't believe Lord Redley will be escorting me anywhere again."

She didn't sound unhappy about that, which was a relief. However, the incident could only have increased Ambrose's hostility toward Brilliance. He looked to where the wretch sat on the opposite side of the theater.

"Do you wish to leave?" Vincent asked.

"Not at all. If you don't mind, I would like to see the play."

He didn't mind in the least, sitting close beside this beautiful, unique woman who apparently was now loyally on his side. It was an uplifting feeling, knowing he was believed and trusted.

The Master of the Theater came out on the stage. Everyone applauded.

"You are in for a special treat tonight," he told the audience. "As you know, Miss Adelaide Biddles will be playing the part of Viola, and Mr. Henry Irving is our Orsino."

Enthusiastic applause broke out for two of London's favorite actors.

"Before the curtain rises, I wish to also welcome a special member of the audience this evening. The composer, Ambrose Castern, is with us, along with his lovely wife."

Again, the audience burst into applause. Vincent seethed quietly while both Ambrose and Lydia rose to their feet and waved at those in the cheaper seats below them, basking in the crowd's adoration.

Sickening! Especially Lydia, since he knew she was the one who had actually taken the pages from his home. If ever a woman deserved to be tarred and feathered, it was that treacherous laced mutton. He was almost ready to ruin Brilliance's evening and leave.

After a few moments, the two pretenders retook their seats.

Then, to his amazement, Brilliance rose to her feet beside him.

"EXCUSE ME," SHE CALLED out into the now hushed auditorium. Since the theater lights were still on, every head swiveled toward her voice. Brilliance could see when Mr. Castern and his wife realized who was speaking. His eyes bulged and Mrs. Castern's mouth opened in a large *O*.

Clearing her throat, she said, "I am Lady Brilliance, youngest daughter of Lord Diamond." She gave a friendly wave of her hand as a murmur went up.

Vincent made a choking sound, and then she felt his hand upon her own, tugging at her to regain her seat. She ignored him.

"That man, Mr. Castern is a good pianist to be sure. However, he is *not* a composer. Every note he plays was written by the gentleman beside me, Lord Hewitt."

There was a general gasp and then louder mutterings all around the theater.

"What is the meaning of this?" demanded the theater manager.

"Since I do not wish to leave and since Lord Hewitt has agreed to explain this play to me, I shall take my seat and you may continue. I simply would find it difficult to sit here all night after hearing such a misrepresentation of Mr. Castern. If he had any decency, he, too, would not wish to be represented as something he is not, but apparently, he has no such qualms. You may now begin."

She took her seat and glanced at Vincent. He was staring at her as if she had grown a third eye.

"You are—" he began.

Brilliance waited with trepidation, wondering what he might say.

"—Amazing," he finished at last. "Not only brave but downright fearless."

Meanwhile, the auditorium was still full of rumbling as people discussed her interruption. The theater manager stared up at her for a long moment. Perhaps he would try to throw her out.

Finally, with an awkward bow, he disappeared behind the curtain.

"Do you know the Duke of Monmouth?" she asked Vincent, while keeping an eye on the duke's box. The esteemed, older nobleman had his arms crossed and was eyeing his guests.

"Not personally," Vincent said. "He no longer serves in the House of Lords."

"His Grace has been in my home. I have dined with him at my father's table. I shall send him a letter tomorrow. He should know what kind of person he is hosting in his theater box."

The gaslights were dimmed, except for a few dotted here and there on the auditorium's outer edge, and the red velvet curtain parted in the middle, swaying open.

"I do not know how to thank you," Vincent said.

"That's simple," she told him. "You can explain to me what's happening."

Brilliance paused and wondered if she dared tell him what she really wanted. Then deciding to listen to her own counsel, she added, "And you may kiss me sometime before we part at the evening's end."

CHAPTER TWENTY-SIX

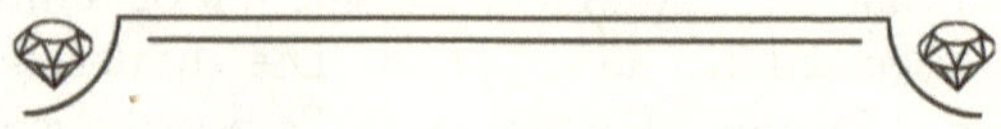

Because of her bold request, Brilliance had put herself on tenterhooks for the duration of the play. Would he kiss her during the play, in the back of their darkened theater box? *No.* Perhaps in the carriage on the way home with Belinda pretending to sleep in the corner? *No.*

Finally, they reached her house on Piccadilly.

"The play was good fun," she said as Vincent walked her to the door. "Even better for your answers to my questions." She'd hardly been confused at all as the characters changed costumes and went from male to female and back again.

"I am glad you enjoyed it." Vincent had barely spoken in the carriage. In truth, Brilliance wasn't sure what he was thinking.

"Belinda, you may go in. I shall join you in a minute," she told her maid.

As the door closed at her back, she looked up at him, silhouetted by the light of the newly installed gas lamps. "I was hoping . . ."

Vincent pressed her back against the solid door and fitted his mouth to hers. At the same time, the front of him crushed the front of her. It was heaven!

She reached up and grabbed hold of him, knowing it could only last a second or two. Or five. Seven long, perfect, heart-pounding seconds later, he bit down gently on her lower lip, tugging it as he pulled away.

"Mm," she said. "I missed that."

"I missed you. And your taste. And your softness. Luckily, I know for a fact no one can see us from inside the house when we are against the door. Your reputation is safe."

Knowing her parents hoped they would marry, she hadn't even worried about that.

"Thank you for your consideration over my reputation," she said. And if that was the case, then why not kiss again. She reached for him, but he hesitated.

"I hate to test fate."

She laughed. "That's exactly what I wish to do. By the way, are you my suitor again?"

"I have been a mulish arse. If you'll have me, then yes, I would very much like to court you again."

The door opened behind her, and she nearly fell on her rear end. Luckily, her father caught and steadied her.

"Good evening, Bri, Lord Hewitt. How was the play?" he asked.

"It was splendid. Even better, Lord Hewitt is now my beau."

She noticed Vincent took another step back, which made her chuckle. Her father was the least hostile man she knew. On the other hand, now that she thought about it, the Earl Diamond was ready to protect his family, particularly his daughters, from any and all threats. She simply had to remind him that Vincent was not a threat.

"We saw Mr. and Mrs. Castern at the theater," she told him.

"Your daughter stood up and told the entire audience that Castern is a fraud."

"That's my girl," Lord Diamond said. "I'll see you inside in a minute. Nice to see you again, Hewitt. We'll discuss the terms of the nuptials soon."

Then he disappeared back inside before Brilliance could even remark upon his hastiness. But when she looked up at Vincent, to her surprise, he didn't seem overly concerned at being rushed into a marriage agreement by an earl.

All but given permission from her father, she crooked her gloved finger, and Vincent stepped close again. Brilliance wrapped her hands behind his neck and held on when he kissed her a second time.

As his hands roamed across her body, she shivered.

"You're cold. What an idiot I am. The nights are growing frosty."

"That's not why I'm shivering. In fact, I'm perfectly warm in your embrace."

"Your father only gave us a minute."

"We've wasted half of it. Kiss me," she ordered.

And he did, a perfect, slow, toe-curling kiss that probably lasted longer than a minute. Brilliance's breasts were aching halfway through, wishing he could touch them, feeling that if he would only caress her nipple, that she would be in ecstasy.

And then it was over, leaving her light-headed with her body in a state of frustration and a persistent throbbing between her legs.

She hoped soon he would ask her to marry him as her father suggested.

"Good night, Lord Hewitt."

"Good night, Lady Brilliance."

And she went inside.

BRILLIANCE SPENT THE FOLLOWING morning writing letters, not only to the Duke of Monmouth, but to other noblemen who were friends of her family. It occurred to her that with court trials taking an exceedingly long time even to begin, that she could assist Vincent in spreading the word of Ambrose Castern's nefarious actions.

Then, expecting a visit from Vincent or at least his calling card being dropped off, when Mr. Dunley presented a card on his salver, she turned it over . . . and gasped.

"Is he here?"

"Yes, my lady, awaiting an audience."

"Is my father home?"

"No, my lady."

"My mother?"

"Again, no."

Brilliance hesitated. "Please send in Mr. Castern *and* Belinda, if you would be so kind."

"Yes, my lady."

Brilliance began wringing her hands with nervousness but managed to stop herself by putting them behind her back. Her fingers met over the top of her bell-shaped skirts.

Mr. Dunley returned, and with a flourish of his hand, he presented Mr. Castern, who was holding his hat in his hand. He bowed deferentially as soon as he saw her.

"Good day, Mr. Castern." Brilliance had already decided to be civil, but she would not offer him tea.

"Good day, my lady." He looked around at his surroundings with interest. "My, my, what a home you have."

"Thank you." She waited. Mr. Castern sighed, and a most put-upon expression came over his boyish face. Yet for a long moment, he still said nothing more.

"Will you sit?" she asked, still wondering how one treated a man in one's home who was neither a suitor nor even invited.

"How kind of you," he said. "And I would love a cup of tea, dear lady. I'm quite parched."

Dear lady! Hm. She glanced at Mr. Dunley who had awaited her next request. "Please bring in the tea service."

"Yes, my lady. Belinda will be in momentarily," he added. Then the loyal Diamond butler sent a sharp glance toward her unexpected visitor before departing while leaving the drawing-room door open.

"I cannot imagine living your existence," Mr. Castern said.

"Really?" Brilliance wondered. "Which part of it and why?" Intrigued, she took her favorite seat.

Surprisingly, he sat at the opposite end of the same sofa, so she had to turn to converse with him.

"My lady, I only mean it must be a different world when you are born to such wealth and luxury. You know only comfort, warmth, and a full stomach. Without a care."

"Whereas you are implying that you haven't known any of that, sir?"

"I didn't whilst growing up. I do now, of course. Regardless of what anyone has told you," he said, then paused meaningfully before continuing, "I have had to struggle and work hard all my life. Now, due to my musical talent, I have earned a comfortable home, and abundance of food, and—"

Belinda came in, and Brilliance, confounded by Mr. Castern's tale, waved her toward the other end of the room.

"Go on," she urged him.

"In short, I am *not* a monster," Ambrose Castern said emphatically. "I am a hard-working pianist who does not deserve this persistent harassment and cruel defamation."

"Defamation?" she mused. "You may not be a monster, sir, and I never said you were, but you are a plagiarist, are you not?"

He shook his head, looking disappointed. "Lady Brilliance, I know you have been influenced by Lord Hewitt, my long-time acquaintance. We were very close at one time."

"Before you stole his music."

Just then, when he looked as though he might become annoyed, a footman came in with the tea service.

"I shall pour," she told him and sent him away. After she'd handed Mr. Castern a full cup and saucer, she said, "You could hardly expect to remain close after what you did."

"My lady, we were as brothers. We worked alongside one another when in the dormitories of Harrow. And we attended Trinity together. After graduation, when he could spare the time from Parliament, at his townhouse here in London and even at his home in Joyden's Wood, we continued to share a passion for music."

He sipped the tea and added, "We never went to my mean, little house, for Hewitt lives like you, with all the ease of a titled, wealthy nobleman. If you can imagine the two of us humming, writing down notes, taking turns at the piano . . ." He shrugged. "I don't believe we knew in the end who wrote what or where *my* composition began and *his* ended."

"I see. You decided to take the music, since you were in the room when he'd composed it."

His eyebrows rose. "Not at all. Who is to say who composed which piece of music?"

"Surely, you and he are to say," Brilliance suggested.

Mr. Castern shook his head. "It's not that simple. We work differently. He keeps music in his head for far longer, whereas I write mine as I am composing. Ultimately, there is no way for *you* to know whether the notes on the sheets of paper were mine or his. But I tell you, they are mine."

"Are you saying Lord Hewitt transcribed *your* music, and thus, in fact, he plagiarized from you?"

"I ask you only to consider the possibility. Simply because I went forward with a career as a concert pianist and he did not, that is no reason to condemn me."

He calmly sipped his tea.

"I saw the handwritten work in his home recently," Brilliance told him, "and I gave it to a music publisher in London. And then suddenly, you were playing at your concert. There can be no doubt that you—"

"My lady, I wrote that piece years ago. When I recently discovered it in the music shop, I could only imagine that Hewitt had published it without the courtesy of using my name but also without the duplicity to use his own. And thus, overjoyed to find my own music, a piece I had forgotten about, I began to play it."

She stared at him, considering what he said. Mr. Castern leaned toward her from his end of the sofa.

"Do you not see how it makes sense? Why would I risk my thriving career?"

Brilliance shook her head. "Why would you?"

"Please, my lady, I have a wife to support, and I do so only by my concerts. If you continue this public attack, we shall lose everything. Neither she nor I have the security of coming from a wealthy family as you and Hewitt. My music is all I have, and you are trying to help Hewitt take it from me."

"I am trying to help Lord Hewitt regain *his* music."

Mr. Castern set his saucer down and rose to his feet. "It is mine I tell you," he declared, waving his arms around. Although he didn't come any closer, Brilliance shrank back, gripping her teacup.

"Why are you helping him?" he asked. "Are you in love with him?"

"I think you had better leave." She could not credit her own ears—a stranger was asking her such an impertinent question!

"You were in his home, you say, when you discovered the music. A nice young lady isn't usually in a gentleman's home. Perhaps you are actually paramours. Perhaps you have made up this entire story in order to help Vincent gain his revenge regarding Lydia."

"I asked you to leave," Brilliance repeated, raising her voice as she rose to her feet. She had no idea about Lydia, nor revenge, but it sounded like the ravings of a madman.

Mr. Dunley appeared and closely on his heels was Lord Hewitt.

"I heard the lady say she wanted you to leave," Vincent ground out. "You will do as she says, and swiftly, before I throw you out into the Piccadilly traffic."

"Look at you, Hewitt, behaving as if you own the place, as if you are her protector. It is quite obvious to everyone in London you are her lover."

"How dare you disparage this lady!" Vincent strode into the room until he was toe-to-toe with Mr. Castern.

Brilliance felt her cheeks warm. Belinda had come closer to offer support, and their absolutely proper and polite Mr. Dunley had heard the ugly accusation. Why, she could not imagine their butler ever taking his clothes off even to sleep. She was sure nothing like this had ever happened in her parents' drawing room before.

"This is your last chance to leave on your own two feet," Vincent threatened.

Mr. Castern sneered. "It seems your ladylove is determined to bestow upon you *my* fame. I warn you, Hewitt, if anyone asks me about your lady's accusations, I shall recommend they consider the source." He looked Brilliance up and down. "And her objectivity in the matter, or lack thereof. Lovers do not make for honest court witnesses."

"Don't they?" Brilliance asked, wondering why that might be so.

At the same time, Vincent grabbed Mr. Castern by the shoulder and, with the man trying and failing to break free, dragged him from the room.

She heard more shouting and then the front door slammed. A moment later, while tugging his sleeves down, Vincent reentered.

"Mr. Dunley would have removed him, my lord, and saved you the trouble."

"Indeed," said the butler. "It is my duty." Then he sighed as if deprived of some amusement. "Do you need me further, my lady?"

"You may take Mr. Castern's cup and saucer and bring a clean one for Mr. Hewitt."

"That won't be necessary, Dunley. I cannot stay for tea."

With the butler departed and Belinda back in her spot at the room's far end, Brilliance took her seat, expecting Vincent to sit beside her. Instead, he paced.

"You promised me you wouldn't meet with him."

"I did, didn't I?" she mused, but the odd circumstance of having Mr. Castern show up had proven too intriguing. "However, neither of my parents were home."

At Vincent's glowering look, she added, "But I had Belinda and Mr. Dunley. I was hardly alone."

Her betrothed swore, seemingly to himself, while looking at the ceiling, down at the floor, then finally at her. And then he took a seat.

"Castern might have threatened you."

"I believe he did, but what of it?" she asked. "As you can see, I am unharmed."

"And you shall remain that way. I don't want your name tarnished by his accusations, nor can I risk your safety."

"What are you saying?"

"I do not want you speaking out against him again," Vincent said.

She thought of the letters she had already sent out.

"And I think it unwise to have you come to court," he continued.

"But then it will be your word against his. Because he is already considered a great composer, you will undoubtedly lose."

He shrugged. "Your safety and good name are worth more than any piece of music."

"What if we were to become engaged so he couldn't suggest—"

She broke off when he started shaking his head.

"That would only make it worse. We would appear to be lovers before marriage. He will make sure his lawyer asks where you were in my home and who was with us."

"Oh!" Brilliance didn't think her parents would be too pleased about that. "Then what is the next step?"

"We must not see each other for a while, and you must stop accusing him of plagiarism at every turn."

"Are you giving in and letting Mr. Castern win?" she asked softly, feeling ill in the pit of her stomach. He could not possibly love her if he was willing to give her up so easily.

"I will go to court with a clerk from Boosey & Co. as my witness. Perhaps that will be enough."

She was almost afraid to ask. "And what about us?"

CHAPTER TWENTY-SEVEN

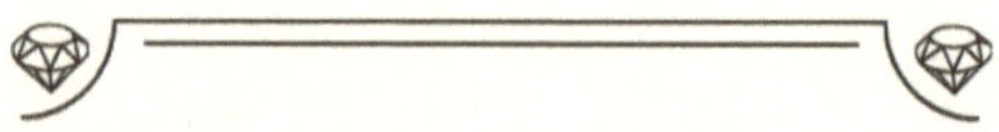

Vincent knew she was disappointed. He was, too. They were at the beginning, or the middle of the beginning, perhaps the second movement, of something extraordinary.

"As soon as the trial is over, we can resume our courtship. Let time and distance cause people to forget you are involved in this."

"That seems as though it may take quite a long time and too much distance for my liking," Brilliance said. "But I suppose you are not dreadfully bothered."

"You misunderstand me then." He crossed to her in three strides and took her in the circle of his arms. "I want you in my life more than ever. You have been my champion, and I am humbly grateful. But I cannot let my problem with Ambrose harm you in any way."

"What about his wife?"

Vincent swallowed. *Did she know about Lydia?*

"What about her?" he asked.

"He said if you take your music away, then they will be impoverished. Unlike us, they live upon his earnings."

Vincent made a face. "He's throwing the hatchet at you."

She frowned. "I beg your pardon."

"Pulling the longbow," he tried again.

Still, she looked perplexed.

"Brilliance, he is lying. He may not be titled, but his family is not impoverished. Moreover, he married into money. His wife had a large dowry as the only daughter in a family heavily invested in railroads and shipping."

She broke out into a lopsided smile. "I like hearing my name from your mouth."

His groin tightened.

"I'm sorry," she added. "I didn't hear anything after you said 'Brilliance.'"

She wasn't listening to him anymore, and he didn't care. Sick of the sound of his own voice, he drew her to him. Some part of his brain recalled that her maid was in the room. Another part, that the door was open.

Lowering his mouth to hers, he kissed her, hoping to impart how much he cared for her and how important she was to him. As their lips fused, he would vow his blood boiled in his veins and his heart began a vibrato beat. *How could he heat up so swiftly and his body be instantly aroused?* All from a rather innocent kiss.

Wishing they were alone so it could become less innocent, he raised his head, watching her delphinium-blue eyes flutter open.

"I don't want distance," she protested.

"Nor do I. But Ambrose will not go quietly. Now that he thinks there is something between us, he will tell each and every journalist that they should be questioning you and your morals. The best course of action is not to speak to any of them. Let me handle this."

He could see she was not happy.

"Why did you come here today?" she asked.

He had come to make sure she knew he wanted to court her properly. That he intended to be her sole and exclusive escort. Mostly, he didn't want her accepting any invitations from Lord Redley or his ilk.

But could he ask her to wait?

Dammit all! In point of fact, he was the one who could not wait. In that instant, he decided to drop the legal action altogether if it meant Ambrose would go away and he could be with Brilliance.

Looking into her eyes, his head filled with Brilliance's floral fragrance and her warmth under his hands, for he was still holding her, Vincent had an epiphany. With absolute clarity, he knew he wanted nothing more than for them to be joined in matrimony if she were willing. Every note he had played in his life had led to this moment, this *crescendo* of feeling.

Ready to drop to his knees and ask her for her hand, he would tell her to forget what he had just said. He would not give her up even for an instant.

"I came to tell you—"

"Bri, dear," her mother said, entering the room before he could step away from Brilliance, before he could even remove his hands from her.

The Countess Diamond gave him a long look, during which he took the opportunity to release her daughter and take a few steps back.

"I knew you were here," Lady Diamond said, "from Mr. Dunley."

"I came to ask Lady Brilliance to go to a ball at week's end, the one at the Earl and Countess Spencer's home. It is rumored that the Queen may honor them with her presence. It's a masquerade, by the way."

"But I thought you said . . ." Brilliance began.

"I was wrong. Why should we alter our lives because of that scoundrel?"

He didn't have to tell her he was going to immediately drop the charges of plagiarism. She would protest because of her kind heart. Instead, he would simply send word to Ambrose.

Brilliance seemed to glow. "I am so relieved. And I look forward to having you escort me at week's end."

Lady Diamond watched this entire exchange. "Mr. Dunley informed me that we had an earlier visit from Mr. Castern. Is there anything amiss?"

"Lord Hewitt was ever so impressive, Mother. Mr. Castern was in the process of becoming belligerent, and then Lord Hewitt arrived and tossed him out."

"Splendid," Lady Diamond said. "Is the tea still hot?"

VINCENT COLLECTED BRILLIANCE from her home. She appeared in the foyer dressed head-to-toe in gold fabric with a tall flourishing headpiece and shimmering golden ribbons woven through her dark hair. Over her eyes was a gold satin mask.

"I should have asked you in advance what your costume was for I nearly didn't recognize you." He was lying. He would know her anywhere, even with a linen sack over her head. "You are a flame, I assume."

"Oh, gracious!" She looked instantly despondent. "I *was* a flame until Mother said it was in poor taste, given the penchant for ladies' dresses catching fire. Father said there are almost three thousand deaths a year around the world. I cannot credit it, but if he says so, then it must be true. Therefore, I declare I am the Sun." Then she shook her head. "But everyone will think I am a flame. Will you wait, my lord?"

"Wait?" He didn't understand. "For what?"

"For me. Of course you will since you came to escort me. Give me five . . . no, truthfully *ten* minutes." Before he could answer, she hurried for the stairs, giving him a tantalizing view of her ankles and sweet gold slippers. On the landing, he heard her call out, "Mother!"

Mr. Dunley nodded to him, neither particularly friendly, nor unfriendly, and then he left for the interior of the house and his other duties. Vincent folded his arms and strolled the foyer, back and forth. He took a moment to examine his appearance in the front hall looking glass. Tightly curled white wig, borrowed from a barrister friend, black velvet knee-length coat with brass buttons down its front and across the wide sleeves, a white lawn shirt with a plain high neck, black knee-length breeches, white hose, and black shoes with gold buckles. *Perfectly ridiculous!*

Another door opened along the hall, and the earl appeared.

"Who are you?" he asked.

"I am Lord Hewitt, my lord," he said with a shallow bow. "Without my spectacles," he added, then wished he hadn't said anything so asinine.

"Are you? Good to see you." And Lord Diamond stuck out his hand for a firm shake. "Fancy dress, I see."

"Yes, my lord."

"I hate costumes. Always uncomfortable, but my wife loved attending a fancy-dress ball. Undoubtedly, we would be going tonight if Brilliance weren't. My countess wouldn't want to outshine our daughter."

Vincent didn't know how to respond, as he would surely insult either one or the other of the ladies. He merely smiled.

Lord Diamond laughed. "You are a smart chap, except for that wig which probably itches like the devil."

"It does," Vincent confessed. "And my shoes are pinching."

The earl laughed. "I bet they are. Where is Bri?"

"She went back upstairs to change."

"Then you have time for a glass of brandy. Maybe two." Lord Diamond turned and walked away.

Vincent trailed after him, soon finding himself ensconced in the man's study.

"Have a seat." The earl poured them each a glass and raised his in a toast. "To your health."

"If I cared about my health, my lord, I would remove this infernal scratchy wig and these overly tight shoes."

"But you love my daughter, so you will not only bear the pain but even dance in those shoes, thereby increasing it."

"Yes, my lord." A split second later, Vincent realized what he'd agreed to. "I mean . . ." He ended with a sigh.

"That's all right. I've been through this with three other chaps." The earl took a long draught of his liquid. "That is good stuff. French gold."

Vincent wasn't ready to leave the topic of the woman he loved. "I haven't told Lady Brilliance yet how I feel, but now that I know you know, I suppose I have your leave to declare my affection and ask for her hand."

"You do."

He wanted to say something reassuring so the earl would believe in his good intentions. "I was going to wait to speak with you after the legal matter was finished, but I have decided to drop the case."

"The devil you say!" Lord Diamond exclaimed. "Why would you do that?"

"Ambrose Castern threatened your daughter's reputation. I believe he will say anything to discredit her and throw doubt upon her testimony."

"Is that so?"

Vincent nodded. "I am sorry I even brought her into this mess."

"Brilliance is not the kind of person who lets herself be persuaded to do something she doesn't wish to do. She is all heart and little head," he mused. "I mean that in the best possible way. My youngest is a treasure. And she helped you because she believes in you."

Vincent felt his heart twinge. He wasn't even worthy of her. He had hurt her when she'd given him the gift of his music printed by the finest publisher in London. And now she might be hurt again unless he made Ambrose stop his threats.

"I have already sent Castern a message that I am not going to sue him."

"Then my daughter is in good hands and has let her heart lead her to the right man. But if you hurt her," the earl said calmly, not raising his voice, "I will destroy you."

Vincent almost missed it. When he realized the import of the nobleman's words, he looked directly into Lord Diamond's eyes.

"I understand, and you need not worry about that, my lord."

"Good. She should be ready soon. I hope you have an amusing evening."

Realizing he had been dismissed, Vincent drained his glass and took his leave of Brilliance's father.

In short order, Brilliance appeared at the top of the stairs wearing purple and gold silk pantaloons with a matching tunic and turban.

"Wearing one of my mother's old costumes," she said, "so I shall not offend anyone."

Vincent thought her a colorful jewel. "You are a Persian lady, is that right?"

"Yes." She clapped her hands. "My costume must be spot on for you to guess on the first try. I didn't want to be one of those ancient queens or historical people because one can never tell who they are." Then she looked him up and down and frowned.

"I confess," he said, "I *am* one of those historical people. Would you care to speculate upon my identity?"

He turned in a circle.

"I have no idea," Brilliance said solemnly. "Someone from the seventeenth century, I would warrant."

"Indeed, you are correct. In my carriage, I have some sheet music with my character's name written largely across it at one end and the name of one of his pieces. 'Canon triplex a 6 vocibus' written on the other end." He stuck out one leg and, with a wave of his hand, gave an exaggerated bow. "I am Johann Sebastian Bach, dressed as he was famously painted in a portrait by Elias Gottlob Haussmann in 1746."

"Bravo, my lord. But I fear you may have to display that sheet music more than once lest everyone assumes by your wig that you are a barrister ready to plead your case before the Lord Chancellor."

Vincent laughed. "Either way, we shall have a good time. Is your maid ready for the carriage ride?"

"Belinda," she called out, and the maid appeared, as all good staff did—instantly, silently, and ready to leave. She was even holding her lady's black mantle, which she draped over Brilliance's shoulders.

They departed in his carriage for the spectacle at Spencer House on St James's Place. Brilliance looked so relaxed and happy, matching his own inner peace now that Lord Diamond had granted his blessing. Vincent thought if there was an opportune moment when they could be alone that evening, he would ask her to marry him.

CHAPTER TWENTY-EIGHT

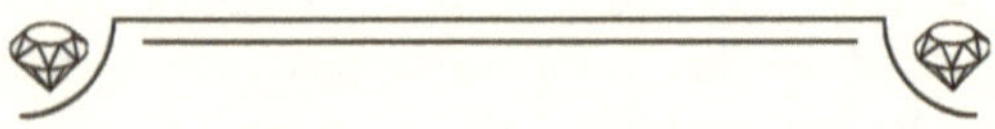

Brilliance was glad she'd changed, if for no other reason than that pantaloons were the most daring and liberating thing she had ever worn. Why, they practically showed the shape of her legs as the silk clung to her, brushed her skin, and moved as she did.

In Vincent's carriage, she even crossed her legs and sat back comfortably, hiding her posture under her thick wool cloak. When they arrived, the area of St. James's Street was congested with carriages of guests heading for the masquerade.

"Shall we walk?" Brilliance offered. Thus, they departed their warm conveyance to stroll the final yards down St. James's Place to the classically inspired home of the Spencer family.

She was free to match her escort's stride as they approached the arches of the ground-floor façade, with her maid trailing behind. Given the time of year, it was unlikely they would get to enjoy the terrace that overlooked Green Park on the building's other side. Yet knowing the luxurious interior that awaited, Brilliance didn't mind.

Upon entering under the arched doorway and through the large paned door, they left Belinda with the other maids in one of the downstairs rooms set aside for them and deposited their coats in another. Brilliance appreciated the chairs lining two walls as she took a vacant seat beside another young lady and changed from her outdoor boots to her purple satin slippers.

"Isn't this one of the most magnificent houses in London?" she remarked when they finally entered the Palm Room, through which all the guests were filtered in order that they could *ooh* and *ahh*. Carved and painted symbols of fertility and prosperity were everywhere, with gild palm leaves rounding the columns and adorning the walls. A domed ceiling and half-vaulted alcoves were also gilded, and the uppermost frieze seemed to be moving with golden griffins, the Spencer family's heraldic supporter. *In a word, breathtaking!*

"I am surprised your family doesn't have a mansion like this," Vincent said.

Brilliance considered. "I do not know about my great-grandfather, but I know my grandfather and my own dear papa have no wish to be burdened with the upkeep. Both prefer to put their time and money into their country properties. Regardless, this is my third time inside Lord and Lady Spencer's splendid home, and I feel as thrilled as the first. In my opinion, the gilding and the carvings are unrivaled."

"You do seem sparkish tonight," he remarked as they joined other guests moving toward the stone cantilever staircase, "and we haven't even reached the ballroom."

Brilliance shuffled her feet on the white Italian marble. "I cannot wait to try dancing in this costume."

"I dread dancing in these shoes," Vincent confessed, as they climbed the stairs under the vaulted ceiling beside white flattened ionic pilasters festooned with white plaster garlands.

His words only made her smile more broadly. "If Herr Bach could wear them his entire adult life, then you can manage for a single evening."

"His probably fit him," Vincent grumbled.

Since they were a little late, the musicians had already begun to play. On Vincent's arm, Brilliance entered the largest of the home's rooms, the Great Room, heavily scented with the guests' perfume and the usual aroma of tobacco.

Crowded with masked and costumed revelers in a constant state of movement, it was impossible to stop and properly admire the red damask wallpaper framed in gilding or even to look up at the three impressive domes making up the ceiling, all of them in green, white, and gold.

Instead, Brilliance managed the barest glance at her environment. Naturally, chandeliers were dripping with crystals, but due to the mystique of the masquerade, only half the candles were lit in each, and the edges of the room were dim except for an occasional sconce. She shivered with excitement.

Vincent tugged her arm so they could make their way around the perimeter. Her gaze landed on females in all manner of fancy dress, from the mundane to the scandalous, seeming risqué as they moved from flickering candle light to the shadows.

"I do not much care for the idea of seeing other women close to you, staring up adoringly, and leaning on you."

"I shall endeavor to keep all my dance partners at arm's distance," Vincent said, surveying the crowd, "if you promise to do the same."

She nodded. Being there with him was the best night of her life so far, although she could imagine even better ones in the future. If she were to become his wife, they would retire to the same bed. Another shiver ran down her spine. Perhaps even as his fiancée, she could experience the mysteries between a man and a woman.

After all, she wasn't entirely ignorant as to what was to come. As the youngest of five siblings, she'd heard her share of romantic, even passionate stories, as one by one her sisters fell in love.

Moreover, her parents had eloped to Gretna Green at Christmas. And while her knowledge of geography wasn't extensive, Brilliance knew that one could not get to Scotland without a few nights spent sleeping at inns. Therefore, they must have had relations, intimate ones at that, before they ever reached the blacksmith's shop.

She could almost shock herself if she thought too much about it. And then, she spotted Martine and her mother. They were precisely where they had arranged to meet—to the left of the large gilded mirror between the first set of windows overlooking the park.

Her friend was dressed as an Elizabethan princess, Brilliance guessed, by the width of Martine's gown and the number of pearls on her stomacher. Her mother, Lady Flowers, who was also dressed as though from the Tudor period, was to be both young ladies' chaperone for the night.

Sharing a mother was Brilliance's favorite type of chaperone, especially someone else's mother who wouldn't truly pay attention to her comings and goings.

After cordial greetings—although Martine's was less-than-enthusiastic when it came to Lord Hewitt—the musicians signaled the next dance was about to begin. Vincent took her hand.

"Come along, Lady Persia, let us dance." And he led her into the throng.

"Am I incorrect in thinking Lady Martine was cool toward me?" Vincent asked as they got into position with the other dancers.

Brilliance hated to admit the truth but did so, anyway. "She has nothing against you, my lord. She is only concerned for me. I have told her about Mr. Castern's perfidy, but Martine is not convinced. And she hopes I am not being led to Fiddlestick's end."

She felt him tense. "I assure you that is not the case."

"I know." Brilliance squeezed his arm, and then the dance began.

Trying not to miss a step, her head was on a swivel, admiring all the ladies' costumes. Spotting a goodly number of milkmaids and two Queen Cleopatras, she wondered what Queen Victoria would dress as should she actually come. And then she took in the men.

"You are the only Bach here, I believe," she told Vincent.

"You are probably correct, although I have seen some other powdered wigs."

"They might be anyone," she said. "I certainly cannot tell." Then she gasped softly. "My apologies, my lord. That was thoughtless of me."

"Lady Brilliance, I honestly do not care about the quality or authenticity of my costume." He gave her a good-humored shrug. "If people think me a barrister or the King of France, it is no matter. I came tonight only to be with you and to make sure you have a pleasant evening."

For some reason, that struck her as the sweetest thing anyone had ever said.

"You have nearly brought me to tears," she told him. And then she saw a familiar face, dressed as a hornet, which snapped her out of her maudlin emotion.

"Is that Lady Georgiana?" She inclined her head in the hornet's direction.

Vincent looked to where she indicated. "I believe so. She ought to be careful. Her true waspish disposition is showing."

Brilliance chuckled. "Then perhaps Ambrose Castern is here dressed as a highwayman."

When Vincent sobered, she wished she hadn't teased. In truth, Mr. Castern might be there, and if he was, she would not call him out as she had before. Holding her tongue would be extremely difficult but prudent, nonetheless.

They danced two dances in a row, and no one noticed or cared, not even Lady Flowers. They each found another partner for the next dance, then returned to dance again.

After the fourth dance, Brilliance was breathless. "I am thirsty, Herr Bach. Can we seek out the refreshment room?"

"Certainly." He tucked her hand under his, while she waved to Lady Flowers yards away in the loud room and mimed drinking.

Receiving a nod of acknowledgment from Martine's mother, Brilliance let him lead her through to the next room. It was smaller, rounded at one end with more pillars, decorated with green and gold wallpaper and covered in classical people, Hera, Athena, and Aphrodite, as well all sorts of objects she knew to be ancient vessels and such.

"A room dedicated to love," she said, looking at the many cupids and the main painting of Venus. Pointing to it, Brilliance told him, "That is reportedly the first Lady Spencer's visage."

"You are prettier," Vincent said.

Her cheeks warmed. "And I am currently thirstier. If I am not mistaken, this is not the right room."

Making their way through the giddy crowd of revelers toward the next chamber, she noticed one thing.

"Don't you think everyone is a little more rambunctious than at a regular gathering?"

"Indeed, you are correct. A costume or a mask gives people leave for their wilder nature to roam freely."

She saw a man dressed as a pirate pulling a winged fairy by both hands. The female was laughing loudly while being drawn toward a darkened alcove. Another couple were dancing a slow waltz in a corner rather than on the dance floor in the Great Room.

"People who are not being themselves is a little frightening," she conceded, "yet also strangely refreshing. The freedom is exhilarating, too. Like my pantalettes."

"Freedom is like your pantalettes?" he asked before sending her a broad grin.

She laughed. "You are so easy to be with. A far cry from the straight-backed pianist who spilled the cherries across your cousin's rug."

Vincent was clearly trying not to laugh, but it burst from him.

"What a peevish, sour, hulver-headed churl I was. And you have fixed me." They found a sumptuous spread of beverages and tasty treats in the blue and gold room that came next. After eating cheese tartlets, small puffs of prawn-filled pastries, and crackers, some topped with minced ham and others with smoked cod, they took a glass of champagne each and left the room.

They went away from the noise, the crowds, and the music along another wing of the house. He took her down the passageway, past one door, and then the next. At last, he grabbed a handle and pushed a door open.

"Blast!" he exclaimed into the pitch blackness and closed it. Still holding her hand, he went farther along to the next door and opened it. "Ah-ha," he said. "In here, Lady Persia."

There was a lamp lit, and a piano, too. Somehow, he had found the conservatory.

"What are we doing?" Brilliance asked.

Instead of a stool, there was a bench, and he tugged her down onto it beside him before setting his empty glass on the floor. The length of their thighs pressed against one another's. She could feel the heat of him through the thin silken fabric of her costume, making her pulse speed up with a delightful pitter-patter of expectation.

Without speaking, Vincent began to play. Brilliance fell silent as the music worked its way inside her soul, expanding within her, filling her with emotions that weren't always comfortable. Intense joy turned to heartbreaking melancholy and back again. Vincent played for, she estimated, about fifteen minutes before he stopped. The last notes were a complex arrangement, making her feel alternately happy and sad before trailing off with a whimsically thoughtful ending.

"I've been working on 'Essence of Brilliance.' I cannot seem to finish it, however. I know the longer we are together, the more I shall wish to add to it and change it because I keep learning more about you."

He put his hand to her chin, tilting her face up and holding her still.

"Lady Brilliance Diamond, will you do me the honor of becoming my wife?"

Brilliance began to cry. She didn't know how the depth of utter happiness snuck up on her or why it brought her to tears instead of laughter.

When he kissed her, she tasted her salty tears along with the champagne and then with relief, she began to laugh.

Unable to keep kissing her, Vincent rested his forehead upon hers as she continued to chuckle.

"I didn't expect either reaction, but I should have. After all, you are the most unusual, unpredictable, changeable female I have ever known. And you haven't given me an answer."

"Oh, Vincent, I thought my answer was obvious."

"I would not presume anything with you."

She smiled. "Very well. I am honored to become your wife. We shall have a happy marriage and lots of babies. And you can compose music all day when you're not in Parliament, or when we're in the country. I'll keep our children away while you do, and then you can play for us each evening."

He started to laugh. "That sounds as though our marriage is all about me. What will you do besides birthing an entire audience of offspring for me?"

Brilliance wished she could think of something spectacular to tell him. Yet she couldn't. Shrugging, she said, "I hope you won't quickly tire of a wife who has no particular skill and cannot sketch or paint or play music." She bit her lip. "Sometime, I shall show you what happens when I try to knit or do needlepoint."

"I don't care about any of that. I just want you to be happy and not bored. Maybe you will take to gardening or wood-carving. Who knows?"

Wood-carving!

"Kiss me again, and this time, I shall neither cry nor laugh."

She set her glass down on the piano, which he promptly retrieved and set on the floor. And while she slid her hands up behind his neck, he put his hands on her back and pulled her close.

Brilliance would vow for the rest of her life that their kiss caused sparks on her lips. She swore they sizzled under his. And the heat of his touch as he caressed her through her layers of silk scorched a trail up and down her back until his hands came around the front of her. Slipping under her tunic, his palms fit perfectly over her breasts.

She moaned softly at his welcome touch.

At the sound, Vincent's tongue sought access, and she parted her lips to grant it. As his tongue stroked hers, an insistent throbbing began between her legs, even as she pushed her breasts more firmly into his grasp. When he sucked on her tongue, her womanly core seemed to melt.

Gasping against his mouth, she quivered, and her fingers tightened in his hair.

"I want . . . I want . . ." She couldn't put into words the swirling sensations making her body tremble. "I am beyond frustrated," Brilliance whispered against his mouth.

"I know. Believe me, I know."

"What can be done?" she asked.

And then his thumbs flicked her nipples, and she drew in a desperate breath.

"That's a start," she said, her tongue feeling dry. "Continue."

He did as requested. Under his ministrations, she could scarcely breathe, nor could she credit how sensitive her skin had become, able to feel the silk sliding over it. As her nipples puckered, she squirmed on the hard bench. "I fear I need something more."

"When we're married," he began.

She groaned. "I cannot live in this state of unbearable dissatisfaction until then. I am actually aching."

"It will fade," he promised, "if I stop touching you." And he drew his large warm palms out from under her tunic.

"That makes it worse. My body wants you not only to keep touching me but to put your fingers elsewhere."

"Dear Brilliance, if I could, I would, but we have been away from the ball for a long time. Besides, anyone who looks at you will know you've been kissed to distraction."

He rose to his feet and did a strange movement, swiveling his hips slightly before shifting from one foot to the other.

"I have some discomfort myself," he confessed.

"Is it your shoes?" she asked.

Vincent grinned ruefully. "No. The part of me that most wants to connect with a certain part of you has awakened quite fiercely." He did another swiveling motion. "A man's arousal is harder to hide."

She looked from his handsome face to his . . . tented breeches, and understanding dawned.

"*Oh!*" Brilliance felt her cheeks heat.

"On your feet, my fiancée," he ordered, handing over her glass that still had some champagne. "Let us toast to our engagement."

Brilliance could not help sighing. "That is a pretty word. French, I believe."

He nodded. They each took a sip from the same glass, and then he set it aside.

"We really must return to the ballroom. Lady Flowers and Lady Martine may be looking for you."

"I do hate to worry them, but I need to stop in the ladies' retiring room first and make sure I am tidy."

Again, her cheeks bloomed with color even discussing such a thing. It was easier to kiss Vincent and let him touch her intimately than to talk about the retiring room where there were facilities for passing water. However, he didn't seem the least bothered.

In two minutes, they parted at the doorway where maids were on hand to assist with anything the female guest needed, even if it was simply making sure her clothing wasn't in disarray.

While Brilliance studied herself in the looking glass to see if Vincent was correct about appearing to have been kissed, Mrs. Castern came in. Their eyes met in the mirror, and the woman walked directly toward her.

"That is a pretty costume," she said.

Brilliance turned and took in her appearance. "Thank you. And you look to be a perfect shepherdess."

"It is an amusing costume," Mrs. Castern said. "We both have the pantalettes."

"Yes," Brilliance agreed. "I love them." She nearly asked the woman if her husband had, in fact, come as a footpad.

"And what is Vincent this evening?" Mrs. Castern asked, touching a hand to her snowy, white cap while she peered at her own reflection.

Vincent? Brilliance examined the woman's face. *Was she being intentionally forward, or had his name slipped out from their earlier association?*

"Lord Hewitt came as Johann Sebastian Bach."

Mrs. Castern laughed. "Unsurprising. He always had an admiration for Bach, almost as much as he had for Handel."

"It sounds as though you were friends," Brilliance guessed. "Was that through your marriage to Mr. Castern?"

The woman stared for a moment of silence. "Didn't Vincent tell you?"

Mrs. Castern had done it again, and plainly on purpose, too.

"Tell me what?" Brilliance asked, ignoring her impudence.

"That he and I were engaged before I married Ambrose."

Brilliance didn't care for the odd swooping sensation in her stomach, nor how the floor seemed to slant. It was unpleasant, as if she were falling from a great height. She didn't want to lie and say she knew, although she ought to have known.

However, she was suddenly struck by the unsettling notion that she had agreed to marry a man whom she knew little about. And she had done so based on her instincts and her emotions.

Not to mention the way he made her sizzle.

Taking a deep breath, Brilliance gave Mrs. Castern the upper hand. "He did not."

CHAPTER TWENTY-NINE

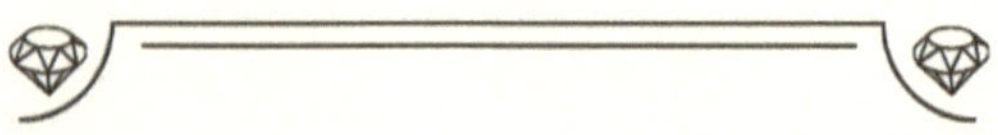

While not intending to be a shrew, Brilliance added the only reason she could come up with. "I guess Lord Hewitt didn't think it was important enough to mention."

Mrs. Castern's lips flattened into a tight line. She even lifted her head and looked down her nose as if insulted, although Brilliance couldn't figure out why a married woman would care whether a man who wasn't her husband spoke of her. Sometimes, people were so befuddling.

Still, Brilliance wished Vincent had mentioned having asked someone else to marry him. It slightly diminished the polish of their engagement. Again, perhaps that's why he hadn't told her, not wishing to dim the sparkle of their own betrothal.

Mrs. Castern gave a small shrug. "I suppose he would keep it from you since it is the sole reason he has been persecuting Ambrose. He probably wanted you to continue to think it was due to plagiarism."

"I do not understand what you mean," Brilliance said. "Mr. Castern stole Lord Hewitt's music, and that is why his lordship filed a lawsuit."

Mrs. Castern shook her head and smiled. It wasn't a particularly cheerful type of smile, either. Brilliance wished she would stop, in fact, as it was making her skin prickle.

A distinctly uncomfortable feeling.

"Vincent didn't write any of that music. Has he told you about his perfect pitch? His gift that he calls a curse?"

Brilliance nodded, wishing this particular shepherdess didn't know so much about him.

Mrs. Castern continued, "And you may have already discovered for yourself what a fabulous memory he has."

"He does," Brilliance agreed, having wondered how he could keep so many sonatas in his head. He also had remembered the names of all Lady Twitchard's guests after that first assembly.

"Thus, he can play anyone's music if he has heard it a few times. He can even write it down due to his powerful recollection." Mrs. Castern fluffed the lace at the sleeves of her costume while keenly watching for Brilliance's reaction.

"You think Lord Hewitt remembered your husband's music and wrote it down years later. Is that what you're saying?"

"I don't know when Vincent set the music to paper. But copying Ambrose's music does not make it Vincent's."

Brilliance didn't know what to say. She had enough sense and decorum not to come out and tell the woman she thought her to be a liar despite that being precisely what she believed.

"I guess the truth will come out in court," Brilliance said and made to go around her.

Against all civility, Mrs. Castern stuck out her hand and grabbed hold of Brilliance's arm, puckering the delicate silk under her fingers.

"It sounds as though Vincent also hasn't told you that he has retracted any claims to my husband's music. He sent a letter to my husband declaring he is no longer pursuing the matter in court."

Brilliance managed not to gasp aloud, but she did feel every muscle in her body tense right up to her jaw tightening, making her clench her teeth. *How dare he!* He said he had another witness who would suffice.

Wrenching her arm away, she rounded upon her tormentor. "Why would he invent all this?" Brilliance demanded. "Why would he lie?"

"I am afraid that is my fault. When I was Vincent's betrothed three years ago, I was lucky enough to listen to both men composing. They were the greatest of friends, and together, we would often spend an evening at Mirabel Manor or at his home here in London. Hours would go by with them calling out suggestions and each taking turns at the piano, sometimes playing a duet. Eventually, Ambrose and I were unable to fight the love we felt for one another despite not wanting to hurt Vincent. Alas, it was inevitable."

She sniffed as if recalling a painful memory. "After I married his friend, Vincent became inconsolable, refusing to speak to Ambrose ever again. I'm afraid his jealousy at losing me got the better of him. He stopped playing and then, it seems, he came up with the lunatic idea that my husband stole his music."

Mrs. Castern shook her head sadly. "I think Vincent is not really angry about stolen music. He is livid because he thinks Ambrose stole me."

Unable to think of anything she could possibly say in the face of this woman's confession and accusation, Brilliance simply turned and left. As she made her way back to the Spencer's Great Room, she realized, to her dismay, that she was shaking.

"Blast," she muttered, knowing it was unladylike to swear. From how happy she'd felt only minutes ago to her current disposition, she was practically a different person entirely. A cloak of anger threaded with doubt had settled over her, and the intensely unfamiliar sentiment was sickening. On the night of her engagement, she ought to be nothing but glad.

Peering around the open doorway into the ballroom, she spied Martine and her mother. Vincent stood near them, watching for her. Their gazes locked instantly. Brilliance was of two minds—confront him now in mixed company or wait until they were in the carriage with Belinda.

Her wobbly legs carried her forward.

"Were you engaged to Mrs. Castern?" Brilliance asked him without preamble.

His dark eyebrows slanted as he frowned. Then he sighed. "I was."

"You ought to have told me."

"Perhaps," he conceded with a shrug.

"Perhaps," she repeated softly. "And did you halt your lawsuit against Mr. Castern?"

Vincent folded his arms, glowering down at her the way he had during his cousin's house party. That seemed an eon ago, and suddenly, Brilliance felt older than her years.

Everything seemed murky and gray where before it had been all bright and shiny. She was his fiancée, a fancy French word that had just lost its sheen.

Shouldn't he have told her everything?

At that moment, Brilliance wished more than anything to go home. "Lady Flowers, how much longer do you think you will remain here?"

The woman's eyes lit up. "I am ready to leave, merely waiting for you two girls to have danced your fill."

"I have," Brilliance said, sending Martine a pleading look, hoping her friend would humor her.

"I have, too," Martine agreed.

With relief, Brilliance took hold of Martine's arm. "Then I hope it is all right if I accompany you two in your carriage. If there is room for me and my maid?"

Lady Flowers looked toward Vincent with open curiosity, especially as he appeared about to protest.

"Of course we will take you," she said.

"I hope you don't mind," Brilliance told him, deciding not to ask nor to give room for him to convince her, "but I intend to go with them."

As expected, he gave her a gentlemanly inclination of his head. This was, after all, not the time for another lengthy discussion.

"In that case," he asked, "may I call upon you tomorrow?"

She didn't hesitate, for she knew after spending the night with her own topsy-turvy thoughts, she would be ready to speak with him again by then.

"You may."

BRILLIANCE HAD BEEN WRONG. She didn't want to see Vincent the following day. She'd spent a sleepless night and got up quite out of sorts. To avoid him, and feeling like a coward, she left early and went to Clarity's home on Grosvenor Square, where she resided happily with her husband of eight years, Lord Hollidge.

"I am sorry to come uninvited," Brilliance said. With her eldest sister being round from her latest pregnancy, it was difficult to get close, but they managed a hug, arms outstretched.

Having almost gone to Martine's home, Brilliance had feared it was too early to impose a visit upon anyone who was not family. In the carriage the night before, she had avoided telling her friend anything about why she was upset in front of Lady Flowers. Besides, knowing Martine wasn't entirely pleased with Vincent's behavior since first they'd met, Brilliance had thought it ill-advised to add fuel to that particular fire. Instead, they'd amused themselves discussing the fancy dress costumes they had seen and speculated whether the Queen had been in attendance undetected.

But today, she wanted desperately to unburden herself. Clarity, who was experienced, understanding, capable of making just about anyone feel better, seemed the best choice with whom to do so.

"You never need wait for an invitation," her eldest sister reminded her. "We Diamonds don't stand on ceremony." In fact, Clarity appeared delighted to see her. "Your visit is a good excuse for a trip to Gunter's."

Brilliance shook her head at the notion. "It's a little early in the day for ice cream, but we could take tea there. Although, I am not sure they open for anything on their menu until ten. Besides, Gunter's is dreadfully drafty this late in the year."

Clarity laughed. "I lost track of the hour and apparently the month, too. You are out and about early. Let's go have a cup of warming chocolate instead."

Just then, the drawing-room door opened and Alice Diamond entered, their clever sister-in-law. Brilliance jumped up again, then turned to Clarity who was struggling to rise.

"No, no, don't get up," Adam's wife said. "I didn't know we would be three, but the more the merrier."

"Indeed," Clarity said. "Is it Thursday again already?"

"Yes," Brilliance and Alice answered together.

Clarity suddenly appeared tearful. "I vow by this time during each pregnancy that I am so forgetful I dare not go out, lest I lose my way home."

Big, fat tears slid down her face, and she yanked a handkerchief out of her thick woolen sleeve. "I am lucky my husband dotes on me when I am a blubbering bundle, more sentiment than sense." She dabbed at her cheeks and eyes before blowing her nose loudly.

Brilliance exchanged a concerned look with Alice, who shrugged.

"Please don't cry," Brilliance told her sister. To see her thusly was an unusual, and unsettling occurrence, except during her other three pregnancies.

"But I forgot the season and thought we could go to Gunter's, and then I forgot it was Thursday and that my own dear sister-in-law was coming at any minute. What a ninny!"

"You are not," Alice protested. "Everything is fine, isn't it? The three of us can as easily have a nice visit as the two of us." Then her eyes widened. "Unless Bri had something private to discuss, only between sisters."

Brilliance knew the right answer. "Then everything would still be satisfactory as you are our sister, too. Hot chocolate for three." She gave the bell-pull a tug. "In fact, *I* am the intruder as I came over without asking Clarity first."

By this time, her eldest sister had dried her eyes and looked more herself.

"Alice and I meet most every week to discuss our lives—mostly our husbands and our children. It is most beneficial to keeping me out of Bedlam."

Brilliance didn't know this. "What about Purity and Ray?"

Clarity tilted her head. "Sometimes Purity drops by, too, but she thinks it impolite to bring up our brother in his absence, so that doesn't help Alice. On the whole, our sister frowns upon gossip, even though I try to explain I am not gossiping about my own dear Alex, just mildly venting. Besides, we often don't talk about the gentlemen at all."

Brilliance nodded and then blurted, "I became engaged last night." And then, like Clarity, she burst into tears.

Alice was the first to reach her while Clarity was rolling back and forth trying to rise to her feet.

"No, don't move," Brilliance said, already wiping her face as Alice sat beside her and draped her arm along her shoulders.

"Why is your engagement making you cry?" her sister-in-law asked.

"And to whom have you betrothed yourself?" Clarity asked. Then she raised a hand to each of her rounded cheeks. "Should I know who it is and have forgotten along with every other sensible thought in my head?"

"No, I don't think you will know him. My betrothed is Lord Hewitt." *Vincent*, she nearly added, as his beloved face seemed to come before her eyes.

"He is a member of Parliament, isn't he?" Alice remarked.

"Yes." Briefly explaining how she met him, Brilliance told them everything up to the dreadful meeting with Mrs. Lydia Castern. By that time, they were on their second cup of chocolate and also munching on biscuits, although Clarity ate more than her share.

"Then, you have not yet heard what Lord Hewitt has to say in response?" Alice asked.

Brilliance shook her head.

"Is that poor man waiting for you at our home?" Clarity asked, still referring so fondly to the residence she grew up in that it made Brilliance smile at her sister.

"Maybe he is. I don't know." What's more, she wouldn't classify him as a "poor man," not feeling particularly generous toward him at that moment. He might be a liar and a scoundrel for all she knew.

"If he isn't there now, most certainly he soon shall be," Clarity persisted. "If he cared enough last night to want to marry you, then he will be concerned today to find out your state of mind. Purity would say it is terribly discourteous to give Lord Hewitt permission to call upon you only to fail to keep the appointment."

Then she shrugged and picked up another sweet lemon biscuit. "However, I would *not* agree with our dear sister. He kept the truth from you more than once, and he may have lied about Mr. Castern, whom I have enjoyed in concert." Then she munched on the sweet treat before adding, "Thus you are forgiven for being a little discourteous toward him. I am sure you are bewildered."

Alice had remained silently listening, but now she spoke, "I had a tangled beginning with your brother, filled with untruths. But nothing that I kept from him was done to hurt him, only to protect him, as well as myself."

Brilliance knew Alice's story of deceit, pretending to be a governess to avoid her deceased husband's brother. "I believe you were dealing with a threatening situation but managed to fall in love with our brother, anyway. But what if Lord Hewitt is only dealing with vengeance over losing Mrs. Castern?"

"You are a good judge of character," Clarity said. "Don't you trust yourself to know the person with whom you fell in love?"

Brilliance startled at hearing her sister say it out loud. "I thought I did."

"If he didn't write the music, would you still love him?" Alice asked.

"Of course. It makes no difference to me whether he composes or not as long as I know the truth." She clamped a hand to her mouth as she recalled hearing the "Essence of Brilliance" when it was a rougher piece and then again last night. "I do know the truth. He wrote all that music. He is an astonishing composer."

Alice smiled. "And would you have wished for him to bring up a prior betrothal while you were still falling in love, or worse, on the same evening as your engagement?"

"No, but in all the discussions we've had about Mr. and Mrs. Castern, he ought to have confessed to once having feelings for her."

"Men, even your dear brother, need some polishing and a little training when it comes to what we women want to know," Alice said. "Wouldn't you agree, Clarity?"

But Brilliance's sister's mouth was full of another cookie, and all she could do was nod.

CHAPTER THIRTY

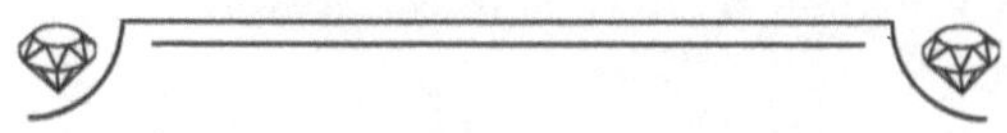

Vincent paced the front hall of the Diamond home. Eventually, their butler informed him that Lady Brilliance was not at home.

He frowned and looked at Mr. Dunley. "Are you saying she is *not at home* as in the lady doesn't wish to see me, or is she truly not here?"

Mr. Dunley's placid expression did not alter. "Lady Brilliance is truly not here."

"But she was expecting me," Vincent pointed out as if that would change matters. He had been ready to beg her forgiveness for every real or perceived flaw in his character as well as for withholding information he ought to have shared.

Mr. Dunley said nothing more. After all, what could the butler do?

Vincent handed him his calling card and left. In that instant, he believed she hadn't intended to snub him, nor even to perpetrate a flagrant act of incivility, but had simply experienced a change of heart. He would give her a little time to consider that his previous engagement to Lydia meant nothing to him now.

And when next he saw her, he would explain how he had stopped the legal proceedings for her safety, so they could spend time together immediately without fear of reprisal from Ambrose.

It all made perfect sense, except he ought to have told her both those things *before* she found out for herself. Moreover, he could not guess how she'd found out between the Spencer House conservatory and re-entering the costumed assembly in the Great Room.

At home, he found himself at his piano, tinkering before inevitably playing the "Essence of Brilliance." It amused him that people would think he considered the piece brilliant.

"What people?" he asked himself. No one heard his work except for Brilliance. Her and the hundreds who attended Ambrose's concerts over the years. *Blast the man!* His fingers came down hard upon the keys.

He had let his hopes rise that he might regain his latest piece and with it, some small satisfaction from a judge announcing in a court that the music was his.

For the first time in years, Vincent felt a little . . . lost. He had grown to accept the thievery and the betrayal over the past three years and had slowly begun to play again while composing once a year for his mother's birthday. But now, he was unsure whether to keep composing when so many of his "children" were in Ambrose's nefarious hands. Even his 'Il Rinnovo,' *The Renewal,* written as he began to let Brilliance enter his heart. Perhaps, he should give up and stop composing altogether.

His butler, who knew not to disturb him in his conservatory unless the house was on fire, tapped gently, pushed open the door, and stuck his sandy-haired head into the room.

"My lord, there is a Lady Brilliance here to see you," Mr. Chambers said. "She claims to be your betrothed."

His heart soared as he rose to his feet. Brilliance still considered herself to be his fiancée. *Thank God!* Vincent had all but convinced himself she regretted everything and would never speak to him again.

"Please show her into the—"

"I am here," she said, stepping around his tall, thin butler and into the room.

As if nothing unpleasant had occurred, she glanced around the room, taking in his sanctuary with her vivid blue eyes—every detail of its disarray including the abandoned brandy glass from the previous night after she'd left him at the ball, the discarded coat and shoes from his costume, as well as the wretched wig. Finally, she looked directly at him.

Her smile allowed the tightness in his chest to loosen.

"You may leave us, Mr. Chambers. And by the way, this delightful lady will soon be Lady Hewitt." Then the dread seeped into him again. "Won't you?" he asked Brilliance.

"Yes," she replied softly.

"Congratulations, my lord, my lady," his butler said with an expression that stated having a mistress of the house was of no more consequence to his day than if a bag of apples had been left on the front step. Then he bowed to each. "Will that be all?"

"Yes, Chambers. And we thank you for your exceedingly warm words."

"Of course, my lord."

"Is the rest of your household so welcoming?" she asked with a touch of irony after he left.

"You know he is merely behaving the part of an unflappable butler, don't you? At this very minute, Chambers is probably dashing helter-skelter toward the basement to tell as many of his fellow staff about you, regaling them with your warmth, kindness, and beauty."

"Not to mention my impatient nature and thus my inability to remain in the front hall, as well as my outrageous impropriety in leaving my maid in the foyer."

"Actually, that will set tongues to wagging. Besides, this room isn't very comfortable for two. Let's go into the drawing room."

Instead of his feet moving forward, however, he drew her to him. She didn't protest. Cradling her face between his palms, he gazed down, knowing he could dive into the blue seas behind her gaze and never tire of swimming in her goodness.

"May I kiss you?" Vincent asked, hearing his voice catch.

"You may," she said, although as he lowered his mouth to hers, he noticed she didn't close her eyes until the last moment. Brilliance wasn't quite the trusting Lady Persia from the night before, nor the same woman he'd known for half a year.

Yet when their lips fused, they were the same two people who had come to care for one another. For his part, he loved her fiercely. The outside world might batter them as a ship in a storm, but Vincent knew in his heart that they would withstand it.

Tilting his head, he took his fill of her, unable to keep from dropping his hands to her waist and pulling her against him. Her lips parted for him, and he tasted her, sucking her tongue until she curled her hips against him and grabbed his forearms.

When he lifted his head, the words came pouring forth like a well-known melody.

"I love you."

Her eyes widened, indicating he'd surprised her. *In a good way,* he hoped. Then in what he assumed was an unmanly fashion, he held his breath for whatever might come next.

Her tongue licked her lips, and his groin tightened.

"I have said it aloud to only one man," she said, and he was plunged again into despair. "But you didn't hear me," Brilliance continued, "because you were walking away, terribly angry at how I'd taken your music from Mirabel."

Vincent recalled that day. "Did you truly say then that you loved me?"

"I did. Afterward, I put my love into a small reticule in my heart, pulled the strings, and kept it safe while moving on. But I never let it go."

"Is your love still in that reticule?" he asked.

She shook her head. "No. I confess it has since escaped and filled my entire heart."

He closed his eyes for a second, then opened them. "I am grateful."

Then he offered her his arm. "Allow me to show you our drawing room. I would like to give you a tour of the entire house, but even Mr. Chambers might protest such flagrant breaking of the rules."

She laughed, a sound that rang through him like a glockenspiel. "I wouldn't wish to get on the wrong foot with him."

He led her into his drawing room, hoping she liked it. Belinda was perched on the front edge of the sofa. She jumped up.

"I am sorry, my lord, my lady."

"There is no problem," he assured her. He turned to Brilliance. "Would you like to have her stay or go to meet my staff?"

"I suppose for the sake of appearances my maid ought to stay."

"Very well." Vincent picked up one of the wing chairs, hoping he was impressing his future bride with his show of strength, and carried it to the other end of the room. Setting it down, he offered it with a flourish of his hand to Belinda. Her cheeks reddened, but she sat.

Rejoining Brilliance, who had taken her maid's place on the gray-and-white striped sofa, he sat beside her.

"The room is pretty," she declared, "if a little sparse."

He glanced at it with fresh eyes. There were no bric-a-brac on the mantel or on the low table in front of the sofa. No tall plants, nor vases of flowers, adorned the room, either. He'd seen all those things in other peoples' homes and appreciated them.

"Will you be interested in bringing a feminine touch and some pretty décor to our home?"

"Yes, I think I can do that. But I'm surprised that Mrs. Castern didn't do that when she was your fiancée."

"That would have been inappropriate. She was never once in this house."

"Was it only in the country when you and Mr. Castern were together, composing and playing duets, with Mrs. Castern lounging around, enjoying the spectacle? It sounded almost as though such entertainment went on in an endless daily and nightly party. Not unlike when Mrs. Shelley wrote her famed story in the company of her husband and Lord Byron during their Swiss summer. That, too, sounded like a constant state of amusement."

Vincent was flummoxed. "I have no idea to what you are referring. Who told you this?"

Brilliance appeared dumbfounded. "I assure you it is quite common knowledge. I even know that Lord Byron's physician was there. And I have read *Frankenstein* twice."

He barked out a laugh at her misunderstanding. "I meant, who told you that Ambrose and I composed together with Lydia, *before* she became his wife, lounging in our company?"

"*She* did. In the ladies' retiring room last night."

"What she told you is blatantly untrue. I compose alone. I assume Ambrose, if he ever writes anything of his own, does the same."

"Then she was not stating facts. She was lying to hurt me," Brilliance mused.

"I promise you that she was. When we were at Harrow, Ambrose and I occasionally met to practice piano in the common music room, and when he visited my country estate, which he often did because I had no idea what a snake he was, we often enjoyed playing for one another. But Lydia was never there."

Vincent suddenly recalled a singular event.

"Wait a moment. I want to be entirely truthful. There was one time when Mrs. Castern, at the time Miss Lydia Drummond, was staying with my cousin. We were engaged, and she visited me at Joyden's Wood."

Brilliance visibly stiffened.

"I swear it was not like when you came. Lydia had her mother as chaperone, and Lady Twitchard and the Colonel were there, too. And so was Ambrose. I think that was the second time they had run into each other, for I first introduced them in London. In any case, he and I did some silly duet, and she was in the room. We both came up with a solo part and then made everyone laugh as we managed to play them at each end of the scale at the same time."

Brilliance nodded. "That would certainly be memorable, but hardly what she described, which seems to have been a gross exaggeration."

Glancing down at her lap, Vincent noticed she was wringing her hands, and he took hold of them.

"What more do you wish to know?"

"How did they become close?"

He was surprised to experience not even a twinge of discomfort as he considered their betrayal. What he felt was relief at having escaped marriage with Lydia so that he was free to be with Brilliance.

"After that evening, I remained at Joyden's Wood. A few days later, Lydia returned to London. I believe they took up with one another at that time. I had met her the year prior and asked her to be my wife after . . . I believe it was six months. Yet only a month after we became engaged, she announced she'd fallen in love with him. It was befuddling and vexing."

Brilliance smiled again.

"Why does that make you smile?"

"Because of how long it took for you to ask *her* to marry you. *We* were close to an engagement after only two weeks in the country."

His beautiful betrothed was correct. Ignoring the maid, he dropped a kiss on her lips. "You are nothing like her. From the start, your helpful, sweet nature shone through. And I saw it clearly as soon as I stopped being afraid of opening my heart. Loving you is as easy as playing the scales."

"I don't find that to be easy."

"For me, it is child's play," he assured her, bringing one of her hands to his lips for a nuzzling kiss.

But her happy mood seemed to dissipate as quickly as it had come.

"Did Mrs. Castern also lie when she said you were stopping the lawsuit?"

Vincent took a deep breath. "No. And if her disclosure had cost me your good regard, it would have been ironic, indeed. I withdrew my suit because I didn't want to wait for us to be together. I have no doubt that Ambrose would have dragged your name through the dirt to protect his income and his own good reputation."

Brilliance appeared thoughtful, then her eyes filled with tears.

"You gave up your music . . . for me?"

BRILLIANCE WAS TOUCHED BY his devotion and his desire to protect her. But in that instant, she knew she would do whatever she could to help him if only there was a way.

Vincent shook his head. "The music will *always* be mine."

"You know what I mean. The world should know that those notes came out of your brain." She reached out and tapped his head. "It is hard to believe we are engaged. I imagined, given my own limited intellect, that I would end up with a kind, but somewhat doltish, husband. Instead, it seems I am to have a smart one with a memory like a hunter's trap and a brilliant musician on top of that."

"Don't forget handsome," Vincent said, pushing his spectacles up his nose.

"I could never forget handsome," she agreed, leaning forward, letting his spicy cologne tickle her nostrils.

"Your maid," he reminded her.

"Is very discreet," she said.

"More than her mistress apparently," he quipped before soundly kissing her again until her toes curled, and low in her body that mysterious throbbing began.

When he drew back, Vincent appeared serious. "Your intellect is not limited," he said. "You operate more on your instincts, but there is nothing doltish about you. I adore the way you speak the truth regardless of the consequences. Such as telling Lady Georgiana she sang like a tomcat screeching during a fight."

She laughed, then shook her head. "I vow I never said that."

"Perhaps not, but we were all thinking it, and only you spoke the appalling truth. Or the way you stood up in the theater and denounced Ambrose. No one but you would think it acceptable, yet alone actually do such a thing. I will have the smartest, fiercest, most brilliant wife in London."

Brilliance liked that description very much. "Even if I am absolutely rubbish at riddles?"

"Even so," he said.

"Should we go speak with my father?"

Vincent's expression appeared sheepish. "I already did, last night before the ball."

She felt her mouth open and snapped it shut. "How forward-thinking of you. I am assuming he gave you his permission."

"He did, in fact."

"I knew he would," Brilliance said. "Still, you may wish to have a private chat with my mother at your earliest convenience."

"I understand. If your mother is anything like mine, then she would appreciate knowing before anyone else in the family."

"Oh dear!" Brilliance thought about having spoken with her sister and sister-in-law earlier that day. "Then I had better go quickly home and tell her."

As she said her goodbyes to Vincent on his doorstep, a carriage drew up behind her father's.

"Here she is, your defender in petticoats," said Ambrose Castern, a moment after he alighted from a cab.

CHAPTER THIRTY-ONE

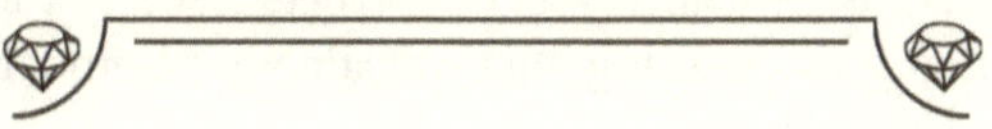

His tone was light, but Mr. Castern's expression was snide.

"We are betrothed," Brilliance informed him, thinking he should definitely not be speaking of what was under her dress. She hoped their being engaged would improve his manners.

Mr. Castern's glance darted between the two of them.

"Then congratulations are in order. Although I cannot help wondering why, with your impending happy nuptials, you both feel the need to continue this unconscionable harassment of me."

"What nonsense are you uttering?" Vincent demanded. "Why are you here?"

"To inform you that I am going to the newspapers with information about a certain Lady B of the Diamond clan who spends her time *alone* with a gentleman."

"But that's me," Brilliance exclaimed.

Mr. Castern laughed. "Your powers of deduction are sharp, my lady, and I am sure so shall be those of *The Times'* readers, especially the ones who study the society pages."

Vincent took a step closer. "Why are you doing this? Have you no honor? I withdrew the lawsuit."

"So you say, and I hope I can trust that you did," Mr. Castern said. "But she," and he pointed a gloved finger at

Brilliance, "has not stopped telling her lies to anyone who will listen."

Vincent looked at her, a question lurking on his face.

"I sent letters to people with whom I am acquainted," she confessed. "Important people, I dare say."

He grimaced, but Mr. Castern swore a blue oath.

"Don't speak that way in front of a lady," Vincent warned.

"A *lady*," Mr. Castern spat out, in a rather disparaging tone as far as Brilliance was concerned. "She is a liar and, after finding you two together outside your home, I would wager a lightskirt, too."

Vincent didn't say a word before stepping forward and striking Mr. Castern a hard blow to his face. Instantly, blood began to flow from the man's nose.

A scream shattered the heavy silence, and Mrs. Castern jumped out of the carriage.

"Ambrose, are you injured?" She drew out her handkerchief and handed it to her husband, who held it against his face. Then she rounded upon Vincent.

"You animal!"

"He insulted my betrothed," Vincent said. "And has admitted an intent to do so in the newspapers like a coward."

"And she continues to slander my husband," Mrs. Castern shot back. "Regardless, his face must remain perfect for the concert stage! Revenues will drop if he appears disfigured."

Brilliance and both the gentleman stared at the incensed wife. Even Mr. Castern seemed surprised that she cared more about his appearance than his bleeding nose or the ownership of the music.

"That hardly seems the primary issue in all this," Brilliance ventured, looking at the irate female. "Although perhaps while Mr. Castern heals, he could give performances at a song and supper room instead. The Eagle, perhaps."

"The Eagle!" both of the Casterns said together with similar degrees of disdain for the popular East End tavern.

"Oh, yes," Brilliance said. "In the newspaper advertisements, it is said to be doing a 'roaring trade.' Regardless," she added, "surely you must understand that the truth is more important than a broken nose, although I do hope Mr. Castern can still breathe easily."

"Breathe easily!" Mrs. Castern muttered, but she looked worriedly toward her husband, nonetheless.

"If you say one libelous word to the papers," Vincent warned, "then I shall reinstate the lawsuit at once."

"The lawsuit hardly matters now that noblemen are canceling their patronage and even some stage managers have said they shall not allow me at their venues. All because *she* is writing letters."

Suddenly Brilliance recalled the lie that had so upset her the night before. "Mrs. Castern, you lied about these two former friends composing together in your presence."

Her face paled. "I did not."

"Last night, when you had me alone, you were a good liar, but today, in the daylight, you seem like a poor one."

"Come along, Ambrose," Mrs. Castern said before turning for the waiting cab. "Imagine a member of the House of Lords brawling on the street," she added as she walked away.

"Not one treacherous lie in the papers," Vincent warned Mr. Castern.

"Can she fix the damage she has done? Will she write more letters and tell those people she was lying?"

"I was not lying," Brilliance said.

"Tell them you were *mistaken*," he corrected himself. "Then you can save face and my career at the same time. Two birds with one stone."

For the sake of peace and undoing any damage she had done, Brilliance was about to agree when Vincent spoke first.

"No. She will not lie to protect you. Not even a little. In this case, the stone is a clear, honest, brilliant Diamond, and I won't let her lower herself to your level. Do whatever you wish, but as an earl's daughter, she is the one who will come out smelling like an English rose."

Brilliance liked his speech but had to point out, "In truth, my fragrance is a blend. Mostly roses, like the Queen's perfume, but with bergamot and clove oils. However, everything else you said was well spoken, my lord."

For some reason, this made Vincent laugh softly, but Mr. Castern rolled his eyes. "I have been taken down by this *creature*." He shook his head. "I will not go quietly."

Vincent growled and appeared ready to strike again, causing Mr. Castern to lurch backward before darting toward the open carriage door.

After the cabbie had driven off, he turned to her. "You didn't tell me about writing any letters."

"I sent them before I found out you had stopped the legal proceedings. Did you mean what you said?"

"I assure you that I did," he promised, clearly still thinking about the unpleasant scene that had transpired in full view of any neighbor who happened to be looking out his or her window. "I shall undoubtedly be blamed for lowering the value of property on King Street," he muttered. Then he asked, "Did I mean which part?"

"About me," Brilliance said. "A brilliant diamond. It truly was very kind of you."

His expression softened. "You are priceless, dear lady." Taking her hand, he bowed over it. "Please ask your mother if I may call upon her tomorrow at one o'clock for a private audience."

"I shall." She didn't want to leave him, but after collecting Belinda, who had managed to remain inconspicuous mere yards away through the entire incident, Brilliance climbed into her father's carriage.

As she headed home, uppermost in her mind were two matters—what it would feel like to have her reputation shredded by Ambrose Castern should he tell the society pages she had spent time alone with a man *and* how she could help Vincent regain ownership of his music.

"I HAD A FEELING Lord Hewitt would be the one," her mother said. "All the way back to last July when you first sent me a letter about him."

Brilliance shrugged. None of Carolyn Diamond's children would doubt her astuteness. She explained to her mother the reason for their earlier cessation of friendship, and how she might now be embroiled in a bit of a scandal.

"We Diamonds have had our share and weathered them all without any loss of status. Do not worry. In the meanwhile, we shall invite his parents over for dinner," her mother added. "I like meeting new people, although your father may quibble, as he says we have enough friends and in-laws."

Brilliance was thinking about the birthday party she had attended. "He is a good son with a seemingly close attachment even to his stepfather. And he gives his mother a piece of original music each year for her birthday."

Lady Diamond's glance sharpened as she looked at her youngest daughter.

"How do you mean 'gives'?" she asked.

Brilliance frowned at the question. "He plays the piece in front of their guests and presents his mother with a . . . *Oh!* He presents her with a hand-written copy!"

"I don't suppose he has dated each one, perhaps along the lines of 'Many happy returns of the day, your loving son' with the month and year?"

"I don't know. Do you think I could go to my future in-law's home without an invitation?"

Her redheaded beauty of a mother nodded, her cat-like green eyes glinting.

"If they are the right sort of people, then yes. And if they don't like their future daughter-in-law dropping by, then they are the wrong sort, in my opinion." Then she added, "I shall accompany you. That's a far cry more acceptable than your maid."

Although Brilliance wanted to run out the door immediately, she had to wait for her mother to change. A countess didn't simply go out into the world willy-nilly.

Then, with hope in her heart, Brilliance and her mother traveled to Lord and Lady Winthrop's home.

"I am prepared to leave my card," Lady Diamond said. "After all, they may be out."

"Do you mean truly out?" Brilliance asked. "Or out to us?"

Her mother bristled. "Out to us? I think not! If they are declared out by their staff, then they had best have taken their carriage and be somewhere on the other side of Town. Out to us, indeed! Bri, I do not understand you sometimes."

Brilliance only smiled. Her mother grew prickly at the oddest times.

Regardless, Lord and Lady Winthrop were not out, and soon, Brilliance and her mother were seated in the drawing room with Vincent's mother. A splendid tea service was laid before them.

As soon as they all had a cup in hand, Brilliance got straight to the meat of the matter. "Lord Hewitt asked me to marry him last night."

His mother leaned forward, nearly spilling her newly poured tea.

"Why, that's marvelous!" Lady Winthrop declared. "I am utterly thrilled for you both. I knew he would make a smart match after the last disaster."

Brilliance decided not to bring Mrs. Castern into the conversation.

"I can scarcely believe it was only last night," she said. "Since then, I have visited with my sister early this morning and then with Lord Hewitt by midday. Now, here I am with you."

She knew her face reddened as the two married ladies exchanged a glance.

"We'd had a misunderstanding that needed clearing up, you see. But my maid was with me the entire time." *Oh dear, that was a lie.* "Except for when I confronted Lord Hewitt in his conservatory."

Lady Winthrop's eyes rounded. "You bearded him in his den. How brave!"

Brilliance shook her head. "No, my lady, in his music room."

Lady Winthrop laughed as did her own mother, although Brilliance had no idea why.

"In any case, I promise that shortly"—*after a few sizzling kisses,* she recalled silently—"we were in the drawing room. He actually moved the furniture, so my maid had a place to sit."

"Bri," her mother said. "I believe Lady Winthrop wishes to speak, dear one."

"My son has not yet had a chance to tell me of his engagement, but I surmised you were exceedingly special to him during my birthday party. It was a shame you had a megrim and had to leave."

Brilliance decided to let that little white lie stand. She blew out a sigh. Life was complicated when one was in love.

"About that party, my lady, I was thrilled yet surprised when he gave the abbreviated concert. Lord Hewitt seems reluctant to play in company—"

"Oh, yes," her ladyship agreed. "My son finds performing to be somewhat demeaning."

"That is a shame," Lady Diamond said. "I had the pleasure to hear him at our home, and I think a great talent like his is a gift from God, intended to be shared. Unfortunately, none of our family, except my second oldest daughter, is particularly musical."

Before her mother bemoaned the rest of her offspring's distinct lack of ability to play anything, Brilliance got on with her request.

"I noticed that Lord Hewitt brought the printed copy of his sonata. Has he always given you a copy as a present every year?"

"Ever since he was a boy. He used to give his father music, too, and then also for his stepfather. We have quite a collection, although the others are handwritten."

Brilliance swallowed and looked at her mother who nodded.

"Have you saved every one?"

"Of course." She looked at Lady Diamond. "I am sure you have kept mementos from all your children, too, be it a lock of baby hair or a childish painting or something recently done."

Brilliance's mother raised an eyebrow at her, offering a tilted smile. "Yes, I have keepsakes from each of my five children."

"My mother is too polite to say it, but she could show you one of my recent attempts at oil painting or watercolor, and you would not be able to tell whether it was from my childhood or last week."

They all laughed. Brilliance asked the final question that would make this a miraculous day. "By any chance did Lord Hewitt put a date on the sheet music?"

"No," his mother said, dashing her hopes. "Although, when he was younger, he would write which of my birthdays it was until I kindly asked him to stop at my fortieth."

The two mothers chuckled about age, but Brilliance was thrilled. "Surely that would be as firm evidence as any date. After all, you only turn each age once."

"I've been turning forty for quite some time," her own mother said. And the two ladies laughed again.

"What is all this about?" Lady Winthrop asked.

"Were you aware that another composer has been passing off your son's music as his own?"

Lady Winthrop paled. "I was not. But if I had to hazard a guess, I would say it must be Ambrose Castern."

"Indeed, yes," said Brilliance. "I take it you have never been to one of his concerts, or you would have recognized your son's music."

"No, I have never heard Mr. Castern in concert, and I never will. I treated him like a son whenever he came home from school with Vincent. But then that awful mess with him stealing my son's betrothed, a terribly disloyal girl. No, I could never lay eyes on either of them again."

She straightened her shoulders. "But now I will have you as a daughter, for which I am exceedingly glad." Vincent's mother looked at Lady Diamond. "As long as you don't mind sharing her."

"My Brilliance is one of a kind, but I will share her with you."

Lady Winthrop patted her chest in the region of her heart. "Thank you." Then she got back to the matter at hand. "Vincent never told me that Ambrose had taken his music. I knew only that my son stopped composing for a while. And of course, he had to let his heart heal so he could fall in love with you."

She rose to her feet. "If you wait a moment, I will get his music. I keep it all in two satchels. They are bulging."

When she reached the drawing-room door, however, she paused. "And if I understand the importance of this sheet music in proving the pieces were, in fact, composed by my son, then you will be glad to know that I personally wrote the year on the back of the first page of every gift he gave me or gave either of my husbands, at each party's end."

And then Vincent's mother hurried out.

"This will prove everything," Brilliance said.

"It certainly shall. We could go directly to the solicitor."

Brilliance considered that. "The last time I took Lord Hewitt's music, he became terribly angry. I learned my lesson. I think I will simply give it to him when he comes to our home tomorrow."

Her mother leaned back in the wing chair in which she sat.

"Why is he coming tomorrow?"

"To speak with you, of course," Brilliance told her. "He spoke with Father last night before the ball."

"I know," her mother said. "Your father tells me everything."

Brilliance hadn't known that. "Do you tell *him* everything?"

"Don't be ridiculous!"

Brilliance laughed. "Lord Hewitt wanted to give you the same honor that he gave to Father."

Her mother tilted her chin. "He is going to fit into our family nicely," Lady Diamond said.

"I must tell you that Mr. Castern has made some dreadful threats about telling the editor of *The Times* that I have been in Lord Hewitt's company without a chaperone. And whether he knows it or not, it is true."

She hoped her mother wasn't too disappointed in her or irritated by the prospect of the family name being tarnished.

"That little worm of a man cannot cloud a clear Diamond. When you were born . . . well, not precisely then because your eyes were scrunched tightly closed, but when I first looked into your blue eyes, I said to your father, 'This baby's eyes are shining like brilliant-cut sapphires.' It is one of my favorite gemstone cuts. If you ask Radiance why, she'll tell you all the whys and wherefores. All I know is that particular cut allows the most light to shine through from all angles." Her mother placed a hand over hers.

"My special girl, you are Brilliance personified, and nothing can change that. Besides, as that wonderful character Jane Eyre said, 'Reader, I married him.' That wipes away nearly every perceived sin, as your father and I found out when we eloped. You will become Lady Hewitt, and no more shall be said of your reputation except as an excellent wife."

Brilliance rose from her seat and threw her arms around her mother just as Lady Winthrop returned, weighed down by two thick leather cases. As Brilliance straightened, Vincent's mother placed these on the table in front of the sofa.

"I certainly hope my son will take all his music to the publisher as soon as he has sorted out this mess with Mr. Castern," she said. "But I want these originals back."

"As one mother to another," Lady Diamond said, "I will personally make sure they are returned to you."

CHAPTER THIRTY-TWO

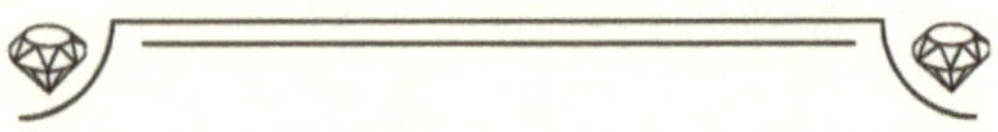

Brilliance was nearly vibrating with excitement, unable to keep from pacing the drawing room and watching out the front window as the big hand of the mantel clock drew closer to one. To her great dismay, even when the small hand was at half past, Vincent still had not shown.

An hour later, she wrote a hurried message and sent it by footman directly to his home. Oddly, the response came from his butler.

> *My Lady,*
> *Seeing how you shall soon be the Viscount Hewitt's wife, I do not think I am speaking out of turn when I inform you that his lordship has been taken by the constable at noon today to Scotland Yard, Whitehall Place.*

Her heart began to race as she finished reading.

> *Lord Hewitt has been charged with assault upon the person of Mr. Castern.*
> *Regards,*
> *Mr. Chamber*
> *Butler to the Viscount Hewitt*

Sweet Mary! "Mother," she called out, rushing from the room.

Lady Diamond was upstairs in her private salon, awaiting the arrival of Lord Hewitt with increasing impatience. However, after Brilliance explained the awful circumstances that had unfolded outside Vincent's home leading to the violence, her mother surprised her.

"I think your father should accompany you to give a statement. Men with their notions of honor and duty, especially a nobleman of your father's stature, can often solve such things better than an irate woman. Therefore, let us find Diamond and see if he is free to go to the jail."

All-over agitated, Brilliance paced whilst her mother sent out notes by their footman until her father was located. Geoffrey Diamond came striding through the door with all due concern and confidence. After sweeping up his wife for a passionate kiss, he let her speak.

She explained any details which she'd left out of her note.

"Yes," he said. "I am sure I can get him released."

Brilliance's mother appeared serene. "Dearest husband, has there ever been a situation that you could not handle to your satisfaction?"

He grinned. "I managed to marry you when all were against us. Everything after that has been easy."

They kissed again, and Brilliance cleared her throat.

Both of them turned to her with dreamy gazes. How she adored her happy, loving parents, but it was not the moment for kissing!

"Please, Father, make haste."

The earl nodded. "Let us retrieve that fiancé of yours."

"Bring him home for dinner," Lady Diamond said.

VINCENT COULD NOT BELIEVE the ignominious state of being held at Scotland Yard. Nor could he comprehend that

Ambrose would do something so fiendish. Surely stealing his fiancée and his compositions was enough, but pressing charges against him seemed beyond the pale.

And then he heard footsteps.

"Come this way, my lord," said the sergeant who had first led him, almost apologetically, to the holding cell.

Vincent followed the man to the front of London's central police station. If he weren't the one being charged, he would have found it interesting to see inside Scotland Yard.

The sergeant ushered him through a doorway, and there she was. *His angel!* What's more, Brilliance didn't appear distraught at his incarceration. Perhaps that was because beside her was the Earl Diamond. And next to him was the constable who had arrested him, seemingly now chums with his lordship.

"All a misunderstanding," Lord Diamond was saying.

Vincent heard no more because Brilliance had launched herself into his arms. Looking over her head at her father's piercing gaze, he tried to push her away, but she kept stepping close again—all wriggling, good smelling warmth and curves which were pressing against him until he wrapped his arms around her back.

He patted it as tepidly as possible before once again trying to push her away.

"Your father," he muttered.

"What about him?" Brilliance asked, lifting her cheek from his chest.

"Bri dear, your betrothed is trying to keep you from making a public display of affection. I would agree if we weren't in this closed room hidden away from prying eyes and among friends." Lord Diamond clapped the constable on the shoulder.

"Indeed," the mustached policeman said. "Indeed, we are."

Regardless, Brilliance did, at last, give him space to breathe. "We have freed you. And I have excellent news."

"Isn't *that* excellent news?" Vincent asked.

"Yes, it is!" She clapped her hands. "Yet this is even better. I have recovered much of your music written and dated. It is proof, don't you see? *Unequivocal* proof—that's the word you used, Father, isn't it?" she asked, glancing at Lord Diamond, before looking at Vincent again. "That *you* wrote the music."

Vincent shook his head, not understanding, thinking only of all the sheets he tore or burned in his rage.

"Your mother had saved them all!" Brilliance gestured to two leather satchels on the desk in the corner. He recognized them as once belonging to his father. And then it dawned on him their import.

"How could I have forgotten?" he asked. "I must be the dullest dolt in England. You cannot possibly marry me."

Her lovely face clouded over. But he smiled at her.

"I am speaking in jest, I assure you."

"He is," said her father, "or I would shoot him."

Vincent startled, but this time Brilliance was the one smiling.

"My father is joking."

"Am I?" asked the earl.

Even Brilliance turned uncertainly toward her father.

The constable watched with rounded eyes before coughing. "Well, Lord Hewitt may leave. And we shall expect Mr. Castern to drop all charges by the morning."

"Very good," said Lord Diamond.

"But the music?" Vincent asked.

"We brought it along to explain the seriousness of Mr. Castern's offense and explain why you had justifiable cause," Brilliance explained.

"Is theft and plagiarism justifiable cause for a punch in the nose?" Vincent asked the sergeant.

"In this case"—and he looked again at the earl—"yes, it is, especially combined with Mr. Castern's slanderous insults toward Lord Diamond's daughter."

In a few minutes, with the satchels tucked under Vincent's arm, he was a free man.

"My father is a generous patron of the police and has been for years," Brilliance told him. "He supports their widows and orphans, too."

That made more sense than justifiable cause for assaulting someone over insults, but he kept those thoughts to himself.

"I am very grateful," Vincent told them both, "but I still need to make Castern drop all charges."

Lord Diamond halted in front of his carriage and folded his arms. "That shouldn't be too difficult now that you have tangible evidence the music he plays is yours. I have no doubt the two of you will wrap this up in time to come back for dinner. My countess is expecting you."

And then he sauntered down the street like he owned it, leaving them to take the carriage.

"Your father is quite a character."

"He is perfect," Brilliance said, staring after him.

Vincent leaned inside the carriage and set the satchels on the seat, noticing her quiet maid in one corner. Then he assisted his fiancée before he climbed in and settled on the luxuriously soft seat opposite. Vincent thought his own conveyance was comfortable, but the Diamonds' town coach was a step above. However, they weren't moving.

The two females looked at one another.

"Shall I?" Brilliance asked. "There is a speaking tube, you see." She pulled the springy contraption from where it passed through the front of the carriage and up under the driver's box. She offered the open end to him.

Taking it from her and leaning forward, Vincent spoke into it, feeling half a fool. "Driver, please take us to 15 Montagu Place, the home of Mr. Ambrose Castern."

The carriage began with a lurch and moved into London's constant traffic, crawling along steadily toward the north side of Montagu Square, a genteel neighborhood but not anywhere he imagined Lady Brilliance had ever gone before.

"You are amazing," he told his future bride.

"Your butler told me what happened, but it was Father who rescued you."

"I am speaking of how you have rescued my music."

Brilliance's pretty cheeks turned pink. "My mother and I paid a visit to your mother yesterday, and I was going to surprise you when you came to tea at one."

"Of all that happened to me today, the worst was disappointing you and your mother by my absence."

"Thus, she invited you to dine with us this evening."

Vincent nodded. "I shall enjoy it if we manage to make Ambrose see reason."

"I have no doubt we will do so."

WITHIN HALF AN HOUR, they arrived at Mr. and Mrs. Castern's home.

"Do you think he will see us?" Brilliance asked.

"That is a good question," Vincent said. "Perhaps we should have brought your father, but I think you are just as formidable."

"Me?" Brilliance had never thought of herself in that way, but then, she had never before been compelled to such a challenge. Because she loved Vincent Hewitt more than she had thought possible to love anyone, she would attempt any task, no matter how arduous.

"Yes, you." He alighted and then turned back to reach for her hand.

"I suppose Belinda should accompany me."

"Indubitably."

Privately, Brilliance thought her perfect reputation was a lost cause, yet she wished to avoid any further improprieties, at least in front of the Casterns.

With Brilliance and Belinda behind him and one of the satchels of music once again tucked under his arm, Vincent lifted and released the door knocker.

"Ridiculous!" he muttered.

Brilliance peered around her future husband as he used the knocker twice more, with increasing vigor. Vincent was taking out his frustrations upon a brass fixture shaped like a musical symbol.

"A treble clef! Such foolishness," he added, about to lift it for the fourth time when the door swung inward.

A young man in the garb of a butler tried to look imposing while staring up at Vincent.

"Tell Mr. Castern that the Viscount Hewitt and Lady Brilliance are here to see him."

Brilliance smiled against his right suit coat shoulder. She had never heard him introduce himself thusly before. The title certainly worked its usual magic, as the young head of staff backed up a step.

"Please come in, my lord, and the ladies, too. I will tell him you are here. If you wish, you may wait in the drawing room."

And he gestured toward an open door across the foyer. Then he bowed shallowly and disappeared along the passageway.

"I counted three errors that an experienced butler would never make," Vincent said.

"Agreed," Brilliance responded. Even Belinda broke her usual silence. "As if I could be a lady."

They strolled into the drawing room, which was chilly with no fire as yet in the hearth.

"A lazy gentleman has untrained staff," Vincent remarked.

Brilliance busied herself surveying the room. It was nicely furnished and decorated. Mrs. Castern had good taste for color and artwork, it seemed. Before she could look more closely at a painting hanging over a credenza, Mr. Castern entered the room, trailed by his butler.

"I cannot credit my eyes that you people are in my home, uninvited."

Brilliance turned to the odd sound of his voice and gasped at seeing the puffy purplish half-moons under each of his eyes, swelling them practically shut. No wonder he couldn't credit them. He could hardly see out of his eyes. Moreover, upon his face was a bandage wrapped over his nose and around to the back of his head.

"You never could take a punch," was all Vincent said, which didn't seem to Brilliance like a good start to the discussion. "Anyway, your damn poor excuse for a butler gave us entry."

"Do you see my face? I had to soak my nose in ice water and must wear this compression bandage for God knows how long. Why are you out of jail?"

Brilliance silently watched, wondering what Vincent would say. Her betrothed grinned.

"Because my future father-in-law is an earl."

"That's outrageous," Mr. Castern said, although it came out thickly and mispronounced.

"There was another reason," Vincent added. He drew the bundle out from under his arm. "And this is only half of it."

"What is *that*?" Mr. Castern asked.

"This is justifiable cause. More precisely, it is my music, written down and dated."

Due to Mr. Castern's bandaged-covered cheeks, Brilliance could not tell if he paled at the words, but he managed to slightly widen his swollen eyelids.

"I thought . . ." He trailed off, and then, in a desperate move, he darted forward and tried to grab the satchel.

Vincent held it high over his head.

"You thought that your treacherous wife had ferreted out all my written work and given it to you. You are mistaken. I have another pile in the carriage. All dated, all in my hand."

Brilliance thought she had never seen a sadder man. Ambrose Castern slumped down onto the sofa.

"Then I am ruined."

"Indeed," Vincent said.

At that moment, Mrs. Castern entered the house through the foyer and found the group in her drawing room.

"What is going on here? How dare you show your face after what you did!"

"I, for one, am sorry your husband looks like Mr. Punchinello," Brilliance said, "but we now have written proof that Lord Hewitt composed all the music."

Mrs. Castern dropped her parcels to the floor. Inside one of them, something made a tinkling sound, and Brilliance knew a piece of glass or maybe crystal had shattered. She felt sorry for the pair. Perhaps Vincent did, too, for he lowered the satchel he had continued to hold high in triumph.

The mood grew worse when tears began to fall—and it was from Mr. Castern's squidgy eyes.

"Stop that," snapped Mrs. Castern without sympathy. "Do not give them the satisfaction."

"All I ever wanted to do was play music for people," Mr. Castern said, letting the tears run into his bandages. "I don't know how it became so twisted and complicated."

Then he raised his head and looked directly at his wife. "Yes, I do. It is your fault."

Mrs. Castern glanced sideways at Vincent and Brilliance, a nervous expression on her pretty face. Then she straightened her shoulders and addressed her husband.

"That's not fair. You wanted the recognition and distinction that comes from being a famous pianist *and* composer as much as I did."

Brilliance was surprised. "But the fame is not yours," she pointed out.

Mrs. Castern wheeled around. "We women have little we can do to make our mark upon the world except cling to a man's coat and hope for a few crumbs of recognition."

Again, Brilliance felt no kinship with this woman's opinion. "What have you received recognition for exactly beyond sitting in the theater?"

Her expression darkened. "I inspire him to—"

"To *not* compose music, apparently," Vincent interjected.

"Are you going to blame me, as well?" she asked. "Is there no one sympathetic to my plight?"

Brilliance could not help the burst of disgusted exasperation that came out as a bark of laughter.

"Your plight! If I understand correctly, you broke faith with Lord Hewitt and ended your engagement—for which I am eternally grateful!—to make a life with Mr. Castern solely for the purpose of this *recognition* you treasure so much. What about your husband's heart? Surely, you love him and would continue to do so even if he broke all ten of his fingers and could never play again. Wouldn't you?"

Mr. Castern gave a startled look at his hands before clutching them together in his lap as if protecting them. Then he, too, watched his wife, awaiting her answer.

Mrs. Castern hesitated, which broke Brilliance's heart on Mr. Castern's behalf. Yet after a moment, the woman's expression softened. She took a seat beside her husband and put her hand over his.

"I would," she said firmly. "Of course I would."

Brilliance felt tears prick her eyes as she looked toward Vincent. His gaze found hers, and she thought they must be thinking similar thoughts of love and devotion. He gave her a small smile.

"What happens now?" Mr. Castern asked into the silence.

CHAPTER THIRTY-THREE

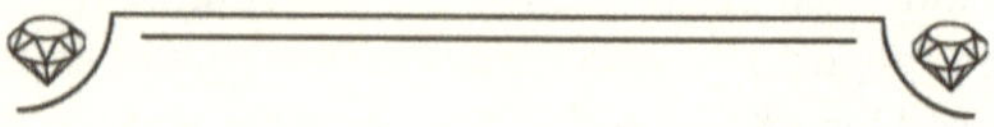

Before Vincent could form an answer, his betrothed spoke up. "We want you to go to Scotland Yard and drop all charges against Lord Hewitt."

He was touched that uppermost in Brilliance's mind was his well-being.

Astonishingly, Ambrose nodded.

"If you try to sue us for the money made from my husband's concerts," Lydia said, "you will be sorely disappointed."

"Going through the profits like flame through dry tinder, are you?" Vincent asked. She'd given him the barest hint during their brief association that she would be a profligate.

"Lydia has been a good wife," Ambrose said, rising finally to his feet. "I wouldn't be where I am today, as one of the most popular pianists in England, if not for her."

Privately, Vincent thought it had been a high price to pay, losing their friendship along with the man's integrity.

"You also wouldn't be where you are today if not for my music," Vincent reminded him. "And without it, I wonder where you shall be tomorrow."

"We are ruined," Lydia cried, tossing herself against the sofa back and covering her face with her hands.

Vincent rolled his eyes. And when he glanced at Brilliance, embarrassment drenched him at her knowing he had engaged himself to such a vain and vapid creature. Now that he loved Brilliance, he could not imagine why he thought he had been in love before. What a tepid life he would have lived had he married Lydia.

"I have a proposal," he said. The timbre of his voice captured their full attention. Even Lydia stopped her caterwauling and lowered her hands.

He looked at Ambrose. "I will allow you to continue playing my music as long as you give credit to me as the sole composer both in the evening's program notes and before you begin each and every concert."

The man swallowed, looking a little ill at the notion. Lydia, however, had a question. "May he still thank his wife and point me out in the audience?"

Vincent shrugged. "I have no opinion on the matter, and thus, no opposition. That is up to your husband."

He was not surprised by the difference in their two demeanors. Ambrose was dreading being discovered a liar, whereas Lydia was satisfied she would remain in the spotlight of each performance.

"And you want no remuneration for the past three years?" Ambrose asked.

Vincent sighed, wishing his old friend hadn't asked such an insulting question.

"None. I don't need your money, nor would I want what you have earned from your playing. It would feel like stealing. And I do not steal."

Both of the Casterns had the grace to appear sheepishly guilty. *At last!*

"But you must drop the charges against Lord Hewitt," Brilliance insisted.

"At once," Ambrose agreed.

"And you have said nothing to the papers about my future bride's reputation?" Vincent asked.

"Nothing," Ambrose promised.

"Then we have concluded our business. I shall not pursue the lawsuit any further."

With an unfamiliar feeling of lightness, knowing this ugly mess was resolved, he gestured for Brilliance and her maid to precede him from the room. With no sign of the young butler doing his duty, they showed themselves out.

When in the Earl Diamond's carriage again, with Brilliance's maid settling to one side and closing her eyes, Vincent's future bride declared, "I am utterly relieved that we are *not* them."

He couldn't help laughing. "That's not anything like what I expected you to say. But I completely agree." Reaching out, he took her gloved hand in his. Just touching her, even with cloth between them, gave him pure happiness.

Brilliance gazed at their joined hands a moment and then her blue glance met his. Instantly, his breath caught in his chest. Her hungry thoughts matched his own, and hers were floating clear as day in her sapphiric eyes.

"We should stop at your home so you can change for dinner," she suggested.

Resist the temptation, he ordered himself. "You must drop me off and go to your own home, lest your reputation be sullied."

Brilliance wrinkled her nose. The adorable movement made him want to scoop her onto his lap. After all that had transpired that day, he wanted her in his arms or, more precisely, in his bed as soon as possible. Their engagement would be a time of excruciating torture, especially if she was so plainly willing to snag any opportunity for intimacy. After all, that evening, there would be little opportunity for any closeness under her parents' watchful eyes.

You are a gentleman, he reminded himself.

"Come now, Lady Persia, don't look melancholy. Everything has turned out for the best."

When they drew up in front of his home, he jumped out and looked back at her. *The devil take him!* Five minutes alone could not hurt anything or anyone.

"If you could help me carry in these heavy satchels, I would most appreciate it."

Brilliance frowned and then . . . she nodded. Climbing down, she took one of the leather cases from him before turning back to her maid who was even then attempting to descend.

"I shall be back momentarily, Belinda." She stepped away, and let him close the door in her maid's face. They hurried up his steps, and the door opened because his butler was as superb as they came.

Mr. Chambers appeared greatly relieved.

"My lord, you have returned."

To Vincent's amazement, his normally staid butler turned to Brilliance and, for an instant, reached out as though he were going to take her hand. He stopped himself.

"The staff and I offer you our deepest appreciation, my lady, and our immense gratitude for freeing Lord Hewitt from jail."

Brilliance appeared touched, and she gave Mr. Chambers her warmest smile.

"It was my pleasure, sir. I cannot wait to live here with all of you. Now, if you will excuse us, I am only going to help carry this into the drawing room, and then I will leave ever so quickly."

"Yes, my lady." Mr. Chambers' gaze flickered to Vincent's before he made a hasty retreat along the passageway. *Superb!*

They practically ran into the drawing room like children doing something they knew was naughty.

Dropping his satchel on the table, he turned to take the one she carried.

"You must be careful with these," Brilliance admonished. "Please get them printed immediately with the original dates of composition, then return them to your mother. My mother assured Lady Winthrop of their safe return."

Vincent laid the second satchel more slowly atop the first. He would not wish to get on the wrong side of either mother, and it nearly quelled his ardor. However, quick as a whip in a horseman's hand, Brilliance plopped herself upon his sofa and held her hands out to him.

"Remember how it was that day at Mirabel Manor, the one before everything went wrong?" she prompted.

He had thought of her in his conservatory more times than he could count. Coming closer, he nodded, and when he took hold of her hands, she tugged him toward her.

"Let's do that again," she said. "Shall we?"

Vincent needed no second bidding. Joining their lips, he tilted his head until they were fused, with hers opening beneath his. Tongues fencing, stroking, teasing, his passion flared, and his arousal grew instantly.

In two shakes, she was under him, but her bonneted head hit the wooden armrest.

"*Oh!*" she exclaimed. "Never mind, carry on." She slid her arms around him. But the sofa was also too shallow and too short. The other armrest was digging just below his knees, and he was in danger of falling toward the table and the precious satchels.

His tumescence softened as the situation worsened when she croaked, "I cannot breathe."

Rearing up, resting one of his arms on the back of the sofa and the other on the table to prop himself, he apologized. "The wood is grinding into my shin bones, so I was resting on my upper body."

She giggled. "Which was resting on me. I fear we must purchase a new couch at once."

"Agreed," he said, looking down into her sweet face. Still holding himself up awkwardly, he dropped another kiss on her perfect lips and then a trail down her neck before he tipped himself over into the space between the table and the sofa.

"That was inelegantly done of me," he said, but it was precisely like the incident in his conservatory at Mirabel. And then she rolled off the cushions on top of him.

"*Oof!*" he expelled all the air in his lungs. When he could breathe again, he exclaimed, "My lady!"

Brilliance's happy face loomed above him.

"*My* lady," he repeated softly.

Threading his fingers into her hair, under the bonnet she wore, he drew her down to meet his mouth in a kiss that promised hot and sensual things to come. Her plump curves were crushed to the front of him. With his arousal swiftly returned in earnest, he raised his hips so she could feel how she tortured him.

They spent the next few minutes prone and panting, their mouths everywhere they could reach without removing layers of clothing. But he could draw her skirts up the back of her and get two handfuls of her ripe, round buttocks. With this leverage, he rubbed her heated parts against his, blazing a scorching path between them.

"Vincent," she moaned, wriggling and squirming like a flame flickering in a breeze. "I . . . what is . . . ? Please!"

For the first time since he was a youth, he was going to disgrace himself. And gladly, but ladies first. Releasing one of her sweet arse cheeks, he managed to get his hand around the front between their bodies and through the opening in her drawers. He found her damp and ready.

Barely touching her, after swift, sinful caresses into her curls, he felt her body tense. Brilliance's eyes closed, and she lay her head on his shoulder while she ground against his fingers.

Entirely spent and limp, she stilled, resting heavily upon him while he finished with a few last arching strokes of his own.

For many minutes, while they returned to their senses, they remained where they were. He wondered if she had drifted off to sleep. She was so tranquil.

"Brilliance," he murmured.

"Mm?" she answered.

"I am wedged and cannot move. Helpless as a newly whelped pup. Unless you get up and release me, I will miss dinner and have to remain on my drawing room floor forever. Which I shall not mind as long as you stay here with me."

Starting to laugh, she raised her head and gazed down at him. "I love you, my pup."

"I love you, my muse."

London, February 1855

IT WAS BRILLIANCE'S FAVORITE time of day, which was an inaccurate notion because the sun had long since set. She lay in bed with her new husband, entwined in one another's arms. Lovemaking usually happened as soon as they shed their clothing. Tonight had been no different.

Would it always be so ardent? Her gown, petticoat, shift, and corset had gone flying hither and yon, while his coat, shirt, and trousers went in all directions. Under a minute, almost desperately, they were pressed together, still standing, kissing frantically with hands roaming each other's bare skin.

Sometimes, by mutual agreement, they would fall back onto the mattress, their mouths still fused. That night, Vincent had swept her up against him with his arm under her knees and carried her to the turned-down bed, laying her upon the downy white sheets of softest cotton.

As their passion increased, they had feasted on one another. And then, with his most capable fingers, he had made her sing his name, and quite loudly, too.

"You are my favorite and finest instrument," he murmured one evening as he played her body so perfectly she was light-headed when she climaxed—a *stringendo,* he called the fast tightening of all her muscles.

That night, when she came back into herself after a heart-pounding crescendo, Brilliance was still breathing hard as he doused the lamp, plunging them into darkness.

This was their time for chatting if one or the other didn't fall asleep too quickly.

"It will be spring soon," Brilliance said, "and I plan to make our garden a showcase."

"Do you?" Vincent asked his lovely bride of five weeks. "Why?"

Her eyes were already adjusting to the moonlight coming in through the window beside the bed. "Because it has been neglected."

"It's still winter. How can you tell?"

"Mr. Chambers told me so. Apart from Cook's small herb garden, he said the rest is in a sorry state."

Vincent chuckled. "He is usually correct. I haven't done anything to it since I moved in. There is a single mature apple tree, which blossoms early, but there are no showy flowers that I can recall seeing around the perimeter. Just a few weedy perennials. Why, I haven't even furnished the terrace."

"We'll have a swing for two," she suggested. "And some rocking chairs. What more could we need?"

He chuckled. "Those will keep us and everyone who visits slightly off-kilter, my love. We ought to have a table and comfortable chairs in case we entertain."

"And I'll plant roses and lilies and forget-me-nots. Maybe a small herb garden for Cook."

"Is that really what you want to discuss tonight? Or are you working your way around to bringing up the Casterns?"

She punched him softly in the shoulder, and he captured her hand, holding it against his chest.

"How did you know?" Brilliance asked.

"I saw the newspaper open in the drawing room."

"What do you think of Mr. Castern's decision to go to Denmark?"

She felt Vincent shrug. "Financially, it was probably for the best. I didn't realize attendance would go down at his private concerts once he disclosed he was playing someone else's music."

"The listeners want to hear and see the composer," she said, freeing her hand to brush her palm over the sprinkling of hair upon his chest.

He tucked his hands behind his head and crossed his ankles, relaxing in a quintessentially manly way that she loved.

"I predict Ambrose will gain new fame as the premiere soloist for the Royal Danish Orchestra," Vincent said. "And Lydia will be introduced to a new legion of concert goers. Unfortunately for that fame-hungry harpy, it is unlikely Ambrose will be allowed to introduce her at the beginning of each concert."

After a pause, he added, "And it serves her right."

Brilliance could not sustain any anger toward Mrs. Castern, but then it wasn't her music stolen, nor her heart broken.

"In truth, I cannot hold a grudge against her," Brilliance said, letting her fingers trace circles across her husband's bare stomach. "Mrs. Castern must love Mr. Castern very much. After all, she gave up the title of viscountess, which she could have had with you. Many women would consider that the grandest prize of all."

"I suppose it depends on what you value." Lowering his hands from under his head, he ran a single strong finger in a line between her breasts to her navel, which he circled, making Brilliance squirm. She batted his hand away to stop the tickling sensation.

"There are dozens of titled ladies in London, after all, but few famous composers' wives. When she realized I didn't have the ambition to become a concert pianist, she betrayed me. And Ambrose went along with it."

"Now that he has left the London stage," Brilliance said, "perhaps you might offer the deprived listeners a concert or two." She hoped he would not discount her idea out of hand.

"Deprived?" he asked.

"Of your music," she insisted.

"I still prefer composing to performing." His fingers had reached her inner thigh. "Except for family and friends."

"And your wife," she added.

"Definitely for my wife." His fingers were working their way to her most sensitive parts.

"I almost feel sorry for Mrs. Castern, missing out on your talented hands."

"You don't care about fame?" Vincent asked.

To her amazement, given what they had just done, he rose over her and nestled between her legs. He seemed to have the intent to make love again.

"Not unless I earn it my—"

His kiss stopped her words. With very little preamble, he entered her once more, and they made their own music long into the night.

EPILOGUE

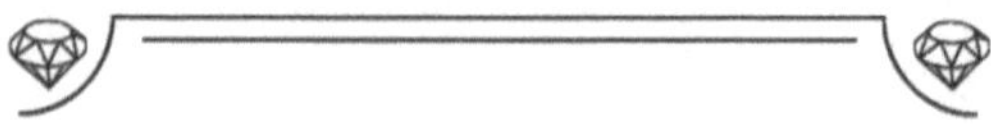

Three months later

Brilliance was pleased with the progress in the garden behind her home on King Street. There was a wickerwork dining set on the terrace and a double-wide swing under the apple tree. She had personally planted flowers and been advised to put in bulbs the upcoming autumn for the following year.

That day, while Vincent was in the House of Lords, she directed a footman in the hanging of lanterns now that the weather was warm enough to be outside in the evening. For she had kept a secret from her husband, which she intended to tell him that night over a garden dinner.

As the hours ticked slowly by, she was tingling with excitement. Thus, when he came in the door, she ran to him. He dropped a package on the tile a second before Brilliance launched herself at his tall, sturdy form.

"Good day, Husband."

"What have you done?" he asked, sweeping his arms around her.

"Whatever do you mean?" she asked.

"Whenever you purchase new furnishings or hire painters and wallpaper hangers to redecorate a room, you greet me in such a good mood."

She hadn't realized that was the case, and it made her smile. Before she could even tell him about the new lanterns, however, his mouth came down on hers. With their usual passion, his hands sought her soft flesh, grabbing hold, while she melted against him.

How blissful was their marriage, she thought. *Thank goodness she hadn't ended up with Lord Redley.*

When Vincent lifted his head, she leaned back in his arms. "Did I ever tell you my former beau, Lord Redley, apologized to me? He was at one of the earliest concerts when Mr. Castern began giving you credit. Apparently, there were some disgruntled audience members who—"

"Did he pay you a visit?" Her husband's eyebrows had drawn together.

"Who? Mr. Castern?" she teased. "Oh, you mean Lord Redley. You are jealous. How sweet!" Resting her cheek on his chest, she added, "It was before we married. He sent me a short missive of apology and asked to come calling." She felt him stiffen. "I declined, but I was glad that he and his aunt and all the world learned the truth about your music."

His hand cradled the back of her head, his fingers gently massaging her scalp. This familiar action usually ruined her coiffure but was well worth it.

She sighed forgetting they were still in the foyer.

"Speaking of my music, I have a surprise to share," he said.

She reared back so she could look into his gray-green eyes.

"Did you lose your spectacles?" she asked since he wasn't wearing them.

"What? No, of course not. I have *never* lost them, in fact."

"I have something to share, too," she said. "I thought to do so over dinner. But you'll need your eyeglasses."

"Very well. I will save my surprise for then, too." He retrieved a package off the foyer floor.

An hour later, after changing for dinner, they were in their garden, sipping wine on the mild May evening. Before them was a wide glass cloche, and under it, a plate of brie and toast points along with slender rhubarb stalks drizzled in honey.

Normally served last, this savory and sweet selection took the edge off Brilliance's appetite before she partook of their cook's rich dinner. She'd found the practice saved her from eating too much and also kept her head clear while drinking burgundy before their meal. Elsewise, the rich wine muddied her thoughts, not to mention making her silly. Neither of which she wanted as a married lady.

A married lady. Vincent's viscountess! The notion still infused her with a mixture of disbelief and gratitude.

"I knew your surprise had something to do with decorating," Vincent said upon seeing the overall charming effect of the lanterns hanging in the apple tree and around their garden wall. "I love what you have done."

"That is not the surprise," Brilliance protested. "Will you show me yours now?" He had brought the same mysterious package outside.

"No. You know my personal philosophy on such matters—ladies come first." Vincent sent her a look that had her cheeks warming. "In bed or at the dining table. Preferably *on* the table," he added, leaning over to nuzzle her neck.

"Vincent!" she admonished before allowing him better access. Eventually, she said, "I will be forced to move to the other side if you do not behave."

"Then show me your surprise, my muse. And I will show you mine."

She liked when he called her that. Lately, he had been composing most evenings with her nearby. As good as his word, he had made a place for her in his conservatory. She had a well-lit area with a wingback chair, a footstool, and even a separate writing desk.

It was the last she had mostly used these past months while her husband played and scribbled notes down on blank sheet music. She was so pleased he was writing it all down for posterity and the public.

Leaning over, she reached under the table. Hidden on another chair was a small book, leatherbound with gold lettering on the spine. This, she withdrew and placed in front of Vincent.

He stared at it, picked it up, and read aloud the words on the spine.

"Hewitt. *The City Beneath the Earth.*" He glanced at her, appearing confounded, but then understanding dawned. "Brilliance Hewitt, not Vincent!" He opened it. "Yes!" he exclaimed, turning past the title page to the next one that had the book title *and* her name.

"Dedicated to my husband with love," he read, scrawled as neatly as she could under her printed name.

"I wasn't sure whether to use my new family name or my new titled name, but then I thought—"

He leaned over and kissed her. "This is fabulous. I am so proud of you."

"You haven't read it yet. It may be awful." But she was pleased nonetheless by her accomplishment. She might not be able to paint or fish, but she was a published author. And that was something.

"Even if it is monstrously dreadful, I shall love it," Vincent promised, deflating her slightly, until he added, "Regardless, I am proud of you for bringing your story out into the open." He shook his head. "And all this time, I thought you were writing letters."

"I wanted to keep it from you until I was certain I could finish an entire novel. When I took it to a publisher, they liked it. Or perhaps they liked my lineage. In any case, at the moment, this is the only copy."

"I shall order one for everyone I know," he vowed.

While she sipped her wine, he perused the pages, slowly skimming and turning, occasionally making a noise of approval. Then she could wait no longer.

"What have you to share?"

He closed her slender tome. "Nothing nearly so exciting, I assure you."

Pulling the brown paper bundle from the center of the table, he handed it to her.

"You may do the honors of—"

Before he could finish, she began to rip the folded edge. When she tore the wrapping quickly, he chuckled. "I thought you only opened packages in such a wild fashion at Christmas time. I see now it is a habit."

Ignoring him, Brilliance didn't slow down until she had uncovered a much larger leather book than her own.

"*The Collected Compositions of Lord Vincent Hewitt, Vol I,*" she read. "Vol I?" Flipping through it, she started to read the titles. And then she got to the sonata he had written for her.

"For my own beloved Brilliance, whose essence cannot truly be captured in music although I shall attempt to do so for the rest of my days."

Closing it with a thump, she leaned over and put her arms around him. "I thought the individual, printed sheet music was impressive, but seeing it like this, as a collection, is splendid."

He shrugged, looking pleased.

"I will order copies for everyone I know," she promised, echoing his words.

"There is something else," he added. "I have booked a concert hall for next month. The manager contacted me, and I—"

Jumping from her seat, Brilliance plopped herself upon his lap.

"I am thrilled. We'll fill opening night's seats with all our family and friends."

"I guess that is one way to ensure I don't open and close on the same night."

"Preposterous!" she said. "Everyone in London will be clamoring to hear my talented husband, the true composer of some of the most beautiful music of our time."

"Some of?" he teased. "I suppose I am not Bach."

"You are *my* Bach," she promised with a laugh. "And on opening night, will you stand center stage and gesture up to me in our box, introducing your beloved wife, the unknown author?"

He cradled her face, his tone growing serious. "Actually, I do intend to sing the praises of my precious muse."

His sage-colored eyes captured her. "Brilliance, I am not speaking in jest. By naming my greatest work—"

"So far," she interjected. "'Essence of Brilliance' is only your best *so far.*"

"Will you hush and let me tell you how much I adore you?" he demanded. "You are my savior, in fact, my greatest patron. Without you . . ." His voice choked.

"Without me," she said, "you would still be a great composer. Although I recommend you do *not* sing on opening night, neither my praises nor any other tune. I have heard you in the bathtub, my love, and you are no better a singer than Lady Georgiana."

Her teasing laughter filled the night air until he stopped it with another perfect kiss.

Finis

ABOUT THE AUTHOR

USA Today bestselling author Sydney Jane Baily writes historical romance set in Victorian England, late 19th-century America, the Middle Ages, the Georgian era, and the Regency period. She believes in happily-ever-after stories with engaging characters and passionate romance.

Born and raised in California, she has traveled the world, spending a lot of exceedingly happy time in the U.K. where her extended family resides, eating fish and chips, drinking shandy, and snacking on Maltesers and Cadbury bars. Sydney currently lives in New England with her family—human, canine, and feline.

At her website, SydneyJaneBaily.com, you can learn more about her books, sign up for her newsletter (and get a free book), and contact her. She loves to hear from her readers.

www.ingramcontent.com/pod-product-compliance
Lightning Source LLC
Chambersburg PA
CBHW060649190726
48289CB00002B/338